"You're absolutely right, you know."

"About what?"

Alanna looked up at him. "Finding the right partner makes all the difference in the world. Makes me wonder what else you might be right about. Which, in turn, makes me wonder how long you plan to make me wait."

The fire in his eyes burned brighter, and his hand pressed more closely in the small of her back. "Wait for what, sweet Alanna?" he asked, his voice caressing every inch of her.

"For you to pull the pins from my hair."

His smile slowly faded as a different, deeper kind of fire ignited in his ebony eyes and the line of his jaw hardened. He looked away, at a point over her shoulder, and began to move them in that direction. His voice rumbled low in his chest when he replied, "Discretion would suggest a more private place."

"Just between you and me, Kiervan," she murmured. "I think it's way too late for discretion."

He muttered something in Gaelic as he whirled her about in a dizzying arc. She laughed and closed her eyes; trusting him, not caring where he took her; reveling in the magical bond which held them in flawless tandem; reveling in the joy that flooded her heart.

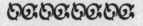

It Happened One Night

Leslie LaFoy

BANTAM BOOKS

NEW YORK TORONTO LONDON SYDNEY AUCKLAND

IT HAPPENED ONE NIGHT
A Bantam Fanfare Book / November 1997

FANFARE and the portrayal of a boxed "ff" are trademarks of
Bantam Books, a division of Bantam Doubleday Dell Publishing
Group, Inc.

ISBN 0-553-57745-X

Published simultaneously in the United States and Canada

Bantam Books are published by Bantam Books, a division of Bantam
Doubleday Dell Publishing Group, Inc. Its trademark, consisting of
the words "Bantam Books" and the portrayal of a rooster, is Regis-
tered in U.S. Patent and Trademark Office and in other countries.
Marca Registrada. Bantam Books, 1540 Broadway, New York, New
York 10036.

PRINTED IN THE UNITED STATES OF AMERICA

WCD   10 9 8 7 6 5 4 3 2 1

It Happened One Night

"Alanna," Bill gasped as he reached the summit of the hill and dropped down on a fallen tree, scattering the powdery snow. "I think I've got altitude poisoning."

Alanna Chapman smiled down at her blond, blue-eyed, red-faced fiancé and shook her head. Bill Boyer was handsome, intelligent, and financially prudent. But he was no backwoodsman, despite the valiant wardrobe assistance of Abercrombie and Fitch.

"You've lived in the Rockies for less than a year," she observed, not for the first time, as she cleared away some snow and sat down beside him. "I warned you that the hike in would be rough and that you might not be up to it." Patting him gently on the knee, she arched a brow and added, "If it's any consolation, the hard part's over. It's pretty much level ground from here on out."

He straightened, pushed his tweed hat back from his brow, and looked about the woods. "What in the name of blue blazes possesses your aunt to live this far off the beaten path? Why couldn't she have built her cabin down by the road like most people do?"

"Because Aunt Maude prefers the isolation," Alanna replied, rising to her feet and extending her hands to help him. As she pulled him from his rough perch, she grinned and said, "And, if you'll recall, I've mentioned a time or two that she's what most people call eccentric."

"I can't believe that you actually spent a good part of your life living up here."

Alanna shrugged and started out again, making her way along an invisible but familiar trail through the snow-covered boulders and answering over her shoulder, "Maude took me in when I had nowhere else to go. And as a life-style . . . I can't complain. It kept me off the streets and out of trouble."

"There aren't any streets, Alanna," he retorted, following her. "And you couldn't have possibly gotten into any trouble, because this is the middle of nowhere."

With a mittened hand, she pointed up and to her right. "Nowhere is over the next rise. You'll be able to catch a glimpse of it from Maude's cabin."

"That's why I'm marrying you," he countered. "Your irrepressible sense of humor."

Knowing from the sound of his voice that he was tiring and falling behind again, Alanna paused on the trail and turned back to watch his progress. "My irrepressible sense of humor and the fact that it'll keep the accounting practice in the family, so to speak."

"Well, yes, of course there are the practical considerations as well," he admitted without lifting his gaze from his feet. "Speaking of which . . ."

"I know, Bill," she admitted, stifling a mildly exasperated sigh. "It's tax season and we have no business being away from the office. But Maude wants me here today. I can feel it in my bones. I had to come."

His vision still fixed on his passage through the snow-slick rocks, he replied, "Of course, Alanna. I understand completely. And it's not as though it were a weekday. Or Saturday. I suppose even CPAs are allowed to rest on the Sabbath. Although I'd hardly call this trek through the Himalayas restful."

Alanna laughed. "The San Juans, Bill. They're the San Juan Mountains. No sherpas or breathing equipment required."

"Speak for yourself," he retorted, reaching her side and finally looking up with a smile of accomplishment. "Mountains are mountains, and if you ever expect me to make this trek with you again, I'll insist on pack mules and oxygen tanks."

"I told you that I'd be fine on my own." She stood on her toes to press a kiss to his cheek before setting out once more. Even as she made a mental note to slow their pace, she said aloud, "You didn't have to come along. I've been in and out of here so many times over the years that I've lost count."

He made a scoffing sound before saying, "Imagine, if you will, my having to report you missing; having to admit to the search-and-rescue people that I let you come out here all by yourself. I'd never be able to show my face in Durango again."

Alanna grinned. "Durango, hell. With your luck, it'd end up being an episode of *Rescue 911* and then there'd be nothing for you to do but board up the windows of Boyer and Chapman and slink out of the *country*." She shrugged and her grin widened. "But then again, I hear the Colombian drug lords are always looking for a few good accountants."

He froze as his gaze shot up from the ground to meet hers. "Alanna, sweetheart, you really shouldn't joke about those things. A joke made in the wrong place and taken the wrong way could be ruinous."

"Yeah, Bill," Alanna drawled, a smile tugging at the corners of her mouth, "You never know which one of the ground squirrels might be into corporate espionage."

Not even a hint of amusement flickered across his well-carved features. "Humor is one thing, Alanna. Irreverence is another. You're going to have to work on that."

"Bill," she countered, arching a brow in warning, "you're going to have to work on lightening up. You're teetering on the brink of becoming a middle-aged stuffed shirt." Without waiting for his response, she turned and resumed her course through the woods. Ahead, through the trees, she could see the brighter light of the clearing. Behind her, she heard Bill muttering as he set off after her.

Maude's cabin sat, as always, at the other end of the wide mountain valley; small and quaint and unobtrusive, it was decidedly picturesque in the snow. And yet there was something different about it today, something that made her uneasy. When Bill came to stand at her side, the realization hit her with a soul-numbing jolt.

"There's no fire," she whispered, her heart thundering as the possibilities raced through her mind.

"Up here, isn't that considered a good sign?"

"No," she answered faintly. "Aunt Maude always has a fire burning in the hearth. And there's no smoke coming out of the chimney."

Alanna heard him respond, knew that he offered some sensible explanation, but she had already left him there at the tree line. Racing across the meadow, her legs lifting high above the snow, she tried to outrun the dark clouds already gathering around her heart.

"Maude!" she cried, dashing through the wintering herb garden that encircled the front porch. Only the sound of her own ragged breathing disturbed the stillness of the afternoon. She bounded up the stone steps, panic edging her voice as she called out again.

"Aunt Maude!" she called even as she lifted the latch on the planked door and shoved it open. "Maude! Are you—?"

She froze, her heart beating frantically as she took in the details of the cabin's interior. The hearth was indeed cold. There were no pots or pans on the kitchen worktable. No bundles of herbs hung on the drying string suspended between the rafters. No lamps were lit. Everything was too neat, too unlived-in looking.

"Please, dear God," she whispered, stripping off her mittens as she darted toward her aunt's bedroom. Two paces into it she froze again and felt the color drain from her cheeks. Maude O'Sullivan lay on her back in the center of the double bed, her body far smaller than Alanna remembered, her hands, resting at her sides, wrinkled and frail.

Slowly, Maude opened her eyes and turned her head to offer her niece a weak smile. "I knew you would come, sweet child."

Beyond her aunt's tremulous smile of welcome, Alanna clearly saw the gray shadowing of her skin and the hollowness of her face. "Oh, Maude," Alanna gasped. Her knees felt weak, her head light. "I thought . . ." she breathlessly attempted to explain as she stripped off her hat and down vest. Tossing them and her mittens aside, she sat on the edge of the bed and took her aunt's hand between her own. The strong, certain fingers that had taught her to spin and weave, to cook and sew, were strangely cold.

"Very soon, Alanna." Maude's voice was soft, but Alanna still heard a trace of its former strength and the quiet notes of acceptance beneath her aunt's Irish lilt.

"Don't talk that way," she admonished, shaking her head and gently trying to rub some warmth back into the too slender fingers. "Remember what you've always said: Believing comes but one heartbeat before reality."

"Death has been patient with me, child. I cannot, in good conscience, ask Him to wait much longer."

Alanna smoothed her aunt's snow white hair off her wrinkled forehead, remembering when the strands had been the color of a raven's wing. Maude had always been a robust woman with unbounded energy. To look at her as she lay in the bed, small and faded, was a shock Alanna could never have prepared for.

"Over on the desk, child—that carved oaken box," Maude said. "Be a dear and bring it to me. There are some important matters we must discuss."

Alanna did as instructed, but even as she carried the box back to the bedside, she protested, "Maude . . . look, I know how you feel about life down the mountain. But I can't just let you choose to stay up here. Not when there are doctors who might be able to help you. Bill came with me today. I left him on the other side of the meadow. As soon as he gets here, I'll send him back down to get help."

"It is my time, Alanna," Maude interrupted gently. "Part of growing up is accepting with grace that all of God's creatures must someday return to Him."

"Acceptance has never been my strong suit."

Maude offered her a patient, knowing smile. "You cannot bend life to your will, child. Neither can you hold Death at bay. What is ordained, must come to pass. It is the way of all things in this realm and beyond." She patted the bed beside her, then said, "Now find your courage, sit back down here beside me, open the box, and let us talk of what I would have done when I am gone."

With numbed but dutiful resolve, Alanna returned to the edge of the heather-filled mattress and placed the box on her lap. The hinged lid made no sound as she opened it. Inside, Maude's brooch lay atop a folded piece of paper. Alanna silently stared for a long moment at the intricate silver dragon that encircled the bloodred ruby before she gently picked it up to cradle it in her hands.

"I know that you have never been able to make the stone work for you, but I also know that you have been given the gift of seeing, Alanna," Maude began. "Someday, when you believe in magic and your own power, you will be able to scry within any quiet surface. But as you learn, it is the Dragon's Heart that will show you the way most easily. It is only right that the ancient tool of the O'Sullivan seers pass into your hands. You have the wisdom and courage to use for good what knowledge it gives you. Within it lies your destiny."

Alanna kept her skepticism to herself. Now wasn't the time to reopen that age-old debate. "I'll guard it well, Maude. I'll pass it to my daughter and—"

"Only if she has the ability to see the future within its depths, child. Your mother did not possess the gift. But that is often the way of seeing. Keep the Dragon's Heart in your care until you are certain as to whom it should properly be passed. It could very well be your granddaughter who will be blessed with the gift. Trust the Dragon's Heart to show you the decision you are to make."

Alanna nodded and placed the brooch reverently on the bed beside Maude. Her gaze dropped back into the box, and she noted for the first time that her name had been written in the center of the folded paper.

"You've always had the most beautiful penmanship," she whispered, lifting the single sheet and opening it. "As hard as I try, I can't even come close." The upper portion of the missive contained instructions for detailed physical movements. Alanna only skimmed them and then dropped her gaze to the lower half of the page. She furrowed her brows as she tried to make sense of the words Maude had written.

"They are the words to an ancient spell, child," Maude supplied. "Written so that you might know how they are to be spoken when you scatter my ashes at the Carraig Cor. Commit them to your memory, Alanna, and then destroy the paper on which they have been passed to you. Share them with no one, for they are sacred."

Alanna looked up, her blood suddenly racing cold and thin through her veins. Part of her wanted to argue the need for the entire conversation. Yet, deep down inside, another part of her knew that it would indeed be their last.

"The Carraig Cor is a Druid's circle which lies on the eastern coast of Ireland," Maude explained, her expression as always earnest and infinitely patient. "In County Wicklow. I want you to take me home to Erin. The urn for my ashes is also within the box."

Alanna glanced down at the green marble amphora cradled in the box, then met her aunt's gaze before she nodded solemnly. "I will, Maude. I promise."

"You must perform the ritual at the height of the moon on the night marking the start of this year's Ehwaz."

Catching her lower lip between her teeth, Alanna momentarily considered pretending that she had, at long last, committed to memory the most confounding of her aunt's many lessons. In the end her sense of honesty prevailed. "Maude, you know I never could make any sense of the Celtic calendar. When, exactly, is Ehwaz?"

"You must be in the Carraig by midnight of March thirtieth."

"In a month? Two weeks before tax day?" Alanna muttered, shaking her head. "Bill's understanding, but even he has his limits. He'll have my hide."

"Bill is not the man who stands at your side through eternity. I have told you this often."

"I remember the conversations, Maude," she admitted with a sigh, carefully refolding the paper and putting it back into the box. "Let's not spend our time talking about Bill and me."

"Child," Maude interrupted, her dark eyes soft, "there is more in living and loving than merely being comfortable in the company of a man. While Bill is a good man, he is not the right one for you. In your heart you know this just as I do."

Unnerved as always by Maude's uncanny ability to know her thoughts, Alanna endured the familiar shudder that raced down the length of her spine. She lifted her gaze toward the window to keep from looking down at the obscenely large diamond weighting her left hand. "I really don't want to talk about Bill right this moment," she said with a long sigh. "Surely we have other things we need to say."

"Humor an old woman, Alanna," Maude whispered. "I am tired, child. And it is important that you understand before I leave you."

Alanna's heart sank at the exhaustion, at the acceptance, she heard in the older woman's voice. Somewhere in the seconds that passed before her gaze met her aunt's, she finally recognized and accepted that Maude was indeed going to die, that there was nothing she or anyone else could do to prevent it. With grace, Maude had said. Accepting with grace, even though it hurt like hell.

Gently, Alanna again took the woman's frail hands into her own. "I'm listening," she said, surprised by the quiet calm of her voice.

"A grand adventure lies in your future and in the end you will find a great love," Maude said, offering her a reassuring smile. "A love worthy of your heart and soul. You deserve nothing less, Alanna. Promise me that you will not marry Bill Boyer before you take me home."

Alanna managed a small but true smile of her own. "That one's easy, Maude. Bill's much too practical to even consider marriage during the panic of tax season. It'd take time away from the business. And a honeymoon? It would be the death knell of our practice."

"Then promise me that which is difficult, child," her aunt said, laying her hand on Alanna's, her eyes searching.

"Swear to me that you will be standing in the Carraig Cor at the midnight marking the beginning of this year's Ehwaz."

"I promise, Maude. I'll do it for you. No matter what."

"As I knew you would." Her eyelids fluttered down as though holding them open had drained her of strength. After a moment she smiled softly. "Bill Boyer draws near. You should go to meet him and send him on to attend to his task. I will warn you though, child, that both his efforts and your hope will be in vain."

Trying desperately to ignore the cold fingers of dread snaking about her heart, Alanna placed the Dragon's Heart back in the box, closed the lid, and set it aside. "I'll make us some hot tea," she offered. "Will you be all right alone for a few minutes?"

"No, child. My time grows too short for tea." Maude softened her words with a gentle smile. "But many a day we have ended sharing a cup of tea and our dreams, haven't we?"

"Too few, Maude. There should be lots more," Alanna whispered. With a deep breath, she added, "You gave me a home, a healthy place to grow roots. God only knows where I'd be if you hadn't found me and brought me here to live with you. I'll always be grateful, Maude. I'll always love you."

"And I you, sweet Alanna. I regret that I did not come for you sooner, child; that I did not stop Oonagh when she decided to go down the mountain to live. But the Dragon's Heart doesn't always show one what is closest to their own heart."

"When Mother's mind was right, she had a will that couldn't be bent," Alanna offered quietly, not knowing what else she could say that hadn't been said a thousand times already. "You did what you could and that's all anyone could have expected."

Maude's eyes burned brighter even as the color of her skin paled another alarming degree and the hands clasped in Alanna's grew cooler. Her words came as though from a well deep inside her, borne on the wings of determination alone. "There is no such thing as a wrong road, child. Remember that."

Maude glanced toward the planked ceiling, then offered Alanna an apologetic smile. She closed her eyes and a peaceful, contented sigh slipped past her parted lips. "Thank you, child," she whispered, "for brightening the later years of my life. Know that I have always loved you as though you were my very own."

Alanna bent to press a kiss to her aunt's forehead and evenly answered, "I never ever doubted it, Maude."

Her aunt's fingers tightened ever so slightly, ever so briefly, around her own, and then, as though from a great depth and dreamy distance, Maude offered, "All will be as it should, Alanna."

"Yes, Maude," she replied, straightening, knowing in her heart that her aunt had carried the promise with her to another place.

Alanna placed Maude's cold hands beneath the blanket and tucked it carefully about her sides. For a long while, she sat there, furiously blinking back the tears while her mind filled with memories of Maude and the years they had shared in the mountains; of watching the sunrises and the sunsets; of winters and springs and summers and falls; of living off the land in times both good and bad. And somehow those wondrous, magical ribbons of remembrance entwined to bear the weight of Alanna's grief and ease the emptiness in her heart.

Finally lifting her chin, Alanna rose from the edge of the bed. She straightened Maude's covers again and kissed her aunt's cheek before she left the room.

She met Bill at the cabin doorway.

"God, Alanna," he began, stomping the snow from his boots and mopping the sweat from his brow with a monogrammed handkerchief. "Distances are deceiving up here. How far is it from the trees to this cabin? A mile and a half?"

"Aunt Maude has died," Alanna began softly and without preamble. "I need you to go down to the Land Rover and use the cell phone to call the sheriff."

His eyes widened and he nodded. "Of course. Of course. Where do I tell them you are so that they can find this place?"

Alanna crossed the room and went to the rough-hewn bookcase that sat beneath the cabin's front window. It took only a moment to find what she needed. Crossing back to her fiancé, she held out the folded paper, explaining, "This is a topo map of the area, Bill. The valley designation is circled. Just read it to them and they'll know where to come."

He took the offered paper and thrust it into the inside pocket of his jacket. "I'll start back as soon as I make the call. Will you be all right while I'm gone?" At her nod, he leaned forward, kissed her on the cheek, then straightened and settled the hat on his head. With a deep breath, he turned and marched off in the direction from which he'd just come.

Alanna watched him only until he'd left the herb garden, then she turned and closed the door. She started the fire in the blackened hearth, and as it crackled and popped to life, she poured water from the storage crock into the cast iron kettle. Once she'd settled it into the edge of the flames, Alanna stood and reached for the tin containing loose tea on the shelf above the mantle.

She would have tea and sit with Maude O'Sullivan one last time. She would keep her promises to the woman who had been the better mother in her life. She wouldn't cry. And while she waited for the world below to intrude on the silence of the hidden meadow, she would practice the magical words Maude had left her on the piece of paper tucked into the box between the amphora and the Dragon's Heart.

1

Clutching the urn that contained her aunt's ashes, Alanna Chapman stood beside the muddy road and watched the taillights of the taxi career into the Irish night.

"Now, why doesn't that surprise me?" she muttered. "I swear, Aunt Maude," she continued, carefully positioning the green marble urn on a wide flat rock on the top of a nearby stone wall, "so far this whole adventure has you written all over it. Two weeks before tax deadline . . . You know Bill's really ticked, don't you? Even promising to do this whole thing on a four-day, over-the-weekend, whirlwind schedule didn't placate him. Can you believe that he refused to drive me to the airport?"

The cool light of the new moon touched the golden band encircling the base of the amphora's gently curving lid. For a moment Alanna had the distinct impression that Maude smiled, enjoying from beyond the mischief she'd unleashed.

A sudden gust of wind caught at her unbound hair, blowing a curtain of honey gold silk across her vision. Muttering in frustration, Alanna shoved it aside and then fished in the pockets of her aunt's woolen cloak for a hair clip. Her fingers found only the cold metal and smooth stone of Maude O'Sullivan's brooch.

Alanna withdrew it and turned it so that the moonlight fell across its face. For a long moment, she studied the intricately woven silver dragon that encircled the bloodred ruby, and then she smiled. As an adolescent she had spent countless hours staring into the stone and hoping to see the wondrous people and things Maude claimed to be within it. No doubt it had been that youthful tendency of hoping for the impossible that had earned her the honor of bringing it and Aunt Maude's ashen remains halfway across the world.

"Not that there was anyone else to do it," Alanna observed wryly. The corner of her mouth lifted in a rueful smile and her gaze moved to the urn sitting on the age-old wall. She felt the now familiar ache of emptiness. Straightening her shoulders, she took a deep, steadying breath.

"You were my rock, Aunt Maude," she whispered. "I'll do it just the way you wanted me to. The way you expected me to." Her attention dropped to the bejeweled pin resting in the palm of her hand. Deep inside the stone, in a sea of swirling fog, stood a warrior of darkness, his hard gaze locked with hers and the shining sword of death clutched tight in his whitened fist.

Alanna dropped the pin. Leaping back, she instinctively brought her arms up, her fists balled in preparation for defense. Only after a dozen seconds had crawled past did she begin to relax.

"Get a grip, Alanna," she admonished. "You're letting this whole hocus-pocus, Irish mythical stuff get to you. There are no fairies. There are no leprechauns." Leaning down, she snatched up the brooch as she added, "And you should know by now that there sure as hell is no such thing as a magical Dragon's Heart. You're just imagining things."

Despite her words of self-assurance, she didn't let her gaze return to the jewel. Instead she turned it over in her hand and freed the pin from the primitive clasp. In a gesture she had seen Maude make a thousand times, she flung a corner of the cloak over her left shoulder and fastened it into place with the brooch. Only then did she permit herself to glance down at the pin again. The stone sat as always in the center of the entwining silver circle, its highly polished surface mirroring the delicate light of the waxen moon, its heart red and empty and still. The sigh that escaped her lips was one of both relief and resolution.

Alanna turned her back on the muddy roadway and looked out across the field. In the distance, slowly rising from the shadows of a small copse of trees, sat a small grassy hillock, its crest crowned by a ring of massive stones. The Carraig Cor. Squinting, Alanna tried to see just what it was about the ancient circle that so obviously alarmed those to whom she had spoken of her mission. No Druids danced about in the full of the moon, and when she listened for the sound of pagan revelry, only the sound of the quiet night wind came to her ears.

Alanna shook her head as she remembered the wide-eyed stares the locals had fixed on her, their quick signing of the cross, the almost panicked refusal of three taxi drivers to bring her to this ancient place after dark. Only the promise of a quadruple fare and a liter of good Irish whiskey had gotten her a ride in the end, and even then she'd had to practically jump from the moving vehicle. Only a good sense of balance born from an adolescence spent climbing around the Rocky Mountains had saved her from a decidedly ignoble exit from the cab. Alanna looked down at her legs and feet. The not-so-incredible foresight to wear cotton knit leggings and a decent pair of boots would save her from an otherwise uncomfortably long walk back into town.

Alanna shrugged and then leaned down to place one hand atop the stone wall. With a single fluid movement, she vaulted over it, landing neatly on the other side. She took up the urn containing the remains of Maude O'Sullivan, and smiled as she cradled it against her side the same way she had carried a football down a sandlot field in her childhood. Somehow she knew that her dear aunt wouldn't mind being carted across the Irish countryside in such a manner. Maude had been nothing if not absolutely pragmatic. Besides, Alanna mused, what really mattered was the ritual to be performed in the circle of stones. *That* she would do exactly as Maude had prescribed.

She glanced up at the moon, noted its position, and then set out across the pasture with long, even strides. Alanna hoped she'd guessed the hour correctly. It would have been damn handy to have had her watch strapped to her wrist. But Maude's instructions had been quite specific, and so she had left in her hotel room everything mechanical and had brought nothing with her but those things which had been simply fashioned from, as Maude had always said, "the bounty of the Earth."

Alanna glanced down at her left hand and wondered again whether she should have put the diamond ring in the hotel vault before embarking on her quest. But it was probably safer on her finger than not, she reminded herself, and it was all-natural. Her new earrings certainly met Maude's exacting requirements. The silver Celtic crosses had simply been too beautiful, too quintessentially Irish, to leave in the little gift shop. Alanna smiled and with her free hand checked to make sure the backings were still secure. The right one felt slightly loose, and as she walked on toward the Carraig, she made a mental note to search her jewelry box for a better-fitting one when she got back to the hotel.

When the wind caught her hair and blew it across her face again, Alanna wished that she'd thought to bring a ribbon or a leather thong to tie it back with. She hadn't anticipated needing it though. In the twenty-four hours since her arrival in Ireland, her mind had been filled with remembering and practicing the strange words her aunt had wanted recited as her ashes were cast to the wind. While her ancestors had been Irish, Alanna had discovered as a child that any affinity for dealing with the Gaelic language had been bred out of the American branch of the O'Sullivan clan. She had no ear for the sound of it and she couldn't make any sense out of the written words either. Thank God Maude had had the good sense to write them down phonetically.

Her musings having carried her to the top of the Carraig Cor, Alanna paused at the outer edge of the stone circle to slow her breathing and order her thoughts. Maude had said she couldn't enter without being both inwardly and outwardly calm. Closing her eyes, she listened to the long sighs of the wind, felt the cool brush of it against her cheeks. It caught the long tendrils of her hair and tossed them gently about her face and shoulders but, unlike before, the sensation didn't irritate her. There was something about the place where she stood, something wild and elemental that came up through the soles of her boots to fill every fiber of her being, something that made the unfettered billowing of her hair seem right.

Alanna brought the urn away from her side and, holding it before her, stepped into the circle. Turning to the right, she began to chant the litany from memory and work her way around the ancient ring. As Maude had prescribed, she made six full counterclockwise trips around the enclosure, each moving her closer to the great stone in the center.

The seventh passage marked a change in the ritual, and Alanna dutifully fulfilled the requirements Maude had set down for her. Pausing beside the central stone, she faced to the east, lifted the urn above her head, and in a clear voice offered up the Gaelic words she didn't understand. Alanna lowered the marble amphora and then moved around the stone to repeat the offering three more times, once to the north, once to the west, once to the south.

Returning to the place where she had begun the final circle, she lifted the urn above her head one last time and chanted into the star-speckled blanket of the night sky. Lowering it, she removed the lid, closed her eyes, and, repeating the final portion of her memorized Gaelic, gently poured the ashen remains of Maude O'Sullivan onto the rock before her.

As though on cue, the wind gusted through the circle, lifting the edges of Alanna's cloak and whipping her hair into a silken cloud that wreathed her head and shoulders. And then, just as suddenly as it had arisen, the wind died completely. Alanna stood beside the stone, her eyes still closed, repeating the words required of her. The chill came without warning, cutting through her clothing to fill the center of her bones. She couldn't restrain the violent shudder that raced up the length of her spine, couldn't prevent the words from sticking on the tip of her tongue. In that single instant, the deep sense of calm she had brought into the circle evaporated and her eyes flew open.

A mist, milky white and heavy, swirled around her. With her heart lodged in her throat, Alanna spun about, straining to see through the dense fog, trying desperately to make out the dark shapes of the stone ring. Every instinct screamed for her to get away, and she obeyed without thought, stumbling blindly forward, her outstretched hands pawing through the thickening mist. She hadn't touched the hard assurance of rock, yet when the ground gradually descended and the mist about her thinned and swirled downward, she knew she'd passed through the ancient ring and on to the hillside beyond.

That knowledge dulled the sharpest edge of her panic but did nothing to slow her progress down the mist-shrouded hillock. Even as the tiny voice of reason within her whispered of her foolishness, Alanna felt her foot slide off a grassy clump. She tried to regain the balance so suddenly lost, but the effort was both short-lived and in vain. Flailing, she pitched forward and down, into the thick milky river that cut across the earth.

As she collapsed against the hardened ground, the air exploded from her lungs in a single painful burst, mingling her angry curse with an anguished cry. She lay sprawled across the wet grass, immersed in the whiteness of nothing, for what seemed an eternity, trying to draw a breath into a body that refused to function. Part of her wanted very much to dissolve into tears. Another part of her wanted to strike out in rage.

The latter easily won. Anger brought with it her breath. With a string of curses concerning the luck of the Irish and her own rash stupidity, Alanna drew her hands beneath her chest and pushed herself up. As she sat, she gazed out across the distance, expecting to see the spine of the stone wall rising through the fog and meandering off in either direction. Despite squinting, she saw nothing.

"Must have come down the blasted back side of this stupid thing," Alanna muttered, disgusted at the prospect of having to go around the hillock before she could even begin the trek across the meadow to the road. "Great," she muttered. "Just great."

With a sigh of resignation, she climbed to her feet. "Well, I've walked through worse," she assured herself as she started slowly down the fog-swept hill. She'd traveled less than ten feet when she was forced to stop. The fog rolled before her, hiding the ground. Attempting to traverse it blindly would only result in another fall, and Alanna knew that simple wisdom lay in patience, in staying where she was until the fog lifted.

Accepting the unavoidable situation, she turned to look back over her shoulder. The ring of stones sat mute atop the Carraig Cor as the moonlit mist poured through the spaces between them and flowed down the hill in her wake like something living, like something in conscious pursuit of her. As she watched, the last of the strange white cloud crossed through the stones and began its undulating descent. Alanna judged the distance between herself and the back edge of the mist advancing toward her and felt relieved. Once the fog lifted, once it rolled past, she would see the ground again and then she could get away from this eerie place.

Sighing again, she prepared to wait. The mist before her swirled up and curled back upon itself, as though propelled by a force far greater than its own. Alanna felt the hairs on the back of her neck prickle as a shudder raced up her spine. The rational part of her mind called her a damn fool, but she barely heard the words.

When the figure strode from the rising wall of mist, Alanna gaped in recognition. The vision from the ruby had taken form and life . . . the warrior of darkness, his gaze locked with hers and glittering darkly, the shining sword of death clutched tight in his whitened fist.

Alanna stepped back in the face of his advance, forgetting the uneven terrain beneath her feet until she caught her heel and staggered backward. With a shriek she tumbled back down into the blanket of mist.

He spoke, the sound so low and hard she felt it pass through her flesh. She shivered and, lifting her head above the plane of creamy fog, fastened her gaze on the man. He stood before her with his sword still raised, looking every bit as though he relished the thought of striking her head from her shoulders.

2

Her gaze swept down the length of him, her accountant's eye recording every detail in a fraction of time. She noted how his curled lips bared straight, strong teeth made even whiter by the raven black curls framing his face and cascading over his shoulders. How over a white shirt with a high collar he wore a dark, well-tailored double-breasted cropped coat with tails, while light-colored leggings that disappeared into polished black boots just below his knees completed the costume. Despite his eccentric appearance, she had been in enough boardrooms to recognize a man accustomed to power when she saw one. He stood above her, his long legs braced wide, the tension of his thigh muscles clearly evident beneath the form-fitting breeches.

Her gaze lifted back to the weapon he held poised beside his head. Straight out of *Ivanhoe*, she thought. The weapon might very well have been an antique, but the man wielding it was anything but. Her mental calculator tabulated late twenties, early thirties. His hand closed around the hilt of the sword with obvious ease, and the weight of it didn't appear to strain him in the least. And his shoulders . . . Alanna arched a brow in appreciation for what no foam-filled shoulder pads on Earth could accomplish.

His eyes narrowed as he considered her, and then he spoke the same words again. This time Alanna recognized the familiar sound of them.

"I don't speak Gaelic," she replied, shaking her head and pushing herself up.

"Stay where you are or suffer my blow!"

Alanna froze at his command. In a land where English was the everyday language, his use of it wasn't all that surprising. And the archaic wording was typical of the Irish penchant for lyrical syntax. What stunned her was the pure vehemence ripping through the order.

"Look," she offered after a quick swallow. "I'm sorry if I'm trespassing, but don't you think you're overreacting just a tad?" She jerked her head to indicate the circle atop the hill as she added, "It's not like I'm gonna make off with one of the great stones or anything."

"You're not the woman I was sent to find," he said through his teeth. "What have you done with her?"

Alanna shook her head. The man wasn't foaming at the mouth, and his eyes were seemingly clear and well focused. Still . . . The Irish lilt to his speech was less pronounced than what she had already become accustomed to hearing, and she wondered if he might be from one of the counties to the north. Certainly members of the Irish Republican Army didn't run about the countryside in the middle of the night, dressed in early-nineteenth-century costumes, committing terrorist acts against unsuspecting American tourists. Or did they? "I came out here alone," she answered softly. "I came to—"

"Where is the Seer of the Ancient Find?" he demanded.

Again Alanna shook her head. "I'm not understanding. Could you possibly put your request into an American version of English?"

A flicker of confusion passed over his finely chiseled features. In the same instant, he demanded, "Where is Maude O'Sullivan?"

Alanna, astounded that he would utter her aunt's name, answered before she could think better of it. "Scattered to the four winds."

His jaw tightened as though she had struck him, and she heard the harsh sound of his indrawn breath. Before he could move, before he could speak, she rushed to add, "Aunt Maude died three weeks ago. It was her last request that I bring her ashes to Ireland, to the Carraig Cor, and release them. And that's just what I did."

He lowered the blade slightly and she saw his gaze slide down the length of her body. The boldness of his open appraisal, the tingling current that passed through her in its wake, suffused her cheeks with heated indignation. "Hasn't anyone ever mentioned to you how rude it is to leer at a woman?"

His gaze came back to hers, and an amused smile spread across his face. Slowly he lowered the sword, then planted the tip of it in the ground between his booted feet and rested his hands atop the knob-ended hilt. "From what region of the American republic do you hail, woman? Your speech is difficult to place."

"If you don't mind, I'd much rather have this conversation while standing on my feet. The ground's just a little too damp to be comfortable."

He shook his head. "For the moment, you'll remain as you are," he said. The evenness of his tone did nothing to disguise the essence of a command. "When I'm satisfied with your answers, I'll give you leave to rise."

"You'll give me *leave*?" Alanna repeated, incredulous. She bolted upright. "I don't think so, Mr. High-and—" The cold prick of the blade against the base of her throat brought an abrupt end to both her words and her efforts to stand. Looking up the length of the sword, she glared at him and clenched her teeth in silent rage. Instincts from a long-ago part of her life slipped instantly into place, their edge still sharp despite the intervening years with Maude. Alanna studied him with narrowed eyes.

"Now, woman," he began, his tone and smile mocking. "I inquired as to your home. I await your answer." He gazed pointedly at the blade at her throat. "And none too patiently, I might add."

"Durango," Alanna answered, refusing to give him so much as a single extra syllable in the way of an explanation. Let him work for it, she thought.

"And where is this village? In which of our states?"

Our? "Colorado," she replied, her thoughts suddenly rac-

ing. He wasn't *Irish* Irish. He was American Irish. Which
went a long way toward explaining his general failure to
abide by the accepted rules of Irish hospitality. Judging by
his abrasive manner, probably big-city American Irish. That
would be New York or Boston. Yet his accent wasn't typical
of either place. Oddly, it had a Southern quality to it.

The sound of his voice interrupted her musings. She
refocused on him. "I beg your pardon," she offered, arching
a sardonic brow. "I wasn't paying attention."

His smile tightened and his tone took on an acerbic edge
when he countered, "I realize that the feminine mind is
prone to weakness, but try to concentrate on the matter at
hand. I should dislike having to scar such a beautiful throat
as yours." He too lifted a brow as he added, "But then, I'm
not known for my restraint."

"Among other things, I'm sure," Alanna observed.

He offered her an unrepentant smile and an abbreviated
bow. "Allow me to repeat my earlier inquiry, mistress. Why
did Maude O'Sullivan select you to bear home her remains?"

Pondering his use of the old-fashioned term of address,
Alanna answered with the simplest of the truths. "Because
she knew I would."

She saw that her answer hadn't been the one he'd wanted.
This time she resisted the impulse to fuel his anger with a
taunt. Instead she focused her attention on the way the hair
curled at his temples, and waited.

"Do you possess the gift?"

Alanna shrugged to the limited degree permitted by the
blade at her throat and replied, "I don't know what you're
talking about."

"Can you see events not yet occurred?"

Unbidden, she recalled how, only less than an hour earlier, his face had swirled in the mists within the Dragon's
Heart. But that had been a fluke if ever there was one. Even
as she prepared her denial, the stranger removed the sword
from her throat. In almost the same heartbeat, she heard it
slide into a scabbard.

"Then you'll do for the task at hand," he stated. "Get up."

Alanna instinctively refused, saying, "You're mistaken. I can't see . . ."

"You're lying, mistress," he interrupted, his tone hard and cold. "Now rise to your feet or I'll be forced to haul you about in the ignoble fashion of a rather large sack of potatoes."

"You wouldn't dare."

He chuckled but Alanna heard no humor in the sound. "Oh, but indeed I would. I have far too much at stake in this venture to allow you to be recalcitrant. I'll permit you to choose only the manner in which you'll accompany me. Would you prefer to walk or that I sling you over my shoulder?"

Alanna clambered to her feet with all the dignity she could muster. Brushing debris from her clothing, she snapped, "This is kidnapping. If you think you can get away with it, you're insane."

He smiled wryly. "This is Ireland, mistress. People disappear every day. That you've vanished like so many others will cause but the briefest of ripples."

"Really?" she shot back caustically. "And do Americans disappear on a regular basis?"

"There are but few Americans amidst this chaos. The relations between our country and England preclude even the slightest concern over their fate. Now . . ." He bowed at the waist and swept his arm across his body in an exaggerated gesture as he mockingly said, ". . . if you please."

She met his gaze and in the moonlight her violet eyes appeared as dark and determined as his. "It's clear that there's no reasoning with you and that my options are limited to say the least. Do you suppose I might ask where you intend to take me?"

With deliberate calm she turned to survey the land about her. The fog had dissipated and before her lay a short expanse of open meadow bordered by a narrow band of stubby trees. It wasn't much in the way of cover, and she had no idea where she might go once she reached the thicket, but it was obviously the best chance she had for escaping him.

From behind her she heard him reply, "I shall say nothing of our destination. Should—"

She didn't wait to hear the rest. With everything she could muster, Alanna sprang away. She raced down the hill and onto the flat open ground, driven by a massive surge of adrenaline, her feet flying over the grassy terrain, her hair streaming behind her like a silken banner. Halfway across the field, she risked a glance back over her shoulder. As she'd expected, he pursued her. But to her alarm, his pace was nothing more than an easy lope, the pace of a man unconcerned with his quarry's speed or direction or plan.

She ran faster, swallowing back her fear as she bounded into the shadows of the trees. Instinctively she veered to her left and raced a serpentine course through the maze of gnarled trunks, ducking beneath the low spreading limbs that lay across her unmarked path. She was only vaguely aware of how the smaller branches snagged her cloak, of how she pulled and twisted out of their reach.

After what seemed a thousand miles, she skittered to a stop and turned back to search through the shadows. Her chest rose and fell as her breath came in hard, desperate snatches while she stared at the utterly, completely, and absolutely impossible. One by one the trees divided themselves and slowly started after her.

Panic raced through her. In the inky moments that followed, Alanna saw only the haunted shapes of the things that moved relentlessly toward her; heard only the pounding of her fear and the shrill demand of her desperate mind. Precious seconds passed before she could will her body to obey the command to move.

Whirling about, she sprinted blindly forward, her arms and legs pumping furiously, her mind tortured with the crawling pace of her flight. That one portion of her brain still rational tried to speak of panic-induced delusions, but her fear drowned it out. She kept running, ducking her head beneath branches she could barely see, holding her forearm before her face to protect it as best she could.

Suddenly, at the edge of her vision, Alanna saw the tree, massive and dark, in her path. Her feet slipped in the woody debris of the thicket floor as she shifted her weight and direction. She felt her shoulder brush against it as she pivoted and dashed past. The sensation came a heartbeat too late, only after the great thing had reached out, caught her about the waist, and hauled her back against it.

The band holding her prisoner had the strength of hardened oak but the warmth and sinewy strength of a man—a man who, despite her thrashing, held her with surprising gentleness.

"Easy now, colleen," he crooned in her ear. " 'Tis naught ye have to fear. The lads an' me are here to protect ye."

The sincerity of his words soothed her as much as the sound of his voice. Casting her lot with instinctive trust, Alanna collapsed against him and choked out, "He's after me. He's got a sword."

" 'Twould be Kiervan of whom ye speak, no doubt. A rough bit of news he is to be sure, but an O'Connell to the center of his bones. He'd not harm ye, colleen. I give ye me word on it."

A chorus of murmured assents filled the darkness around her. She turned her head to peer into the shadows, to separate the human forms from those of the trees. An even dozen men, dressed rough and dark, stood between her and freedom. No wonder her attacker hadn't pursued her with any urgency. He had let her run into the waiting arms of his fellow terrorists. "Please," she pleaded. "Let me go. Holding me for ransom is useless. Bill won't pay it."

" 'Tis that what ye think we're about, colleen? Did Kiervan not offer ye an explanation of our need?" He made a sound in his throat that spoke eloquently of his displeasure.

"I'm an American citizen," Alanna went on.

"And a poorly mannered one at that," said a chillingly familiar voice.

She molded herself against the broad expanse of man at her back. If he spoke the truth about protecting her . . .

"Kiervan, lad," her benefactor said, his voice low but carrying well across the wooded space. " 'Twould be difficult for anyone to be gracious under dire threat. We sent ye up there thinkin' ye would keep yer own wits about ye."

"You sent me up there because I'm the only man who would go."

She felt the chest behind her rise and fall in the quick measure of silent mirth. After a moment he answered, " 'Tis true enough, to be sure."

"And if you'd care to take a closer look at that bit of baggage you're clutching, you might notice that she's not an old woman like Maude O'Sullivan was to have been."

The giant at her back chuckled again and shifted his hold, lifting her up and settling her against his side. "Neither a priest nor an old man am I, Kiervan me lad. If Maude sent another, a younger woman, in her stead, I'll not question her wisdom in the matter and I'll not be ungrateful."

A chorus of agreement rose around her, fueling Alanna's sense of desperation and loosening her tongue. "I have no idea who you people are or what you're about, but Maude did not send me. Now put me down before you break my ribs."

"I'd suggest you refuse, my friend," said Kiervan. "While she plays the docile maid, she plots her escape. If you value her as you say, you'd be wise to bind and gag her for the length of our journey."

"You can't just haul me off like . . . like . . ."

"A sack of potatoes?" Kiervan supplied. Even in the darkness she knew the taunt had been accompanied by a grim smile.

" 'Twouldn't be right to do such a thing," said the man who held her. " 'Twouldn't be showin' the proper respect for a Seer of the Find."

"As I've already explained to Kiervan, the King of the Irritating," Alanna protested, trying to wiggle out of the man's embrace, "I'm not any seer of some find."

"No?" His voice had a sharper edge when he asked, "Did she come alone, Kiervan? Was there another in her company?"

"She's the only one I saw. If there's a second, then she came wearing a fairy cloak."

A low murmur of awe and fear rippled around the ring of men beneath the trees.

"For heavens sakes, guys," Alanna muttered. "Try to get a grip on reality here. I'm Alanna Kathleen Chapman, a flesh-and-blood certified public accountant from Durango, Colorado, in America. I came to Ireland and the Carraig Cor to release my aunt Maude's ashes like she wanted. I don't give a damn about your Irish politics. Now we've reached the point where enough is enough. Put me down and let me go."

"Maude is dead?"

Why were these people so fixated on the subject of Maude's demise? "Yes. Three weeks ago," Alanna ground out.

The man who held her drew a breath as though to speak, but a distant, soft whistle stalled his words. He turned with such speed that for an instant Alanna's world blurred. In the haze of her righting vision, she saw a shadow bolt from the trees and slide to an abrupt stop before her protector-turned-captor.

"A patrol of twenty, Paddy," the newly arrived man whispered breathlessly. "Comin' up the draw from the east."

"Then 'tis time we be puttin' the Carraig behind us, lads," answered the man who held her, the man named Paddy. Spinning about to address the others, he continued in the same breath, "Eoghan will lead us out of here. Brian will bring up the rear."

Alanna nearly collapsed as Paddy suddenly dropped her to her feet. Catching her balance, she stepped beyond the immediate reach of his arms. She saw the men melding into the thicket of shadows and motioned Paddy to join them as she whispered with calm assurance, "You didn't hurt me, so I won't tell them which way you went. I'll lead them away."

"You'll be comin' with us, colleen," he said, shaking his head. "Ye have no choice. Ye of all women mustn't fall into their filthy hands."

Alanna planted her feet and folded her arms across her

chest. "Dragging me kicking and screaming is really going to slow you down."

"That it would, mistress," growled Kiervan from behind her. In the same moment of time, he grabbed her shoulder and spun her about to face him. His features were hard, his face a mask of determination. Suddenly, without any other warning, his fist sent her into a well of reddened pain that ended abruptly in blackness.

3

Kiervan des Marceaux stood at the gunwale and angled his open palm into the moonlight. The tiny Celtic cross glimmered softly, the bright silver in stark contrast to his work-darkened and callused hand. Alanna Chapman's earring could very well have been fashioned as a companion piece to the pendant he kept locked in his desk.

His brows furrowed as a long-ago night came back to him: the last memories of his mother, pale and weak, her fingers twined through his, her eyes bright with fever, her words desperate whispers that tore her parched lips. She had paused in her passing to press her most valuable possession into his hands, to admonish him to keep it always safe. She had been too young to die, he thought, barely thirty-five years old. He'd been only half her age that horrible, stormy night but he'd calmly sat beside her, held her hand, and at the last, swore before God that he would see done everything her heart had ever wanted. And when she'd left him forever, he'd gazed down at the pendant in his hand, at the emerald-studded silver Celtic cross, and railed against the cruelty of her kinsmen and an uncaring God. Her hands had grown cold when he had finally released them. Then he stood, squared his shoulders, brushed away the last tears he swore he would ever shed, and went to comfort his brother and sisters.

Kiervan lifted his face to the night wind and let it caress him, remembering his mother's gentle touch, remembering the sacred pledges of that night, the promises that had set his course in life and finally brought him to Ireland and his mother's kinsmen. Had it not been for the peace of her soul, he would have gladly died without ever having set eyes on any of the dark-hearted O'Connells.

Kiervan resolutely tucked his memories away. Then he refocused his gaze on the earring in his hand.

Since Alanna Chapman wore only the one earring and both her earlobes had obviously been pierced, the explanation was relatively simple: the other had been lost. He tried to remember whether she'd been wearing one or two when he'd held her at blade point, but try as he might, he couldn't seem to recall any details of those moments other than the fire in her violet eyes.

His blood warmed as the most recent memories of his prisoner assailed him. Clenching his teeth and willing his mind elsewhere, he examined the earring again, noting the time-honored, simple construction, noting with considerable interest the innovative rolled clasp which secured it. Should, in the days ahead, Mistress Chapman prove herself a more gracious guest than she'd been thus far, he could easily fashion her another earring to match. Although he'd brought aboard only the simplest of his silversmithing tools, they'd be entirely sufficient for such a simple task.

"Considering the risks, that's a rather paltry bit of booty, Captain," offered a familiar voice.

Kiervan smiled as his First Officer came to stand beside him. "It's only paltry, Richard," Kiervan parried, "if you choose to ignore the ravishing young woman from whose earlobe I had the pleasure of removing it."

"Any self-respecting pirate would have taken both earrings," countered Richard St. John with a grin, resting his elbows on the railing and gazing out over the night sea. "I do believe you're becoming a shade of respectable, Kiervan. Must be your pending—"

"Mistress Chapman had only the one," he interrupted, deliberately diverting the direction of their conversation. "Besides, any self-respecting pirate would have taken the woman and let her keep the earring. Of course, it's a mystery as to why she wears ear bobs of such simple design and materials with a ruby-and-silver brooch worth a king's ransom on her cloak and a diamond the size of a robin's egg on her hand." He slapped the railing and with wholly feigned surprise, moaned, "Damn! I am slipping. I should've taken the brooch and the ring too, shouldn't I?"

"A diamond the size of a robin's egg? Kiervan, I've never known you to tend toward exaggeration. I think perhaps you've been around your kinsmen too long."

His gaze sliding to the rocky shadow rising up from the ink-dark water, Kiervan sobered and answered quietly, "I didn't believe their cockeyed stories either, but I watched her come across time with my own eyes, Richard."

"Could it have been trickery of some sort?"

Kiervan shook his head and slipped the earring into the inside breast pocket of his coat. "I felt the unearthly cold as the door opened. I stood against the stones and watched her stumble through the mist. There was no trickery, Richard. Her manner and speech alone mark her as being from another place and time."

"Well," Richard St. John said with a shrug of his capable shoulders, "Paddy O'Connell seems sufficiently convinced. Some of the others are grumbling, but he's assuring them that this woman will suffice for the purpose."

"Are they settled for the trip back to Bantry?" Kiervan inquired, straightening and turning to gaze at the stern, noting the dark shapes moving about in the shadows.

"Aye, Captain. And I reiterated your orders for quiet. As soon as we can be reasonably assured that the British patrol boats have passed, we'll be on our way."

Flashing his First Officer a grin, Kiervan said, "Until then, Mr. St. John, I'll be in my cabin . . . seeing to the various needs of Mistress Chapman. Call me when we're ready to open sail."

"Aye, aye, Captain," Richard murmured, staring out over the water.

Kiervan ignored the note of disapproval in his friend's voice and walked away. Halfway to the blockhouse, he paused, turned slightly, and pointed to the newest cannon at midship. "Toss a blanket over that thing before it lights up the bay for the British and gets us all killed. And tell the well-meaning soul who's been polishing it to stop. Just because Paul Revere made it, doesn't mean that it should gleam like your aunt Polly's tea set."

He had just pulled open the blockhouse door when the sounds of the night sea were drowned by Paddy's raucous laughter. With his blood pounding in his temples, Kiervan temporarily set aside his original destination and moved silently and resolutely toward the stern.

Alanna struggled to slip back into the abyss of nothingness, but the pain wouldn't permit the escape. Everything hurt too badly to be obliterated by sleep. Her jaw pounded hard and hot where Kiervan had struck her. Her teeth ached, and with each breath she took, her neck muscles protested. And her midsection . . . Even though she lay still and flat on her back, her torso felt battered and bruised, almost as though she had spent considerable time bouncing up and down on something as soft and yielding as a concrete post.

Kiervan's shoulder instantly came to mind and in the wake of the image rode a host of unsavory adjectives. She clenched her teeth in anger, and pain, white and piercing, shot around the length of her jaw. She immediately released the pressure and vowed that no power in heaven or on Earth would save him if she ever got her hands on him. But, she reminded herself, revenge would have to wait. She needed to put first things first, needed to figure out just where the hell she had been taken. Resolutely she opened her eyes.

A lantern? Surely not in this day and age, she assured herself, blinking to readjust the focus of her vision. The effort produced no change in the sight above her head. The roof was low and constructed of what appeared to be tongue-in-groove oaken planks. Just beyond the foot of her bed, the lantern hung from a hook three-quarters of the way up a curved wall made in the same fashion as the ceiling.

A curved wall? Of course, she thought, like on a really old ship. The realization went a long way toward explaining the gentle rocking motion of the room, the twin tangs of salt air and pine pitch, and the long, mournful creaking of wood that reverberated all around her. *Lord,* she thought, *if I don't pull it together pretty quick* . . .

The oil-fed flame cast a meager pool of light, and yet there was more illumination in the room than that afforded by the single lamp. Moving her head produced a wave of pain down her neck and across her shoulders, but the effort was rewarded with a wider view of the world she had awakened in. On the opposite wall, three identical lanterns glowed with brighter lights. She decided her prison probably measured ten feet square. The massive beam running across the width of the low ceiling just made it seem smaller.

Alanna inventoried the contents of the room with a quick glance. A washstand had been placed against the opposite wall, and a basin and pitcher sat atop the sturdy piece of furniture. Along the same wall, just a short distance away, rested a large wooden box, the color deepened with obvious age and marred by rough travel. A russet and powder blue braided oval rug covered most of the planked floor, extending almost to the door at one end of the room. On the other end, it stopped just short of the biggest desk Alanna had ever seen. Antique and definitely executive quality, she thought.

Kiervan. Hadn't one of her first impressions of the man been of his sense of power and command? This had to be Kiervan's room. Not room, she reminded herself. On ships, personal spaces were called either quarters or cabins. "Cell, in this case," she muttered. The effort of speech, just the gentle contact of her tongue against her teeth, sent a wave of pain over her face.

Alanna freed a hand from the bed coverings. Gingerly she touched her jaw, finding the flesh beneath her fingertips swollen and hard. The bastard. If she looked as bad as she felt . . . "Wow," she whispered, her gaze fastening on the delicate lace trimming the cuff of her sleeve. "Gorgeous stuff." But how and when had she gotten into a linen and lace nightgown?

The likely answer came swiftly. He had dared to take

such liberties? Another thought followed instantly. Kiervan could return at any time. Prudence dictated an immediate escape.

With a low groan, she flung aside the bed coverings. Sitting upright strained her already abused midsection, but she willed herself to ignore the discomfort. Despite her resolve, climbing from the bed became considerably more than a matter of simply throwing her legs over the side and standing on her feet. Like quicksand, the mattress seemed to pull her deeper into itself with every move she made. In exasperation, Alanna grabbed a handful of the thing and jerked it back to view the monster lying hidden beneath.

Ropes? A net of woven ropes? That was odd, she thought. Her gaze came up. An honest to goodness feather mattress? Like in "The Princess and the Pea"? She shook her head, tossed aside the bolster, and then flopped onto her stomach. As she wiggled toward the outer edge of the feathery pit, she added masochism to the already lengthy list of Kiervan's faults.

Gaining her feet, she paused only a moment to orient herself and to rearrange the yards of linen which had twisted around her body in the struggle to be free of the bed. She glanced down at the fabric pooled at her feet. Obviously the nightgown had been made for a much taller woman. Alanna gathered up handfuls of the cloth, lifting the hem above her ankles, and moved across the braided rug toward the door.

The door latch lifted easily but no amount of pushing or pulling would budge the steel-banded panel. "Locked from the outside," she muttered, abandoning the task and turning back into the room.

Her gaze swept over the two round windows set high in each of the exterior walls. She padded toward the one under which a heavy chest had been placed. Standing on her tiptoes on the chest, she could see the world beyond the confines of her cozy prison.

The sight did nothing to soothe her growing panic. A pale moon hung low in the sky, its subtle light reflecting off the glassy swells of a jade green sea. In the distance, silhouetted against the night, rose a rocky shoreline, its spine rimmed by moon gold, its face dark in unapologetic, unyielding melancholy.

Alanna swallowed and, laying her head against the coolness of the windowpane, silently grieved for the loss of her greatest hope. She straightened a moment later and, with a deep breath, lifted her chin and squared her shoulders. "All right," she whispered, turning away from the window, "Plan B."

She slipped behind the huge desk, pushing the chair aside so that she had clear access. The work surface, covered with papers, looked as though the occupant had been called from his tasks unexpectedly. Alanna studied the map lying half unrolled atop the other things. A navigational chart? she wondered. Hand drawn?

Shaking her head in consternation, she lifted up one corner to peek at the papers under it. As she did, a bright object slid from the still-coiled end of the parchment and fell to the floor with a heavy, metallic thud. She stooped to retrieve it, suddenly picturing the classic picture of Christopher Columbus facing bravely into the wind and the setting sun, a rolled chart in one hand, a sextant in the other.

"Damn," she muttered, turning the device over and over in her hands. "Who would've guessed it'd be this heavy?" Lifting it up, she squinted into the eyepiece for a long moment, saw nothing of any particular significance, then lowered it with a quick shrug.

The long, neat columns of a ledger caught her attention, and she set aside the sextant. Running her finger down the list of goods stowed within the cargo hold, Alanna noted the use of both American and British symbols for weights and monetary values. A man with a foot in both worlds, she noted. But what an incredibly odd assortment of commodities to be collected in one place: rice and silk, dried peaches and wheat, salted cod and hides. All the notations had been entered into the accounts in a strong but elegant script.

Probably a secretary who does handwritten wedding invitations on the side, biding her time and hoping for deliverance, she thought. Another poor artistic soul trapped in the world of having to pay the rent.

Another book, also open on the desktop, caught her eye. At a glance Alanna knew the same hand that had filled the ledger had also penned the entries in what appeared to be the ship's log. She bent forward to read the words, her gaze instinctively seeking the date of the record.

"No way!" she cried, suddenly straightening and rubbing her eyes. She bent forward again. No, she had seen it right the first time. The last entry was clearly dated 20 March 1803. "That can't be right," she sputtered. Then an explanation came to her. Of course! The ship was a living diorama! Undoubtedly used so that unsuspecting tourists could fund the wackos' revolutionary efforts.

Relieved, she focused her attention on the short paragraph under the date and read the account of the ship's sailing from an unnamed port and its arrival at an unnamed destination. And at the very bottom, with a line between it and the passage, was a name. Kiervan des Marceaux.

A Frenchman? She shook her head. No, she believed him to be an American like herself, and his accent had a truly Southern quality to it. But hadn't the man called Paddy claimed that her assailant was an O'Connell to the bone? She arched a brow at a sudden wry thought. Irish-French-American, a true Heinz Fifty-Seven.

Tracing an invisible line beneath his signature with her fingertip, she said softly, "Kiervan des Marceaux." She repeated it again, letting his first name lilt off her tongue in the Irish fashion and then shifting to a rounded, full French pronunciation of his surname.

"Well done, Mistress Chapman."

She started, jumping back from the desk, embarrassed at being caught snooping. He stood in the doorway, one shoulder resting against the jamb, his arms folded over his chest, his weight resting casually on one leg.

Alanna caught her breath as her gaze swept the length of him. Even in the open space of the Carraig Cor, even in the darkness of moonlight, she had known that he possessed an indomitable vitality and will, that his rugged features had been chiseled by an artist's hand. But within the confines of the ship's cabin, bathed in the warm light of the lamps, he was far more handsome, and more frighteningly powerful, than ever.

"Are you a student of languages as well as witchcraft?" he asked, straightening his long frame and stepping across the threshold.

His words shattered the spell his physical presence had woven over her. Alanna crossed her arms defensively over her chest. "How long have you been standing there watching me?"

Turning, he pulled the door closed as he replied, "You were perusing the manifest when I returned. Did you discover anything of note?"

Alanna recognized his attempt at civility, but her well-honed instincts understood the danger of letting another set the terms of a conflict. She had every right to be angry, really angry, with him. In her most imperious tone, she demanded, "Hasn't anyone ever told you it's rude to watch someone without making your presence known?"

He cocked a brow derisively. "Has no one ever mentioned to you that it is equally rude to rifle through another's personal effects?"

"I'm a prisoner," Alanna replied, lifting her bruised chin. "The rules of etiquette don't apply to me."

"I'm a warden," he shot back, crossing the room with easy strides, his dark gaze holding hers. "The rules of etiquette don't apply to me either."

"Well, Mr. Sing Sing," Alanna snapped, backing up in the face of his advance, "if it isn't against your regulations, would you mind telling me why in hell's name I am being held against my will? Why have I been kidnapped and stashed in this floating naval museum?"

Stopping at the end of the desk, he studied her for a long moment before he answered, "Because certain members of the O'Connells needed Maude O'Sullivan, and she sent you in her stead."

"Damn it!" Alanna cried, flinging her hands up in irritation. "You make it sound like some top secret spy mission!

How many times do I have to tell you that my aunt Maude is dead? How many times do I have to tell you the story of bringing her ashes to the Carraig Cor? When are you going to listen?"

"I would suggest that you are asking the wrong questions of the wrong person, Mistress Chapman."

"Well, if you'd be so kind as to enlighten me, I'll just haul my little fanny out of here and get this whole mess straightened out."

"Patrick O'Connell is the man who can provide you with an explanation," he replied, reaching down and pulling open the center drawer in his desk. She watched as he took something from an inside pocket of his coat and deposited it inside before closing it and then opening one of the deeper drawers on the side of the massive piece of furniture.

Removing a decanter of amber liquid and two crystal glasses, he set about pouring drinks as he continued, "Not that I wholly accept the possibility of your mission, mind you. While traveling through time is a most interesting notion, it's nevertheless one I could share only in a wharfside tavern and then only after the other patrons were so deep into their cups as to be far beyond reason."

Refusing to be sidetracked, she asked with fraying patience, "And might I inquire as to the whereabouts of this Patrick O'Connell?"

"Paddy?" He shrugged. "Well into *his* cups."

"The Paddy from the woods?"

"The same. Would you care for a drink?" He lifted his gaze to meet hers and offered one of the glasses.

Alanna straightened to her full height. "I don't drink with strangers."

A knowing smile barely touched the corners of his mouth. "We're hardly strangers, Alanna." His gaze glided slowly down the length of her, and she knew that the linen gown hid nothing from him. A strange and wholly unwelcome jolt of excitement shot through her, and she railed against the traitorous warmth spreading through her limbs.

Angry and indignant, she took another step back. "You don't possess a single shred of decency."

"You're a perceptive woman, Mistress Chapman," he replied, his expression hardening. Setting the second glass down on the desk, he lifted his own in salute. "To Maude's wisdom, Paddy's dream, and my profit. May you play your part well."

4

Arms akimbo, Alanna demanded, "And just what part is it that I'm supposed to play?"

His response came without the slightest hesitation. "A traveler from another time and place."

"Really?" she scoffed. "Like what? Mars in the year 2525?"

He took a slow sip of his drink before responding, "As Maude foretold before she left, America in the year 1997."

Making no attempt to disguise her sarcasm, Alanna clasped her hands together and said, "Golly gee, I just don't know. It'd be such a stretch. I'm not sure I can pull it off."

He glanced down at his whiskey and offered it a smile of pure appreciation, a smile that instantly transformed his face. "Damn fine whiskey the Irish brew," he said, shaking his head slowly. "Smooth as arctic ice and just as dangerous. It'll creep up on a man from behind and without the slightest of warnings. Leave him reeling and trying to make sense of nonsense."

"I'm impressed by your eloquent description of Irish spirits, but I'd much prefer to continue with the previous subject."

He chuckled and took another sip of his drink.

"Forgive me," Alanna snapped, "but I fail to see anything humorous in either my situation or my expectations."

He tilted his head to the side and studied her for a half dozen heartbeats before his smile faded and he said, "I apologize for my amusement." He straightened and set aside his glass. Facing her squarely, he fastened his gaze on her. "Let us attempt to begin anew."

"It it's all the same to you, I'd much rather just part company."

"Alas, that won't be possible for some time yet. Perhaps in a fortnight or two you shall be permitted to leave."

"You've been part of this little museum project a tad too long, Mr. des Marceaux. Your attitudes have become as archaic as your speech."

"It's *Captain* des Marceaux."

"President of the International Association of Maritime Wardens, I'm sure," Alanna shot back. "You've been out to sea a very long time, *Captain*. Spending a day or two on land might do you good. You know, let you get caught up on the latest news and all. Like finding out that the word 'alas' died a well-deserved death a couple hundred years ago."

He reached for his drink and, shaking his head, lifted it to his lips. Instead of taking a sip, he downed the remaining whiskey in one long swallow. Refilling the glass from the decanter, he asked, "In what year were you born, mistress?"

Alanna looked to the ceiling, hoping for heavenly intervention. "In 1969," she replied on a long breath. "And let me save you the math work. I'm twenty-seven. Twenty-eight in October."

He stared into his drink and nodded. Without looking up he declared, "I'm a score and twelve. Or, as you would say, thirty-two." Slowly he lifted his gaze again. "I was born in Plaquemines Parish, near New Orleans," he said. "In the year 1772."

"Yeah, right."

"You doubt my word?"

"I figure I have three choices here." Alanna held up her index finger. "One, you're the ghost of a long-dead, guilt-ridden sailor who believes that the rest of the world is as stuck in time as he is." She added a second finger. "Or two, you're a schizophrenic who's lost all touch with reality, having become trapped while vacationing in an alternate personality." Adding another finger to the count, she went on, saying, "Or three, I took a *really* wrong turn coming out of the travel agency. Now, my jaw hurts like hell and I've never heard of a ghost who could deliver that kind of a wallop. Which, all in all, eliminates the first choice. And while I don't mean to denigrate the New Age crystal clutchers, I know that waltzing through an open door in the space-time continuum is scientifically impossible. That pretty much eliminates the third option."

"I gather you're convinced that my mind is deranged," he finished dryly.

Alanna shrugged. "It works for me."

"And what proof might I offer to convince you otherwise, mistress?"

"Offhand I'd say that it would have to be a personal message from God."

He chuckled, and a most human smile brightened his face. Alanna felt the tightness in her chest soften at the sight, but quickly reminded herself that the man was her enemy.

"Words from the Lord, mistress?"

"More like from Lucifer," she retorted, spinning about and presenting him with a view of her back. His chuckle came softly to her ears and sent a flush of heat across her cheeks. It bothered her that she wasn't sure of the source of his amusement. Rather than have him believe her a coward, or let him ogle the contours of her backside, she gathered up her nightgown and resolutely stomped away. The folly of her action occurred to her only after she had committed herself to the course. The one place to go was the bed. And she wasn't about to provide him with even the slightest room to misconstrue her feelings about him.

As she reached the edge of the oval rug, she spun back to face him. He met her gaze and lifted an expectant brow. "Normally I'm better mannered, Captain," she began coolly, "but I'm beginning to tire of this whole melodrama. And quite frankly, I don't feel obligated to be especially polite anymore." She paused to add emphasis to her next words. "Just who the hell are you and what gives you the right to hold me prisoner?"

"Kiervan des Marceaux, captain of the *Wind Racer*, an

American privateer sailing out of the French port of New Orleans," he offered with another of his short bows. "And I have no right to hold you prisoner beyond my ability to do so for as long as it pleases me and those with whom I seek to do business."

"Then you're holding me for ransom."

"In an indirect manner, yes."

"How much are you asking for me?"

A devilish smile lifted one corner of his mouth and amusement danced in the depths of his dark eyes. "Your worth depends entirely upon your specific talents, mistress."

"You're a . . . a . . ." she sputtered, unable in the end to find a word adequate to express her raging indignation.

"Rogue?" he offered.

"Bastard!" she retorted, spitting the malediction through her teeth.

His smile turned bitter. "Indeed I am, mistress. Recognized and bound by no man's laws."

"The accident of one's birth is no excuse for hooliganism."

"Hooliganism?" he asked, both brows rising and the corners of his mouth twitching. "While I consider myself a man of wide experience, I'm not familiar with that particular curse, Mistress Chapman. Would you be willing to define it for me?"

"It means behaving like a ruffian or a gutter rat or a—"

"I have an acceptable understanding now. Thank you."

"You're welcome," Alanna shot back. "Can I explain any other words for you?"

He appeared to think for a moment, and then nodded slowly. "I'm curious about what you call 'New Age crystal clutchers.'"

The muscles beneath her eyes twitched as she replied icily, "It would take far more time than I have."

"You have at least a fortnight," he reminded her, shrugging his massive shoulders and settling himself on the corner of his desk. "And I'm reasonably patient."

"Well, I'm not."

"So I've noticed, mistress. So I've noticed."

"And neither do I have the inclination to explain one damn thing to you."

"Then permit *me* to enlighten *you*, mistress," he replied, his tone cooling.

In his words, Alanna heard the ominous rumbling of a gathering storm. In his eyes, she saw the unmistakable spark of lightning. She took a deep breath and, with bravado as her shield, said, "I don't care to hear a single thing you have to say, Captain des Marceaux. I'm tired of all this, and talking has made my jaw hurt even worse than it did before."

"Then allow me to do the talking, Mistress Chapman. You need only nod your understanding and assent from time to time. I'll tell you when."

She glared at him and silently called him a horse's ass.

"Perhaps you might like to be seated while we conduct our business?" he asked, gesturing toward the chair she had shoved aside earlier.

Alanna lifted her chin and widened her stance. "Aunt Maude warned me about jerks like you."

He shrugged and crossed his arms over his chest. "Another curse, I assume. We'll come back to it some other time. At the moment, I have more pressing concerns."

Alanna stared at him in stony silence.

"It matters not one whit to me whether you were a willing party to what transpired on the Carraig Cor this night. You are here and Paddy believes you to be the representative of Maude O'Sullivan. His certainty is sufficient for my purpose."

Representative? His purpose? Alanna willed her face to remain an impassive mask, refusing to give voice to her curiosity.

"Revolution is always alive in Ireland, mistress. There's a profit to be made in such circumstances for a man willing to take the risks, for a man willing to seize the opportunities before him, to fashion his own fortunes when the Fates have been cruel or the spirits of other men falter."

She gave him points for poetic expression but nothing else.

He went on, apparently unconcerned by her silence. "Five

years have passed since the last Irish attempt to throw off the yoke of English rule. Five years is an eternity in Ireland, mistress, and the day draws near for yet another effort to be free of their masters. The cautious and timid among them fear the consequences of failure. They seek assurances, both earthly and non, before they'll commit their hands to the bloody task.

"I'm a privateer, Mistress Chapman, a merchant in cargoes forbidden and desired. I care little to nothing for who purchases my offerings but only that I profit from the transaction. If my cargo assures some Irishmen of success, it's in the best interest of my financial venture. However, that they refuse to pay for my goods without a blessing from the ancient gods is not."

He pinned her with a dark look. "Are you understanding thus far?"

Yeah, I got it, she thought. *You're a gun-running mercenary supporting a bunch of delusional terrorists.* Alanna met his gaze with cool detachment. She'd be damned before she meekly surrendered to this man's control, choke before she uttered a word in response to his cue.

"Well done," he said as though she had actually spoken. "Now we come to your role in the enterprise. Maude O'Sullivan was to have returned from 1997 to the present time to bless the revolution which would end English rule. Since you've come in her stead, the task falls upon your shoulders. You're to provide the Clan O'Connell with a favorable prophetic vision, convincing those of faint heart that the Irish pantheon of gods favor their efforts and that success will be theirs if they but take up arms."

The man was a . . . a . . . Lunatic seemed such a gross understatement and far too benign. Not only did Kiervan des Marceaux believe in the idiotic notions of the present being the past and of traveling through space and time, but he hadn't the slightest qualm at making a profit from supplying the means of wholesale death and destruction. That he truly expected her to help him accomplish the grisly task was beyond contemplation.

"Not in this lifetime or the next," she muttered. Anger,

white hot and seething, coursed through her. She opened her mouth, intending to fire a barrage of aspersions both upon his heritage and his character, but before she could launch a single one, he shook his head and rose smoothly to his feet.

"Gambling against great odds is my forte, Mistress Chapman," he said, his tone silken, sure, and amused. "And I'm wagering that you'll change your mind before our time together is done."

"Like hell," she retorted.

"That choice is yours to make, mistress. But be forewarned, I can be a most persuasive man."

Once more his face was transformed by a smile, the soft and gentle smile she felt to the tips of her toes. But, she realized, he was fully aware of its effect; the expression was calculated and without true warmth. He used it as a weapon, a means of disarming women, of drawing them into his arms, his bed, and under his control. That she had so easily fallen under his spell rankled her pride.

Alanna drew herself up to her full height and balled her hands into fists at her side. Meeting his gaze, she said slowly and clearly, "Touch me and die."

5

Never had he encountered a woman of such fire and spirit. She stood before him poised for battle, clad only in a white linen gown; her hair, the color of the first spring honey, cascading over her shoulders, her violet eyes flashing in defiance. To Kiervan she looked every bit an avenging angel. *Touch her and die?* He started toward her. "I have lived a full life, mistress."

At his first step, her eyes widened, a flicker of fear in their haunting depths. In that instant he knew beyond any doubt that she hadn't expected him to take up her challenge. The advantage was unexpectedly his, and he seized it. There was much he wanted to know about this exotic creature.

"I have but one request ere I die, sweet Alanna," he said softly, closing the distance between them. "I would hear you whisper my name, feel your lips—"

"In your dreams!" she replied, taking a step back and nervously glancing over her shoulder toward the bed.

"Alanna, I would know how a woman of your time loves a man of mine; I would know the fullest measure of your passions."

The rosy hue that flooded her slender neck and her cheeks, the panic in her eyes as she looked past him in search of escape, caused him to stop and consider her in genuine wonder. "Have you never bedded a man, Alanna?"

Her chin jutted defiantly and the fear in her eyes vanished. In its stead shone wounded pride.

"No. I haven't. And just in case you're curious, I'm not

the last one in America. There's a nun in Poughkeepsie, Sister Mary Agnes. We're pen pals."

Although her voice was strong and even, he heard the telltale quaver buried beneath the veneer of bravado. "I meant no slight, mistress," he offered.

"Tell me something, Captian. Do rogues score extra points for debauching virgins?"

God help him, she had somehow and without warning managed to gain the upper hand. He stood as though rooted to the cabin floor, his mind struggling for the words that would rescue him.

"I suppose," he ventured, "that among some men, the taking of a virgin is considered a noteworthy act. Personally . . ."

"Personally, you can sell guns to the highest bidder for wars in which helpless men, women, and children are slaughtered, but you do draw the line at forcing virgins into your bed?"

"Mistress," he answered, chasing away the purer instincts of a better man. "I prefer women of experience. They require little seduction, can please a man without instruction, and expect far less afterward."

"So why don't I feel reassured?"

Kiervan studied her. Had no man ever told her of her beauty? Had no man ever begged for the honor of being her first? He knew the answers, of course, knew that she had spent most of her life tearing to shreds the desperate desires of men both good and bad. He'd slit his own throat before he followed their path of humiliation.

"Your instincts are finely honed, Alanna. You do indeed have good reason to fear me. A bastard learns well to take what he wants, when he wants it, and without apology."

She met his gaze, and though she kept her silence, he heard her reply ring as clear as if she had spoken aloud. *And you want me.*

"Aye, Alanna. But only for a time. I'll be bound to no woman."

"You'll pay for it."

He shrugged. "I'm a man of means. I'll gladly forfeit your price and count it a bargain."

Her eyes narrowed, but even through the dark fringe of her lashes, he could see her anger.

"I'll fight you tooth and nail."

"Only for a time, Alanna. And then you'll surrender to your desires. I know the truth, for I have this night already sampled the sweetness of your promise."

As he expected, she gasped and stepped back. He moved forward to shorten the space between them as he continued, "Shall I tell of disrobing you and gowning you for sleep? Shall I speak of your pleasured sighs at my touch? Or the manner in which your flesh welcomed and invited my own?"

"How dare you take advantage of an unconscious woman! You lowlife!" she yelled furiously.

Kiervan lifted his hands in mock surrender. "Though the temptation was strong indeed, I swear I did naught but properly clothe you, Alanna." He smiled devilishly because he knew it would increase her anger, which would in turn goad her toward action. "The pleasure is ever greater when your lover is awake and can fully appreciate your skills."

She sputtered for words and then finally ground out, "I'll kill you."

"Ah," he whispered, "I do recall your threat. I also seem to remember that there was something required of me first." Even as he reached for her, she moved to dart past him. Laughing, he sidestepped into her path and caught her to him. With her arms pinned against his chest and her shoulders wrapped tight within his unrelenting embrace, she fought for a moment before stiffening in passive resistance.

"Little fool," he whispered, shifting his hold on her to free a hand. Mindful of her injury, he gently lifted her chin to gaze into the fiery ice of her eyes. "I told you I take what I want."

Through bared teeth she snarled, "You'll burn in hell for this."

He offered her a quick shrug. "The fate of my soul was sealed long ago, Alanna. I'm beyond redemption and well past caring." Her hair tumbled silken and cool over his arm as he held her to him, its coolness wondrous in contrast to the heat and strength of the flesh pressed against his. Their clothing might as well have lain scattered upon the floor for the meager separation it offered. The scent of lavender and lemons drifted over him, and Kiervan inhaled the intoxicating mixture as he closed his eyes and lowered his head. "I'll not hurt you," he whispered, brushing his lips over hers. "Fight me not, Alanna."

She trembled in his arms and a soft cry strangled in her throat, but she made no forcible effort to free herself. Her surrender sent a surge of molten need through his veins, a bolt of heat he tempered with the thought of her inexperience and fear. The voice of his conscience, raspy from long silence, urged him to release her, to set her free from him before the path awaiting them could no longer be abandoned.

But the delicate scents of her had woven their magic about him and the warmth of her breath against his lips beckoned with a call too elemental to resist. He surrendered to desire, taking her mouth with his, thoroughly laying claim to the softness of her lips, moaning low when she curved into him and yielded to the questing of his tongue, struggling to breathe when her arms slipped up around his neck and her lips moved over his in response.

The slender tethers holding him in check having frayed to the breaking point, he drew back and took a long steadying breath as he gazed into her upturned face.

"Kiervan."

The whisper tore through him like a raging wind, scattering his doubts beyond recall and sending the sweet wave of victory coursing through his veins. Once more he lowered his head to brush his lips over hers. "I await my death, mistress. Do with me as you will."

She moved with such speed he had no time to react. A brilliant fire exploded at the apex of his thighs, crushing the air from his lungs and draining the strength from his knees. Awash in a wave of pain, he could do nothing to keep her in his arms, could do nothing but moan as he sagged toward the floor in misery and wordless fury.

Alanna raced to the door of the cabin, fighting back panic and daring not a single look back. She knew with absolute certainty that it wouldn't be long before he staggered to his feet and came after her, that the seconds between now and his vengeance were precious. The latch lifted and the door opened without resistance. Barefoot, with her hair streaming behind her, she fled down a dimly lit corridor toward a short flight of steep stairs. Hiking the gown above her knees, she clambered up the worn wooden steps, taking them two at a time. Her breath ragged and her heart pounding, she burst from the bowels of the ship onto the deck. Sliding to a sudden halt, Alanna glanced about the now clouded night, quickly noting the silent activity of shadowed male shapes and the world which lay beyond her floating prison. No light, of either man or heaven, sought to break the darkness. Her sight adjusted as she gazed to her left and out across the open sea. Turning to her right, she saw, beyond a wide expanse of green water, the rocky shoreline she had glimpsed from the window of Kiervan's cabin.

Ahead of her the ship narrowed to a long thick pole that stretched out over the sea. Alanna whirled about. The doorway from which she had emerged onto the deck sat in the center of a squat, flat-topped blockhouse. A few feet to her left another steep but short flight of stairs led upward. With relief, she noted that the structure didn't fill the entire width of the ship. On both sides, between it and the railings, a wide space permitted easy passage to the rear of the vessel. Pivoting to her right, Alanna dashed for the corner.

She was three-quarters of the way down the deck, with the unmistakable silhouette of a dingy in sight, when a human shape stepped from around the corner and squarely into her path.

She stumbled to a halt. "Colleen, 'tis dangerous for ye to be topside, don't ye know? Where be Kiervan?"

Paddy. And he showed not the slightest signs of being inebriated. With a sigh of relief, Alanna moved toward him, keeping her voice low as she said, "He's a madman, Mr.

O'Connell. He thinks it's 1803. He thinks he's some gun-running privateer."

"But for the first, 'tis all true, colleen. The lad's mind be far sounder than that of most men."

She froze and then managed to sputter, "It's 1997!"

He shook his head. " 'Twas before you climbed the Carraig Cor, to be sure. Least 'twas that time from which Maude promised to return to Erin. Now come along, colleen," he said, stepping forward and extending his hand, "an' I'll be a seein' ye safely returned to Kiervan's cabin."

She stared at him, shaking her head and backing beyond his reach. "You're just as crazy as he is."

" 'Tis a long day ye've had, to be sure, an' 'twill be only a long rest which makes the edges of the world a wee bit smoother. 'Twill be easier for ye in the mornin'." He moved toward her again as he added, "Let's be about findin' Kiervan now."

Again Alanna shook her head. "I don't think so."

"Ye canna stay up here. My lads will do ye no harm, but Kiervan's have no respect for what ye are. And a British patrol could come upon us at any time. 'Tis not safe for ye to be remainin' topside."

She wasn't safe anywhere aboard this floating loony bin. Alanna glanced toward the rocky island in the distance. The impulse and the decision came in the same fraction of time. Without a word she spun about, grasped the railing, and vaulted over the side. In midair she righted herself and entered the water with knifelike precision.

Kiervan started up the stairs with his teeth clenched through the pain. Seer of the Find or no, and Paddy O'Connell be damned, he'd throttle her the moment he could slip his hands around her lovely little neck. He heard the low buzz of excited men as he reached the deck, and without pausing he strode toward the starboard side, toward the hands clustered along the gunwale.

As he approached, Paddy whirled about to face him. "She gave me no warnin'," he cried, as he gestured toward the sea. "I couldna stop her."

"Lower your voice," Kiervan commanded, moving through the throng to stand at the rail.

"Drowned, she did," Paddy lamented from behind him. "Not a sign have we seen of her. Poor, wee colleen."

"My ass," Kiervan growled, unbuttoning his coat. "Look to the darker waters, men, and keep an eye for a sudden whitecap." Stripping his jacket from his shoulders, he turned to a young man waiting at his elbow. "Fetch both pistols from my desk and the oilskin bag from my chest, quickly."

The youth sprinted away and Kiervan set to the task of removing his boots. "Mr. St. John," he called as he worked, "set sail as soon as I'm away. Stay well distant from the British patrol lanes as you take our passengers back to Castletownbere. I'll bring the woman to Bantry. Meet me there."

"Aye, Captain."

Kiervan nodded at the First Officer's easy response, certain that both the *Wind Racer* and his fortune were in capable hands. He let his gaze travel over the water. A flash of white two-thirds of the way to shore caught his attention.

"There you are," he muttered. Her start was considerable, her strokes easy and strong. Yes, she'd make land well before him, but in the end he'd catch her. Of that he was most certain.

The cabin boy skidded to a halt beside him, offering him the bulky pouches he'd demanded. Thrusting his coat and boots into Paddy's hands, Kiervan said, "Place these and the smaller bag into the larger, bundle it well, and drop it down to me when I call."

"Ye will bring her to us safely, Kiervan, lad? Ye will keep yer pledge?"

"I'll have her there by the appointed time," he vowed, climbing to the top of the rail. "I make no promises beyond that." Then, without a backward glance, he launched himself into the dark sea.

6

Her teeth chattering from cold, Alanna planted her feet on the rough sea floor and paused to scan the narrow beach and the rocks rising before her. Although she saw signs of nothing human or animal, she twisted the nightgown askew anyway and tugged at the bulky knot which secured its length around her waist. As the fabric floated freely about her, she cast one more glance back over her shoulder. The ship had sailed away. Relieved to have escaped the insanity of the *Wind Racer* and its Machiavellian captain, Alanna started forward, her attention shifting to what lay before her.

Once on the beach, Alanna wrung the water from her gown and rubbed some warmth back into her chilled limbs. The pool of sopping linen around her feet soon caught her attention. The too long length of the garment would present a problem in traveling. The solution to the dilemma also provided a remedy to the problem created by her bare feet. Quickly she located a rock sharp enough for her purpose and set to work. Only minutes later she stood with the ragged lower edge of the gown fluttering fashionably above her knees, and the linen remnants padding the bottoms of her feet, held in place by thin strips that crisscrossed up and around her calves in the chic style of European sandals. Another strip, tied at the nape of her neck, held her hair back from her face.

"Trendy yet functional," she muttered with a smile. "Perfect attire for that unexpected getaway weekend."

Her smile faded as she turned to the rocky face of the cliff before her and carefully picked a route up through the rocks. After a moment she nodded, laced her fingers, and flexed them back. The cliff might well be Irish, but a rock was a rock, whether it was in Ireland or Colorado. Maude had always said no experience in life was ever wasted, and she accepted that once more her aunt's words had been proven true. A thought nagged at her but she resolutely drove it away. The climb was too precarious to have her mind occupied with regrets. When she got to the top, when she had put a good many miles between herself and this dark cove, then it would be time to rail against the loss of Maude's ruby brooch, time to consider how she'd manage to get the precious piece back from the nefarious Kiervan des Marceaux.

She pulled her engagement ring off her finger and for a long moment studied the stone in the moonlight. Odd that her greedy would-be captor hadn't taken it. Surely he'd known it to be valuable. "Like I care why he does what he does," she muttered, reaching for one end of the cloth strip she'd used to bind back her hair. Knotting the ring securely in the length of the fabric, she tossed it back over her shoulder, then tucked a loose tendril of hair behind her ear. She paused as she checked her other earlobe, then shook her head.

"Take a simple pair of earrings and leave the diamond. The man's the world's most pathetic criminal," she scoffed, stepping up to the rocky cliff and selecting her first handhold.

Pulling herself up and over the edge, Alanna collapsed into a patch of wind-toughened grass, her arms and legs quivering with exhaustion. A salted breeze passed over her and she shivered against the chill. With a deep breath, she sat up and faced inland.

Not a single light broke the darkness of the land which lay before her. Somewhere in the back of her mind, she hoped that a widespread power outage had occurred. The more cynical side of her asserted that she'd had the miserable luck of casting herself on the shores of an uninhabited island.

"Way to go, 'Lanna," she groused, adjusting her make-shift footwear. "Out of the frying pan and into the fire." She half smiled. "At least I'm alone. It could be worse." At her back the sea was a rolling roar.

Another chill momentarily possessed her, but she knew its cause hadn't been the wind off the sea. She turned to look over her shoulder, out across the water to where the ship had been anchored. Nothing. Shaking her head, she finished retying the laces of her impromptu sandals.

Climbing to her feet, she studied the land before her. The sky was lightening with the promise of another day, and in its pearl gray light she could see the faint outlines of a path that cut across the rock-strewn hillock, a path which disappeared into the shadows marking the edge of the world.

"Buck up," she chided herself sternly. She refused to look back, but instead took a deep breath and then marched forward, her sight fixed on the path that had to lead somewhere. "To civilization," she promised herself. The reassurance sounded hollow to her ears. Alanna frowned but kept going. Behind and below, the ocean rolled on, its sound deep and rhythmic.

Kiervan, treading water and holding afloat his water-proofed cache, watched her disappear from sight and then resolutely continued toward shore. Hauling the oilskin bundle had slowed his progress from the first, and Alanna's penchant for caution had delayed his advance even more. She had looked back twice after reaching the beach and each time he'd halted to wait motionless in the dark waves, hidden beneath the wet dark mat of his hair.

Only a desperate man would have bound his fate to Irish revolutionaries, he mused, not for the first time. And only a damn fool would be swimming in a cold Irish sea in pursuit of a woman who'd likely be the death of him. Kiervan clenched his teeth against the bone-numbing cold, hugged the bulky pouch closer to his chest, and turned on his side.

Kicking with angry determination, he pulled himself through the water with one arm.

Paddy O'Connell claimed the woman was a Druidess, an ancient sorceress with magnificent magical powers. God knew she had more cunning, strength, and stamina than any female he'd ever encountered. And courage. Even the stoutest of the men in Paddy's troupe had quailed in the face of the cliff Alanna Chapman had apparently attacked with relentless confidence. The Irishmen had insisted on trudging up and down the rocky beach in search of a safer, easier path upward. From what he could tell, she hadn't paused to consider that another course might exist, but had set herself against the rock and won.

"A true witch would have flown to the top," he muttered. A mouthful of bitter brine rewarded his sarcasm. Sputtering, he sighted on the nearing shore and remanded his thoughts to the effort immediately before him. Her lead had lengthened and it would grow even longer before he too reached the top of the black rock. But catch her he would, and before the sun reached midmorn. He pictured her facing him in defiance, the sun at her back, haloing her wild golden tresses and lighting her supple contours through the tattered remnants of her nightgown. The blood in his veins warmed. Resist as she might, Mistress Alanna Chapman would surrender.

The smoke rose in tiny wisps from the ruins to drift in the early morning breeze. Alanna stood at the crest of a hillock and examined the small farm before her. Clearly the structure had once been a simple home; the yard about it had been neatly walled and the smaller outbuildings had obviously housed fowl and other livestock. Nothing remained now except for smoldering shells of wattle and daub, broken fences, and a few scattered household items. An eerie stillness hung over the destruction like a lamenting cloud.

"Like souls not yet ready," she whispered. Shaking her head to dispel the grim thought, she lifted her face into the soft warming light of the sun and closed her eyes.

Long moments passed before Alanna could take a deep

breath, open her eyes, and start slowly down the hill. The coward within her begged to go around and beyond the burned-out farm. Other instincts, nobler and stronger, pushed her toward the devastation.

"Hello!" she called, pausing at the breached fence. "Anyone here?" Her words drifted into the yard and disappeared into the silence. With a sigh of resignation, she climbed through the opening in the stone wall.

Small feathers, downy and white, rolled past her feet as Alanna crossed the yard. "Hello?" she called, her voice no louder than a whisper. Only the morning breeze answered. When she neared the sooted remains of the dwelling's walls, she stopped and strained to hear through the unearthly stillness.

It occurred to her in that moment to cross herself, to make some sign to ward off evil spirits. In the same instant, she dismissed the impulse as both ludicrous and hypocritical. Her mother had been a devout Catholic, but try as she might to believe, Alanna had always felt as though she were standing on the outside of the cathedral and looking in. To call upon the saints now might result in a brilliant bolt of lightning, one she'd fully deserve.

The place was positively eerie, but she assured herself that she could be away from it as soon as she had done her Samaritan duty. If someone was injured, she had to help. If someone was dead . . .

With a deep breath and clenched fists at her sides, Alanna stepped around the corner of the house. In the same instant, she closed her eyes and whirled about, gasping. The image remained before her, branded in her mind's eye. An old woman at the base of the stoop, a simple rosary in her twisted, gnarled hand, and two men, one undoubtedly her husband, the other most likely their son . . .

Alanna gagged and then spilled the meager contents of her stomach at the base of the wall. Her hands trembling and her knees threatening to crumble beneath her, she pushed tendrils of hair back from her face and brushed away the tears coursing over her cheeks.

"Okay," she said, sniffing, "I can do this. I have to do this. They deserve that much."

Without looking back at the gruesome scene, she went in search of something with which to cover the bodies.

Alanna carefully, reverently placed another rock along the edge of the dirty blanket, on the last of the three small efforts she'd made in the yard. It had been more than a matter of destroying evidence. It had seemed so cruel, so unfeeling to cover these people with the heavy stones, and so she had shielded them only with the charred remnants of woolen blankets and used the stones from the rock walls to weight the edges so the coverings wouldn't blow away. She consoled herself with the knowledge that she hadn't flung dirt over them, that she hadn't been able to commit what had felt like the greatest of sacrileges, but that she had made some effort to protect them from wolves and vultures.

The police would have to undo her work, she assured herself as she positioned another chunk of limestone. This was a crime scene and they would likely rope it off, take pictures, and then take the bodies away to the morgue. Eventually a priest would bless the departed souls and consecrate the ground into which they would be laid in final rest. Her duty was simply to protect their bodies, their dignities, until the authorities arrived. And she hadn't disturbed the crime scene all that much. Not as she would have by digging big holes and dragging these poor people to a makeshift graveyard.

Alanna sat back on her heels and wiped the palms of her hands on the soft woolen pants she'd found in what remained of the tiny barn. She glanced at the second mound of rock and offered the younger man an apology and an explanation of her need.

A horse nickered, the sound jolting her and shattering the silence. Alanna spun quickly about, tumbling ignobly to her backside in the process.

The man sat atop a dappled gray stallion, gripping the reins with leather-gloved hands and watching her with a disdainful smile twisting his pale lips. She took in everything about him at once and pegged him just as quickly. The quintessential upper-crust English country gentleman. Everything about him was purely classic: the smooth simplicity of an English saddle, the riding costume complete with lace jabot and shiny black leather boots, the neatly arranged sandy blond hair, the blue eyes that gazed down an aquiline nose in contempt.

With all the poise she could muster, Alanna climbed to her feet and brushed the dust from the legs of her borrowed trousers. She knew she had a lot of explaining to do; she would have to provide the details of how she had come to be found with the victims of a brutal murder. But she'd be damned if she babbled like an idiot to this man who sported an attitude of social superiority.

"Most touching," he said dryly. "Who were they to you?"

Beneath the cultured British tones, Alanna heard the resonant threat of a rattlesnake. Tensed for flight, she replied, "I just happened along and found them. Do you know whether the authorities have been notified?"

He tilted his head slightly to one side and studied her for a long moment, then he smiled and replied, "A Yankee Doodle. How very interesting. When did you wash ashore?"

Alanna had a mental image of a rat paddling furiously toward land. A pithy rejoinder died at the tip of her tongue. After all she had been through in the last eighteen hours, she probably did look like a semidrowned rodent. Before she could think better of it, she reached up and tried to push her fingers through the hair at her temples. The strength of the tangles made her wince and abandon the effort.

"I went overboard," she answered. "Apparently no one in my tour group noticed." For a fraction of a second she wondered at the ease of the lie that tumbled so smoothly, so unexpectedly, from her lips. Why hadn't she told him the truth?

"Then you are alone?"

Said the spider to the fly. Alanna lifted one shoulder in a gesture she hoped he would take as unconcerned assent. "I was heading inland when I came across this horrible scene and I thought it my Christian duty to cover them before I went on. Do you know whether the local authorities are on their way?"

He smiled sardonically. "*I* am the local authority."

"Something kinda like the Sheriff of Nottingham?" she quipped.

Incredulity flicked over his angular features for a moment, then disappeared behind a placid mask. "Permit me to introduce myself," he said, swinging down off the horse.

The creak of the saddle leather ricocheted across the yard, then melted into the rocky rim of the hills above. Alanna saw little clouds of dark dust rise around his feet as he dismounted. She watched him glance down and frown at the dirt dulling the shine of his boots.

With a sigh of resignation, he lifted his gaze to meet hers. "I am Graeme Ashton, fourth earl of New Canraterian." He inclined his head ever so slightly toward her. Alanna fully understood the meaning of the gesture. Kiervan's bows had been obvious mockeries, but he had at least implied no disrespect with them. This man had.

"You have come ashore on my property, mistress. That which is on my land belongs to me by right of claim."

Alanna blinked up at him and quickly opted for obtuseness. "Then you knew these poor souls," she said, glancing over her shoulder at the makeshift graves.

He shrugged. "Tenants who resisted a lawful eviction."

His answer chilled her. She forced herself to speak. "You had them killed?"

Again he offered a dismissive shrug. "The interests of the Crown and my rights as a landlord grant me considerable discretion in dealing with such matters."

Alanna stared at him, appalled. "Are you saying that you think their murder was legal?"

Brushing at the sleeve of his jacket with long, gloved fingers, he replied, "The Crown does not concern itself with the details of how the minions are managed."

"There's a slight difference between 'managed' and murdered, Mr. Ashton," she replied tightly.

"Not in Ireland, mistress," he answered, his voice cold

and flat. He fixed her with a hard stare and added, "Henceforward, when you speak to me, you will address me as 'my lord,' and your tone will be appropriately servile."

"I'm an American by birth and temperament," Alanna retorted evenly. "We don't do servile."

"You are not in America, mistress. And I will remind you that what stands on my property is my property."

Alanna offered him an abbreviated salute. "Then I'll be exiting your property with all due speed. Good day, Mr. Ashton." She turned to go, but an iron band clamped around her right arm and held her back. She glared at him over her shoulder.

"You are free to leave when it pleases me to grant you permission, mistress. At the moment, I choose to seek other pleasures where you are concerned."

A strength born of anger welled up, pounding through her. Meeting his regard squarely, she said with all the calm she could marshal, "I don't like being manhandled, Mr. Ashton, and I won't stand for being told when I may come and go. I'm officially warning you that I have been professionally trained in personal security techniques. Now release me or I'll be forced to defend myself."

He tightened his grip on her arm and laughed. "This will be much simpler than I had ever dared to imagine."

Alanna's eyes narrowed. In the next instant, she jerked her arm upward, simultaneously rotating it out, toward his thumb. She heard his gasp of surprise and outrage as she broke free, saw his startled expression fixed on his empty hand. Knowing the advantage would be fleeting if she didn't continue the assault, Alanna drove her left fist into the pit of his stomach and, when he doubled over, gasping and pale, caught him firmly beneath the chin with her right. He toppled backward into the dirt with a garbled but most unaristocratic oath.

Wasting no time, Alanna dashed past him, sighting on the green rock-strewn hills rising a short distance beyond the yard. She had just cleared the fence when the sounds of pounding hooves rolled across the verdant landscape from the west. Without slowing her pace, she sought the source.

Even at a distance, Alanna could tell that the group riding hell-bent toward the farmstead were Ashton's men. In the same instant, she heard the dappled stallion coming at her from behind. Panic flooded through her veins, and with a burst of speed, she sprinted for the rocks at the top of the hillock.

She had barely begun to climb the rise when the earth under her feet shook with the force of the approaching horse and rider, and she knew she wouldn't make it to the top in time.

7

Alanna was suddenly airborne; a massive steel band wrapped about her midsection, and a scream burst from her lungs in a short, painful explosion. Ashton didn't bother to sling her across the saddle, but drew her up only enough to hold her pressed hard face-down against his side. Alanna felt the muscles of the horse bunch and spring, smelled the twin tangs of sweat and leather. The stallion pivoted sharply, and the world became a sudden blur of black-studded green. She could feel her bones grinding hard against each other, and her head seemed to wobble in all directions at once.

He was taking her back to the farmyard! The realization struck her like a physical blow. With strength born of desperate fear, she twisted and pushed at the arm about her waist, swore vehemently and lashed out with her feet. Her captor pulled her up and settled her closer to his side, squeezing the remaining air from her body until Alanna heard roaring in her ears. With every pounding beat of the horse's hooves against the turf, her reality grayed.

She couldn't let herself slip into the peaceful, dangerous void of nothingness. To surrender now would only assure her an end like those she had buried such a short while ago. As long as she could fight, there would be hope.

Desperately, Alanna grasped for something, anything, to anchor her conscious mind. The smooth leather of the saddle slid beneath her fingertips. She clawed at it, found purchase, and instantly pulled herself forward and up. The arm about her middle tightened, shifted its hold, and then without warning, flung her outward.

Her world spun at a crazy angle and the hard-packed dirt of the farmyard seemed to rush up to meet her. A cry escaped her lips as she instinctively closed her eyes and reached out to control her fall. Her efforts came too late and she hit the ground with a suddenness that ripped the air from her lungs. For a long moment, she lay motionless, unable to breathe.

As she lay fighting for breath, sounds came to her as though filtered through a drainpipe stuffed with cotton. Horses stamping and neighing. Men laughing, throaty and coarse. Clanging metal. The hair on the back of her neck prickled, and fear drove new life into her limbs.

Alanna scrambled to her feet. Dirt billowed everywhere. She could taste it, could smell it, could feel the grit on her lips. Amidst the powdery clouds, men scurried and animals shied from the melee. But even as she sought an avenue of escape in the confusion, the chaos slowed and the men began to turn toward her. In a heartbeat she found herself in the center of a ring of sweat-streaked, dirt-encrusted faces. She whirled about, searching for a sympathetic expression among them, and found only glittering, feral leers. One unbuckled the sword at his side and let it fall to the ground. The others followed suit.

Part of her wanted to cry, to drop to the ground and curl into a ball until the nightmare ended. Instead, Alanna locked her knees, clenched her hands into fists, and prepared to defend herself.

"We will come to you in good time, rest assured. At the moment, we have a more pressing amusement."

Keeping a wary eye on the other men, she whirled toward the sound of Ashton's contemptuous voice. He stood some ten feet away, apart from the circle and beside one of his men. Another man knelt at their feet, his figure draped in a dark cloak, his shoulders slumped and head bowed in submission.

Ashton chuckled and gestured toward the man at his feet. "And who might this be?"

To her surprise, Alanna's voice came strong and even as she replied, "I really have no idea."

"Are you certain, mistress?" Ashton taunted. "My men tell me he seemed most determined to assist your escape."

Even as the words left his mouth, Alanna sensed that all was not as it appeared to be. She studied her tormentor carefully. Ashton had the numerical advantage, and, heaven help her, she could never equal the viciousness that blackened his soul. But she couldn't kneel at his feet, bow her head, and silently surrender. She had no choice but to act.

"I asked you who the man might be, mistress," Ashton snarled. "Have you suddenly become deaf?"

"I don't know him," she answered evenly, "but I'll say he's proof that there's at least one decent man left in Ireland." She paused and met Ashton's gaze squarely before she added, "Which makes it obvious that he's not an Englishman."

Angry murmurs rose from the circle around her. Alanna acknowledged the sound but kept her attention focused on Graeme Ashton. As much as his men might be enraged by her insult, she knew the wolves wouldn't move against her until their master gave the command.

"Your tongue is sharp indeed, mistress."

Alanna nodded. "And don't forget my quick wit, either. If I move too fast for you, let me know and I'll slow down."

Snarling, Ashton snatched a handful of the prisoner's long, dark hair. Jerking the man's head up, he gestured toward Alanna and said, "Had you Irish curs half the courage of your women, the contest would be ever so much more interesting."

Kiervan. The man at Ashton's feet was Kiervan des Marceaux. How . . . ? Her heart twisted at the sight of the blood trickling from the corner of his mouth, at the dark swollen patch that had been the right side of his handsome face, at the long ebony lashes that lay spiked and still on his high cheekbones. She willed him to his feet, silently begged him to rise and continue the fight at her side. But he didn't move.

"Oh, Kiervan," she whispered.

"Ah, I see that I was correct. He is a friend of yours."

Alanna lifted her chin. "I thought not at the time we met," she replied, "but I can see now that I greatly misjudged the man." Shifting her weight onto one leg, she met Ashton's glare, shrugged a shoulder, and offered him a sardonic smile. "Then again, I didn't have a low mark to measure him against. I hadn't met you."

She saw one corner of Kiervan's mouth twitch upward in the slightest smile. His voice came, low and cracked and dry. " 'Lanna—"

The rest of his warning was lost as Ashton drove a booted foot into the center of his chest.

Alanna closed her eyes at the sight and turned away. *Kiervan. Poor Kiervan.* Trembling and queasy, she opened her eyes and sought Ashton.

He stood facing her, his hands on his hips, his feet spread wide and a predatory light blazing in his eyes. Behind him, Kiervan lay unmoving, a crumpled, beaten mass sprawled in the powdery dust of the yard. The man who stood guard over Kiervan's prostrate form moved to join the circle around her, removing his sword as he went.

"I wish that I could permit you to live," Ashton said, moving toward her, "but the price would be far too high. I will, however, toss your corpse beside that of your champion when we are finished with you. Quite magnanimous of me, wouldn't you agree?"

Vengeance and anger strengthening her resolve to fight, Alanna drew a deep breath and then forced a derisive laugh. "If that isn't a cigar in your pocket, Ashton, you're going into battle unarmed."

Ashton's eyes darkened with rage. She heard the muffled sounds of his men's laughter around her and then saw Ashton's face flood crimson.

Alanna forced herself to continue. "Tell me something," she goaded. "Is raping a woman the only way you can keep her from giggling at you?"

Goaded, he charged at her, his arms outstretched, his hands thin gloved talons. Alanna waited. She heard the men around her suck in their breath, saw Kiervan move. But none of it mattered as much as the violence bearing down upon her. She could hear the rasp of Ashton's labored breathing, could feel the anger radiating from his fingertips when she stepped back and twisted to the side. In the same instant, she threw her leg across his path with all the speed and strength she could muster.

Ashton pitched forward, his feet slipping in the loose dirt, his arms flailing as he sought in vain to right himself. The circle of men broke and scattered before him, leaving their weapons behind in their haste to save themselves.

Alanna sprang forward and scooped up an abandoned sword, drawing it from the scabbard the instant her hand closed about the hilt. The ring of metal filled the yard only a moment before sunlight glinted off the polished steel. For an instant, time seemed to stop. Men froze at the sight of her, their jaws slack. Alanna stared back at them, numbed by the slight success.

And then the world exploded in a blurred frenzy of noise and motion. Ashton scrambled up from the dirt roaring obscenities and commands. His men leapt forward, searching amidst the rising clouds of choking dust for their swords. Horses screamed in high-pitched panic and thundered past her, giant streaking banners of red and black and gray.

Alanna heard her own voice above the din, heard the howl of her battle cry. As though watching a movie from the safety of a darkened theater, she saw herself charge into the confusion like a woman possessed, holding the sword in both hands, swinging it in a broad swath, mindless of the destruction left in her wake. Men screamed in pain and rage, but in her panic and the clouds of dust, she could see nothing except the blur of the blade she swept in a protective arc before her.

Where had Ashton gone? She strained to separate his voice from the others. The sound of his curses came from behind and she half pivoted to seek him out.

He held a sword high above his head, gripping the hilt with both hands as he charged a man on horseback. Alanna watched in horror.

Kiervan sat astride Ashton's own mount, one hand holding the reins, the other grasping the reins of a second animal. Alanna saw him recognize the threat of Ashton's advance, watched in growing panic as he turned the horse to meet his adversary.

He had no weapon. The realization came like a thunderbolt. Kiervan would be slashed to ribbons unless . . .

"No!" she screamed, scrambling forward. "Ashton! Over here!"

Both men turned in the same instant. Kiervan's gaze caught and held hers. His dark eyes sparkled and a crooked smile lifted the corners of his mouth, a smile of confidence and something akin to camaraderie. He drew the reins of the second horse forward and then flung them in her direction.

His hand remained up and open and Alanna clearly understood his wordless request. She lifted the sword to her shoulder and with a prayer for control, pitched it toward him. She watched him stand in the stirrups and held her breath. She sighed with relief when his hand closed about the hilt.

Even as he brought the weapon down and turned the blade into the sunlight, she heard Ashton's raging call. She knew that she couldn't help Kiervan any more than she already had. He was strong, she assured herself. He was a warrior. He could handle Ashton on his own. He needed her to be ready to make a run for it, and so she focused her attention on the horse dancing before her, on catching the reins and mounting him.

The animal towered above her, his nostrils flaring and his eyes wide with terror as he backed away. Alanna grabbed the reins dangling to the ground and seized the forward edge of the saddle, but as she reached for the stirrup, the frightened animal spun about, pulling the metal piece beyond her grasp. The speed of his unexpected movement swept her off her feet and she snatched frantically for the saddle with her free hand to keep herself from falling beneath his hooves.

And then he bolted. Alanna clung to him as he rocketed forward, tossing her against his muscled side and then up into the air like a hapless rag doll. Somewhere in the first moments of his flight, she realized that the reins had been ripped from her hands. She closed her eyes and choked back a scream as her fingers slipped against the smooth leather. God, she was going to fall. Every bone in her body would be broken, and her brains would be smashed against the gray rocks of Ireland.

And then suddenly she felt a force at her back grasp her by the waistband of her woolen pants, lift her up, and drop her across the saddle. Instinct and desperation made her lean forward and snatch at the mane flying out along the horse's neck. She twined her fingers through the coarse, tough strands and forced herself to look up from the ground flying beneath the animal's hooves.

Kiervan rode close beside her, his black cape billowing out behind him. Leaning from the saddle, he snagged her mount's reins, then squared himself and tossed them back to her with a quick, crooked grin. Alanna glared at him and caught the leather strap with her right pinkie. If he thought she was going to let loose of the beast to take the reins with both hands, he had another think coming.

He shook his head and his grin broadened as he urged his horse ahead. Above the thundering of hooves, she heard him laugh. The blood heated in her veins. When she got off this carnival ride from hell, she'd kill him.

8

Kiervan judged a good many miles to have passed, and as he neared the crest of the hill, he decided they had time enough to rest themselves and their animals. As expected, there had been no signs of their being followed. His fearless companion had wounded to varying degrees most of the men in the yard, and even had one or two been capable of it and inclined to do so, he'd made sure they would have been hard pressed to find a mount on which to pursue them. He slowed his horse. Behind him he heard Alanna's horse ease its pace as well.

Once on the other side, just below the hilltop, Kiervan stopped and swung down from the saddle, his ribs aching and the side of his face throbbing. Alanna's horse ambled on and he had to duck beneath his own mount's head to catch the reins as it passed. The roan gelding halted with a long, deep puff of fatigue and lowered his head.

Kiervan studied the pathetic figure atop the animal. The fire in her had burned itself out, leaving behind only an exhausted woman. She half sat, half lay on the back of the horse, her shoulders slumped forward and her face hidden by a tangle of dirty golden hair that had slipped from the frayed cloth strip she'd used to tie it back. Her legs clung tightly to the sides of the animal, her feet covered in tattered rags and rammed into the stirrups.

A pang of guilt shot through him. He'd pushed her too far, too fast, too hard. "Alanna," he said softly, reaching up to touch her arm. "We can rest a bit now. Climb down."

She didn't move and offered him no sign that she knew he had spoken. Kiervan glanced down at her hands. Twisted in the coarse strands of horsehair, her fingers were blue and swollen. "By the saints, woman," he whispered, grasping her wrists gently, "turn loose."

She stiffened and tightened her grip.

He pushed aside the mat of hair hiding her face and laid his hand along the curve of her cheek. "I'll not let you fall, Alanna," he murmured, watching her unfocused stare. "Trust me."

She blinked once and glanced at him, but for only a moment before turning away, tears welling in her eyes and her shoulders shaking with silent sobs.

His gaze passed over her, noting the diamond ring tied to the strip of cloth in her hair, the dark spatters staining the linen of her tattered nightgown, the tear that opened the front of it in a perfect arc from her shoulder down to the center of her chest. Beneath the soiled and ragged edges of cloth, he glimpsed one of the rounded, satiny curves that had been the undoing of his judgment aboard the *Wind Racer*.

Seeing her so defeated, he questioned whether the woman he had held in his arms the night before was gone, gone forever. That Alanna Chapman had been of fire and ice, daring confidence and naive fear. Had the qualities which had so attracted him been beaten out of her so quickly by the cruelties of English Ireland? No, he told himself. For the moment, she needed care and compassion. But when that time had passed, he'd issue a challenge and she'd find the strength to rise to it. The Alanna Chapman he was coming to know wouldn't allow herself to be broken by anything.

He put his hands about Alanna's waist. "Come down," he crooned, drawing her toward him. "Lean into me and let me do the work."

"I can't."

The whispered admission sliced at his heart. "Yes you can, Alanna. Close your eyes and release your hold on the mane. Put your arms about my neck."

She nodded weakly, but it was a long moment before he felt her muscles begin to relax. Easing her closer, he slipped one arm around her waist. With his free hand, he clasped the nearest of her wrists and gently drew her fingers from their tangled hold.

She came to him with a strangled cry. With her arms tight about his neck and her face buried in the curve of his shoulder, Kiervan stepped back, hugging her to him as he drew her down from the animal, at once fully aware of both her feminine softness and her uncommon strength. Carefully he lowered her to her feet, but when her legs crumpled beneath her weight, Kiervan bent down, slipped his arm behind her knees, and lifted her up to cradle her against his battered chest.

No woman had ever clung to him as a savior and protector. He'd always been careful to choose those who clearly understood the fleeting nature of their relationship. None had ever cried in his arms. He hadn't permitted it. And so as he stood on the Irish hillside, he realized that he had no idea what to do with Alanna Chapman.

Of one thing he was most certain, his own body sorely felt the effects of the battle in the farmyard and the breakneck flight which had followed. If he didn't put Alanna down, he'd soon drop her. A nearby limestone outcropping provided a ready solution, and he carried her across the short expanse of grass.

With Alanna arranged across his lap and her arms still tightly about his neck, Kiervan leaned his back into the curve of the hill. He knew better than to close his eyes. Sleep had been too long denied, and his body demanded a fuller rest and would take it if he even blinked too long. He would sleep tonight. After they had put a full day between them and Ashton.

He felt Alanna sigh, felt her arms relax their hold on him. "You were magnificent," he whispered, brushing the hair back from her face. How many times had he whispered those words? he suddenly wondered. They came easily to his lips, the compliment expected in the awkward lull which often followed lovemaking. He had never before offered them with the sincerity he now felt, had never uttered them to a woman beyond the confines of a bed.

Alanna sat up, released her hold on him, and sniffed quietly before she replied, "I bet you say that to all the girls."

He tucked a lock of hair behind her ear and mockingly chided, "It's customary for you to tell me that I too performed brilliantly."

She smiled softly. "Is that what all the girls tell you?"

He grinned as best his battered face would permit and let that answer suffice.

Rolling her eyes, she shook her head in good-natured exasperation. Then she fell silent, her attention fixed blankly on the ground at her feet. "I went slightly berserk back there," she said after a few moments. "I've never done that before."

The pain of his bruised ribs cut short Kiervan's chuckle. "A most appropriate time to sample the experience if ever there was to be one," he observed. "And you were indeed a credit to that ancient order of Viking warriors. None could have wrought any more damage than you did."

She faced him squarely, her eyes huge, her cheeks coursed by wide, muddied tracks. "I didn't kill anyone, did I?"

"Would you regret it so very much if you did?"

"Of course I would," she replied. "Wouldn't you?"

"No." Her startled expression prompted him to add with more patience than he felt, "They intended to kill us, Alanna. We were entitled to use like force in escaping."

Her lower lip caught between her teeth, she stared into space for another long moment before she suddenly returned her gaze to his. "But did you see any bodies that you knew were really dead?"

Her childlike innocence touched him and sent an unexpected warmth radiating through his soul. Kiervan smiled lopsidedly. "If it makes you feel any better, when last I glanced that way, they were all still twitching."

She fixed him with a penetrating look. "You have a very dark sense of humor, Captain des Marceaux."

"It's likely to become much darker before the swelling goes down," he said dryly.

"I'm so sorry," she murmured, reaching up to gently cup the injured side of his face in the palm of her hand. The tenderness of her touch, her compassion, sent a wave of pleasure down the length of his body, weakening his already tired muscles. "Are you hurt anywhere else?"

He found the regret in her violet eyes oddly disquieting. He chose to avoid any consideration of it, telling himself it would pass if not dwelt upon.

"Quite honestly," he replied, keeping his manner far more buoyant than he actually felt, "I believe that the soles of my feet are the only parts of me that weren't thoroughly pummeled. You have the honored distinction, mistress, of being the only woman for whom I've ever accepted a beating."

"Accepted?" she repeated, dropping her hand, wariness evident in her tone.

"Do you believe that six Englishmen could have bested me had I not permitted it?"

A smile of skepticism touched her mouth. "You're telling me that lying on the ground like a heap of dirty laundry was all part of your plan?"

"It was most effective, was it not?"

"Oh, yeah," she agreed, nodding. "And just what would you have done if I hadn't created a diversion for you? What if I'd keeled over in a dead faint?"

He shook his head. "I can't imagine that you would ever give anyone the satisfaction of making you faint, Alanna. I knew you'd fight impressively."

"And if I hadn't managed to send ol' Ashton sprawling? What if he'd caught me?"

"I'd have killed any man who attempted to take you by force."

Her eyes narrowed as she studied him, and only after a long pause did she ask, "Why?"

"Because no man takes what I've claimed as my own," he said, and instantly regretted his loose tongue.

With both hands flat against his chest, her skin flushed with anger, Alanna pushed herself off his lap. The unexpected pressure against his bruised bones and muscles left him gasping in pain and powerless to stop her flight, left him unable to lean forward quickly enough to prevent her from crumbling at his feet.

"I hate you!" she cried, falling forward into the grass as though the effort to remain even partially upright were beyond her. She grabbed handfuls of turf and her knuckles turned white. "I hate you! I hate this place! I hate this time! I want to go home!"

In her words he heard frustration and anger and finally an acceptance of reality. Alanna had come to the hard truth at last and finally believed that she had crossed through time. Kiervan took a deep breath and then rose to his feet. His own belief had once been weak. Had he not witnessed her crossing, were her manner and speech not so unlike any woman of his time . . .

"I don't have the power to return you to the life you had, Alanna," he said with gentle firmness. "And even if I did, I wouldn't permit you to go."

"I hate you. You're a . . . a . . ."

"Blackguard," he supplied. "Be that as it may, you have a responsibility to fulfill, and I'm the man who will see it done. Can you rise to your feet now?"

"No," she retorted petulantly. "I'm never going to get up. I'm going to lie here until I die."

It hurt to laugh. Kiervan winced and sobered. "Which might well be quite soon if you're still lying there when Ashton comes in search of us. He doesn't strike me as the sort to forgive and forget what we did to him."

Reluctantly, Alanna loosened her hold on the grass and dragged her arms back to position them beneath her shoulders. Bending down and taking her upper arms firmly in his grasp, Kiervan helped her to rise, the effort costing him a good measure of his own strength.

They stood together, his hands still wrapped about her arms, neither of them looking at the other but both finding their balance in the space they shared. Kiervan's instincts urged him to draw her closer as his conscience and good sense argued that now was not the best time.

Alanna was the first to break the silence hanging between them. "Don't think that I'm ungrateful for your being there back at the farmyard. But my thanks are the only reward you're going to get."

"A fortnight is a long while," he replied with a slight shrug, visually tracing the delicate curve visible through the tear in her gown. Then, releasing her to draw the cloak off his shoulders, he added, "And as I told you last night, I can be a patient man."

She looked up at him, her eyes dark. "Don't you ever think about anything except dragging me off to your bed?"

He arched a brow. "Would you prefer Ashton have the honor?"

"That's a low blow!" she countered, poking a finger in the center of his chest. "You know damn good and well I'd rather not—"

"Alanna."

She stopped and stared up at him, her finger still pressed against his flesh. "What?"

"You're prodding a particularly painful spot."

"Sorry," she offered, dropping her hand and looking at the ground. After a moment she looked up at him again. "Look," she began. "I'm glad you were there to help. Why you came after me I'll never know, but . . ."

"I came after you because I had no other choice."

She shook her head and closed her eyes. "I don't want to hear it."

"And because you have no other choice," he finished quietly.

She stepped away from him on unsteady legs, still shaking her head. "I'm going back to the Carraig Cor and figure out how to reverse this god-awful mess," she vowed, pulling the loose cloth strip from her hair. The diamond glinted in the sunlight as she untied it and then rethreaded it onto the fabric scrap. "I'm going back to where I belong."

"No, Alanna," he said evenly, shaking out the folds of his

woolen mantle. "You'll accompany me to County Kerry and—"

"Help you get your blood money?" The words were more statement than question. She turned and limped toward their horses, strips of her makeshift footwear trailing through the grass in her wake. "Not in this lifetime or the next," she called back as she tied the fabric strip loosely about her neck. "You're on your own, Captain des Marceaux. Good luck."

Kiervan swore beneath his breath and went after her. If only the greatest plans of his life didn't depend on this cargo of munitions. If only Maude O'Sullivan had been the witch who had come through the portals of time and not her obstinate, fiery-tempered niece. If only he weren't so attracted to her.

Alanna was shortening a stirrup strap when he came up behind her and shook out his cloak.

"Do you want something?" she asked without looking away from her task.

"Your willing company on the journey to County Kerry."

"Sorry."

Her indifferent, casual dismissal fed his anger. "You are the most troublesome, independent, contrary woman I've ever had the misfortune to encounter."

She straightened and faced him squarely, her hands on her hips and her chin held high. "And you are the most obstinate, single-minded, cold-blooded, mercenary man *I've* ever had the misfortune to encounter."

He offered her a curt nod of acknowledgment. "I'm also one of the few men you'll meet in this time who'll protect your right to choose the time and place of your surrender. In that you should be grateful."

She started to speak, but he held up his hand and continued, saying, "I've already granted you far more latitude in other matters than is either customary or wise, Mistress Chapman. Our relationship will be significantly altered from this point forward. It will be on my terms and my terms alone."

She flashed him a look that clearly conveyed annoyance and defiance, and replied, "You can eat dirt and die."

With a well-practiced flick of his wrist, Kiervan billowed the fullness of his cloak into a cloud of his own making and then dropped it neatly over the struggling body of Alanna Chapman.

9

Knowing it was a familiar dream did little to calm her, did nothing to ease the terror coursing through her bones.

Alanna clung to the rock face, perspiration sliding in rivulets down the length of her body, her hold buffeted by the wind that whipped through the narrow valley. No woven rope of nylon secured her, no piton gleamed dully from the shadows of rocky crevices. Far below, a river ribboned a dark path along the verdant valley floor, its laughing gurgle playing off the canyon walls and mocking her desperation.

Her foot slipped and a shower of stony debris plummeted into the void. Alanna scratched about blindly until she found another, even less stable toehold and then lifted her vision skyward. The azure heavens faded into white where they touched the shimmering edges of the canyon rim, and overhead large, sharp-winged birds glided across billowing gray flannel clouds. Still she waited, bearing with silent fortitude the crystalline film of sand burning her skin, abrading the tender flesh beneath her breasts and along the inner surface of her thighs.

And then Maude O'Sullivan suddenly appeared, strands of her gray hair dancing in the breeze. A serene and knowing smile deepened the lines radiating out from the corners of her hazel eyes as she peered calmly over the edge of the precipice.

Alanna breathed deeply in the assurance that everything

would now, as always, turn out right. Maude would extend her hand and from her fingertips would flow a sparkling mist of magic, a twinkling cloud that would spin its power about her tired body and bear her upward to the safety of Maude's sheltering arms.

Alanna called up, begging her aunt to weave her magic, pleading to be saved from a certain death. Shading her brow with her hand, Maude lifted her eyes to stare into the noon-day sun. Alanna called up to her again, her voice small with terror and cracking from thirst. A long moment passed before Maude looked back down. With a tender smile the old woman blew her a kiss, then turned away.

The one part of her consciousness that remained tethered to reality marveled at the sudden twist in the scene that had haunted her sleep since Maude's death. The other half recoiled in frightened confusion. The dream had never gone like this before. This wasn't what was supposed to happen. Why had it changed?

In disbelief and horror, her body slipping against the hot granite face, the woman that was herself watched the flutter of Maude's skirts disappear. Willing her fingers to hold her among the living, Alanna pressed herself against the burning wall and pleaded for a miracle, for Maude's intercession. The laughter of the stream grew louder, and the wind paused to stroke her cheek and whisper her name.

She knew then that her fate had been cast to the elements and that she had neither the skills nor the strength to resist the forces set against her. Her racing heart stilled and she felt calm as the Alanna of her dream took a single deep breath and then stepped out into the wind.

Alanna awoke with a heart-wrenching start. Instinctively she cast herself against the solid warmth at her side, clung to it by sheer force of will while she fought to calm the frantic beating of her heart.

" 'Twas only a dream. You're safe."

Kiervan. The rumble of his voice against her cheek instantly eased the panic and she relaxed into the gentle curve of his embrace. Part of her felt disgustingly weak and guilty for accepting the comfort of his arms. Another part suggested that it might not be criminal to let someone else be strong for a change. She accepted the middle ground, consoling herself with the firm assurance that her dependence would be only momentary, just until she recovered enough to get her act together.

Reality slowly filtered in. She and Kiervan shared a horse. She sat across his lap, her legs dangling down one side of the animal, her head resting against Kiervan's shoulder and her back supported by his arm. The cloak had been loosened so that it no longer bound the movements of her arms.

She didn't move or look up at him. They were already too close. She could feel the heat of his body all along the length of hers and could hear the beat of his heart, feel it against her cheek. She found his nearness comforting and strangely invigorating. Alanna deliberately shifted the focus of her attention to the world beyond Kiervan's arms. They had stopped beside a wide stream.

"I was falling," she offered when she finally decided her voice wouldn't quiver.

"An unpleasant dream is quite understandable," he replied, his tone soothing. "You've suffered a great many upheavals this past day. Any woman would have been undone."

The remnants of the dream evaporated in a flash of indignation. Alanna bolted upright and turned about to glare up at him. "Any *woman*? *Undone*? And a *man* would've done so much better?"

His obvious shock lasted only a second and then he shrugged. "I simply meant that men are more accustomed to rugged experiences and are thus better suited to enduring them. Women lead sheltered lives and are grievously ravaged when they encounter the sordid aspects of a larger experience."

"What a crock."

"I beg your pardon?"

"I'm not going to sit here and listen to another word of

your sexist drivel." Arching her back and pushing against the saddle, Alanna launched herself free. She landed neatly on her feet beside the stream and instantly put additional distance between them.

"Sexist?" he repeated, swinging down from the horse. "Would that be another insult?"

The laughter in his question might have been subdued, but she heard it nevertheless. Alanna whirled about to face him, her hands on her hips. "Yes! It means thinking that men are inherently superior to women."

"They are."

She ripped the cloak from her shoulders and flung it on the ground between them. "Maybe in the brute force department, Captain des Marceaux. But physical strength is hardly the most significant measure of a person."

"True enough."

"There's also intelligence and perseverance. Accommodation and—"

"I accept your argument," he said, lifting his hands in mock surrender.

"No you don't. You're patronizing me. It's the tell-her-what-she-wants-to-hear-and-she'll-quit-harping-about-it strategy. It's based on men thinking women are too stupid to understand what's really going on."

He cocked his head to the side and shifted his weight to one leg as he crossed his arms over his chest. Alanna had the distinct impression that he would have regarded a two-headed cat in much the same manner. "Are all the women of the twentieth century so shrewish?" he asked after a moment.

"Women are shrewish. Men are focused and determined. Same behavior, Captain. Different standards."

He shook his head gently. "Mistress," he said with slow certainty, "you are going to encounter some difficulties in adjusting to life in this time."

Alanna rolled her eyes. "No kidding. Is this your first clue?"

"You'll have to alter your manners and beliefs if you hope to find a husband to take care of you."

Bill! Oh my God, I forgot about Bill! He'd be worried sick when she didn't come back on time.

"Okay, Captain," she managed to say, quickly gathering her wits about her, "let's get something clear from square one here. First off, I don't intend to spend the rest of my life in the early 1800s. I'm going back to where I belong as soon as I can figure out how to do it."

She lifted the cloth strip hanging around her neck to show him her engagement ring. "Secondly, I have a man waiting to marry me back in 1997. I spent the better part of twenty-eight years thinking that I'd rather die alone than shackle myself to a man, and while Bill Boyer isn't perfect, he's a decent human being. He knows how to say 'please' and 'thank you' and wouldn't ever dream of telling me what I could and couldn't do." *Only because he knows it wouldn't do him any good,* her inner voice added. She ordered it into silence.

Again Kiervan fixed her with the gaze that made her wonder if he'd heard her caustic thought. "Have you suffered cruelty at the hands of men, mistress?" he asked. "Is that the cause of your vehemence?"

Alanna sighed at the dark memories the question brought her. Refusing to surrender to the pain and anger that always accompanied them, she replied evenly, "Cruelty? No, not of the punch and kick variety. Their self-absorption? Yes. Their complete disregard for the feelings of others? Yes. The consequences of being bound to them as they careened through life? Most definitely yes."

Frowning, he inquired, "And so you consider all men as callous and foolish as those in your past?"

She replied evenly, "I've yet to meet a single one who didn't think of himself first. Nor have I found one who regarded me as his equal."

Kiervan smiled as he asked pointedly, "Not even your Bill Boyer?"

Alanna stared at him, stunned by the realization that she had indeed lumped her fiancé with all men. And try as she might to find some reason to qualify Bill's general attitudes and behaviors as being the exception, she couldn't. She'd spoken without thinking, but she'd spoken honestly. Alanna tried desperately to think of a way out of the corner into which she'd inadvertently painted herself.

"You aren't likely to find a different kind of man in this century, either, Mistress Chapman. Not in Ireland. Certainly not in America."

Shrugging, Alanna observed, "Well, if I can't get back to America and Bill, I assure you that my life will go on, Captain. I'll simply have to muddle through on this side of time without a man to assist me. I'm not about to marry someone just because it's socially expected."

"Permit me to be brutally direct, mistress," he countered, straightening and broadening his stance. He met her regard, his eyes raven dark. "You are now of this time and so you must survive within its limitations. Women have but few choices to make regarding the course of their lives. Once chosen, the path can't be easily altered. You may be a wife, a nursemaid, a domestic servant, a mistress, or a whore. In any case, you'll be at the beck and call of a man. There's no escape from that truth. Give your decision due consideration."

"Thank you for sharing your great wisdom. I couldn't have possibly figured all that out on my own," she returned, instinctively deciding that sarcasm would be safer than letting him know how deeply his words had disturbed her.

"I offered advice in sincere concern, mistress. I meant no insult."

She knew that in his own way, he had indeed been offering sound advice. She had let the ghosts of her past interfere with present good judgment. Maude had warned her. Alanna pushed matted tendrils of hair away from her face and sighed. "Look, Captain. For the time being, you and I appear to be stuck with one another. I don't exactly relish the idea of having to deal with the repercussions of that Ashton incident alone.

"On top of that, there's this thing I'm supposed to do for Maude. It's obvious she sent me here in her stead, and since I owe her a helluva lot, I'll do whatever it is without a fight. If we have to endure each other's company for the next fortnight or so, then so be it. All I ask is that you don't treat me like a child or the village idiot. Do you think we can declare a truce on those terms?"

"I shall make the attempt, mistress, and trust you to remind me when my efforts fall short."

"You can count on it." She stuck out her hand in what she thought to be a universal and timeless way to seal an agreement. Kiervan's puzzled consideration of her hand very quickly suggested that she was wrong. Still, she refused to withdraw it, to lower it to her side and surrender the opportunity to make a point with him.

"One does not shake hands with a lady."

"Take a walk on the wild side, Captain." He arched a brow in silent question and Alanna tried again. "Take a chance, Captain. Live dangerously."

Fighting a smile, she watched him take a deep breath and gather himself. Slowly he lifted his own hand and then, ever so gently, clasped her hand in his. The warmth of him enveloped her from head to toe, softening her bones and threatening her resolve. His gaze met hers and she felt herself being drawn into the darkest depths of his soul, into a place where her own would be forever lost to the power of his.

Alanna swallowed hard and straightened her shoulders. Tightening her fingers about his, she would have quickly completed the gesture, but he slowly, deliberately tightened his own grasp and, in the space of a heartbeat, stripped away her control.

She saw the promise of danger in his eyes, felt unspoken words caress the steely bonds which had always held her safely in check. Heat radiated up the length of her arm, through her body, and down through the soles of her rag-wrapped feet. A knowing smile lifted the corners of his mouth as he stroked the back of her hand with his thumb and then released her.

Too grateful to have escaped to muster any anger at his insolence, Alanna stepped beyond his reach on legs that had become as unsteady as her pulse. She forced herself to ask lightly, "That wasn't so bad, now was it?"

"I found it most enjoyable, mistress, and will make it a point to sample the experience again. As soon as possible."

She refused to respond to his taunt, looked away from the sparkling eyes that seemed to so easily ensnare her and steal her presence of mind. "Now that we've gotten that straightened out . . ." she managed to offer in a voice that sounded too loud to her ears. "Is there any particular reason why we've stopped here?"

Kiervan nodded and shifted his sight to the horizon, his smile gone. "A town lies ahead. Judging by the depth of the ruts in the road, it should be of fair size."

Her heartbeat beginning to slow to a less painfully erratic pace, Alanna focused on the rock she nudged with her toe. "Large enough for us to get lost in?"

"We can't hope to pass through any community unnoticed. Americans seldom stray this far from the coast."

She dared to glance up at him when she asked, "So why are you mentioning it?"

"We must go in for a time," he replied, turning to study her, all traces of amusement gone. In its stead a distant kind of caution, almost a cold challenge, burned. He looked away abruptly and continued, "For a time as brief as possible. We're riding stolen mounts whose colors and quality will be noted for the duration of our journey."

"Making it much easier for Ashton to trail and eventually find us," Alanna observed, her gaze returning to the rock and the efforts of her toe, but the larger part of her awareness puzzling the unexpected expression in his eyes.

"You're quick," she heard him say.

The approval she heard in the words seemed at such odds with the hard look in his eyes only moments before. She glanced up to find him surveying the length of her, and a not unpleasant warmth flooded her cheeks.

He turned abruptly away and said harshly, "You're also most improperly clothed."

The captain was apparently as uncomfortable now as she had been when he had held her hand hostage, and she enjoyed the realization that she had that kind of power over him.

"What?" she asked, barely containing the smile that threatened to spread across her face. "You don't like my attire?" she pressed. "I'll have you know that where I come from, this would be considered by many to be the cutting edge of fashion. It's called the Waif Look."

"It draws unnecessary attention to you," he responded, his voice cool and matter-of-fact.

Reined in tight, Alanna thought. "Ah," she said, nodding and watching the well-chiseled lines of his profile. "The Ashton concern again."

His jaw clenched and only after a long, slow breath did he reply, "That among other concerns no less troubling. There's also the incidental matter of food and the provisions necessary for traveling."

She let him off the hook. "Okay, I'll admit to being just this side of starved," she said.

"I think it well considered to make ourselves somewhat presentable before we venture into the village. Aside from drawing unnecessary attention to ourselves, the appearance of desperation always weakens one's bargaining position."

She nodded. Obviously he intended for them to bathe in the stream. Her mind raced ahead, filling with certainties and dire possibilities. The linen of the nightgown she wore now as a blouse would cling when wet, and then she wouldn't be able to hide a precious thing from his scrutiny.

Kiervan des Marceaux was absolutely right about desperation. It did weaken one's bargaining position. She looked down at the soiled and torn gown she wore and then fingered a dust-coated lock of her hair. "It's going to take a good deal of time and effort for me to look even halfway decent," she muttered.

"You'll have what time you need," he answered, taking up the reins of their horses. Leading the animals toward the stand of slender trees growing along the bank, he added, "We don't want to approach the town until well after dark. It will lessen the number of people to note our passage and ease our search for a man whose business lies in taking risks."

Alanna pivoted and watched him tie the reins around a

low branch. He was loosening a cinch strap when she commented, "I can't help noticing that you're pretty good at this fugitive stuff."

"Stuff?" he inquired, shooting her a quick glance.

"Thinking about things that will . . . you know . . ." She floundered in silence for a moment, then sighed and began again. "I mean that you seem to have some experience at being a fugitive, at being pursued by the hounds of hell, if you will."

He straightened, laying one arm across the saddle of the stallion, and leaned casually against the beast while studying her with open curiosity. "And how is it you recognize the characteristics of an outlaw, Mistress Chapman?"

She flashed him what she hoped was a dazzling smile and countered, "Let's change the subject, shall we?" Not waiting for his reply, she pointed toward the river. "Why don't you bathe first? I'll see if I can't find some soaproot growing along the bank."

The sparkling light of devilment returned to his eyes. "We could bathe together."

It bothered her that her heart leapt at the offer. "Don't take the equality thing too far, Captain. Pop off those boots and into the drink with you." Turning away, she started down the grassy bank. Over her shoulder she called, "Back in a couple."

Kiervan watched her go, his brows knit. *Back in a couple?* Lord, what had she meant to say? Surely not the imaginings that were blazing across his mind at the moment.

10

The cold water had restored a good measure of his calm and helped to cool his blood by the time he saw Alanna coming up the bank. Kiervan shoved the locks of hair from over his eyes and, treading to maintain his position in the current, watched her make her way through the trees. She moved with a natural grace, ducking beneath low-hanging limbs without slowing her long-legged stride. He saw that her feet were now bare and that she had fashioned a makeshift bag out of the rags. What she had placed into it, he could only wonder. If it was soaproot alone, she had gathered enough to clean half of Ireland.

He studied her as she glided through the thin shadows of the trees. She'd rolled her pant legs to just below her knees, exposing the lean, well-muscled curves of her calves for his appraisal and appreciation. A smile lifting the corners of his mouth, his gaze traveled slowly upward. The contours of her thighs were hidden from all but his memory by the too large fit of the woolen breeches. The waistband was another matter entirely. While it hung loosely about her, it fell in a lopsided way that dramatically accentuated the narrow expanse of her waist and the graceful sweep of her hips.

A searing image came to him: his hands resting on those curves, drawing her closer, the warmth of her bare flesh caressing his palms and tempting his control. His body responded to the vision with a suddenness and intensity that startled him. No woman had ever fired his desires as this one did. And the seduction of no other had required the tenacity this one would. Alanna Chapman was a rogue's challenge indeed. And he knew enough about her to be certain that he'd be ill served if she were to see the hunger in his eyes. Alanna was an intelligent woman, a woman with the most disconcerting ability to see into his heart and soul. The twin sisters of virtue, Prudence and Patience, had already warned him of the ground to be lost with bold looks and rash advances. And so far his experience with the fiery honey-blond creature had proven them unerringly correct.

As she emerged from the stand of trees, Kiervan stopped treading and let his body sink toward the river's bottom. Only when the pain in his lungs had become unbearable, and the desperate need to fill them with air forced him, did he trust himself enough to push for the light overhead. He broke through, lunging above the glittering surface, gasping and shaking the water and hair from his face.

His eyes were drawn to her instantly. She knelt on the bank beside his clothes, her slender hands resting on her thighs, her golden hair tumbling over her shoulders, the afternoon sun lighting the thin linen of her torn gown and shadowing curves that beckoned his touch. He looked away, focusing his attention on the horses nibbling the tender grass that grew beneath the trees, and resented the faceless man named Bill Boyer.

"Here," she called. "Catch."

Kiervan turned to see the oddly shaped object leave her hand, and lifted his own just in time to do as she had bidden. He saw her press at the tear of her gown and hold it close to her skin and knew wisdom lay in keeping his eyes averted.

"I've been thinking," he said, kicking his feet to keep himself afloat while examining the pounded root she had tossed him.

"Uh-oh."

The sound of her amusement tempted him to glance in her direction. Her smiles were beautiful and wide, the kind that could make a man do and say foolish things. He concentrated on making the root produce its characteristic foam along the length of his arm as he continued, "Perhaps it'd be for the best if you remained here while I conducted business in the town."

"Don't worry. I'll behave myself. I'll pretend to be a dutiful little maid. Three paces behind and eyes downcast."

"I have no doubt you could play the part for a short while, Alanna. My concern rests in the nature of the men with whom I must do business. I'd prefer to keep you from the dangers inherent in such a situation." *And away from those who'd want to take you from me,* he added silently.

"I appreciate the gallantry, Captain, but if you think I'm going to let you and some lowlife pick out clothes for me, you can guess again."

"Was the linen gown in which I dressed you last night not of good taste and considerable quality?"

"Yeah," she admitted quietly. "But the important question is whether the woman you bought it for liked it. If it suited her tastes and looked decent on her."

"She never received it."

"Hmm . . ."

At the contemplative sound, he risked a glance in her direction. She lay on her stomach watching him, her chin propped in her hands and her knees bent while her crossed ankles swayed slowly forward and back above her rounded derriere. The torn fabric of her gown had fallen open to reveal the soft upper swell of her breast. His mind ordered his eyes elsewhere, but they refused to obey the command.

"So who is she?"

"Who?" he heard himself ask.

He was only vaguely aware that she arched a slender brow and offered him an amused but patient smile. "The woman you bought the nightgown for."

Her simple question brought a host of memories flooding back, memories that seemed to have been torn from the life of another man. Instincts well honed by danger warned him to keep his wits about him. Kiervan pulled his gaze from the enticement on the bank. Soaping his battered and bruised chest, he winced and eased the diligence of his scrubbing. When the sharpest edge of the pain had passed, he finally replied, "The lady is the daughter of a wealthy and socially prominent Charleston merchant."

"Does she go by 'daughter' or does she have a name?"

He knew that he possessed the answer, but where had the knowledge gone? Kiervan frantically ransacked his mind searching for the bit of information Alanna had requested. It seemed to take forever, but at last he remembered. "Eglintine," he answered in both triumph and relief.

"C'mon," she challenged on a snort of laughter. "What's her name?"

"Eglintine," he repeated. "Mistress Eglintine Terwilliger-Hampstead." He had the distinct impression that Alanna laughed into her hands, but he couldn't be sure.

"Does she look anything like her name sounds?"

He hadn't considered the idea before her suggestion, but . . . Kiervan shook his head to refocus his thoughts. Far too much rested on his plans. He couldn't afford to entertain even the slightest of doubts. "I wouldn't know the lady were we to meet. I've seen her only from a distance. She's reputed to be a gentlewoman, reasonably fair of face and decidedly sound of limb."

He heard her mutter something about teeth, but the rest of the words drifted beyond his ears. "Pardon?" he asked, splashing water across his shoulders and rinsing away the suds. "I couldn't hear you."

A long moment passed before she replied, "Don't you think a nightgown's a little personal for a gift to a woman you've never even met?"

Kiervan hesitated, considering the wisdom of truthfulness. In the end he shrugged and replied, "I'd planned to give it to her after we were married."

"You're going to marry someone you don't know?" she blurted incredulously. The sound of her disbelief drew his attention back to her. Now she sat cross-legged on the bank, her elbows on her knees and her chin once again propped on her fists. Her eyes were wide with fascination when she continued, "You'd actually marry a virtual stranger? For real?"

"It happens quite frequently," he answered. "There's

nothing the least unusual regarding the arrangement." He watched the play of emotions across her face, each clear and sharply defined for the moment they possessed her: surprise, amazement, bewilderment, disappointment, and finally vexation.

Kiervan smiled. Alanna was unabashedly herself, childlike in her forthrightness and thoroughly comfortable with how she dealt with the world. An observant man would always know where he stood with Alanna Chapman. Only a blind fool would be caught off guard and unprepared. He studied her, noting that she furrowed her brows as she considered him in return. Altogether not a good sign.

"Sounds to me like you and her father sat down with a couple of good brandies and negotiated a deal."

Kiervan rubbed the battered root through his hair and congratulated himself on having foreseen the tack of her comment. Still, it wasn't wise to have her know that he could so easily anticipate the nature of her discourse. "I gather that you disapprove," he offered, his tone carefully controlled.

"Did anyone happen to ask Eggie how she felt about being traded like a prize hunting dog?"

Eggie? He forced the smile from his face. The young woman was to be his wife before the summer's end, and if nothing else, he owed her a modicum of public respect. "Mistress Terwilliger-Hampstead understands the expectations and the duties of a woman of her social class."

"What about love?"

The hair on the back of his neck prickled at the question, and yet the reckless gambler within him refused to be intimidated for a single moment. The words were out before he could stop them. "What about love, mistress?"

"Maybe I'm wrong, but don't you think it would be easier, not to mention a helluva lot nicer, to spend the rest of your days with someone you felt something for?"

Alanna had posed yet another of the many questions he'd steadfastly refused to allow himself to consider; questions that now, as always, set his teeth on edge and stirred his ire. Deciding the time had come to put an end to the discussion, he gave her a dismissive shrug and said, "An arranged marriage isn't without emotion. A certain fondness often develops over time."

"Now, there's something to look forward to," she scoffed. "When you're old and gray and on death's doorstep, there's nothing quite like your wife patting your hand and telling you that she's learned to feel a certain fondness for you over the last fifty years."

Kiervan turned to face her squarely and glowered. "Despite the fact that you're to be married yourself, it's apparent from your words you've very little experience with affairs of the heart. I, on the other hand, have had sufficient involvements with women to have learned a few hard truths.

"The fondness which you so disparage is preferable to a relationship begun in passion and then suffered long after the flames have been extinguished," he continued. "Such fleeting emotions are an acceptable basis for one's relationship with a lover. If chosen with caution, she won't encumber a man for the rest of his days. She'll gracefully accept a parting of the ways once the desires have ebbed. A wife isn't so easily . . ."

"Disposed of," Alanna finished, her tone even but edged with contempt. "You're one mercenary son of a bitch, Kiervan des Marceaux. Tell me, do you intend to keep a string of mistresses after you marry poor Miss Eggie?"

"It's commonly done," he answered defensively, deciding she had all the tenacity of a terrier in pursuit of a burrowed rat. Even as he presented her with a view of his back, a vague but nagging sense of chivalry prompted him to add, "There's a degree of discretion expected, of course."

"Oh, of course," she retorted. "Does Eggie know about your views on fidelity?"

Lord, if only he'd managed to catch some sleep within the past twenty-four hours. His wits were far too dull to effectively battle the indignant woman perched on the bank. Kiervan sighed. "I'm sure Mistress Terwilliger-Hampstead is aware of the customary relationship between men and their wives. Women do tend to talk with one another with regard to such matters. Surely her own mother has discussed the nature of marrige with her."

"Does Eggie get to keep a string of handsome young men on the side?"

"For her to have liaisons would be quite unacceptable. A man must be assured that the children his wife produces are his own."

"Why?"

"So he may pass his property to his rightful and true heirs."

"His male heirs."

Her words contained far more than the recognition of legal fact. In them he plainly heard the accusation of favoritism. What had she called it? Sexist? Kiervan turned to face her and offered an olive branch. "Female children have value as well. Often equal to or exceeding that of their male siblings."

"Oh, yeah," she answered as she nodded in false agreement. "That's right. You can marry them off. What's the term? Advantageously?"

His patience gone, Kiervan considered her in aggravated wonder. "Look at the ring your beloved Bill Boyer has given you and tell me that your future hasn't been bartered. How could you have an objection to a father securing a young woman's financial and social future?" He saw pain flicker across her face, but in a heartbeat her expression was neutral.

"You're absolutely medieval," she replied evenly.

"And you have not answered my question," he growled.

"All right," she shot back, climbing to her knees. Sitting back on her heels, she began, "What does Eggie gain by being married to you?"

He looked along the course she seemed determined to pursue, and for once the reckless side of his nature heeded the cautious instincts of wisdom. "I fail to see how—"

"Just answer the question," she cut in, holding her hand up to prevent further protest. "I'm on my way to making a point."

Let her, he decided in anger. He had reasons enough to

marry Mistress Terwilliger-Hampstead. All of them sound and quite acceptable. "She'll receive a household of her own and be assured of a future of certain and generous financial support," he snapped.

"Yeah, a woman's always so secure with her husband's lovers hanging around the wings," he heard her mutter. Then more loudly she asked, "And what do you gain by being married to her?"

He glared at her, all the bitter memories, all the sacred vows he had made, boiling up from the past to scald his soul. No one had ever been privy to the devastations of his life. He had no need of pity. To no one had he confided the dreams harbored in the deepest corners of his heart. To share them would lead to their utter destruction. What would he gain by marriage to Eglintine Terwilliger-Hampstead? *Everything a bastard could ever hope to achieve.* But he would go to his grave before he admitted that truth aloud. Slowly, evenly, he gave Alanna no more honesty than he gave any other. "Through the marriage I stand to gain a partnership in her father's mercantile firm."

She considered him for a moment, her gaze locked with his, searching to see beyond the walls of his resistance. Kiervan smiled. Try as she might, she'd have no success. He'd built his defenses well and strong enough to withstand the meanest of assaults.

Without looking away, her scrutiny no less intent, she posed yet another question. "And what does Mr. Terwilliger-Hampstead get out of the 'arrangement'?"

"A ship's captain willing to take great risks for his exclusive benefit."

She nodded and finally looked away. Counting on her fingers, she began, "Okay, let's see what we have here. Daddy doesn't have to feed, clothe, or house Eggie anymore and gains a son-in-law who'll make him a lot of money. You get all the advantages of marrying into a wealthy, prominent family, which is a big social step up for a bastard sea captain, wouldn't you say? Eglintine gets a house to clean and a philandering husband.

"The way I see it, you and her father have the social and

financial security. All Eggie gets is the thrill of being sold into slavery and then spending the rest of her days with a master who values her only for the status her family gives him and the number of marketable children she can produce."

With clenched teeth, Kiervan flung the soaproot onto the bank. It landed precisely where he'd intended. As she stared down at the ground before her knees, he grated out, "My personal affairs are none of your concern, Mistress Chapman, and I'll discuss them with you no further. I care nothing of what you think of me or of my motives for marriage."

"I understand why you'd like to close the subject, Kiervan ol' boy," she replied, looking up and arching both brows in an expression that conveyed a curious mixture of both disapproval and acceptance. "You don't exactly come out of the conversation looking too noble or too gallant."

Did nothing daunt this woman's spirit? he wondered. Was there anything he could say or do to keep this fiery creature from delving into the well-ordered corners of his life? The inspiration came suddenly, like a brilliant beacon of light through the fog. There was indeed something he could do. Kiervan averted his face to hide his smile and started for the riverbank. He had placed both hands on the grassy edge before she reacted.

"What are you doing?" she demanded, her voice trembling with barely controlled panic as she glanced wide-eyed between his chest and the pile of his clothing lying in the grass beside her.

"My bathing is done," he replied evenly, lifting himself upward. "I'm getting out of the water."

She gasped and her eyes grew even wider. Scrambling to her feet, she announced, "Now it's my turn." Without pausing she took a single step forward and then dove headfirst into the river.

"It'll be your turn in due course, sweet Alanna," he murmured, turning about to sit naked on the grassy bank. "We've yet to discuss your reasons for marrying Bill Boyer."

$\bullet \quad \bullet \quad \bullet$

Determined to escape Kiervan's view, Alanna swam upstream, struggling against both the current and her thoughts. Okay, so Eggie wasn't exactly getting the Hunchback of Notre Dame for a husband. Kiervan des Marceaux had biceps, triceps, and pecs to die for. And his abs . . . The guy had abs that would guarantee him a place of honor in the Poster Babe Hall of Fame. She instantly amended the observation. "Guy" was a term too neutral and soft. "Babe" implied a kind of dewy youthfulness that Kiervan had lost years ago, if he'd ever possessed it at all. He was a man in every sense of the word, rough textured and hard as rock, world-worn and scarred. Against him, Bill came up sadly lacking in manly qualities. Deliberately setting aside the memory of her weakness and her lack of curiosity concerning her fiancé's attributes, she reminded herself that Kiervan's attitudes toward women were both prehistoric and predatory. And if they handed out awards for arrogance, he'd have to hire a moving van to haul them home.

Still, she admitted, given the present circumstances, Kiervan was probably the ideal traveling companion. If she were to meet Ashton again, she'd be damn glad to have someone big, capable, and self-assured standing beside her. And Bill never need know about the time she had spent with Kiervan des Marceaux.

But the security of his presence was a double-edged sword, and she knew it. Kiervan was a dark knight, a man who had vowed to protect her from the assaults of others while at the same time committing himself to laying his own siege against the fortress of her will. Alanna grimaced at the analogy. Knights and fortresses? When had she ever thought in such fairy-tale terms? Her marbles had to be loose, a very vulnerable condition to be in around Kiervan.

She glanced back through the trees to see if he still sat on the bank watching her, but found that Kiervan had disappeared and taken his clothes with him. Keeping a watchful eye on the shadows of the nearby trees, Alanna allowed the slow current to carry her downstream to the place where she had thrown herself into the water and where the makeshift sack containing the soaproot remained.

The bag also held other roots and plants she had gathered in her search, herbs that Maude had always used in poultices. Grabbing the bag from the bank, Alanna glanced over them and sighed. They'd reduce the swelling around Kiervan's eye and ease some of the discomfort he had to be feeling around his ribs. Their proper administration would require that she touch him. The thought of applying them to his injuries sent a quiver down the length of her that was as disquieting as it was exhilarating. For a moment she considered taking the coward's way out and pretending she didn't have the knowledge to treat his battered body. But even as the impulse came to her, she denied it. Letting him suffer would be cruel. She'd have to deal with the situation as best she could. She would simply have to keep her wits about her, do what must be done, and then move well beyond his reach.

The decision was accompanied by sensations not at all unlike the ones she had felt when Kiervan had begun to climb from the river. Part of her had eagerly anticipated adding another stunning physical attribute to Kiervan's already impressive list. Another part of her had been scared that she might do or say something she would instantly and forever regret. The last thing in the world she needed was for him to think she might consider letting their relationship move to a more intimate level. And what else could a man think when a woman sat on the bank gaping at all his glory in open-mouthed wonder? Squeaking like a frightened mouse had been involuntary, but hiding in the river had been a considered, albeit hasty, decision to escape. Odd, she suddenly mused, she'd never even been tempted to catch Bill unaware.

Soaproot in hand, Alanna swam upstream once more. While there was obviously much she had yet to discover about this new life into which she'd wandered, she'd already learned one invaluable, primary lesson: being around Kiervan des Marceaux tended to rattle her good judgment. The man had the uncanny ability to ignite all of her emotions at once, to set her normally sound instincts warring against each other. When he was near, her heart beat too fast and her mind didn't work quite right. As she paused in midstream to unfasten her woolen pants, Alanna knew with absolute certainty that staying beyond Kiervan's reach would become her watchwords over the next fortnight.

With a nod of conviction, she began to scrub herself with the soaproot. She'd find some neutral ground with him, engage in conversations less argumentative than those of their brief past. And she'd start by asking him just what the hell a fortnight was.

11

Alanna awoke and stared up at the night sky. The new moon seemed like a watery ghost floating amidst the million bright stars sprinkling a black velvet sea. For a long while she traced the outlines of the constellations, remembering how she and Maude had passed many a night studying the skies together. The shadows of loss came swiftly in the wake of the happier memories. The years with Maude had been too few; the years in the mountains had come so late in her life.

With a wry smile, Alanna consciously put away the past and sat up. *Look to this day,* Maude had always said. *For yesterday is but a memory and tomorrow only a dream. Look well therefore to this day.*

Glancing up at the sky once more, Alanna judged the hour to be one or two past midnight. A new day had indeed come. It was time to face it and whatever it held in store for her. *Hopefully some food,* offered her eternally optimistic inner voice. Her stomach rumbled at the prospect and she pressed both hands over her abdomen in a futile attempt to keep the sound from echoing through the grove where they rested.

Beside her, Kiervan mumbled Gaelic in his sleep and then bolted to a sitting position, the poultices she had lain across his face and chest falling away; the cloak that had covered him slid down. He searched the shadows of the trees and across the open land beyond. In the glimmer of the moon and stars, he seemed more mythical than real. Blue-black locks of hair curled across his brow and spilled over his broad shoulders. The normally hard, angular lines of his jaw had grown smoother, shaded by the dark growth of a new beard. The gentle light washed across his bare torso, creating an intricate pattern of dusky shadows threaded with thick, corded bands of gold.

Despite reason, despite wisdom, her senses demanded more. Even as she silently decried the act, her gaze traveled along the narrowing line between his shoulders and his waist, down to where the breeches hugged his hips, down to where the rippled muscles and the trail of dark curls disappeared beneath the taut expanse of pale fabric. The inky folds of the cloak lay bunched across his lap and legs, protecting him from further ravages of her brazen regard.

Merciful heavens, Alanna thought, what had gotten into her? Never in her life had she surveyed a man with such . . . with such . . . enthusiasm, she admitted, clenching her teeth and deliberately shifting her focus into the darkness beyond him and clasping the ring hanging about her neck. She was engaged to another man. It was absolutely shameful to look at Kiervan that way. *And damn dangerous,* she added in the next instant.

She saw his shoulders relax, and before he could seize command of the moment, Alanna said softly, "The sound that so rudely awoke you was my stomach. It just decided to remind me that it's been neglected the past twenty-four hours."

"You shouldn't have let me sleep," he replied, glancing over his shoulder at the shirt he'd tossed across a branch to dry.

Alanna shrugged and climbed to her feet, wincing at the quivering of her muscles. "There really wasn't much I could do about it," she explained, bending back to stretch. "By the time I finished cleaning up, you were already lying here, out like a light. Genghis Khan could have come tearing through here with his screaming horde and you'd have never known. Obviously you needed the rest."

With a finger, he nudged the damp sacks of herbs lying on the ground beside him and asked, "What are these?"

She couldn't control the wicked impulse. "Poison, my pretty," she cackled. He gaped up at her, eyes wide with alarm. "Not really," she assured him. "They're poultices to take down the swelling and draw out the bruises. Maude used to make them for me on a regular basis." She sobered and studied him for a moment before she asked quietly, "Do you feel any better?"

He continued to look up at her, but his eyes became a shade darker than the night, as brilliant as the stars overhead. Softly he replied, "Yes. Thank you, Alanna."

Her muscles, painfully tight only minutes before, went suddenly soft. If he reached for her, it would all be over. She would sink down beside him in the grass and . . . "Yeah, well . . ." she started, struggling to regain her scattered wits. "You looked kinda pathetic lying there, and I took pity on you."

She stepped away from him, putting a safer distance between them, and then swung her arms about as though they too needed to be stretched. Afraid that he might see through her facade of nonchalance, Alanna forced a measure of buoyancy into her voice when she added, "I can't take much credit for the improvement, though. To be perfectly honest, Maude's Magic Herb Blend probably didn't do as much for you as the sleep did."

He glanced up at the night sky. "It is late," he pronounced, gaining his feet. The cloak fell away and Alanna deliberately averted her eyes from the sight that had beckoned her earlier.

Taking his shirt from the tree branch, he continued, "We'd best be getting straight on toward the village and conduct our business."

Her stomach chose that particular moment to contribute a rumbling gurgle to the conversation. Alanna rolled her eyes and grimaced. "No argument from this end," she said. "But what made you change your mind? I clearly recall that yesterday afternoon you were dead set against me going into town with you."

Stuffing his arms into the sleeves of his shirt, he answered, "I changed my mind because the circumstances changed.

Yesterday afternoon your stomach wasn't as empty as it is now. It would be cruel to leave you out here hungry while I'm dining in the pursuit of new horses and clothing."

Her stomach didn't exactly growl. It made a sound something like a gurgling whimper. Silently cursing her traitorous anatomy, she grimaced apologetically.

He gave her a wide smile and winked his unswollen eye. "I promise to feed you before we do any business."

Damn the handsome bastard. With no more than a boyish expression and a few kind words, he'd destroyed her illusion of safe distance. "I've been dozing off and on most of the afternoon and evening," she offered, trying to sound unruffled, "but from time to time I had a lucid moment. One question keeps coming back to nag at me. If you wouldn't consider it impertinent to ask, might I inquire how you intend to pay for food, clothing, and new horses? I don't think they'll take American Express."

He poked his head through the neck opening of his shirt and looked at her quizzically while he drew the rest of the garment down the length of his torso. "American Express?"

"A form of credit in my time. I was attempting to make a joke."

He offered her a smile of good-natured patience and then slowly reached up to touch his face. "The pain has indeed lessened, Alanna. I didn't think healing to be among your powers."

"Well, you've seen the full range of my medicinal talents. And unless you want me to go over your ship's account ledger, you're going to be real disappointed with whatever other powers you think I might have."

"Must you always confound me, woman?" he demanded, his voice exasperated. "Are you telling me that you have some experience with simple bookkeeping? Or that your witchcraft is as weak as a woman's head for business matters?"

"I'm telling you that I am a certified public accountant," she retorted, her anger washing away her discomfort. "It may not be the most glamorous profession in the world, and it certainly leaves a lot to be desired in the excitement department, but it does mean that *this woman* has one helluva good head for business matters. I'm also telling you that I don't have any mystical powers. Maude might have had them in spades, but I didn't inherit a single solitary one. If you expect me to conjure up raging storms or to quiet the sea, you're flat out of luck, Captain. I wouldn't know what to do with bats' wings, lizards' tongues, or the eyes of newts even if I had a bazillion jars of each. I don't know any magic spells and I sure as hell don't dance naked in the moonlight."

"But you can prophesy, Mistress," he countered, his voice soft and calm, his eyes searching hers. "You can see events that have yet to occur."

"We've been over this before. In your cabin. Remember? I told you I don't have any special powers."

"And you're lying now just as you did then," he persisted with a gentleness that drew the breath from her body. "I can see it in your eyes, Alanna. Prophesy is the power required of you. That you possess the gift is the reason Maude judged you suitable to come in her stead. For my purposes, your single power is sufficient." He began to shove his shirttails down into the waistband of his breeches but paused to look up at her and add, "Although I would have no objections to watching you dance naked in the moonlight."

"Don't you ever give up?"

He grinned widely, teasing her. "Never. And when might I expect your capitulation?"

Alanna retorted hotly, "When they ice skate in the streets of Port-au-Prince."

He considered her, his expression sobering only slightly. Both amusement and patience were evident in his tone when he said, "Since you have such limited experience with men, Alanna, I think it only fair to warn you that we're irresistibly drawn to great challenges."

"More like hopeless dreams," she replied.

He shrugged. "They often tend to go hand in hand, but not always."

"Well, don't get any ideas about holding my hand . . . or any other part of me for that matter."

He grinned and swept the length of her with appraising eyes. "Are you cut of the same cloth as was Maude? Was her spirit as feisty as yours?"

"Maude had the patience of a saint. But even she would have been tempted to turn you into a toad by now."

"I'm familiar with that old folk tale, mistress. Are you suggesting that in my present state I'm a handsome prince?" he taunted.

"Handsome, yes. There's no point in denying it. But if you're a prince, it's only among scoundrels."

"Speaking of which . . ." he returned, his smile unaffected by her insult. "We should be off in search of my royal subjects." With a wide gesture, he indicated the horses. "Shall we go?"

"If I had any other choice—"

"Which you do not."

"Not at present," she agreed. "But once we reach County Kerry, it'll be another matter entirely."

His smile changed, subtly and slowly. And Alanna knew that he envisioned a far different ending to their relationship than she did. Loathing surged through her, but the true cause wasn't Kiervan's roguish hopes. No, Kiervan had provided only the initial spark for the ferocious fire that consumed her. She was disgusted with herself, furious at the tingling wave of anticipation that had rolled over her the moment she had recognized his thoughts, furious because she had no heady, breathless memories of Bill with which to fight the temptation of Kiervan des Marceaux.

She whirled about and marched into the shadowy grove of trees. "I need to remake my shoes," she declared without a backward glance.

He chuckled and called softly after her, "Don't berate yourself overlong, Alanna. The night grows short."

Alanna swore beneath her breath, calling him every name she could think of as she snatched her linen rags from the tree branches. A small measure of calm returned while she fashioned the first sandal. He couldn't have known for sure what she'd been thinking, she assured herself. His taunt had been based on a guess and that was all. If she stayed away too long, he would think he'd been right.

When she'd finished her task, Alanna rose to her feet. Kiervan des Marceaux wasn't going to get to her again. It had been years since she'd hidden behind a mask of cool detachment, but she remembered the protection it afforded and remembered exactly how to play the part.

Kiervan waited with the horses some ten feet or so beyond the edge of the trees, and yet she felt the intensity of his scrutiny the instant she emerged from the woods. The fit of the mask wasn't quite as comfortable as she remembered it being in the past, but the sudden narrowing of his eyes told her that he'd detected the shift in her manner. She knew then that she had at least achieved the first requisite for self-protection. Her attitude showed in the way she walked, the way she held her shoulders, the way she surveyed him in return.

"Were there any signs of Ashton or of English patrols while I slept?" he asked, his words quiet, his manner thoughtful, as he handed her the reins of her mount.

She took them from him, keeping her fingers well distant from his. "Some riders passed by a couple of hours ago," she replied, her voice controlled and devoid of emotion. Satisfied with the degree of calm she presented, Alanna pointed into the distance on their right as she added, "They were over that way."

"And you didn't think to mention this to me earlier?"

"It didn't seem to merit the status of crisis information. And besides, Ashton and his men aren't the only ones allowed to travel the roads of Ireland."

"How many riders were there?"

She waited until she had swung up and across the saddle before answering. "I don't know. Maybe a half dozen, give or take two or three."

He gained his mount and for a moment regarded her in a silence so intense that she had wanted to look away. *No*, she remanded herself, *I won't crack. I can't let him control me.* It took every ounce of her self-discipline, but she met his gaze squarely.

"In which direction did they travel?" he finally asked.

The coolness in his voice matched her own, and Alanna realized that Kiervan was also quite adept at hiding himself, and that being deliberately shut out hurt a lot. A lot more than she had ever imagined.

She swallowed and replied carefully, "They were heading into town."

He nodded once and then turned his horse toward the roadway.

Alanna rode at his side through the darkness, hating the silence hanging between them more than their noisy contests of wills. At least when they were arguing with one another, she felt she had some measure of control over herself and the situation, however fleeting it might be. In the silence she couldn't escape the nagging sense that her mastery of her emotions was nothing more than an illusion; that her fervent pledges to remain beyond Kiervan's influence were only hollow words. All he had to do was look at her or say the right words and she reacted without thought.

It'll get better, Alanna promised herself. She wasn't herself and hadn't been since she stumbled out of the stones atop the Carraig Cor. Maybe, when she got something to eat and a decent night's rest, she'd be more in control.

A thought came to her suddenly, bringing with it instantaneous understanding and relief. *Of course, it only makes sense,* she thought, relieved. Traveling through time had to be as hard on a person's mind and body as rapid altitude changes. Only a fool would attempt to climb mountains before they'd become acclimated. A couple of days to adjust to this new world was all she needed. When she got used to being in another century she'd get her strength back and she'd regain command of her emotions. Until then, the smartest, and safest, thing to do was to remain behind her protective mask of cold reserve and wait.

12

The impact of horseshoes against the rough cobble-stones reverberated through the dark and otherwise silent streets. Kiervan kept them to the deeper shadows cast by the ramshackle buildings on their left, keeping their pace through the village unhurried. He cursed the Irish penchant for paving stones and hoped that, should anyone awaken at their passage, they'd dismiss them as late-night travelers trusting their mounts to carry them homeward.

Alanna rode behind him. Kiervan fought the urge to glance back at the silent, cloak-draped figure and offer her some sign of reassurance. There was no point in making the effort. He knew what he would find. She would be sitting atop her mount, her head held at a haughty angle and her back ramrod straight. She would meet his gaze without emotion, returning it in equal, maddening measure.

At his gesture of encouragement, she would only dip her chin in silent acknowledgment. It had been all she had accorded him when they'd stopped at the edge of the town and he'd lain before her both his course and a suitable tale should there be questions concerning their traveling together. She hadn't bothered to respond at all when he'd removed the coins from the hem of his cloak and pressed several into her hand.

Glowering at the empty street before him, Kiervan decided the woman was surely one of the most nettlesome creatures ever to cross his path. A good half of what she said made sense only after he'd pondered the words and the context in which she'd used them. Her attitudes regarding men and women and marriage were eccentric to say the very least. And she'd chosen now of all times to play the withdrawn regal lady, now when he had neither the time nor the latitude to show her the futility of her charade.

A wry smile touched his mouth. It wouldn't take much effort to undo her game. Mistress Alanna Kathleen Chapman was a woman of passionate disposition, and despite her considerable self-discipline, in the end she wouldn't be able to suppress her innate temperament. He had only to choose the avenue of his approach from among the many her nature afforded him and then watch her cool reserve crumble.

But it wouldn't be enough to make a brief mockery of her pretenses. He fully intended to inflict such damage on her protective facade that she'd never again be able to hide from him, so that never again would she attempt to make him feel inferior. His conscience instantly deplored the ruthlessness of his course, but his wounded pride quickly silenced it.

He smiled dangerously as he considered the most certain of the possibilities. Alanna's tempestuous emotions were stirring in and of themselves, but he sensed that their potency would be far surpassed by the physical passions she'd so long refused to explore.

Lord, he suddenly wondered, how had she managed to stay chaste for so long? Her fiancé couldn't be much of a man if he'd allowed her to keep his passions in check. Perhaps Bill Boyer simply hadn't had the wherewithal to press Alanna into surrendering herself and her maidenly virtue. Could Bill Boyer be one of those dandy men who possessed no real hunger for women but kept one nonetheless, just to still the wagging of gossiping tongues? Kiervan frowned. From what he already knew of her and from what he could readily surmise, Alanna Chapman wouldn't like being a convenient decoration. So why would she have agreed to marry the man? Judging by the ring the man had given her, Bill Boyer was a man of considerable means. But again, what he knew of Alanna's character told him that she wouldn't marry for money alone. What had drawn her to the man she'd left on the other side of time?

Suddenly he heard the music of an Irish pipe drifting to his ears on the cool night breeze. Kiervan frowned and then deliberately focused his attention on the pool of pale light spilling across the road some distance ahead of them. Thoughts of bedding Alanna Chapman were dangerous; they led him down puzzling paths, clouded his thinking, and dulled his perceptions. And unless he could keep his wits about him long enough to take them safely through the next few hours, imagining would be the closest he would ever get to either solving the mystery of Alanna's heart or sampling her deeper fires.

With their mounts tethered among the donkeys and the other horses at the shadowed rear of the pub, Kiervan led the way up the dark alleyway. He paused beside the door, listened for a long moment, and then turned to Alanna. "Keep the cloak about you and do nothing to call attention to yourself," he said, keeping his voice low. "Remember, you're an innocent maid kidnapped from her father's home. I was employed to find you and am—"

"I got it the first time," she said softly. "I can do timid and withdrawn."

Kiervan studied the violet eyes lifted to his scrutiny. He needed to be sure of her, to be certain that she could keep her ire in check. If, as he feared, an English patrol had passed through the village in search of them and offering rewards, she could with one wrong word, one wrong action, put nooses about both their necks.

"Alanna," he began, not caring that quiet desperation was evident in his words. "I know not why you've become so distant, but I beg you to set it aside until we're away from here. I give you my word that I'll answer for my crimes before sunrise."

She blinked and her aloofness fell away. Every instinct within him spoke at once, demanding that he take her into the shelter of his arms, that he hold her and assure her that all would be well. Gently whispering her name, he reached for her. Even as he did, she stepped beyond his touch, her eyes downcast.

"We're wasting time, Captain," she said quietly. When she added, "And I'm hungry," the measured tones had returned to her voice.

With a sigh and a nod of acceptance, Kiervan turned and stepped into the doorway.

The main room was small for a pub, no more than twenty feet square and bounded by stained and deteriorating plaster walls. Into the space were packed an odd assortment of tables and chairs and men and women, all of which needed washing with a strong lye soap. Kiervan peered through the peat and tobacco smoke, noting the blackened hearth on the far side of the room, the pipe, drum, and fiddle players idling in the corner, and the bar on his left which had been made of two barrels and a few broad planks. Centered in the wall on his right was a post and lintel doorway opening into what appeared to be a corridor. He well imagined what business was conducted in the rooms which undoubtedly lined the dark narrow hall.

This place was like a thousand others he had entered in the course of his travels around the world, places in which treachery had been refined to an art, places from which he had extracted many a friend and most of his crewmen. But this time was different; he had Alanna with him. Never had he brought a woman with him into such a den of squalor.

He looked at Alanna. As he did she lowered her eyes, but not before he'd noted that she too had conducted a swift survey of the pub and its occupants. Saying nothing, she glided from his side and then gingerly settled herself at an unoccupied table situated midway between the front door of the establishment and its wide, grimy front window.

He frowned as he realized she'd claimed the seat against the wall. Kiervan stepped to the table and pulled out the sticky chair opposite her. "Perhaps you'd prefer to sit here."

She didn't look up as she quietly replied, "You sit with your back to them. I'm not."

Dragging the chair around to her side of the scarred tabletop, Kiervan studied her. She hadn't turned a ghastly shade of green nor had she wrinkled her nose in disgust. In fact, she appeared calm and poised, not at all affected by the strong odors of old ale, smoke, and unwashed humanity. It was almost as if she could ignore the wretchedness about her. Clearly, Alanna was a woman of quality, and yet she seemed oddly unaffected by the squalor around them.

The approach of a serving maid interrupted his thoughts. Kiervan judged the young woman to be roughly the same age as Alanna and of similar physical stature. Her curves were fuller than Alanna's, the span of her waist and hips still narrow but showing the ravages of a poor and hard life. She had pulled her bodice well off her shoulders, revealing a slender neck marred by a line of fading bruises, and breasts that had been pushed high and artfully molded by the tight lacings about her midriff. The thin, yellowed fabric of her blouse hid naught from his inspection, and the knotted hem of her skirt exposed a pale calf and a good expanse of her thigh.

Kiervan allowed his gaze to linger over her breasts for another moment and then looked up into her face with an appreciative smile.

She smiled in encouragement and placed her hands on the table across from him. Leaning forward to provide him with a better view of her wares, she fluttered her eyelashes and asked, "An' how might I serve a fancy gent like you?"

Out of the corner of his eye, he saw Alanna stiffen. "An' what might yer name be, darlin' girl?" he inquired of the maid, assuming the lilting tones of his youth. He felt Alanna's attention dart to him and then skip away.

"Mary," the woman replied, raising first one shoulder and then the other to emphasize her already ample display of flesh.

"Ah," he offered on an almost reverent sigh, "Named no doubt for the Blessed Virgin Mother." He immediately let his eyes fall back to her chest and again he sighed, this time in feigned resignation. " 'Tis a shame indeed, Mary dear, that I must be about less pleasurable business this night."

Mary turned as though newly aware of the other woman's presence and swept the length of Alanna's cloaked form with open disdain. Kiervan noted the rapid rise and fall of the shoulders hidden beneath the dark fabric of his mantle and knew without looking that while his companion's hands rested in her lap, they'd been balled into tight fists.

"Sad it is to say, but the life of a bounty man is not his own, darlin'," he interjected in an effort to distract both women. "Rescuin' the Lady Elizabeth has been a trial to me patience, to be sure. Now . . ." He looked to Mary's hips and sighed in pained regret. "To have to ask ye only for a meal an' a pint o' ale is surely a chafin' me body most sorely regrets."

" 'Tis simple fare we have to offer," Mary returned, still glowering at Alanna. " 'Tis hardly good enough for a *lady*."

"She will eat whatever ye bring her," he countered, leaning forward to lay his hand over Mary's. Her attention instantly focused on him. Kiervan smiled up at her and stroking her knuckles with the pad of his thumb, set about the second of his tasks. "An' if 'twouldn't be too great a favor to ask of ye, darlin', would ye be willin' to sell some of yer clothes? The Lady Elizabeth's father might be well tempted to short me purse if I was to return her to England in rags." He frowned and added, "To me way of thinkin' 'twould be a shame of the worst sort not to have the coin to travel this way again."

Refusal danced for only a moment in Mary's eyes. Kiervan watched as a malicious light suddenly flickered to life in the depths of them and knew that he'd played his hand with skill. The prospect of his money now and in the future, combined with the temptation of dressing an English lady in the raiments of an Irish barmaid, had been inducements Mary couldn't resist. Alanna would be furious, but at least she'd be covered in more appropriate garb.

" 'Twouldn't be no hardship on my account," Mary replied with a sly glance in Alanna's direction. "I've a piece or two that might be to the lady's likin'."

"Ye be sainted in me heart, Mary dear," Kiervan went on, still stroking the back of her hand. "Mayhap, when the lady's eaten her fill, ye'd be kind enough to take her to yer room an' see to her proper wardrobin'. An' while ye'd be from me side, I might find a man here 'bouts known fer his horse tradin'."

" 'Twould be Eth ye'd be seein', then," she supplied, indicating a bearded, wiry little man seated in the darkest corner of the room. Sitting in a circle of men with his back to the corner, the man had been the first to note their entry into the pub and the longest to study them. From experience, Kiervan knew immediately that this man would be the force with which he must eventually reckon.

Nodding and patting the young woman's hand before he leaned back in his chair, Kiervan crossed his arms over his chest and stared into the smoky haze. "Ah, Mary, ye have no idea how a man feels to be among his own kind after bein' parted by time an' distance. 'Tis indeed food for the starvin' soul."

In the full tones of the King's English, Alanna muttered, "Food for the starving body would be even more welcome."

Kiervan looked at Mary, shrugged his shoulders, and sighed in deep apology. "Do be a darlin', Mary, an' fetch us somethin' for our bellies. Lestwise there'll no' be a moment o' peace for any of us."

She glowered at Alanna one more time, then sauntered toward the hearth, her hips swaying in continued invitation.

Kiervan frowned as he turned to Alanna and whispered, " 'Twas no idea I had that ye possessed the gift of mimicry as well, darlin'. But ye took a chance I'd prefer not to see ye do again."

Her voice low and her English affectation gone, Alanna countered without looking at him, "Then stop inviting the woman to lay her merchandise on the table for you. It's a sight *I'd* prefer not to see."

Kiervan said nothing. Instead he leaned forward, propping his elbows on the table and his chin in one hand. Behind the artful curve of his fingers, he allowed himself a genuine smile. While he watched Mary return with a steaming trencher in each hand and a loaf of bread tucked beneath her arm, he found himself hoping Alanna would momentarily abandon her study of the floor. He wanted to see her eyes, wanted to see if the violet of them had become flecked with green.

Alanna stared down at the platter and fought back the impulse to gag.

"Are you unwell?" Kiervan asked quietly, working a bit of the food onto his wooden spoon.

"I will be if I eat this." She prodded what looked like it might be a chunk of potato. A pool of grease encircled it, glistening in the lantern light. Her stomach roiled and she resolutely put her spoon down and set the wooden plate aside. "I neglected to mention that I'm a vegetarian," she offered in explanation for what she knew had to be outwardly odd behavior. At Kiervan's sidelong look, she tried again, saying simply, "I don't eat meat."

"Try," was his only response.

Alanna ignored him and reached for a piece of the bread he had sliced earlier. Chewing a bite, she decided that the experience couldn't be that much different from eating paper towels. The absorbency of the stuff was incredible. She didn't have the spit to swallow. The only solution, other than choking to death, seemed to be to wash it down with ale. Although warm and bitter, the brew did, in the final analysis, accomplish the task of getting something reasonably solid into her stomach.

Halfway through the loaf of bread and with three-quarters of the pint gone, Alanna sat back in her chair and sighed in utter contentment. Her stomach was finally full and a delightful sense of well-being had drifted over her. Yes, she decided, the idea to wait until she'd adjusted to life in 1803 had been a sound one. She was feeling much better already. God only knew what Bambi the Bouncing Barmaid would scrounge up in the apparel department, but she'd deal with that situation when it came. In fact, Alanna reflected, she felt good enough to handle just about anything right now.

She snuck a look at Kiervan through her lashes. Despite his admonition that she try to eat the stew, he'd made very little progress with it himself before pushing it away. He sat beside her, both forearms resting on the table, and absently turned his empty ale glass between his hands as he watched a group of men depart.

Her scrutiny drew a glance from him, and she quickly looked away, focusing her attention instead on the dirty table. Before her rested the remaining bread and the deadly little knife Mary had provided for hacking it into pieces. It was more of the short, efficient hunting variety than a proper bread knife. She'd watched Kiervan test the balance and heft of it the moment the maid's back had been turned. There had been a hard light in his eye as he'd considered it, and at the time she'd been certain he intended to appropriate the weapon. But as yet he'd made no move to take it. She told herself that she could trust his judgment, that he simply hadn't had the chance to move it out of sight.

But even as she reassured herself, she saw the barmaid advancing toward them, and the decision was made. Turning slightly toward Kiervan, she leisurely pushed her own glass across the table to him with her left hand, saying as she did, "You might as well finish this. I've had more than enough already." In a single fluid motion, she palmed the knife with her right and slipped it into his waistband at the small of his back.

The look he shot her was of pure surprise.

"Steady, Captain," she whispered, looking down again in the manner of a modest gentlewoman. "Buxom Bimbo at two o'clock."

13

Holding the cloak closed, Alanna followed Mary through the doorway and into the hall. She couldn't name the exact cause, but she had the very real sense that something was wrong. Kiervan's tones had been flawlessly lilting and his manner had been easy, but Alanna knew when she'd been given the bum's rush. Glancing over her shoulder, she saw him moving, ale in hand, toward the man Mary had called Eth. Kiervan's stride was relaxed, his expression confident, like a bored man wandering toward an open pool table, she decided. And yet there was something about his manner that she found disquieting.

Her contemplation of Kiervan came to an abrupt end as Mary led her farther down the corridor. Suddenly regretting the ale she'd consumed on a virtually empty stomach, Alanna drew a head-cleaning breath and focused on the more immediate situation.

She found herself in a hallway that couldn't have been any more than three feet wide and was lined with doors spaced at regular intervals. She counted twelve in all, six down each side. The number became thirteen when she included the grungy windowed door at the end of the hall that led outside. She shuddered at the mythical implication of the number, then chastised herself for falling prey to superstitions. Numbers had nothing to do with a person's luck. She continued in Mary's wake, observing the narrow bands of weak light showing along the bottom edge of five of the once-painted panels, noting that all of them clustered in the center of the passageway: three on her left, two on her right.

Mary passed them, then paused to open the next door on the right side of the hall. *Three and three,* Alanna thought, crossing the threshold after her. Enough moonlight filtered through the dirty window glass to let her see the other woman cross the room and lift the globe from an oil lamp. While Mary's attention was occupied, Alanna adjusted the door, leaving it ajar should she need to escape, but closing it enough to hide her presence from anyone who happened by. With the simple task completed, she edged toward the center of the room, noting that its only contents were a rumpled bed and a low chest of drawers.

Suddenly, from the other side of the wall, came the sound of steady thumping. *Headboard,* her mind supplied. Alanna grimaced and willed herself selectively deaf. She had a fairly accurate idea of what went on in the rooms in a place like this. She'd scurried through them more times than she'd care to remember, taking money to her stepfather, to her stepbrothers. Neither the exposure nor the general nature of her knowledge had ever made being in them any less uncomfortable for her.

As the wick caught flame, a man's throaty cry of triumph reverberated through the room. Alanna wished herself a thousand miles from this awful place.

"He's a man, yer companion is, to be sure," Mary said.

Alanna stood in the center of the tiny room and murmured something noncommittal.

"What's 'is name?"

With a sigh, Alanna resigned herself to the fact that she wasn't going to get away with standing there pretending to be deaf and mute. Affecting her upper-class English accent, she replied, "I really do *not* have the slightest idea."

Mary put her fists on hips and arched a brow. "Yer sayin' yer travelin' with a man who's never told ye his name?"

"Oh," Alanna said, stalling. Her mind raced. Kiervan hadn't mentioned using an alias, but under the circumstances, it seemed a prudent thing to do. "O'Hara," she offered, supplying the first Irish name that came to her. But

Scarlett wouldn't do for a man, and for the life of her she couldn't remember Scarlett's father's name. Another memory saved her just in time. "Danny," she added. "Danny O'Hara. I have, on occasion, heard him refer to himself as Dan-o."

An appreciative expression settled over the other woman's face as she turned back to the lamp on her crude dresser. Adjusting the height of the wick, she smiled and said, "That Dan-o be the kind ye'd be a willin' to leave the light on fer, if ye know what I mean."

Alanna felt her stomach tighten, but she swallowed past her misgivings and put on a brave face. "The effort would likely be in vain. I have observed that he is not at all reliable."

Laughing and shaking her head, Mary opened a drawer in the chest. " 'Tisn't what I mean a'tall, darlin'," she countered when her amusement had faded a bit. "I mean he'd be worth lookin' at while he's buckin' 'tween yer legs."

Alanna's jaw dropped open as a searing heat flamed up her neck and across her cheeks. If the Happy Hooker noticed her embarrassment, she didn't seem to care about it.

"I imagine many a woman's done drawn her breath at the sight," Mary went on, pulling various items from the drawer and tossing them onto the bed. "Sure 'twould be the last bit of air ye'd have 'til he was done, though. He looks to be the size of a—"

"I *really* do not want to continue this conversation," Alanna interrupted, her accent faltering slightly in her haste to stop the woman's words.

Mary looked up at her, clearly amused. "He ain't laid ye down yet, has he darlin'?"

Lord, Alanna groaned, how had this gotten so out of hand? Pointing to the articles on the bed, she began, "That skirt will do nicely and the blouse seems quite—"

"A special bit of baggage ye must be indeed," Mary said, considering her with narrowed eyes. She cocked her head to the side and added, "A man like Danny O'Hara ain't usually given to waitin' fer his pleasures."

"I need something for my feet," Alanna hurried on.

"Might you happen to have an extra pair of shoes you would be willing to sell?"

A knowing smile lifted the corners of the woman's mouth as she surveyed Alanna from head to toe. With a deprecating snort, she pronounced, "Ain't ever been had by any man, have ye?"

Alanna stood silent before the censure, her hands balled into fists. She owed this woman no apology for a chastity preserved against incredible odds. "I have inquired as to the possibility of footwear," she answered icily.

With a shrug, Mary bent to open the bottom drawer of the chest. "To be sure, nothin' draws a bee like a new flower," she observed, straightening to add two large but softly shaped items to those already on the bed. Pulling a petticoat from the middle drawer, she continued, saying, " 'Tis a sweet prize they can't resist takin'. 'Tis only a short matter of time 'fore he's rubbin' yer petals."

"I am not interested in—"

"Then 'tis a fool ye be, yer ladyship," she snapped, whirling about to face Alanna. Wagging her finger, she continued, "Ye may be high an' mighty born, but ye don't know a damn thing about what goes on 'tween men an' women. A whore I am, pure an' simple, but I got more man sense in me left pinkie than ye'll ever have in yer whole body. If'n ye were only half-witted, ye'd take a bit o' me advice. Lift yer skits fer Danny O'Hara an' beg him to take ye to heaven whenever an' however he wants. Straddlin' that man will be the grandest, most glorious ride, o' that ye can be sure."

Alanna squared her shoulders and, with all the haughtiness she could muster, replied, "I shall give the idea the consideration it is properly due." Having made her last pronouncement on the subject, she stepped to the bed and began to gather the clothing into a manageable bundle. She felt Mary's eyes follow her, but she clenched her teeth and ignored the woman's scrutiny.

" 'Twill be sad in a way, as well, darlin', an' ye might as well know it. His bein' yer first is a goin' to ruin it fer ye ever after fer sure. No other man's ever goin' to be enough to fill ye like he will."

"These are quite interesting," Alanna said evenly, placing a pair of homemade boots in the center of the neat little pile she had made. "Are they sheepskin?"

"An' ye might as well know, 'tis a sure bet he'll no' be stayin' with ye either. He's the kind can have any he wants an' when he wants 'em. Once yer bloom's worn off, he'll be searchin' fer other fields where he can sow his seed. When he's done with ye he might even come to nestle with me awhile."

"Hope springs eternal," Alanna muttered, knotting the sleeves of the blouse about the other articles. Kiervan had his shortcomings, but a lack of class certainly wasn't one of them.

"The things we could do, him and me . . . "

"Spare me," Alanna groaned. From the pocket of her pants, she fished the coins Kiervan had given her before they'd come into town. She had no idea what each was worth, but as she tossed them down on the bed, she prayed they'd be enough. If she'd had more, she'd have gladly offered them in exchange for the woman's promise of conversational silence.

As Mary bent to scoop the money from the sheets, footsteps pounded down the passageway. Alanna spun about, a feeling of danger crawling up her back. The cloak was still swirling about her feet when the door swung open to reveal Kiervan standing in the shadowed hall.

Considering the urgency in his eyes and the determined set of his jaw, murmuring "Thank God" was hardly the most germane or intelligent thing she could do, but at that moment she had never been more relieved and grateful to see him.

He held out his hand in a wordless request for her to hurry. With the bundle of clothing in her right hand, she put her left in his, trusting him to lead her. Her feet barely touched the floor as he drew her down the corridor toward the windowed door at the end. They were less than a half dozen paces from their goal when excited English voices from the yard ripped through the thin wooden panel. As the black silhouette of a man on the other side filled the glass,

Kiervan swore and, without the slightest pause, pivoted, grasped the handle of the second door from the end, and dragged her inside.

Alanna stumbled into the darkness.

"Wait here," Kiervan commanded, leaving her in the space between the bed and the door.

She watched as he vaulted across the room and peered around the window frame. He darted back with an oath, surveyed the room with a desperate glance, and then swore again. Her heart pounding and her legs shaking from the rush of adrenaline, Alanna struggled to pull the hem of the cloak from under her feet without upending herself.

"Damn it, Alanna!" he whispered harshly.

She blinked up at him just in time to see him fling his jacket to the floor. "What?" she asked, watching in stunned fascination as he yanked his shirttail from his breeches.

"I said take off your cloak and shirt and get into the bed."

She understood his request instantly. Given their circumstances, it was the most logical thing to do. Nodding, she said, "I get the drift of—"

"Do it!"

Alanna blinked once at the harsh command and then glanced about for a darkened corner into which to hide her bundle of clothing. He was before her in a heartbeat, stripping the bundle from her hand and the cloak from her shoulders in the same instant, flinging them to the floor in the next. He didn't waste a motion. The moment the mantle and her newly acquired clothes had been discarded, he reached for her shirt and yanked it free of her pants.

"I can do it," she protested as she pushed at his hands. Her meager attempt didn't slow him in the least. The makeshift shirt came up and over her head with such speed and force that she rocked back on her heels, her balance gone. Even as she stumbled backward, he caught her to him, pinning her arms between the heated flesh of their chests. Then he pivoted and fell with her onto the bed.

Alanna landed on her side, cushioned within the circle of his embrace, pressed hard along the length of his body. The sensations had barely registered in her brain when he rolled her beneath him. She gasped at the jolt of fire that shot through her, at the sudden tightening low in her belly. Clenching her teeth, she stiffened her body and pressed her knees into one another, finding only scant comfort in the fact that her breeches remained to separate them.

"Damn it, Alanna," Kiervan growled in frustration, propping himself on one elbow to gaze down at her. With his other hand, he reached behind him and gathered a handful of the bed coverings. " 'Tis a ruse," he said, dropping the covers over them, then settling his arms on either side of her tousled head.

She stared up at him, a defiant look in her eyes.

"There's a bounty on our heads and they know we're here. They'll search the rooms, 'Lanna," he hurried to explain. "Play along and we may yet save our necks from the hangman."

She nodded, but the eyes that searched his were uncertain and the body beneath him remained rigid. If his plan was to have a hope of success, he needed her pliant and soft, an accommodating partner. He needed Alanna to the point of surrender, and he hadn't the time to go about it with the tenderness he would have preferred. She deserved better of him, deserved to be slowly led down the paths of pleasure.

Even as he cursed the Fates for making this dangerous game necessary, voices echoed down the corridor, and at the other end of the hall, a door slammed. Alanna cringed at the sound.

Kiervan leaned down and lightly brushed his lips over hers. "Do you trust me, Alanna?" he asked on the barest whisper.

"Yes," she answered, her voice soft against his cheek. He felt her swallow, heard the tremor in her voice when she added, "Show me what you want me to do."

14

"'**T**is a charade that must be only a shadow from the truth, Alanna. There's no other way they'll believe it," he explained, lowering his head to kiss first the corner of her mouth, then cover her trembling lips with a gentle but certain caress. "Follow where I lead and resist me not," he begged, nipping at her lower lip with his teeth. "I'll take us only far enough. I give you my word."

Another door slammed in the corridor, the sound of it slightly closer than the first. Alanna flinched. His heart hammering, Kiervan took her mouth, kissing her with urgency, tracing the inner edges of her lips with bold strokes of his tongue. She yielded to his request without hesitation, opening to him the dulcet regions of her mouth.

Kiervan explored the honeyed sweetness of her, his tongue dancing and darting about her own, stroking, tasting every delectable treasure within the soft cavern. Alanna moaned and he accepted the sound, feeling the resonance pass through his chest and into the center of his soul.

Alanna softened beneath him, the curves of her body molding around the hard angles of his own. The heat of desire flooded from his fingertips to his chest, then shot down the length of him, taking his breath and hardening his need. Her flesh burned against his, branding and claiming him. The taste of her intoxicated him and muddled his senses, made him want to forget restraint, made him want to forget all but taking her, all but becoming lost in her sultry fire. He knew he was teetering on a dangerous precipice, that control was quickly slipping from his grasp and that his seduction of Alanna was moving beyond pretense and into the realm of his fantasies.

She was untried, he told himself, a maid submitting rather than suffering certain forfeit of her life. The ring she wore about her neck pressed hard against his flesh, reminding him that she belonged to another. What he was doing with her wasn't right. And yet he recognized all the reasoned words as false. Never had any woman felt so right in his arms.

As if she'd sensed he needed reassurance, Alanna drew her arms from between them. Her hands caressed his chest, then slipped up to his shoulders and about his neck. Fiery shivers raced through his flesh at her touch and he deepened his possession of her mouth, his questing rough and compelling, demanding her total surrender.

She answered in equal measure, twining her fingers through the hair at the nape of his neck, welcoming his advance with a moan of need as hard and desperate as his own, turning his doubts to ashes and releasing them into the winds of their desire.

In the distance he heard another door slam, heard the sound even nearer than the last. Through the roaring of his blood in his ears, Kiervan heard the percussion and marked it as still toward the upper end of the passageway. The better man within him recoiled at the callous speed with which he pressed Alanna, but the bold and ruthless survivor conceded to the necessity and spurred him on.

He laid a trail of fevered kisses across her cheek and jaw, then down onto the delicate curve of her neck. Whispering his name on a ragged breath, she turned her face into his shoulder, yielding yet another part of herself to his rough possession. Kiervan reveled in the silken feel of her, tasted the heady potion of sky and sea and earth and woman that clung to her skin, that pooled in the hollow at the base of her throat.

Another door closed. Midway.

Kiervan continued downward, roughly pushing aside the corded ring, laying kisses over the creamy swell of her breast, wanting the time to sweeten and savor the pleasure, his heart cursing the necessity of haste. And then Alanna arched up, offering his lips a dark, pebbled peak, and his regrets were lost in a low, hard moan. He suckled her, teasing the hardened crest with his tongue, and she arched higher, holding him to her, softly calling his name and shifting beneath him to settle him against her.

He ached, wanting her passion sheathing him, yet knew that he couldn't ask that of her. Not now. Not here. Not like this. Kiervan slid up to rest his arms on either side of her slender shoulders. She looked at him, her eyes large and a brilliant liquid blue, her lips swollen and still wet from his kisses. He felt the searing heat of her body everywhere it touched his, felt the throbbing demand of his manhood against her yielding warmth.

" 'Tis far enough, 'Lanna," he rasped, brushing back a lock of golden hair that had tumbled over her shoulder. "I'll not take you any farther here. There'd be no stopping if we don't stop now."

She lifted her head to kiss his neck, and when she drew him down to her softly parted lips, he was powerless to resist. Holding him to her, she explored him, the bold caresses of her tongue sending bolts of molten desire spiraling through his body. He closed his eyes and abandoned himself to the exquisite torture of her lips, to the soft ravaging of her hands. The world would come crashing in upon them soon enough, but until then, he was hers and she his, and nothing else mattered.

Her hands slipped slowly, deliberately down the length of his sides, drawing him to her. When they came to rest on his hips, he could no longer control his passion. Her body responded instantly to his movements, matching perfectly the rhythm of his urgency and desire. She arched up into him as her hands held his hips against her own.

Kiervan took her quiet cries into himself, feeling them spiral through and tear apart the last remaining shreds of control. With a low moan, he rolled them onto their sides, drawing Alanna close and hard against him. His hand slipped down to the curve of her waist and then lower, one part of him drowning in the satin softness of her skin, another part nearly frantic to find the edge of her trousers and move them aside. The instant his fingertips found it, he slipped them beneath. Moaning in satisfaction, he quickly slid the woolen fabric down and over the sweep of her hip.

She trembled and gasped in the same heartbeat that she tore away from his possession of her lips. Kiervan gazed down into the moonlit pools of violet bright with desire, felt the tantalizing rise and fall of her breasts against his chest. He moved his hand across the swell of her belly and watched her eyelids grow deliciously heavy with expectation. They closed as his fingers slid lower, into her damp curls. With a strangled sigh, she eased back, granting all that he cared to take and offering all that she had to give.

Kiervan's gaze caressed the length of her bathed in moonlight, marveling at the perfection of her, feeling his need throbbing through every fiber of his being. Leaning down, he captured a pebbled breast with his mouth and suckled, the rhythm of his lips and tongue the same as his fingers that touched and stroked Alanna's sweet welcome.

She reached for him as she called his name in a low moan containing a plea as old as their dance, a desperation as sharp as that driving through his own veins. With one hand she held his lips to her breast. With the other she swept the hard angle of his hip and then dropped to the buttons on his trousers. His head swam with anticipation and primal urgency.

From somewhere in the pounding maelstrom, he heard the weak voice of his conscience, but he ignored it and rolled Alanna onto her back. As he settled against her, capturing her lips in a fierce warning of what was to come, she roughly pushed away the barrier of his trousers. The sensation of the knife she'd tucked there earlier sliding down his side and into the bed coverings was lost as the heat of their skin met and he drew her breath into his own lungs.

She arched against him and her hands came to his shoulders. With a ragged whisper of her name, he drew away from her lips and, with every ounce of what remained of his control, willed himself to pause, to let her feel and accept the hardness of his wanting against her. He gazed into her wide eyes, silently promising her all he had to give. Her lips parted and the fire in her eyes burned as hotly and invitingly as her need.

The light came without warning, spilling across them and momentarily blinding him.

"Get out!" Kiervan bellowed into it, his anger at the intrusion fiercely real. Alanna tensed, pressing herself against the length of him, and he lowered himself to shield her body with his own.

"We are searching for two American colonials. A man and a woman."

His heart hammering painfully in his chest, Kiervan squinted at the figure in the doorway. A single man stood on the other side of the threshold, a lamp in one hand, a flintlock pistol dangling toward the floor in the other. He looked young, his shoulders the width of a boy not quite a man. His accent marked him as English.

"They're no' here!" Kiervan challenged. "Now close the door an' be gone!"

"Have you—?"

"Are ye deaf or merely dull witted?"

He saw the Englishman's gaze drop to the bed, recognized the sudden gleam that came to his eyes. Kiervan glanced down into the patch of light that fell over them, to the dark-budded mound of Alanna's pale breast. Rage, raw and seething, shot through him. The jackanape was ogling her as if she were a common—

Realization swept through him like a gale wind, instantly tempering his wrath and bringing back his reason. He wanted to cover her, to protect Alanna from the leering eyes at the doorway, but he could not, not if they were to play their parts. Whores expected chivalry from no one, and few granted it to them. His heart twisted for her, for the indignity she was suffering. Swallowing back the bitter taste of his forced indifference, he prayed she would understand and forgive him. Kiervan glared at the other man, silently vowing to kill him if he moved to touch her.

"A tempting bit you've got to nibble there," the stranger commented, still gaping at Alanna.

"Go buy your own woman," Kiervan retorted. "This one's mine for the night."

"Not the sharing sort, are you?" the other said, finally tearing his attention from the delicacy trapped between Kiervan and the bed. He leaned forward in an obvious attempt to see past Kiervan's shoulders, asking, "What say you, mistress?"

Kiervan tensed, but he'd barely opened his mouth to offer words in her behalf when Alanna laughed and carefully peered between his chin and his arm at the stranger. In a flawless Irish accent, she replied, " 'Tis a fine night indeed when a girl has two strappin' men fightin' o'er her. But ye've come too late, me lad. Go home an' leave Sean an' me to finish what we've well started. If'n ye come tomorrow, Sean'll return the favor, to be sure." She slipped back beneath him and ran her fingers through the hair at his temples as she cooed, "Won't ye, Sean, me darlin'?"

"Aye," Kiervan snapped, glowering at the young man. " 'Tis a point I'll make to throw open the door an' gawk at the two of ye like an oafish schoolboy."

He reached beside him and drew the knife from the twisted sheets. Flipping the weapon about, he grasped the point between his fingers. "I've an itch I'm well past scratchin' an' me patience is at its end, lad." Lifting the knife up in preparation for throwing, he growled, "Now get the hell out an' close the bloody door or I'll drop ye where ye stand."

"No whore's worth dying for," the other observed, reaching for the door. As he drew it closed he paused, poked his head through the opening, and asked, "How much does she cost?"

"Everythin' you got, lad," Kiervan answered evenly, honestly. "An' then some."

"Is she worth it?"

"Aye," he assured him with a certain nod. "She's worth a man's soul."

When the door had closed and darkness had fallen over them, Kiervan laid the knife beside the pillow and gathered Alanna to him, then rolled them onto their sides. Nestling her head into the protective curve of his neck and shoulder, Kiervan felt the rapid hammering of her heart against his chest, the fierce trembling of her limbs. He drew her closer and smoothed the hair that cascaded down her back as he stared helplessly up at the ceiling. Words whirled about in his mind, disjointed and fractured words of thanks and wonder, of apology, reassurance, and desire—words he wanted to give to Alanna in the darkness but couldn't.

The morning would see his mind clearer, he told himself. The storm swirling within him would have calmed by then; the words could be collected and ordered so that Alanna didn't think him a blithering fool. With what remained of the night, he'd take her as far as he could from this wretched place, would find a secluded haven where he could hold her again and make everything right.

His course charted, Kiervan pressed a tender kiss to her temple and said, " 'Tis time we go, 'Lanna. They'll be widening the search and we have but to slip through the holes in their net."

Alanna distantly heard the sound of Kiervan's voice, felt its soothing vibrations pass through her body, but his words were only tiny pieces of flotsam in the roiling currents of her awareness. Her heart was beating too fast, too hard, slamming painfully against her ribs. Her breath came in shallow, quick snatches that were still too much for her lungs to hold. But more than anything else, there was a terrible ache, twisted and hot, centered low in her belly. Its power radiated through her, drawing her inward at the same time it propelled her out toward something unknown.

It was the ale, she told herself. She wasn't much of a drinker and she'd had too much of it. And being caught like a rat in a trap probably had something to do with it too. If this hideous night hadn't come right on the heels of a warp drive through time, she might have handled it better. That's why being in Kiervan's arms had affected her so deeply. It was nothing more than a mild version of post-traumatic shock. She didn't really want him. Once they weren't touching anymore, it would be all right.

Then Kiervan shifted against her as he rose from the bed,

and the truth, searing and inescapable, came between them. No man had ever pushed his way past her reserve; none had ever put so much as a chip in the walls of her self-control. Not Bill, not anyone. But this man had seized her mind and her body with terrifying ease, as if she'd had no defenses at all. She'd accepted his kisses and the bold intimacies of his touch with nothing but welcome sighs and without so much as a decent moment's hesitation. And not because she'd had too much to drink. Not because she'd had a bumpy ride through time. She'd been fascinated by the taste of him, by the feel of him, by the way he'd made her blood sing.

Alanna blinked back tears of shame and humiliation. Kiervan didn't want anything more of her than to possess her body. She'd already given him far too much of herself. To cry in front of him . . . Never. Never in a million years. For now, she wouldn't think, wouldn't let herself dwell on what had happened. She wouldn't deal with her raw emotions. Willing everything away, she sat up and then climbed off the bed.

Her nightshirt lay atop the jumbled heap of their discarded clothing, and she snatched it up, suddenly frantic to shield herself from Kiervan's gaze. He stood less than an arm's length away, his brows furrowed and the corners of his mouth edging down as he pushed his arms into the sleeves of his shirt. The moonlight danced over the muscles in his shoulders, kissed the long, silken strands of his hair. He looked up and, catching her perusal, smiled.

The tension in her body coiled tighter. Alanna turned away and tried to draw a breath into her lungs. She needed to get her shirt on, she told herself, needed to put everything she could between herself and the molten experience just past. And of course the damn thing was wrong side out. She muttered a curse and almost dropped it in her haste to turn it right.

"Alanna," he called softly.

She ignored him. She wasn't even close to being ready to talk to him yet.

"You have no reason to be afraid. The greatest danger is past."

No reason? She jerked the neck opening of the shirt over her head and shoved her arms into the sleeves. *No reason?* How about his being the most dangerous man she'd ever met? How about the way she'd melted in his arms, huh? Like a two-bit streetwalker. Hell! She hadn't even asked him for the traditional two bits!

"Our circumstances aren't as desperate now as they were moments ago."

Yeah, right. She jabbed the ragged lower edge of the linen gown into the waistband of her pants. Maybe his circumstances weren't desperate, but she was more desperate than she'd ever been in her life. She was bound to this man for the next fortnight, whether she liked it or not. The damn problem was that a treacherous part of herself found the man tantalizingly attractive and the circumstances intensely appealing. He could make her sigh, make her forget everything in the universe except the wondrous feel of his callused hands on her skin, the delicious taste of his kisses and—

God! she inwardly railed. What would Bill think if he ever found out? She was like a drug addict, drawn to the poison that would lead to certain ruination and death. Well, she silently vowed, snatching up the cape from where Kiervan had flung it, she'd resist the temptation. She'd exert her own will and defy the wanton part of her that desperately craved a full taste of him. She would avoid him, keep distance between them at all times, at all costs. Never again would he catch her unaware, weak.

"Here, Alanna," he said, handing her the bundle of clothing she had acquired from Mary. "Are you ready?"

She took the lumpy packet with a crisp nod, then spun about and stepped to the door. Her hand on the latch, she paused and looked over her shoulder at him. "One question before we head out of here," she said. "Just how long is a fortnight?"

He smiled mischievously and, cocking a roguish brow, replied, "Not long enough, Alanna. Not nearly long enough."

"You can bet the bank on that one, Captain," Alanna

agreed with quiet tartness. "What I want to know is, how many days are there in a fortnight?"

"Fourteen."

"Then it's two down and twelve to go."

"If you'll recall, I've always said 'a fortnight *or so*.' It may well take us longer to reach County Kerry."

"Not if we really put our minds to it." In the half second it took for her to turn and yank at the door latch, Kiervan had blocked her escape. She glanced up at the hand on the door above her head, noted how casually he leaned his weight against it.

No, "casually" wasn't the right word, she instantly decided. He looked as though he had a definite purpose in mind. His jaw was set and his attention was focused entirely on her. And if the darkness in his eyes was any indication, he wasn't happy.

So what? demanded a defiant voice. So what if he didn't like being given the brush-off? With every bone in her body, Alanna knew that they'd come to a do-or-die crossroads. It would either be his agenda or hers from here on out. Let him do his Kiervan-the-Dark expression. Let him brood and say whatever nasty things he wanted. She wasn't going to cave in just so he wouldn't be unhappy about losing the contest of wills.

" 'Tis a most confoundin' woman ye are, Alanna Chapman," he whispered.

The unexpected huskiness of his voice sent rippling waves of warmth from her head to her toes. He lowered his head and Alanna knew what he meant to do. Her heart raced at the prospect even as her rational mind recoiled in anger and fear. She felt the heating of her blood, the softening of her knees. An outraged voice ordered her to turn away, but the demand fell on deaf ears. She wanted to be wrapped in the promise of his embrace again, wanted to taste him, to feel the seductive command of his lips on her skin just one more time.

He kissed her with a gentleness that undid what little remained of her resolve. Alanna closed her eyes and curved into him, her hand pressed to his chest to steady herself, to keep her legs from buckling beneath her. Every nerve and fiber of her being remembered his touch and responded without reserve. Her spirit soared upward, drawn toward the promise of something compelling, something she couldn't see or name, something she craved more than life itself. And then Kiervan withdrew his possession with a low sigh that caressed her lips. She clung to the warmth of him, struggling against the looming horror of standing alone, of spiraling into the cold void of emptiness and abandonment. Then Kiervan stepped back and her fortitude shattered.

Alanna let him take her hand and lead her out of the room, let him guide her down the hall, through the door, and into the darkened yard as she desperately searched her memory for a glimpse of Bill, for an image to calm the storm raging within her.

15

Alanna watched Kiervan ride between two large stones and disappear from sight. Praying that he'd at last found a suitable place to camp, she nudged her sturdy little mount up the track after him. Her back ached from the strain of riding for hours with her shoulders resolutely squared. And her face . . . her face felt as if it might crack and fall off. She had cried buckets of tears in the gray hours that had passed between leaving the pub and the first light of the new day. Silently railing at herself and swiping at the fiery trails coursing down her face hadn't accomplished anything even remotely positive. Not only had the self-inflicted mental bashing left her physically and emotionally exhausted, but her cheeks felt raw and sore.

Still, Alanna reminded herself, she hadn't shed a single tear since sunrise. She smiled grimly in rueful self-congratulation. It didn't matter that her eyes were so dry that blinking had become downright painful; she could take considerable pride in knowing that she hadn't so much as sniffled or whimpered or choked back a sob the whole time she had followed Kiervan through the earliest hours of the morning. So far he didn't have a clue as to the damage he'd done to her psyche back in that grungy little room. And if she could avoid a face-to-face for a while longer, he would never know.

Looking over her shoulder, Alanna scanned the lake lying below them. It was huge. Positively huge. And the most beautiful shade of blue-green she had ever seen. It had to have magical restorative powers.

" 'Twill do, will it not?"

Alanna blinked at the sound of Kiervan's voice. Lord, she finally understood what people meant when they said their eyes felt like sandpaper. Turning her attention away from the lake, she tilted her face down so that he couldn't see the ravages of a night spent crying. A quick sidelong glance told her far more than she wanted to know. Kiervan stood before his horse in the center of a miniature, rock-ringed meadow complete with a tiny waterfall. It was nothing short of an earthly garden created by the Celtic gods. And every inch of Kiervan des Marceaux belonged in it.

Alanna quietly cleared her throat and answered, "I think it probably fits the term 'picturesque.' " Determined to keep her face from Kiervan's scrutiny, she quickly swung down from her horse. With the animal between them, she quipped, "It's positively right out of an Irish tourism brochure." Even to her own ears, her voice lacked its usual buoyancy and she cringed.

"The grass is sweet and the water's from a spring," he commented. "So there'll be no need to take the horses down to the lake. We can remain hidden for some time if need be."

Alanna nodded but her attention was focused on making an escape, on working at the accursedly tight knot which bound her bundle of clothes to the saddle. "The horses might be thrilled with it," she began, hoping to distract him enough to cover the frantic fumbling of her fingers. "And I'm sure it'll fit the bill for a middle-of-the-night drink, but I'm afraid that little trickle ain't gonna cut it for doing the wash. Not by a long shot. No siree."

Alanna knew she was babbling, but the words simply kept coming and, God help her, there didn't seem to be any way to shut off the faucet. "I don't mean to be nasty or anything, but I think Mary's areas of expertise are rather limited. Judging by the look of these things, I'd have to say that doing laundry isn't on her 'To Do' list very often. Not that I got a very good look at them. It was kind of dark in her room, even after she lit the lamp. And in all fairness, these probably aren't her best clothes or even things she wears very often. I mean, I wouldn't sell my best or my favorite clothes. Would you?"

"No. I wouldn't."

God, didn't he recognize a rhetorical question when he heard one? Had that been amusement she'd heard in his voice? Alanna gnashed her teeth and silently swore at him, at herself, and at the leather thong. The knot finally, mercifully, worked loose and, jerking the lumpy parcel free, she announced, "I'll be down at the lake if the President calls."

Clutching her bundle of clothes and holding Kiervan's cloak above her ankles, Alanna whirled about and walked out of the circle of rocks without another word. She felt his gaze follow her, felt it slowly caress the length of her. Sheer willpower kept her pace even and unhurried, but there was absolutely nothing she could do to slow the rhythm of her heart.

She shaded her brow with her hand and looked out across the smooth surface of the water. So serene, she thought. So unlike her thoughts and emotions. The water seemed to beckon her, to whisper of a world in which raging turmoils and bitter doubts didn't exist. She listened to its call for only a moment, then shook her head. No matter what happened, she'd endure. Whatever they expected of her in County Kerry, she'd handle it. Whenever she finished fulfilling Maude's obligations, she would return to the Carraig Cor and somehow find her way forward in time. And Kiervan . . . Kiervan des Marceaux could be damned six ways to Sunday for all she cared.

Suddenly he stood behind her, as though the thought of him had brought him to her. The warmth of his body filled the space between them, and Alanna felt the tension in her shoulders ease, felt the ragged edges of her exhaustion smooth. An inexplicable mixture of hope and longing settled over her, gently quelling the turmoil of her thoughts.

He cleared his throat softly, calling Alanna from her

peace. "I've unsaddled your pony," he began, "and left her hobbled up in the enclosure."

She knew it wasn't what he'd really wanted to say. In her heart she'd heard more beneath the amiable offering. Perhaps they could find their common ground in commiserating over their mutually wrecked mental and emotional states. Even as the thought crossed her mind, she rejected it. She had come perilously close to giving him her body. She could never let him into her heart, never let him glimpse the shadows of her soul.

Alanna lifted her chin and turned to face him. Behind him waited his own horse, its reins dangling to the ground. A bolt of fear shot through her. With far more poise than she actually felt, she arched a brow and serenely asked, "Are you leaving me?"

Surprise flickered across his features for a fraction of a moment and then disappeared behind his mask of self-control. He scanned the perimeter of the lake before he answered, "Only for a brief while. I thought to give you some time alone, and I want to do some scouting for Ashton's men. I'll return before midday."

Alanna nodded and turned away. She unfastened the clasp of the cloak and then slipped the garment from her shoulders. A thousand pounds seemed to go with it. "Take what time you need, Kiervan," she said, tossing the woolen mantle over a boulder. "I'll wait for you here."

"You'll return to the circle as soon as you've completed your washing?"

She looked over her shoulder to find him studying her. The sadness in his eyes, the worried angle of his brow, wound about her heart. "I'll be careful," she promised quietly. "You do the same, okay?"

Again he looked away, out across the lake. "If for some reason I don't return by nightfall, you must go on without me. Travel to the west and remember to stay off the roads. Your destination is O'Connell Hall near Castletownbere. There are more coins in the hem of the cloak. Use them as you see fit."

Alanna nodded. There wasn't any point in telling him

that if something awful happened, she'd come to find him. It would only lead to another raging argument, and they were both too battered to go about it with any sense.

"I'll be in the circle when you get back," she promised, kneeling beside her bundle of clothes. "You might consider hooting like an owl or something to let me know it's you coming up the trail. Otherwise you might just get a good-sized chunk of rock upside your head." She undid the knotted sleeves that held the packet closed.

"It might be that you'd choose an even larger piece if you were certain it was me."

"I might," Alanna agreed, setting the boots aside. Looking up to offer him a teasing smile, she added, "Guess you'll have to take the chance and find out."

His gaze touched her lips and then lifted to her eyes. Suddenly the corners of his mouth tightened. "I'll return before long," he said, his tone perfunctory. After a stiff, abbreviated bow, he turned on his heel, picked up the reins of his horse, and led the animal away.

She watched him until he rounded a curve in the bank and traveled beyond her sight. Shaking her head, Alanna went back to sorting through her new wardrobe. Hopefully, he'd have his act together when he got back. The side of Kiervan des Marceaux she had just seen was flat-out scary. She could handle the Calculating Mercenary side of his personality. It was at least predictable, and he wasn't even close to being the most predatory businessman she'd ever met. She could deal with the Relentless Rogue aspect of him as well. It might well be exasperating and sometimes frightening, but it too was incredibly predictable. The Fearless Warrior and the Dauntless Risk Taker had protected her, had saved her. She owed those parts of him her very life. But the Lost Man . . . The Lost Man tugged at surprisingly tender heartstrings.

But her emotions were hopelessly muddled, and her instincts . . . Kiervan stirred instincts within her that she'd never known were there, instincts that weren't the least rational.

If only Kiervan weren't so Kiervan. If only he didn't deal

in the means of revolution and death. If only he weren't committed to marrying Eglintine Terwilliger-Hampstead. If only he believed in love and fidelity. If only he were a tiny bit like Bill, safer, then she might be able to let herself fall in love with him.

Love Kiervan? Alanna shook her head and launched herself into sorting her newly acquired clothing. Loving Kiervan des Marceaux would be a sure ticket to a guest appearance on a TV talk show. Beneath her breath she mumbled, "Sensible women who let surging hormones make bad decisions . . . Is it a genetic predisposition or just stupidity?"

Yeah, she could sit on the stage, in the lineup of that day's other incredibly pathetic women, and tell all of America how she'd fallen in love with a gorgeous hunk of man who was bad news from the start. She could tell them of his mercenary business dealings, of how he'd broken her heart when he'd dumped her to marry another woman for her money and social standing.

Yeah. And Americans would shake their heads, wonder at how such an apparently together woman could have done something so unbelievably moronic, and then congratulate themselves on having infinitely better common sense than Alanna Whatshername. Mothers across the nation would point to their TV screens, eye their daughters, and ask, "Have you learned anything from this miserable creature's story?" It would be humiliating, of course, but it would be a worthy sacrifice of dignity if it prevented just one woman from stumbling down the same tragic path.

Unfortunately, she reminded herself, the next day would have the show's host moving on to people who switch the braille labels on soda machines, and she'd be alone to deal with the shredded remnants Kiervan had left of her heart. No, all in all, even thinking about loving Kiervan des Marceaux was a really bad idea. Public service be damned. And Maude could be too if she thought her niece was naive enough to trust this nineteenth-century gigolo. Bill might not be exciting or adventurous or even remotely dangerous. But he was safe. He'd never break her heart.

"Because I don't love Bill and never will."

At the sound of her admission, Alanna took a deep breath and closed her eyes. She needed to get a grip on herself, to rationally line up one more time all the reasons that made marrying Bill Boyer the right decision for her to make. She lifted the diamond from beneath her tattered nightgown and studied it, trying desperately to recall even a fragment of the rationale Bill had offered her along with the symbol of their intent. Nothing came to mind other than the thought that she had needed to take it off and put it away, that she no longer had the right to wear it.

She also knew she couldn't go anywhere near Kiervan until she got herself under some semblance of control. After all, he'd done nothing wrong . . . lately . . . and she sure didn't want to have to offer an even semitruthful explanation for her sudden confusion. He couldn't help being so damn good-looking, and he couldn't change his ways any more than the proverbial leopard could change its spots. That made the problem hers and hers alone. The only smart thing to do was to keep it to herself.

Alanna tried to still her thoughts. Regardless of how hard the bottom line of her situation might be to accept, it couldn't be denied. Kiervan would never be able to commit to her. And despite her resolution of only moments ago, Alanna knew she cared for him far too much already. To let him into her heart any further would be committing emotional suicide, would lead to such heartache that she'd never have the strength to drag herself out of bed, much less anywhere near the talk show circuit. Besides, she assured herself, she was going home soon.

Alanna rose to her feet and brushed the damp sand from the knees of her pants. As she started her search for soaproot, she decided that if Kiervan was still plagued with questions when he returned, she would have no choice but to give him honest answers. It was a simple matter of self-preservation.

Kiervan had selected Eggie Terwilliger-Hampstead for her social position and her wealth, but mostly for her pedigree. Obviously those things mattered a great deal to him. Alanna sighed and shook her head. God knew she couldn't claim so much as a tattered shred of any of it. If ever there had been a waif from the wrong side of the tracks, it was she. If she played her cards right, if she went about the task with real finesse, she wouldn't have to worry about Kiervan slipping past the walls she had spent the night rebuilding around her heart and soul. He would recoil when she told him, or at least curl his lip in distaste as all the kids had done in grade school. Yes, once he knew where she had come from, he would quickly lose interest in her.

Alanna frowned as she realized that Bill had never asked about her life before she had gone to live with Maude in the mountains. And she had never once considered telling him. Maybe Kiervan wouldn't want to know either, she thought hopefully. Even as she considered the possibility, she resolutely tamped out the spark. She needed to push Kiervan away before he did permanent and serious damage to her heart. Telling him about what passed for her family life would be painful, no doubt about it. But at least it would be a pain of her own choosing.

"You were supposed to hoot, remember?"

Kiervan reined in his mount as he spun about and sought Alanna among the rocks above his head. "Where are you?" he demanded after a quick but fruitless search.

"A mere stone's throw," she replied, stepping from behind a rough-edged boulder. "I could have nailed you right between the eyes. You'd have never known what hit you." With a mischievous grin, she casually tossed away a rock.

The order he had spent hours imposing on his mind drifted away on the breeze that threaded its way through Alanna's honeyed hair. She was indeed an Irish fairy woman, a woman who could muddle his thoughts and steal his resolve with but a single smile. Kiervan mentally shook himself. "Your new clothes seem to fit you well." He cringed at the insipid sound of the words.

"Thanks. But you can't really get the full effect from down there," she countered. "Meet you in the clearing." Then, without waiting for his reply, she vanished.

Kiervan scowled at the trail ahead and then the narrow cleft between the rocks. His thoughts traveled back over the paths they had taken for the better part of the morning. Only days ago he had been a man in full control of the world around him, a confident master of his own destiny. And then Alanna Chapman had come into his life, turning his well-ordered universe on its ear and cracking the stalwart defenses which he had built around his heart years ago.

But, he reminded himself again, the time had well come to put matters in their proper place and on their proper course. Nudging the horse forward, he vowed that nothing would distract him nor detour him from the achievement of his goals, not Alanna's eccentric ways, not her stoic endurance, not even her winsome smile.

His resolution collapsed the instant he entered the ringed meadow. God hated him. God truly hated him. Alanna stood barefoot in the center of the grassy circle, her golden hair tumbling over her shoulders, her arms held out from her sides, her eyes bright with excitement. Certainly Mary's hips had never looked as enticing beneath the folds of the deep blue skirt, nor her breasts as delectable as Alanna's did, gently swelling above the gathered edge of the sun-bleached linen bodice.

He instantly noted that she no longer wore the ragged cloth necklace. His gaze darted to her left hand and he felt an unexpected wave of satisfaction when he discovered her third finger unadorned. She'd put away the ring, the symbol of her betrothal. Kiervan saw it as a hopeful sign. She had apparently come to her senses, had finally decided to stop using poor Bill Boyer as a shield. Not that it had been a very effective shield, Kiervan mused, remembering Alanna's impassioned response the night before.

"So what do you think?" she asked, slowly turning about for his inspection. "Are they awesome or what?"

He knew her well enough to know that she'd die before asking him to assess her physical attributes, but his mind steadfastly refused to consider anything else. "Awesome?" he heard himself muse, swinging down from the saddle.

"Yeah, awesome. I feel like I oughtta be in the cast of *Brigadoon* or something."

"Brigadoon?" Kiervan clenched his teeth the instant the word left his tongue. He'd met parrots with more expansive vocabularies than he seemed capable of using at the moment. Frustrated, he reached for the bulky sack draped across the cantle.

"*Brigadoon*'s a play about the Scottish Highlands," she explained. As she spoke she lifted one arm above her head, folded the other across her laced and narrow midriff, and stepped into the intricate footwork of a Scottish fling.

Kiervan watched her, mesmerized by her grace and skill, by the spritely abandon with which she moved, by the joy that brightened her face. And then her gaze caught his and she froze in midstep. A rosy blush swept up from the edge of her bodice to tint the long, slender column of her throat and color her cheeks. She cast him a look of utter embarrassment before fastening her attention on her toes.

Kiervan chuckled and his world suddenly came about on a straight and even keel. Hefting up the sack, he said, "You've no cause to blush, Alanna. Nor to stop. You dance beautifully."

"Thanks," she replied, glancing up at him through her lashes and offering him a quick and grateful smile, "but I'm really not all that good." She looked down again and, burying her toes in the grass, continued, saying, "I only took a couple semesters of dance in college to meet my Phys Ed requirements, and the instructor made a point of discouraging me from switching my major. She said I wasn't built to be a dancer."

He couldn't have explained the meanings of more than half of the words Alanna had used, but he understood the gist of the whole. "Might your instructor have been blind?"

Laughing quietly, she lifted her head and met his regard. "She could see perfectly well. And I'm not built like a dancer of my time. I'm not tall and willowy. And I can't even come close to touching the back of my head to my heels."

"Permit me to share a truth with you, Alanna. Men find

little satisfaction in watching a willowy woman dance. And I can't imagine why it would be necessary for you to be able to so contort yourself for any dancing you might do in public. Now, it would be another matter indeed in the privacy of—"

"Don't you dare say it, Kiervan!" she challenged, smiling and holding her hand up to stay him. "Your mind's slipped into the proverbial gutter again."

"The gutter, ye say, darlin' Alanna." He shook his head in feigned innocence and pressed his hand to his heart. " 'Tis wounded I am, to be sure. Let a man try to broaden his artistic horizons just the weest bit an' he's accused of harborin' low an' lascivious thoughts."

"Puh-leese," she countered, rolling her eyes. "I'm not buying it. What's in the sack?" she added.

" 'Twas somethin' I had in me head to share with ye, but now . . ." He shrugged and opened the bag to peer inside while he went on. "There's a little farm down a ways the other side o' the lake, ye know. Neat as a pin an' the farmer's wife a kindly soul. But surely ye'd no' be stoopin' to dine wi' the likes o' me."

"You have food in that bag?"

"Aye," he answered wistfully, rummaging through the contents as though he'd forgotten what he'd purchased. "Here be a loaf of bread, crusty an' still warm from the oven. Ah, yes, an' the cheese. 'Tis a heavenly yellow. An' a few thin's the dear sainted woman pulled from her garden. 'Tis carrots I see an'—"

"Enough, Kiervan! You're torturing me."

He slapped his hand over his heart again and regarded her with widened eyes. " 'Twasn't me intent a'tall, Alanna darlin'."

"Oh, bull cookies," she retorted, her hands on the curve of her hips, her eyes twinkling with amusement. "Now give up the blarney . . . and the bread."

"It occurs to me," Kiervan replied, smoothing the lilting tones from his voice, "that I'm in a position to set the terms of the exchange."

Her eyes narrowed and she tilted her chin slightly to regard him with good-natured suspicion. "Don't push your luck, buster. This is Ireland. I can always find another rock."

He nodded and smiled. "I haven't lived as long as I have without knowing when to exercise a reasonable degree of common sense, Alanna." Sobering, he added, "And I won't withhold sustenance even should you refuse my request."

She swallowed and drew a deep breath before she asked warily, "So, what do you want from me?"

"To begin again. To begin as we should have." The words were not those he'd chosen earlier that morning, but his stunned regret lasted only a fleeting moment, vanishing before the power of Alanna's smile. Perhaps God didn't hate him so overly much after all.

16

Sitting beside the trickling waterfall, Kiervan waited until Alanna had spread their provisions between them before he asked, "How is it that you acquired the skill with which you passed me the knife in the pub?"

She didn't look up, but he thought he saw a tiny smile playing at the corners of her mouth when she replied, "A skill acquired from a youth tragically misspent."

"You were permitted to play with knives as a child?"

With a delicately arched brow, she met his gaze, handed him a chunk of bread, and said, "If you want to know the story of my life, Kiervan, just come right out and ask me for it. I figure you're about to burst with questions, and I've come to the conclusion that you have a legitimate right to answers."

Why did he feel as though he were being led down a path of her conscious choosing? It didn't really matter which of them chose the course, he decided in the next instant. There *were* a good many questions that he'd like answered. He took the bread from her, laid it aside, and pulled the knife from the top of his boot. Cutting a slice from the half wheel of cheese before them, he said quietly, "I sense that it may be a subject you'd find . . . difficult . . . to discuss. A gentleman should always afford a lady an avenue of escape."

Alanna shrugged and tore a small piece of bread for herself. "What's in the past is over. It can't be undone." With the morsel a scant breath from her lips, she paused to add,

"And besides, I'd like to think that it's something I've risen above."

"I won't pry, Alanna," he promised, putting the knife aside. "I can't demand your secrets. I have no right to them."

She placed the piece of bread in her mouth, chewed, swallowed, and then replied, "I appreciate your sense of gallantry, but I do think that you have every right to know about the rather odd woman accompanying you across Ireland. Do you want the *Britannica* or the *Reader's Digest* version?"

"What would be the difference?"

"Long and detailed or short, bare-bones."

He leaned his back against the sun-warmed rock and studied Alanna for a moment before he asked, "There's no middle ground?"

"Not with me," she admitted with a smile. "I seem to always find myself at one extreme or another."

Kiervan nodded, briefly considering her observation. "A difficult position to maintain for any length of time, mistress."

"Would that be the voice of experience I hear, Captain?"

With a slight shrug, he crossed his ankles and considered the bread he held in his hands. "Let's simply say that in our brief time together, I've often seen aspects of myself reflected in you. I believe we're something of kindred spirits."

She tossed her hair back over her shoulder and then reached for one of the wedges of cheese. "And of the same beginnings too," she declared, her voice soft.

Raising a bite to his mouth, he countered, "Not unless you be bastard born." At his words she lifted one shoulder in a gesture that spoke eloquently of a riddle guessed. His meal forgotten, Kiervan quietly offered, "If it's painful for you to remember, Alanna, you needn't for my sake."

"Hey," she admonished with a stalwart half smile, "I'm nothing if not tough. Bastards have to grow up quicker and harder than those, as Maude used to say, 'born on the right side of the sheets.' "

"Your aunt raised you?"

Alanna shook her head and consumed another bite of the cheese before she explained, "I went to live with Maude when I was sixteen. Until then I didn't even know I had an aunt. According to Maude, she and my mother went to America together." She paused and then added with wry amusement, "Apparently across time. Talk about a well-kept family secret. Neither she nor my mother ever gave me so much as the tiniest little hint."

With a dismissive shrug, she continued, "Anyway, they had a fight soon after arriving there and never spoke again. My mother wanted to adopt the ways of their new country." A faraway look came to her eyes.

"And their new time," Kiervan supplied, hoping to draw her back to the telling.

Alanna nodded slowly, her vision fixed in the sparkling fall of the water, her brows knit. Kiervan waited in silence, watching her eyes darken, wanting with every fiber of his being to take her into his arms and banish the memories that shadowed her heart, but knowing in his own that he needed to allow her both time and a safe distance.

Suddenly her gaze came up to meet his. She smiled in wordless apology before she reached for more food and continued with her tale. "Maude refused to change how she'd always lived. When I went to stay with her, I had to learn about oil lamps, hauling water, cooking on a hearth, and all sorts of other 'old ways.' I'll have you know that I make one impressive Irish soda bread."

"Perhaps you might make some for me when we reach County Kerry?"

"Yeah, okay," she agreed, nodding. "It'd be nice to spend some time in a kitchen again."

He saw her focus once again shift into the past.

"Isn't it strange," she commented, "how things once foreign to you can become comfortingly familiar?"

She shook her head as though to dispel the ghosts that haunted her. "Oh well," she drawled with a quick arch of her brows. "Pitch that knife this way and I'll carve up some more of this cheese."

He leaned forward to hand her the weapon, asking as he

did, "The life you lived before Maude took you in was so very much different?"

She laughed, the sound both amused and a bit bitter. Whittling at the yellow block before her, she said, "When I was just over a year old, my mother married a man with two half-grown sons. Mom was seldom a strong woman. Some days she could barely drag herself out of bed. Others . . ." Her voice faded away; the knife slowed and then stopped.

"Alanna," Kiervan whispered, reaching out and placing his hand over hers.

"She was institutionalized quite often," she continued, her eyes downcast, her voice flat and distant. "On average twice a year. She'd be better when she got out, but little by little, she'd slide into the shadows that were always there. When I was twelve, she drowned. The authorities officially ruled her death accidental, but I've never been convinced it wasn't suicide. I think she just walked to the edge of the lake and decided to keep on going."

Kiervan watched as Alanna bit her lower lip and struggled for control. She had looked much like that in the aftermath of their charade the night before—struggling to impose control on her emotions. He had pushed her then and regretted the action since. Kiervan stilled the impulse to gather her into his arms, to soothe her sadness with the balm of his kisses. Her trust was too new, too fragile, to endure a challenge of that magnitude. In silence he gently squeezed her hand.

Slowly she lifted her chin and raised her eyes to his, whispering, "So many more things make sense now that I know where and when she came from. Things I never understood before. She just couldn't cope with the complexities of life in the twentieth century, Kiervan. I can't help but think it must be so much easier to travel backward in time."

He shook his head and smiled gently. "I'm more inclined to believe that you're a stronger person than your mother was. You have an uncommon resilience, Alanna, a spirit that won't be broken."

"Thanks," she replied, offering him a smile as she drew

her hand from beneath his. Buoyancy had returned to her voice and manner when she added, "But like I said, bastards grow up hard and fast. Those that can't, don't make it to adulthood."

"Your father must have—"

"Stepfather." As she chopped a chunk of the cheese away from the whole, Alanna made a sound of disgust and dismissal. "Wayne. Wayne the Wanderer. He's a long-distance trucker, what would probably be a wagoner these days." She looked up at him, anger flashing in her eyes like a storm at sea. "I'm assuming he's still alive," she explained. "Guys like Wayne are too mean to do the world the favor of dying.

"Anyway," she went on, glaring at the rocks behind Kiervan's shoulders, "Wayne was seldom home when I was growing up, and when he was, I couldn't wait until he left again. He drank a lot and gambled, badly. And those were the most public of his many shortcomings."

Kiervan considered Alanna, for the first time understanding the reasons she'd become so cynical about marriage and the privileges of men. He knew the answer, but because he sensed Alanna needed to say the words, he asked, "Did he love your mother?"

"No." As she added more slices of cheese to the pile before her, she elaborated, "He only married her so he'd have someone to take care of Aaron and Paul when he was on the road."

"Your brothers?"

"Stepbrothers. Aaron's the one who taught me how to palm things. They were pretty much your everyday, garden-variety sneak thieves until they hit their late teens, and then they graduated into the big time. When they were in their mid-twenties, they pulled an armed robbery, pistol-whipping the female liquor store clerk. She survived but with such severe brain damage that the doctors say she'll never regain consciousness. The state took me away from Wayne during their trial. I was almost fifteen."

"But you were sixteen when you went to live with Maude O'Sullivan," Kiervan said.

Alanna nodded. "It took the courts over a year to decide

that Maude was a fit guardian. They had a problem with her 'rustic' lifestyle." Shaking her head in wonder, she went on. "While they were shoveling and stamping the mountains of paperwork, I went through a series of foster homes. Some good. Some remarkably like living with Wayne and the boys.

"Anyway," she continued, "between Wayne and Aaron and Paul, I spent a good part of my formative years in bars, pubs. They would've felt right at home in the one we were in last night. They had an incredible knack for finding a true hole-in-the-wall. By the time the courts declared Wayne an unfit parent, I'd been in enough bar fights to qualify for professional status."

She offered him a bright smile, but Kiervan had worn the expression far too often himself not to recognize the ragged emotions behind it, the painful memories it was meant to conceal. As he expected, her next words tumbled out. "Actually, though, the experience wasn't all bad. It had some unique advantages. I'm probably the only woman you'll ever meet who can rebuild a short-block Chevy."

"And what might a Chevy be?" he inquired, not because he wanted to know, but because he sensed Alanna desperately needed him to.

"Sorry," she offered with a quick grimace. "It's a car, sort of like a carriage, but instead of using horses, it's driven by an internal combustion engine. History wasn't one of my favorite subjects in school, but I kinda doubt that you'll see one in your lifetime. You'll have to take my word for it, but trust me, the twentieth century wouldn't be the same if they hadn't been invented."

Kiervan tore a bit of bread from the larger piece he held in his hand. "Do you find it difficult to live without these cars?"

"Not really," she answered. "Maude didn't have any and there's a certain kind of tranquility when they're not around. Actually, I rather like the pace of things. . . ." She smiled. "Although I must say that, early 1800s or not, life's hardly been at a peaceful, pastoral pace since I met you."

He grinned as he countered, "I've always taken great

pride in being known as a man who can make events happen."

"A real-life Captain Chaos." Chuckling softly, she picked up the rough cloth sack and peered inside. "If I dug deep enough in here, would I find anything resembling either a cooking pot or a cup?"

"The woman had too few for her own use," he answered absently, his mind occupied with other, far more important matters. It was obvious that Alanna had chosen to close the doors on her memories. He well understood the need to keep the pain of the past locked safely away, knew that pressing her further now would serve only to fray the fragile cord of trust developing between them.

Reaching for the loaf of bread, he decided that for the moment, both kindness and wisdom lay in respecting her wishes. There would come a time when he could ask her about her fiancé, about the other men in her past, the men who had held her and taught her much about the pleasures of loving. The Alanna who had lain beneath him last night hadn't been inexperienced. At least not wholly so. She'd known what he'd been about, had welcomed his advance, had . . .

"Are you going to worry that question to death before you ask it?"

He started and, before he could think better of it, replied, "It's something of a rather delicate nature, Alanna. Perhaps the matter would be best left alone."

"Sometimes, Kiervan, your face is remarkably readable. You want to know about what happened between us last night, don't you?" She met his gaze unflinchingly. "Something like, 'You seemed to know the routine surprisingly well for a virgin,' right?"

"Alanna, I think we should leave this be."

"And if you were into being honest, you'd admit that's where you were heading when you started asking me questions about my family." He opened his mouth to offer another objection, but she shook her head and added, "It's okay, Kiervan. I can understand how you'd wonder, and it wouldn't bother me to talk about it. We're rather open about sexual matters in the twentieth century."

"Apparently," he muttered, his chest tightening.

"Look, Kiervan. Where I come from, you'd have had to have spent your life wrapped in cotton and stuffed in a really dark closet not to know the basics of making love. As you've no doubt noticed, I wasn't the least bit sheltered and there were a good number of guys who tried desperately to give me some personal experience on the subject."

She sighed and muttered something about truth or consequences. Taking a deep breath, squared her shoulders and said, "I've never aspired to being a nun, Kiervan. But I've never wanted to be a whore either. It's the one and only area of my life where I haven't gone to extremes. Only heaven knows why."

It didn't matter whether heaven knew the reason; he did. Kiervan watched her tear another bit of bread from the loaf. Her movements were unhurried, her fingers steady at their task. They were much alike, he and Alanna; their temperaments honed by the demands of survival; their early lives woven on the looms of poverty and circumstance.

But they were very different in one fundamental respect. He'd made love to countless women without ever loving a one, had long ago learned to separate what his body did from what his heart felt. Alanna had chosen another path. Her heart and body remained entwined, whole and unsullied by the callous world in which she'd existed. She had given nothing of herself to any man, would give nothing until she could give all. And he envied her.

Something arced through the air before his face. Instinctively, Kiervan put his hand up to shield himself. A small chunk of bread tapped against his forearm and then fell into his lap. Alanna chuckled quietly, calling his attention back to her.

Settling herself onto her side and propping her head in her hand, she said, "I asked if you have any family."

He nodded, giving himself time to marshal his thoughts and find his tongue. "Twin sisters, Riona and Dominica, and a brother, Donal. All much younger than I."

"Where do they live? In Charleston?"

"A proper lineage means far too much to the good people of Charleston. It would have been cruel to ensconce them there. Riona and Dominica are at a school for young ladies in New York. Donal is fostering with friends and studying law in Boston."

"Did you foster with a ship's captain?"

He laughed outright, the contrast between Alanna's images of his childhood and the truth painfully comical. "No, Alanna," he answered softly. "I didn't foster with anyone. I went to sea when I was eight as a cabin boy for the man who was then my mother's . . . occasional paramour."

She blinked and he saw understanding in her eyes. He steeled himself for the certain question, reminded himself that his mother's past was done and that honest words couldn't hurt her.

"And you worked your way up the ranks over the years?"

Kiervan studied Alanna for the span of a half dozen heartbeats, gratitude for her compassion swelling in the center of his chest. When she cast him a patient look, he pushed past his emotions and replied, "I took my first vessel by right of might. I was but twenty at the time, rash and impatient with stupidity, intolerant of abuse. Rather than accept the lash, I mutinied."

Her eyes darkened with concern. "I'm no legal scholar, so correct me if I'm wrong, but couldn't you have been hung from the yardarm or something for that?"

"Aye," he agreed, wondering if she'd know a yardarm from a mizzenmast. Then he flashed her a broad, rakish smile. "It never occurred to me that I might fail."

For a moment she smiled in equal measure, and then her smile faded. As she shifted her gaze to the waterfall, Kiervan admonished, " 'Tis a sad thought you're harboring, Alanna. Burdens shared are more easily borne."

She shrugged and, without looking at him, replied, "I was just thinking that your mother must be proud of the man you've become. But I get the impression that you don't like to talk about her." Her regard arrowed back to his as she hurried to add, "And that's okay, Kiervan. I really do understand how you'd rather not discuss her."

"Her name was Saraid O'Connell," he said even before the decision to speak had been consciously formed. He focused on the toes of his boots as the rest of the words tumbled from his lips. "At fourteen her brother sold her into English bondage and she was transported to the American colonies. I was born the following year. She died when I was seventeen."

He glanced up to find Alanna's eyes wide, her lower lip clenched between her teeth again. Fighting the urge to brush his thumb across her mouth, to take her face gently between his hands, Kiervan shook his head and said softly, " 'Tis a common story, Alanna."

"But to be sold by your brother . . ."

" 'Tis Ireland," he answered with a shrug. "Among any people long brutalized, treachery often becomes a way of life, of surviving. Selling each other for a price is but a small step further along the same road." He stared at his boots again as he mused aloud, "I suppose that's the reason I've always found a certain irony in the ancient Celtic crosses. To my way of thinking, nothing better symbolizes Irish history: Christianity and paganism, piety and deceit, loyalty and betrayal."

"I think you're being rather hard on them."

"It's true that not all the Irish have a penchant for betrayal," Kiervan admitted, "but in dealing with them, it's far better to be pleasantly surprised, Alanna, than bitterly disappointed. 'Twas Eth who sent the men for the English patrol last night, you know. And then sold me the horses and supplies while he waited for them to arrive."

She nodded and then quietly countered, "Don't forget that we've both got Irish blood." She suddenly smiled. "Irish blood that's probably been diluted somewhat. You're at least half French."

Kiervan grinned. "Not really. A cook on one of my first voyages was Jean des Marceaux. I liked the sound of it. Rather befitting a pirate, don't you think?"

"It fits you perfectly," she said with an appreciative smile.

She sobered and considered him for a moment, her brows knitted as though she were making a difficult decision. Finally, slowly, she said, "I might well be full-blooded Irish. I have no idea who my father was either."

"Your parentage doesn't matter to me, Alanna," he softly assured her. "And you're as American as I am. Neither of us belongs to this place."

She looked at him, a wary light in her eyes. "Your mother was Irish. Did she ever try to come back?"

Memories of the hard-scrabble life he'd shared with his mother tumbled through his awareness. Deliberately pushing them back, Kiervan reached for a chunk of the yellow cheese. Tearing it in half, he replied, "She endured her circumstances with the grace of a true chieftain's daughter, and in the end she found a measure of happiness with a good man. Riona, Dominica, and Donal are their fruit."

"A chieftain's daughter?"

"Aye. You'll have the pleasure of meeting my uncle when we reach Castletownbere. He now leads the O'Connells. It's his decision I await with regard to my business."

Staring at him and slowly shaking her head, she muttered, "Every time I think I'm beginning to know you, Kiervan des Marceaux, something pops out of your mouth that absolutely astounds me. Are you telling me that you willingly deal with the man who sold your mother?"

He closed his eyes and leaned his head back against the solid warmth of the rock. "It's as she asked when she lay dying. For the peace of her soul, I vowed to bear no malice for Phelan O'Connell. I'll not lie to you, Alanna. 'Tis no easy pledge to keep. But honor it I will, just as I'll honor my vow to care for my sisters and brother."

"Ahh."

"Ahh, what?" he asked, opening his eyes to regard her.

"You promised your mother that you'd take care of your brother and sisters. That explains why you're so hell-bent on marrying Eggie Terwilliger-Hampstead. I take back most of the nasty things I've been thinking about your motives for marriage."

Kiervan sat away from the rock, the corners of his mouth edging upward. "Most of them?" he repeated. "Not all?"

Rolling onto her back, she cradled her head in her hands and stared up at the sky. "Well, I still think your general attitude is rather cold-blooded. In the end you're marrying her for social standing and money, no matter how honorable your reasons for doing it." She paused to turn her head and smile at him, a smile he found delightfully bedeviling. "Kinda Irish of ye, don't ye think?"

He wanted to be angry, wanted to take offense, wanted to ask about her reasons for marrying Bill Boyer, but in his heart he knew Alanna spoke only the truth. Except for denying her ability to see into the future, she'd always been boldly forthright with him. Given her sudden change in circumstances, he could understand and forgive her the single lapse in honesty. He might well have done the same had their positions been reversed. And he knew, to the center of his bones, that Alanna would always face him, and the truth, without flinching.

"Some heavy-duty thinking's going on in that head of yours, Kiervan."

He glanced at her long enough to see that she still studied the sky and wasn't about to pursue an immediate explanation. "A matter that will require additional pondering," he supplied, returning his gaze to the toes of his boots, and his attention to the questions that continued to haunt his mind.

"Ponder away. And while you're at it . . ." She stifled a yawn with the back of her hand. "Give some thought as to how we're going to cook those potatoes. They're too new to bake over hot coals."

A companionable silence draped over the idyllic meadow, broken only by the melodic notes of the waterfall and the discordant sounds of Kiervan's own inner turmoil. His thoughts pitched and rolled, leaping up one moment and plummeting the next. Despite his grim determination to steady them against the gale, he found himself unable to hold a course.

With a frustrated sigh, he abandoned the effort and rose to his feet. "Alanna," he began, intending to offer her a believable reason for his woolgathering. When she didn't answer, he turned to find her eyes closed, her breasts rising and falling in the slow, even rhythm of peaceful slumber.

Kiervan crossed to their packs with easy strides. If Alanna continued to pillow her head with her hands, they'd be numb when she awakened. He returned a moment later, folding his cape into a neat bundle.

Kneeling beside her, he gently eased the makeshift pillow beneath her head. As he did, she curled onto her side without waking and brushed her hand over the sun-warmed wool. Alanna smiled, soft and accepting, then, in sleep, murmured his name.

He closed his eyes, fighting the desire to lie down beside her and take her in his arms, fighting the surging, raging winds of his thoughts. Suddenly the storm broke and he found himself becalmed.

In that moment a certainty illuminated the battered wreckage of his life. Alanna wasn't the kind of woman to be kept as a mistress. She would never suffer being a shadowy presence in any man's life. But she would consent to being a man's lover . . . until that man took a wife. Kiervan nodded, finding reassurance in his more customary line of reasoning. In all likelihood the passion that held Alanna to that man would burn itself out before they parted company, and neither of them would suffer so much as a twinge of regret when he walked down the aisle of a church with another woman on his arm. Yes, he told himself with relief and satisfaction, that would be the way of things.

She watched the Alanna of the dream cling to the rock and waited; waited for Maude to appear at the edge of the cliff as always. This time the dream would take its normal course, she assured herself. Maude wouldn't walk away. The Alanna pressed against the stone wouldn't choose to die.

And suddenly Maude was there, above her and leaning out to assess the situation. The stream meandered across the valley floor like a ribbon of glittering diamonds. The wind

*swirled up the narrow canyon, scattering shimmering waves
of heat as it went. A sharp-winged bird rode the current up
the gorge, its plumage iridescent in the sunlight, dark
against the brilliance of the azure sky. Maude shaded her
eyes and watched its progress. The dream Alanna called out,
but Maude paid her no mind.*

The rational, detached part of Alanna's consciousness
protested, struggled frantically to impose rightful order on
the dream. Maude had never worn a long white tunic before. There had never been a bird winging up the canyon.

*After a while, Maude looked down and studied Alanna.
Slowly the old woman placed her fingertips on her own
smiling lips. Her eyes brimming with tears, she nodded
once, and then cast her kiss into the wind. Alanna watched
the sparkling mist spiral upward and beyond her reach. Her
fingers slipped against the granite as she molded herself
against the wall and begged Maude to try her magic one
more time. Only the wind answered, whispering her name
as it brushed across her cheeks. She called out again, arching
her neck to peer desperately up at her aunt. But Maude was
not there.*

Watching the woman who was herself press her forehead
against the blazing heat of the stone, Alanna willed strength
across the chasm that separated dream from reality. The
Alanna of the other world straightened her shoulders and
pushed away from the rock.

*Her passage through the wind made no sound. Silence
enveloped her mind, her body, as she spun toward the sparkling river below. Only her heart spoke, its words certain
and calm. It was done. There would be no going back, no
salvation from her fate. It was as it was meant to be. From a
great distance came a voice of terror and desperation, a
voice demanding that she fight, that she fly.
And suddenly she rode astride the back of the dark bird,
her arms about its neck, her body bound to its by the glim-*

mering threads of Maude's magic. It soared upward on a draft of wind, carrying her high above the canyon and beyond the reach of the mortal world. She nestled her cheek into the silken feathers, breathing deep the scent of sun and sky. And then, beneath her, the great bird flexed its wings and its unearthly power rippled through her, setting her blood racing.

Alanna started awake with the beat of her heart hammering in her ears and her breath short and ragged. Kiervan knelt beside her, his hand resting gently on hers, the lines of worry fading from around his mouth as she looked up at him.

" 'Twas only another dream, Alanna," he said quietly. "You're safe."

The sun rode low in the sky at his back, and in its mellowing light, Kiervan's locks tumbled over his shoulders in muted shades of midnight black. But Alanna remembered how they gleamed in the full light of day, remembered the silken feel of the strands between her fingers the night before, remembered the heady scent of sky and sun that had clung to the skin pressed against hers in the darkness of the little room off the pub.

"Was it the same dream as before?"

Alanna blinked and her thoughts focused back to the present. The lines had returned to the corners of Kiervan's mouth, and a deep furrow creased the space between his dark brows.

"The same," she replied, her voice raspy from sleep. "Only different." At his doubtful expression she traced her lips with the tip of her tongue, then added, "Every time it comes, it changes a bit and progresses further."

He seemed about to speak and then apparently changed his mind. Squeezing her hand instead, he nodded once before rising smoothly to his feet. As he turned toward the horses, he finally spoke. " 'Twill soon be dark enough to travel. I'll prepare the horses if you'll see to yourself and our provisions."

"Okay," she whispered, watching him stride across the

tiny meadow, feeling again the shuddering power of the bird beneath her in the dream.

Had Maude O'Sullivan sent her back in time knowing Kiervan would be there to keep her from harm? Is that what Maude had meant when she'd said Bill wasn't the man for her?

Alanna clenched her teeth and lifted her chin. Damn her resolve. If she didn't keep it tightly leashed, it wandered away and left her surrounded with nothing but stupid, mushy emotions. And those emotions, where Kiervan des Marceaux was concerned, were dangerous, pure and simple.

17

Heavy clouds scuttled lower across the early morning sky. Kiervan sighted on a distant mound of rocks and then considered the gathering storm for a long moment before glancing over at his companion. Alanna sat astride her stout little Kerry pony, the reins hanging loosely from the fingers of her left hand, her gaze fixed blankly between the animal's ears. She'd ridden at his side through the night, her thoughts as clearly weighted as the thunderheads now massing above, her responses to his efforts at conversation brief and forced. What dream haunted her? he wondered for the hundredth time. Why did she so steadfastly refuse to share the burden of her fears?

He cleared his throat quietly in an effort to gently call her from her thoughts, and then voiced the question that had nagged at him for the better part of the night. "Is it death you see in your dreams, Alanna?"

She didn't look at him, but shrugged her cloak-draped shoulders and shook her head.

Kiervan narrowed his eyes. "Ruin?" he asked, watching her carefully. When she again shook her head, he continued. "Destruction perhaps?"

Again she wordlessly answered no.

"Perhaps it's the fruit of a decision you see," he offered, determined to prod until she either admitted the truth or angrily told him to mind his own business. "Could it be the misery and disappointment of a life with your Bill Boyer?"

She shot him a hard look that told him more than he

knew she'd intended to reveal. A wondrous exhilaration tingled through his flesh and brought a smile to his lips. "I've been wondering, Alanna . . ." he began, trying to tamp down his elation. "I've explained my reasons for marrying Eggie, but you've yet to tell me yours for choosing Bill as your mate."

"He's kind and sensitive," she replied almost too quickly. "He works and plays well with others. He doesn't run with scissors. He'll be a faithful husband and a good father."

Kiervan waited to answer, watching the warring emotions play across her features and feeling a wholly unexpected wave of relief flood through his veins. "Forgive me, Alanna," he said at last, "but your Bill sounds rather dull. Does he possess all of his faculties?"

She straightened her shoulders before haughtily answering, "I'll have you know that he's a brilliant accountant."

Kiervan made only a bare attempt to stifle his laughter. Through it he offered, "I'd suggest that his passion is misdirected."

"You don't even know Bill," she countered, turning her head to meet his scrutiny. "How can you pass any sort of informed judgment on his passions?"

Kiervan sobered and cocked a knowing brow. "If he hasn't seduced you, Alanna, the man's priorities are out of kilter. Either that, or he's a spineless excuse for a man to begin with."

"There's nothing wrong with Bill," she retorted, her tone still defiant but her eyes clouding. "He's a decent man."

Kiervan slowly shook his head and evenly observed, "A stranger would be tempted to say that the problem, then, obviously lies with you. But I've danced at the edge of your fire, Alanna, and I know better. Your betrothed doesn't stir your senses, does he?"

She shot him a murderous look as she replied icily, "The nature of my physical relationship with Bill is none of your concern, Kiervan."

Kiervan reached out, caught the reins of her pony in his hand, and drew both their mounts to a halt. He offered her a sardonic smile. "And you dared to call me a mercenary?

When you're marrying just as much for money and social position as I am?"

Her chin came up sharply and she fired back, "I'm not marrying Bill for either of those reasons. I happen to love him. Very much."

Kiervan's heart softened in the face of her bravado. "Sweet Alanna," he chuckled. He slowly, tauntingly brushed the pad of his thumb across the tempting fullness of her lower lip. "You're such a miserable liar. You shouldn't even make the attempt."

"I'm not lying," she insisted, closing her eyes. "I'm not—"

The rest of her denial faded away as he drew his thumb across her lips again. She made a soft sound deep in her throat, and her lips parted in seductive, irresistible invitation.

Kiervan drew a deep breath, his body quivering with want. "Tell me that Bill Boyer makes you feel the things I do, Alanna," he demanded softly. "Tell me that you think only of him when you're in my arms."

"Kiervan . . ." she began. The rest was lost as her voice broke.

Tenderly he tilted her face up until she met his gaze. "Tell me for which of us your blood burns hottest, Alanna."

The truth shimmered in the depths of her beautiful eyes, resonated through the scant distance between them. Joy, sparkling and splendid and pure, swept through his veins.

"God, that you'll look at me like that forever, woman."

Even as he offered up his hope, her eyes darkened. He'd been in too many battles not to recognize the color of fear. His newborn happiness cringed in the face of it, and he searched madly for the words to reassure her. He hadn't found any when she pulled away from him, and so he let her go, knowing that to hold her against her will would only drive her beyond his reach.

Kiervan straightened in the saddle and fixed his gaze on the storm gathering above their heads. He heard the creak of Alanna's saddle and then nothing. The silence looming between them ached, and he finally broke it without looking at her.

"Why are you so afraid of me, Alanna?" The answer, crystalline and piercing, came to him on a sudden gust of cold wind. Kiervan clenched his teeth and nodded before the power of the obvious truth. " 'Tis betrayal you see, is it not, Alanna? A Celtic cross." He turned to face her. "And 'tis me that you vision as the traitor, isn't it?"

She started as though he'd driven a knife between her shoulder blades. For a moment, her eyes, troubled and confused, met his, and then they darted away. "We're going to get soaked," she replied, looking at the tempest building above them. In the next second, she assessed the land around them.

"There's a decent stand of rocks over that way," she said, pointing to the northwest and the site Kiervan had already selected. "We might find some shelter."

A fat drop of rain spattered on the back of his hand, and Kiervan quickly nodded his assent. Kicking his horse in the flanks and trusting Alanna to follow, he raced toward the distant formation. In only minutes his coat was plastered to his back and icy water coursed from the ends of his hair. The discomfort of his body, however, barely bothered him. His thoughts were focused elsewhere. Who did he betray in Alanna's dream? What must he do to force the story from her lips? What could he do or say to allay her fears?

What roughly formed options he'd considered were lost as lightning arced between the inky clouds and thunder filled the air in the heavens above with a resonant crack.

In what remained of the late-afternoon light, Alanna leaned against the rocky wall and tried to ignore the fact that she was more miserable than she could remember ever being. She tried to find some comfort in knowing that, at least for the moment, she had on relatively dry clothing. It was more than the man standing beside her could say. She looked across at Kiervan and found him with his arms folded across his chest, staring into the rain- and twilight-shrouded hills rolling out before them, his brow furrowed with thought.

While less than an arm's length separated them physically, Alanna sensed a deep gulf separating them emotionally. His mood had taken a wholly unexpected and inexplicable turn into brooding silence when she'd changed from her sodden skirt and blouse into the tattered remnants of the nightgown and her borrowed woolen pants.

She'd told herself repeatedly that this distance was exactly what she'd hoped to accomplish in telling him her life's story. But it wasn't her past that had achieved the consequences she'd wanted, and she knew it. The wedge between them had been driven into place by her refusal to be honest about her relationship with Bill, by her refusal to share her recurring dream with Kiervan. She told herself again that she shouldn't care how she'd accomplished her goal. She should simply be glad that she had.

But part of her didn't like it at all. It was one thing to keep Kiervan from flinging her into his bed and another entirely to endure his complete withdrawal. Somewhere there had to be a more comfortable halfway point. If she had to spend the coming night the way she'd just spent the day, she'd either go nuts or explode.

"Certainly the rain can't go on like this forever," she ventured. "Once we get going again, we can make up the lost time."

He didn't reply and Alanna sighed quietly. "Kiervan?" she began, "What are you thinking about?"

He turned slowly toward her, resting his shoulder against the rock wall and crossing one booted ankle over the other. "I'm thinking about you."

Well, at least he was talking. It was more than he'd done for the last ten or twelve hours. "Geesh. That could be scary. Reach any earth-shattering conclusions?"

"Quite frankly, Alanna, at the moment I have no idea what to think of you," he answered, his voice caressing her like rich velvet.

She considered him for a moment and then slowly smiled. This was much better than the painful silence. If she was careful to keep their conversation on fairly neutral topics . . . "Well, I do seem to recall that you've already started a list and that none of the terms were particularly flattering. Let's see, wasn't 'troublesome' on it? And 'contrary'?"

"Aye. I included 'independent' at the time as well. But 'twould seem that I have neglected to add a few others in the days since that conversation."

"Oh, yeah?" she retorted, smiling and mimicking his position against the rock. "Like what?"

Kiervan considered her while his smile broadened, " 'Foolhardy,' for one."

"No argument here."

"And 'reckless,' " he added softly.

Alanna grinned up at him. "Always."

" 'Challenging,' comes to mind as well."

"That's me," she admitted. Alanna lifted her chin proudly and quipped, "There's never a dull moment when I'm around."

An unfathomable light ignited in the depths of his eyes, and his voice lowered seductively as he added, " 'Daring and brave.' "

"Now, Kiervan," she teasingly admonished. "Be careful. That one sounds dangerously close to being a compliment."

"And 'beautiful to distraction.' "

Alanna felt the words arrow into her heart, felt the warm current that eddied from them to oddly both soothe and ignite every fiber of her being. God, he knew just what buttons to push. She knew enough to be instantly wary. Alanna rolled her eyes and shook her head. "Beautiful? You've *got* to be kidding," she laughingly retorted, stepping away from the wall and lifting her arms out from her sides. "I have to look like I've been drug through a knothole backward. At least a half dozen times."

Kiervan closed the distance between them with one smooth motion, slipped his hands about her waist, and whispered, "And so very, very tempting."

"It's the stress, Kiervan," she countered flippantly, placing her hands against the hard planes of his chest in an effort to keep at least a tiny bit of distance between them. In the pale twilight, the finely chiseled lines of his face seemed softer, more touchable than she remembered.

"The adrenaline's pumping through you, des Marceaux. We've been through the paces the last few days," she offered in a desperate attempt to divert her thoughts from the path they'd so suddenly taken. "Give it some time and it'll pass."

"Is that what it's called in your time, 'Lanna?" he asked, leaning down to press a lingering kiss to the center of her forehead.

Alanna closed her eyes and savored the heady ripple slowly cascading down the length of her body. "What do we call what, Kiervan?" she absently inquired, fighting the mesmerizing sensation of his heartbeat against her palms. The corded muscles of his chest rippled beneath her arms as he wrapped her in his embrace.

He leaned down and brushed his lips along the curve of her ear, whispering, "Shall I add 'difficult and exasperating' to my list?"

"No," she replied solemnly, arching her back in an attempt to reclaim the distance between them, distance in which she hoped to marshal the scattered remnants of her earlier determination. She looked up to meet his smoldering gaze, moistened her lips with the tip of her tongue, and then added, "I'm serious, Kiervan. What do we call what?"

"By all the saints, woman," he groaned, the lines at the corners of his mouth tightening. Then, slowly and deliberately, he drew her back to him and captured her lips with his own.

Never in all her life had she felt so liquid, so wondrously weak. Kiervan's possession deepened and her resolve scattered as her spirit soared with the heavenly magic of it. She leaned into the certain strength of his embrace, shuddering with every molten caress of his lips.

He drew away with a suddenness that left her senses reeling and her legs trembling. She felt the fleeting warmth of his lips against her temple and then he swallowed.

"Alanna," he whispered, his voice thick and rough. "Look at me."

She couldn't answer, couldn't move, couldn't lock away the emotions still swirling through her heart and her mind and her soul. He shifted his hold to take her chin gently between his thumb and finger and then tilted her face upward.

"Open your eyes, Alanna."

She obeyed and instantly realized that their chests rose and fell in the same desperate rhythm; saw the hunger burning in the depths of his ebony eyes and knew that he could see the same need in her own.

"What's between us, Alanna? Is it adrenaline?"

"Yeah," she managed to answer on a ragged breath, hoping he wouldn't see the lie in her eyes.

He smiled, the expression doing little to soothe her spirit. " 'Tis no reason you have to fear it," he said, stroking the curve of her jaw with the pad of his thumb. "Or me."

Pain shot through her, jolting her. What had she been thinking? He was a mercenary, a rogue without conscience, a man betrothed to another. Not fear him? Baiting Lord Graeme Ashton had been risky. Not being afraid of Kiervan des Marceaux would be certain suicide.

"What fear has caught at your mind, 'Lanna? Deny it not. I can see it in your eyes."

She opened her mouth, but no sound came when she attempted to speak. Alanna shook her head and stepped back, tried to break the circle of his arms.

Confusion clouded his expression for only a moment, and then the hard lines of determination furrowed the space between his brows. He tightened his arms about her, drew her into his renewed embrace, and slowly leaned down, his intent evident. Alanna stared up at him in disbelief and growing panic.

"No," she said with a firmness that surprised her. "This isn't right, Kiervan. We're both engaged to others." She ducked out of the circle of his arms and stepped away. "This is too close to adultery for me."

He crossed his arms over his chest and considered her. She braced herself, knowing that the dark clouds wrapped around the Irish hills were nothing compared to what loomed before her.

"Alanna," he finally said, "listen to me and know that what I'm about to say is offered with the very last bit of patience I possess. You can deny it with your dying breath, but you're not pledged to Bill Boyer because he's the passion of your life. You're marrying him because he doesn't threaten the walls you've built around yourself. He's safe and you won't ever have to worry that he'll outthink you or hurt you."

She lifted her chin and swallowed. "And is that so awful?"

"No."

Her heart hammering high in her throat, Alanna willed herself to ask, "Then why is it so important to you that I admit it?"

He cocked a brow and very slowly, very gently, said, "You'll never know the flames of a true fire with your Bill Boyer. And you can have much more than you're settling for, Alanna."

God, enough of the beating around the bush. Let's just say it straight out. Alanna spoke before her courage could fail her. "What you're saying is that I can have you?"

"We can have each other," he countered, his voice velvety, his gaze caressing hers.

We can have each other. For how long? An irrational spark of hope ignited deep within her. She instantly banked it and warily asked, "And what about your plans to marry Eggie?"

"They cannot be changed," he answered, his tone no less beckoning than before.

Hope died with his words. "Mercenary to the end," she cynically observed, turning away with a shake of her head. "At least you're consistent."

He caught her arm and turned her back, saying, "No, Alanna," with such gentleness that she wanted to cry. "Hear me out. What exists between you and me is uncommon. You know it as well as I do. Only your silly resistance prevents us from taking each other as lovers."

Silly? Her pride bruised, she met his ebony gaze and countered, "So you've decided that I'd make a nifty little mistress, have you?"

The corners of his mouth lifted in a smile tinged with regret. "I've considered the idea and find that I feel a definite attraction to it, but I also know you wouldn't be content being another woman's second."

She arched her brow. "So just exactly what do you have in mind? A torrid one-night stand?"

If he caught her sarcasm, he apparently chose to ignore it. "One night with you would never be enough, Alanna."

She tilted her chin up another notch, determined to see the contest through to the ugly end. "Two nights then? Or maybe three?"

"God, but you can be prickly," he said, drawing her back toward him and slipping his arms about her waist. His gaze searching hers, he asked, "Can we not simply agree to be lovers until the fire burns itself out?"

"And then we would just go our separate ways, right?" She saw the flicker of triumph in his eyes and something in her rebelled. Before he could offer a reply, Alanna added, "Can I count on you to leave twenty dollars on the dresser when you say your final farewell?"

The look of victory vanished. A coldness came into his eyes. "Perhaps we could consider it your wedding gift to me," he replied mockingly.

Anger and pain surged through her, and with every ounce of strength she could muster, she wrenched herself from Kiervan's embrace. In the next instant, she spun about and strode out into the rain. Heading out across the sodden meadow, she called herself the worst kind of fool with each rain-drenching footstep.

Her perfectly rational little plan had backfired. She'd poured out the tale of her miserable childhood circumstances, and it hadn't stopped him. Oh, no. He'd considered her past and decided that everything in it allowed him to have whatever he wanted. Kiervan des Marceaux had no problem with stepping into the long line of men who had no respect for her. As if to taunt her, the image of the dark room off the pub, of arching up beneath Kiervan's powerful body, blazed before her eyes, then was mercifully washed away by her scalding tears.

The ground swam before her watery eyes, dark green and inviting, and in her misery she yearned to have it swallow her, to allow her to disappear beneath the blanket of its silent oblivion. She pushed on across the meadow until she stumbled, only vaguely noting the fact that she made no effort to catch her balance, made no effort to break her fall.

In midair, her downward momentum abruptly stopped and then just as suddenly reversed. Even through the blur of her misery and the horrible rending of her heart, she recognized the heat and power of Kiervan's hands.

"Alanna, please . . ."

"Don't touch me," she commanded, twisting free of his grasp and backing away from him. Turning to flee, she yelled, "Leave me alone!"

He caught her by the upper arm and spun her back to face him. "We will finish talking about this," he pronounced.

"I don't have anything to say to you," she retorted as she pried at his fingers with her free hand. Her effort produced no results.

" 'Tis not just in my bed that I want you, Alanna," he asserted, pulling her squarely before him.

She ceased struggling and glared up at him. "God! That one's a classic!" Alanna railed. "You're a smart man, Kiervan. I expected something a bit more original out of you. Next you'll be telling me that you'll still respect me in the morning."

" 'Tis the truth, damn it," he snapped, taking her shoulders in his hands and giving her a shake.

All right, she decided. If he wanted a fight, she'd give him one to remember for the rest of his days. Alanna planted her feet and squared her shoulders. Cold rain sluiced down her back. "You're a bastard to the center of your black heart!"

"I admitted that the night we met," he replied impatiently. His eyes narrowed and she saw a vein pound at his temple, saw the rain dripping off the ends of his hair like black pearls. "And the matter of my soul we will discuss some other time."

Without looking away, Alanna replied through the bitter ache wrenching her heart, "We're not going to discuss anything. Not now. Not ever. Go away. Go find some town. Go find some other woman."

She bore the intensity of his gaze for what seemed an eternity and then he said slowly, and with a hardness that made her flinch, "Perhaps I will. At least one who's not afraid of being a real woman."

Heat exploded through her. Standing captive before him, her hands balled into fists at her sides, she glared up at him. "And just what are you insinuating, Captain?"

He shook his head and then abruptly released her. "Go on, Alanna," he said, gesturing toward the encampment. "While I'm gone you can wrap yourself in your safe little blanket." He offered her a cold smile as he added, "Dream of your beloved Bill Boyer who's not man enough to stir you."

It took a long moment to quash the impulse to strike the smirk from his face, but when she finally possessed an acceptable measure of self-control, she retorted, "He's a better man than you'll ever be! At least he understands the concepts of honor and fidelity and . . ."

"We've had this conversation before, Alanna," he interrupted, leaning down to bring his furious gaze even with hers. "I'm fully aware of how gallant you find your fiancé."

"Make fun of him all you want. At least he's capable of thinking of something other than . . ."

"Lovemaking?" he provided, slanting a mocking brow. "Is that the word you're stumbling over, Alanna?"

"It's a lot nicer than the one I was thinking, but it's close enough. And for your information, in case it ever occurs to you to wonder, I happen to believe that there isn't much point in being a *real* woman unless there's a *real* man around to appreciate it."

"And would that be adoring Bill who stands on the other side of time?"

She raked him up and down with open disdain. "It sure as hell isn't you."

He folded his arms across his chest, and his voice rumbled low in his chest when he said, "Prove it."

He looked for all the world like a pirate facing a mutiny of drunken sailors, like a man not the least surprised, nor the least concerned, by the turn of events. Caution and fear pricked her in the same moment, and Alanna suddenly sensed then that she'd been drawn into a finely woven trap.

"I don't have to prove anything to you," she announced with far more poise than she felt, "and I'll be damned if I let you goad me into thinking that I do."

"Coward."

"Think whatever you like. I don't care."

"Yes you do. Your chin always leads, 'Lanna." He unfolded his arms and traced the line of her jaw with the tip of his finger. He brushed his thumb across her lower lip as he added, "Did you know that your mouth gets small when you get angry? Like a little ripe cherry begging to be nibbled."

"Stop it!" she demanded, swatting his hand away as she turned her head aside.

He caught her chin in the palm of his hand and forced her to look up at him. "No, Alanna. I've made the mistake of stopping too often of late. 'Tis not a thing I'll do this night."

Even as the thought of running crossed her mind, he clamped his free arm about her waist and roughly hauled her against him. Alanna pressed her hands against his chest and pushed with all her might. He laughed low and hard as he drew her closer and bent his head down until she felt the warmth of his breath caress her cheek.

"You say that I've not the ability to play man to your woman," he growled, holding her fast, his fingers tightening about her chin. " 'Tis a grievous insult. I demand that you prove the truth of it."

She knew what he was about, foresaw the likely outcome of his intention. A bolt of anticipation shot through her, heating her blood and tingling through her flesh. Instincts honed in her youth screamed of the danger in surrendering to temptation.

"Don't you dare!" she sputtered over the staccato rhythm of her heart. "Don't you—"

He took her defiant words into his mouth, his kiss punishing, his tongue boldly thrusting past her resistance. She pushed against his chest and tried to twist from the arm pinning her body to his. But her mind reeled before the speed and demanding force of Kiervan's advance, leaving her powerless to control the savage, primitive sensations he always awakened within her. And as always, the strength ebbed from her limbs in a single breathtaking moment.

She leaned into him, her body molding around the hardened planes of his, unable to resist the relentless waves of exquisite fire rippling through her soul. His name mingled with her moan of denial and acceptance, to be lost in his greedy possession of her mouth. Alanna clung to him, her heart thundering and her breathing ragged, as she rode the heated tide.

"You're mine, Alanna," he whispered into her ear.

Mine? A spark of indignation began to smolder. Surely he didn't consider her in the same light as he did his ship or his cargo? She stiffened, but if he noted her reaction, he gave no outward sign.

"I claimed you as mine the night I brought you from the Carraig Cor."

Alanna's pride intervened and she pushed away from him with all her strength. He let her go, his brows knit in open puzzlement as he considered her. She met his gaze squarely and stated, "You don't *own* me, Kiervan des Marceaux. No man owns me. And no man '*claims*' me without my consent."

"A consent which you readily give," he reminded her with a sardonic smile. "Every time."

The cold fingers of shame touched her briefly. Then a wild fury swept over her, crushing all reason. Through the white-hot haze, she saw the blur of her hand, heard the resounding impact of flesh against flesh, felt the burning sting across her palm. A pain, sharp and rippling, shot up her arm, knifing through the shield of her outrage.

Kiervan held her wrist in a viselike grip between them. She looked beyond it and saw his lips set in an unforgiving line, his eyes dark coals burning with the fires of anger and bruised pride. Alanna's heart recoiled in regret.

"Suit yourself, Alanna," Kiervan answered, his gaze never leaving hers, the anger in his eyes never wavering. "Your precious virtue has nothing to fear from me."

A cold mask instantly settled over his features. He released her, slowly opening his hand as if ridding himself of something which he held in utter contempt. "I will never touch you again."

Then he took a deliberate step back, turned on his heel, and walked off into the rain, taking the greater part of Alanna's heart and the last feeble rays of daylight with him.

18

For the fifth morning in a row, Kiervan awakened to aching need. He gritted his teeth, gathered the blanket under his chin, and rolled onto his side. Pressing his eyes tightly closed, he ordered his mind and his body into the realm of dreamless sleep. Both ignored him. As if to deliberately add to his agony, his mind filled with images of Alanna, of her riding beside him for the past five days in silence or stiff-backed anger, of how she blinked at him in confusion or glared daggers at him whenever he attempted to pull her into a conversation.

Other memories came as well, memories he found infinitely more torturous. His body pulsed with a primal rhythm as he remembered the warmth of her body against his, the taste of her honeyed mouth, the scent of her skin, the sweet, innocent eagerness of her acquiescence.

With a muttered curse, he flung the blanket aside and sat up. On the other side of the fire lay Alanna, wrapped in his cloak. God, but she muddled his thinking. He could maintain a clear head and purpose when alone, but the moment she stood before him, every bit of his good sense drained out the soles of his boots.

"Are you all right?"

Kiervan started at the soft sound of Alanna's voice. His gaze instantly found hers across the banked embers remaining from the night before. She rested on her side, watching him with gentle violet eyes, her golden hair tumbling over her shoulder and splayed out over the bundle of clothing that served as her pillow. If there was ever a woman meant to be awakened with a kiss . . .

"I'm fine," he groused, grabbing his blanket and rising to his feet. With his back to her, Kiervan flicked it about his shoulders in the fashion of a cape, a cape wholly designed to preserve his dignity and pride. God knew he was warm enough without it.

"Are you sure? You seem a little tense to me."

"I'm simply anxious to be on our way," he answered crisply, moving off from their encampment without looking back at her. "You'd best prepare for the day ahead. We'll ride hard again."

When well beyond her sight, safely screened by a massive jumble of rock, Kiervan expelled a long, hard breath and tore the makeshift wrap from his shoulders. In a heartbeat his coat and shirt lay atop the gray woolen mass at his feet. The cold air prickled against the burning heat of his bare skin, and for a too brief moment the sensation distracted him. But, as always, his thoughts quickly and unerringly turned back to Alanna.

How in hell's name had she managed to remain a virgin for twenty-seven years? He rubbed the five-day growth on his chin and decided that the explanation had to lie in the nature of twentieth-century men. Either they were blind dullards or they were indeed eunuchs. He considered the possibility that perhaps they were both. Another thought occurred to him in the same instant, bringing a hard line to his lips. Then again, maybe they were just as he was, quick-tempered fools who'd allowed Alanna to box them into the corners of their own pride. The likelihood that he was but one among many such men in her life further prodded his already bruised self-regard.

It didn't matter, he angrily assured himself.

The vow he'd made in anger had come from the wisdom of his instincts. Their beliefs were too different, their pasts and their temperaments too much the same, for there to be anything of substance, of even relative permanence, between them. It was best that he not touch her again, that he avoid tasting the tempting promise of her lips. Nothing good would ever come of it. There were other women. Kiervan snatched up his shirt. Turning the garment right side out, it occurred to him that the words had become a daily affirmation; the redressing in a cold wind, a morning ritual. He scowled and, pulling the shirt down over his head, made a mental note to find another way to start tomorrow.

The noon sun tickled the back of his neck. Kiervan let his hand slide along his horse's back in the wake of the brush. The coat felt silken to his touch, and his mind drifted to other hair, longer and golden, and he wondered how it would feel bathed in sunlight and slipping through his fingers.

As though his thoughts had summoned her, he saw Alanna leave the tumble of rocks serving as their midday resting place and come toward him. Kiervan leaned against the side of his mount, watching her approach. He noted the gentle sway of her skirts, how she hugged her arms about her midriff, how the shadows washed across her features. In the days since he'd made his ill-considered vow, he hadn't regretted it more than he did at that moment.

She stopped some five feet or more from him and took a deep breath before asking, "Are you trying to kill the horses?"

"Never," he answered. "A good horse is too hard to come by."

Her chin came up and, as he'd expected, she took two bold steps forward. With her fists on her hips, she looked up at him and demanded, "Then is it me you're trying to punish?"

Kiervan fought back the urge to cast his pride to the wind, resisted the impulse that demanded he sweep her into his arms. Instead he shook his head and quietly chuckled. "Were it you I wanted to punish, Alanna, I'd have taken an entirely different tack. 'Twouldn't have been a horse you'd have spent the last five days riding." He noted the crimson that instantly flooded her neck and cheeks, the fire that suddenly lit her eyes.

"How crude," she retorted, her tone too carefully disdainful.

"And how exhilarating you find the very thought," he taunted. " 'Tis a shame you can't bring yourself to admit that you want me to take you."

"I'd die first."

"Even if you found the courage to put truth into words, Alanna, my sweet," he replied, leaning down until but inches and the strength of his will separated their lips, "you'll grow old and pass to the world beyond without knowing my touch again. Though you may beg me for another kiss, another caress, I've made my vow and I won't break it."

"Your vow is the best thing that ever happened to me."

Deliberately he straightened and let his gaze wander downward. A slow smile lifted the corners of his mouth as he watched the rapid rise and fall of her breasts, as he noted the twin pebbled crests straining against the fabric of her blouse. "So I see," he offered quietly without looking away from the feast she provided him.

She crossed her arms over her chest and stepped away, retorting, "You're a despicable lowlife."

"You forgot 'bastard,' " he reminded her. "I'm a despicable lowlife *bastard*."

She whirled about and stormed away. Lord, he mused, watching her high-spirited retreat, she was beautiful any time, but especially so when angry. With a sigh of resignation, he went back to brushing his horse, finding what small comfort he could in knowing that in all likelihood, she suffered only slightly less frustration than he.

Alanna headed toward the bank of the small stream. "Despicable, lowlife, *handsome* bastard," she amended as she went. He probably hadn't shaved in the last five days simply because he knew just how much his beard intrigued her. The damn thing made him even more mysterious, more unfathomable, and far more attractive than she found comfortable.

It wasn't enough that her traitorous heart raced at the thought of him, that the sight of him actually heated her blood, that the memory of his touch left her weak and breathless. No, by far the worst humiliation came from the undeniable fact that she hadn't the power to banish something he'd stirred to life within her, something quiet and yet compelling, a nebulous weight and presence that completely filled her body and saturated her will.

It occupied her awareness at every moment, and every nerve and fiber of her being hummed with the expectancy of a forbidden, dark discovery. But she knew better than to dwell on it. The one time she'd tried to analyze the feeling, the sheer power, the absolute inescapability of it, had scattered her wits to the winds. Pure self-preservation demanded that she ignore it, that she pretend she didn't know it possessed her. Maybe if she concentrated on how angry she was with Kiervan . . .

Alanna dropped down on a rock beside the stream and buried her face in her hands as the truth washed over her. Kiervan controlled the restless hunger inside her. His dark eyes stoked it and made it stronger and more insistent. His touch made it leap up and dance, left her powerless to check the impulses which drove her into his embrace, that sent her seeking the intoxicating wonder of his possession. The certain knowledge that he knew the effect he had upon her, that he fully understood the relentless nature of the feeling swelling inside her, touched a fear far deeper than any she had ever encountered before.

For a wild moment, she considered facing the situation squarely, considered asking Kiervan straight out about the strange feelings taking control of her. But her pride bristled at the thought, warning her that such boldness would deliver her completely into Kiervan's power, that the next time she stepped from his arms, she'd be a person forever changed. Exactly how she'd be different, she couldn't guess, but a part of her wanted so very much to find out.

Alanna sighed resolutely and turned about on the rock, deliberately placing her back toward Kiervan—a fact he would note if he happened to look in her direction.

Her chin in her hands, Alanna gazed at the smooth surface of the water and willed her thoughts to still. The vision came with a sudden clarity that left her gasping. Ashton with a figure who remained hidden in the shadows. The figure whispered. Ashton nodded and handed it something that gleamed dully in the shadows. A second set of images came in the wake of the first. Ashton's sword glinting in the sunlight. Kiervan dragging her toward the protection of higher ground; the throaty screams of men and horses charging a rocky hillock on the Irish countryside.

And then the vision disappeared as suddenly as it had come.

Alanna vaulted to her feet and spun about, fighting back a rising sense of dread. The rocky hillock of her vision rose not more than a fifty feet away. She turned, frantically seeking Kiervan. He remained where she'd left him only moments before, calmly combing his horse.

The decision made, in the next moment she was running toward him, her skirts held high above her knees, shouting his name. He whirled about and, at the first sight of her, started forward, his expression grim. It took her several seconds to realize that his attention focused on a point beyond her. A glance over her shoulder sent ripples of stark terror racing down her spine. A dozen dark shapes spilled down the slope of a nearby hill. Before them one rode separately, a glimmer of steel flashing between him and the cloudless sky.

"It's Ashton," she told him needlessly, throwing herself into the protection of his arms. "I saw him in a vision in the stream. He's found us."

He took her hand in his and sprinted for the rocks. Alanna tried to keep up with him, but her feet barely touched the ground. Without breaking stride, he asked, "Did you happen to see whether or not we survive?"

"Sorry," she replied breathlessly. She thought she heard him say something that sounded like "Great," but her heart was thundering too loudly in her ears to be sure.

When they reached the base of the rocks, Kiervan shoved her ahead of him, saying, "Climb as high as you can. Go."

Alanna skittered to a stop before a natural channel in the rock and whirled back, the world spinning as she tried to find her balance and her breath.

Kiervan flung the reins of Alanna's mount back over its neck. "Yah!" he shouted, slapping the horse on the rump with the flat of his hand. It immediately wheeled and vaulted for the open land beyond the hillock, clods of turf shooting from the animal's hooves as it raced away.

Kiervan whirled back around to face her. For an instant, time ceased, and in that moment, she accepted the difficult truth: Kiervan des Marceaux was unlike any man she had ever known, a man wild and untamable, a man dangerously powerful no matter the game or the stakes. And that was why she loved him.

"I told you to climb!" he bellowed. "Now go!"

She did as he commanded, scrambling up the rocks as best she could in her long skirts. Kiervan came behind her, urging her to hurry every step of the way. When she reached a flat spot sheltered by another rock, she paused and reached for the hem of her skirt.

" 'Lanna," Kiervan pleaded, placing his hand at the small of her back. "We haven't time."

"I can't move with a ton of fabric in the way. It'll take me only a second," she promised, quickly gathering the lengths of cloth into a haphazard knot about her thighs.

Kiervan muttered an oath as she started upward again, but she kept moving and didn't glance back. A thin whining sound suddenly creased the air and exploded against the rock behind her. Even as she hurried on, a boom of thunder rolled up from the ground below.

"Guns," she gasped, racing faster up the flume. A second whine, closer than the first, split the air and she heard Kiervan grunt in reply even as the report volleyed up and through the rocks.

Alanna kept moving, kept climbing, twisting through narrow passages and around smooth-faced obstacles. She heard Kiervan behind her, heard the rasping of his breath and the scrape of his boots and clothing against the rock. Only when she rounded a tight bend and entered a pocket with high sheer walls did she stop. Gasping for breath, she turned back just as Kiervan shoved himself through the narrow opening and into the sheltered cavern.

Blood soaked the left sleeve of his jacket and ran in rivulets down the back of his hand. It dripped from the tips of his fingers, making brilliant crimson splatters on the weather-washed limestone.

"Apparently I've had a small climbing accident," he offered with a wry smile, lifting his wounded arm slightly.

She wanted to rage at his cavalier attitude, and she wanted to cry. She chose a third option. "Cuts don't bleed like that," she countered, fumbling with her knotted skirts. "Why didn't you tell me that you'd been shot?"

"I didn't think there was much point in mentioning it until something could be properly done about it."

Alanna frowned. "I hate it when you're so damn rational."

"You mean you hate it when I'm right."

The amusement in his voice buoyed her own spirits. The return of their easy banter felt good. "All right. Yes, I hate it when you're right," she admitted, working one of her petticoats over her hips and down her legs. As she straightened with the garment in hand she eyed his arm and asked, "Can you get out of your jacket or am I going to have to cut off the sleeve?" God, he looked awful. His face had noticeably paled in the moments since he'd entered the cave. Blood pooled at his feet.

"You needn't look so grim, Alanna," he assured her, leaning his good shoulder against the wall of the cavern. " 'Tis only a flesh wound. The ball passed cleanly through."

"Yeah, right," she muttered, putting the edge of the petticoat between her teeth. "Strip, buster. I want to see it for myself."

"Alanna," he chided with a wan smile, "I'd suggest that the present is probably not the best time for you to have decided to end your foolish reticence."

The sound of tearing fabric echoed around the smooth stone walls. "Quite frankly, Kiervan," she retorted mildly, "I'm far more interested in keeping you from bleeding to death than I am in ravishing you. I need to bandage your wound. Now, sit down before you fall down."

He winced as he straightened and considered the entrance

to their lair. "We haven't the time for caring for the wound as you'd like, Alanna. For now, you'll have to be content with tying a bandage about the outside. Should Ashton or his men come up in pursuit of us, we must be ready."

"We'll hear them coming long before they get here," she interrupted, tearing another long strip of linen and watching him sway. "And they'll have to come through the same opening we did. We can take them out at our leisure. What's your next objection?"

He looked up and she followed the line of his sight. "Try again, des Marceaux. The overhang protects us from an aerial assault. Unless," she added, bringing her gaze back down and edging toward him, "they're contortionist trapeze artists."

He blinked hard and fast, shook his head, and then rubbed his good arm across his forehead. "You seem to have a great deal of experience in matters such as this," he said at last.

"Hiding out? You bet." She tore a third length of cloth and took another step closer, never taking her eyes off him. "No one can find a rat hole deeper or more quickly than I can. There was a point in time when my life depended on it. You don't ever lose those kinds of instincts."

He closed his eyes and leaned his forehead against the wall of stone. "And so now what do we do, mistress?"

Alanna quickly tossed down the fabric and stepped to his side. "You know the answer just as well as I do," she said, slipping an arm about his waist and drawing his uninjured arm across her shoulders. "Why are you asking me?" she inquired, easing them both down the wall.

"I like to see your mind at work," he whispered. " 'Tis a fine mind, in case I've never said so."

"We wait," she answered, settling him on the floor, basking in his compliment despite their desperate circumstances.

"How long are you prepared to do that?" When she shrugged, he added evenly, "They have water, Alanna. And food. And fire. They can last considerably longer than we can."

"But we have each other. That's something."

She glanced up when he offered no reply. His face was ashen and his brows were furrowed in pain. "But while we're waiting for a minor miracle," she whispered, gently pulling away from his side, "I'm going to bandage your arm. And if you want to pass out while I'm doing it, I promise never to tell a soul."

He didn't speak again until she pulled the knife from his boot top. "Alanna . . ." he called weakly.

She straightened and leaned forward to cup the side of his waxen face in the palm of her hand. He felt cold and clammy and she knew that he was going into shock. Despite her resolve, she couldn't keep the fear from her voice when she asked, "What is it, Kiervan?"

His lips began to form a reply, but not a sound came out before his shoulders slumped and he slipped into unconsciousness. With trembling hands and a prayer, Alanna grabbed him by the lapels of his jacket and maneuvered him until he lay flat on the floor of their little cave. Only after she'd elevated his feet with a rock did she slit open the sleeves of both his coat and his shirt and set to binding his wound.

19

The reality playing before him had the fragmented quality typical of dreams and yet there existed about it a
sense of something significant and compelling, something
that he knew he needed to understand. Kiervan watched in
fascination as a narrow valley passed far beneath him and
he marveled at the effortlessness of his flight.

*Gliding on the eddying currents of the canyon winds, he
felt the warmth of the sun on his back and wings, felt the
power of his freedom and the sureness of his control. Still,
he sensed that he was not his own master. A force, elemental, nameless, and beyond his ken, drew him up the rocky
cleft.*

*And then, from nowhere, an old woman appeared at the
edge of the canyon. Dressed in a long, billowing robe of
white, she leaned forward and gazed down the rocky wall at
her feet. He dipped a dark wing and circled, studying the
woman, wondering at her purpose. Then he saw Alanna
and terror wrenched his soul.*

*She clung to the side of the cliff, her fingers white and her
feet scraping for purchase, as she pleaded with the woman
above her. Kiervan strained to hear her words, but felt only
her desperation. He swept closer on determined wings,
praying that the dream would alter at his command, praying
that he would be granted human form and the ability to
reach down over the edge of the cliff and draw Alanna to
safety. But he remained as he was, silent and dark, a master*

of the currents, a creature apart from the world he surveyed. Kiervan's heart ached at his powerlessness.

As he approached, the woman straightened and shielded her eyes with her hand. Her gaze met his and she smiled knowingly. With tears shimmering in her eyes, she put her fingertips to her lips and then cast her kiss into the canyon wind. A glittering, swirling, ephemeral mist flowed from her hand, instantly enshrouding him. The brilliant dance of color and light blinded him, and his internal compass spun as though the entire world had been abruptly upended.

Then, as quickly as he had been dazed, his senses cleared. The old woman had disappeared; the mystical strands of magic clinging to his wings were the only evidence that he had not imagined her. He righted himself and sought Alanna. Even as he found her, still clinging to the rocky face of the canyon, he saw her shoulders relax, saw her draw a steadying breath, saw her release her hold and step into the wind. His soul screamed in denial, but the cry died within him.

He awoke with a violent start, his heart hammering and his breath ragged, every muscle in his body rigid with panic.

"I'm right here, Kiervan, I've got you. You're all right."

Warmth and comfort instantly flooded over him. He lay with his head cradled in Alanna's lap. She held his hand tightly in one of hers. With the other she gently smoothed his brow. Pins and needles pulsed through his muscles, and his heart was still thundering when he turned his head to look up at her.

"Bad dream, huh?" she asked, offering him a tender smile. "Been there myself a time or two."

"You let go," he accused, his voice harsh. "Damn it, Alanna. You deliberately let go."

"Of what?" she asked absently, running her fingers through his hair.

"The cliff," he snapped, squeezing her hand. "You let go and stepped out into nothing. You chose to die."

Her smile faded and wariness flickered in her eyes. "It was only a dream, Kiervan. I wouldn't do something like that in real life. You know that. Or at least you should by now."

Kiervan pulled his injured arm closer to his body, ignoring its throbbing. "There was an old woman on the ledge above, but she wouldn't help you."

Alanna's face paled. "Maude," she whispered.

"It could have been anyone," he countered through clenched teeth as he slowly flexed the fingers of his injured arm.

She shook her head. "Was she wearing a long white robe? Did she throw a kiss into the wind that . . ."

"Shimmered," he supplied, his mind reeling before the apparent truth, the effort to work his fingers forgotten.

"It was Maude."

"Alanna," Kiervan began, sitting up.

She placed a hand in the center of his back and assisted him while she admonished gently, "Watch your arm. You don't want to start it bleeding again. You've lost a lot of blood already."

"I don't give a damn about my arm," he retorted, turning to face her squarely. His heart hammered more painfully than his wound. "How is it that you know the particulars of my dream, Alanna?"

With a quick shrug, she replied, "I've had the same one. Remember when I told you that I kept having a bad dream that changed a bit each time I had it? That every time it went a bit further than the time before?"

He remembered. Pressing her for the details of her recurring nightmare had been his immediate goal when they had entered into the horrible, ill-fated discussion of their feelings for one another. For five days they'd kept their argument alive without a direct word, each of them intent to let it simmer between them until they parted ways at Castle O'Connell. But now Ashton had them trapped, and the possibility loomed large that they'd never reach County Kerry.

He sensed that the time had come for them to face the truths of themselves, the truths in their shared dream. He also knew absolutely that the exchange would alter the nature of their relationship. Beyond that, the course was uncharted. He drew a deep breath and committed himself to the certain perils and potential glories of discovery.

"You've not answered my question, Alanna. How is it that your dream has become mine?"

She shrugged again and studied her toes. With an air of nonchalance, she answered, "I suppose it's the nature of magic. You kind of come to accept those sorts of things when Maude's involved. I can only assume that there's some specific reason for giving you the dream too."

If he'd ever needed reassurance that he was pursuing the right course in pressing Alanna on the matter, she'd just given it to him. Kiervan nodded. "Do you believe that if you die in your dreams, you die in reality?" he asked gently. "Is that what frightens you?"

"Nothin' more than an old wives' tale," she countered, flashing him a brief, halfhearted smile.

"I don't want to watch you die each night in my dreams, Alanna," Kiervan admitted. "Can the dream be altered? Is Maude trying to warn us?"

She smiled at him again. "I don't die. Obviously you didn't get that far. I didn't either the first time. Relax, Kiervan. You swoop down and catch me in what is nothing less than a masterful move."

Something inside him began to ease. He met her gaze for a long moment before he trusted himself enough to ask, "Are you quite sure?"

"I remember it quite vividly. It was . . ." She blinked and a rosy hue colored her cheeks as she shifted her attention to the opening of their rocky chamber.

"I won't permit you to evade the subject this time, Alanna. Far too often we have set the matter aside. It was . . . what?"

She answered without looking back at him. "It was intense."

He lifted a brow. "Intense?"

"When I remember that part of the dream, I can still feel the feelings just like they were then . . . strong."

"What kind of feelings?" he pressed.

She turned back to meet his scrutiny. "I'd prefer not to

talk about it," she answered flatly. "They're rather unnerving."

Kiervan chose to ignore her resolution. "In what manner?"

"Look, Kiervan, I really don't want to talk about this." Her eyes darkened to the color of a storm gathering at sea. "It makes me uncomfortable."

"It makes you uncomfortable?" he parroted, the blood beginning to pound in his temples. "With all due respect, Alanna, you have no idea what truly uncomfortable is. Imagine watching you commit suicide in my dreams and being unable to stop you, only to awaken and find that you know more about my nightmare than I do myself.

"You tell me that I save you from death but that remembering the feelings you had upon being rescued unnerves you. Are you trying to avoid telling an unpleasant end to this dream? Do I fling us both into the side of the ravine and break our necks?"

She drew her knees up beneath her chin and wrapped her arms about her legs. "No," she replied quietly.

"Then what? If your dreams are invading my sleep, I have a right to know," he persisted. "I deserve an explanation. And I believe Maude gave me the dream to this very end."

Her voice was but a whisper and her gaze remained focused blankly on the opposite wall of their chamber when she answered, "I don't know how to put it into words."

His heart softened and he pushed a tendril of honey-colored hair off her shoulder. "I ask only that you make the attempt," he promised quietly.

"It's part physical, part emotional, and separating the two isn't really possible," she began. "Each feeds the other. It's . . ." She closed her eyes before she continued. "It's a lot like when you kiss me. It's something I want, something that, deep down inside, I know that I need. It's also something that scares the hell out me. It feels wonderful beyond words. And it makes me feel very, very out of control."

"I frighten you?"

She shook her head. "I frighten myself, Kiervan. I'm afraid of surrendering to you, to the power that part of me is so willing to grant you. If I do that, I'll be lost. I wouldn't be able to stand on my own ever again. I'd be a part of you."

"And that's bad to your way of thinking, Alanna?"

"It would be beyond horrible when you walked away. I don't think I could endure it." Her eyes remained closed when she leaned her head back against the wall and took a ragged breath. He sensed the incredible strength of her will as she continued, "And you've already told me you'd eventually leave me. You said it flat out, remember?"

She gave him no time to reply, but continued on, saying, "You're going to marry Eggie for her money and her social position. Even though I don't condone what you're going to do, I understand your motives. But you also intend to have a string of temporary lovers just like you've always had. And while I understand that that's considered acceptable in this time of yours, I just can't be one in a long line of them. You don't believe in forever, Kiervan. And as strange as it seems, I do."

He shook his head and as gently, as evenly, as possible, countered, "You think you believe, Alanna, because you know no differently. But I don't lie to you when I say that the nature of passion changes over time. There always comes a time when a man and a woman wish to go their separate ways."

She heard the tenderness in his words, felt the earnestness of his beliefs, but she couldn't bring herself to accept them as her own. She opened her eyes and met his gaze. "I learned early on that if you care too much, you'll hurt too much. I've spent a lifetime keeping the walls around me strong, keeping myself safe from cynics like you. I'm not going to let you into my heart, Kiervan, not knowing that someday you'll tear it into a thousand little pieces. No matter how wonderful being your lover might be, it wouldn't be enough to balance out the loneliness of the ever after."

He lifted both brows in an expression of puzzled incredulity. "So you'd prefer a lifetime of wondering what might have been, of not knowing?"

"Yeah. That's pretty much the gist of it." She climbed to

her feet, hoping that he'd take a pointed hint and let the discussion die a timely death.

He stood as well, moving slowly and holding his injured arm against his side. He swayed for only a moment and then braced his feet wide apart. "And if I believed in forever as you do?"

Alanna sighed and scowled at her feet for a long moment before looking back at him and replying, "But you don't, and there isn't much point to discussing a situation that's not only hypothetical, but also highly unlikely."

"Humor me on the matter. What if . . ."

"Then we'd have a whole different ball game goin' on here," she snapped, knowing that anger was safer than reason when it came to dealing with Kiervan des Marceaux. "I'd be willing to chuck it all and take the chance of loving you. Okay? Is that what you wanted to hear?"

One corner of his mouth twitched slightly. "Loving and being lovers are not the same thing, Alanna."

His calmness frightened her. Dashing headlong into the relative safety of anger, Alanna countered, her hands punctuating each word, "Why are you so obsessed with making me your lover? There's hundreds of women in the world who'd literally leap at the chance. They'd be more than willing and you wouldn't have to work nearly as hard at getting the deed done.

"Mary's still waiting for you back at the inn. Hell, you wouldn't have to try at all for her! What is it about me, Kiervan? What makes me such a valuable prize? What makes me worth so damn much effort?"

His answer came in the same unruffled calm that so frustrated, so panicked her. "You're fire and wind and storm. To make love to you would be like . . ."

"What?" she demanded. "Like bagging an elephant on safari? A real trophy to brag about to all your friends?" She ignored the questioning furrow between his brows.

Affecting a stuffy English accent, she continued, "Yes, I took this particular virgin while touring in Ireland last spring. Put up a helluva fight. Native boys fled in terror, of course, but I stood my ground and finally took her down.

Dangerous undertaking, all in all, but bloody fine sport, ol' boys. Bloody fine sport."

He considered her, his eyes unreadable. After a moment he asked, "What manner of men have you encountered in your life that you'd consider all of us capable of such contemptible conduct?"

"Gee, I don't know. Maybe they were contemptible. What do you think?"

"Do you consider Bill Boyer to be cut from the same cloth as all men, Alanna? Or is he alone different?"

His barbed question doused the last of her anger. "Bill isn't into competitive hunting," she answered distantly. "It's not a trophy thing with him. He doesn't share the stories of his conquests. He's not into carving notches in his bedpost."

"I think that you misjudge me," Kiervan said, his tone even and calm and yet somehow more animated. "Have I spoken to you of my past lovers? Do you know their names? The circumstances of our meeting? Our parting? Have I described the times I spent in their company?"

"No," she admitted quietly, grudgingly.

"Then obviously I possess a sense of discretion. What's passed between us since we met will go with me to my grave. It's a private matter and not a subject for public discussion. What might yet pass between us will be held in equal regard."

"Chivalry lives," she muttered beneath her breath.

He smiled and the corners of his eyes crinkled. He had the most fascinating eyes. And when he smiled like that . . . Alanna straightened. Devilish smile and roguish eyes or not, she wouldn't let him turn her into mush.

"I'm also capable of appreciating the uniqueness of your passions," he went on, his expression sober, his voice an intoxicating blend of smooth and husky, caressing her faltering anger. "Never have I met a woman with the spirit you have. Never have I encountered a woman whose strength of will so closely matches my own. You're the only woman I've ever found who possesses the power to utterly destroy me."

Stunned and wary, Alanna studied him. "Destroy you?" she repeated, her inquiry barely a whisper. Even as the words left her lips, a faint warning began to sound in her mind. Despite her resolve, she was being drawn back under Kiervan's power.

"Have you not considered that *I* might become lost in *you*? That after you leave me, I could very well spend the rest of my days searching in vain for a woman who can ignite the fires within me that you can? The difference between us, Alanna my sweet, is that I'm willing to accept the risk."

Sensing a finely woven net closing about her, Alanna desperately sidestepped the challenge. "You have no idea what kind of lover I'd be," she scoffed. "Considering my lack of experience, odds are I'd be downright lousy. A real disappointment."

He shook his head and chuckled. "Good Lord, woman. How can you utter such absolute nonsense? I've sampled only the smallest tastes of you, and on each occasion you stole not only my breath but every last shred of my good judgment as well. Were I you, I'd be more concerned that my passions would be wasted on a lover who couldn't equal them."

"I don't think I'll have anything to worry about in that respect, Kiervan."

He slanted a brow and she instantly felt her cheeks warm. "I didn't mean . . ." she stammered, looking everywhere but at him. "That didn't come out quite right. What I meant to say was . . . was that . . ."

"You amaze me, Alanna," he interjected, admiration and amusement ringing through his words. "I've seen you pass through the portals of time, fling yourself into the Irish sea, climb cliffs, and bait Ashton. I've watched you blithely play high stakes games and boldly risk your very life and limb. And yet you're afraid to step into my arms."

Staring at the floor of the chamber, she shrugged and observed dryly, "Well, we all have our flaws."

"But it rankles you. I see it in your eyes as we speak. I feel it in the air betwixt us." He slowly lifted his hand and took a tendril of her hair between his fingers. She felt the strength of his simple possession, felt the nebulous weight she had long harbored begin to lift.

"I'll say it plainly so that there's no misunderstanding," he said softly, holding her gaze with tender force. "I want you, Alanna. And I'll wait for you however long I must. Please come to me."

The intensity of his request wrapped about her heart and sent warm, wondrous tremors through her soul. In their wake rose an enveloping cloud of unfamiliar emotions. Suddenly she found herself wanting to laugh, wanting to cry, wanting to lay her head on Kiervan's chest and stay there forever. "I . . . ." she began in a dazed attempt to ground herself.

He twirled the strand of hair between his thumb and forefinger, but his eyes never left hers. "Please come to me, Alanna."

"You swore that you'd never touch me again," she offered, inwardly cringing at the small, desperate sound of imminent surrender in her voice. Her pride wounded, she swallowed past the tears tickling the back of her throat and lifted her chin to add with woefully thin bravado, "You said I'd die before you touched me, remember?"

If he found the least satisfaction in her weakening, he carefully concealed it. Only a warm invitation shone in the depths of his ebony eyes, and his voice rumbled low and husky as he answered, "They were ill-considered words spoken in anger and regretted more deeply and more often than you can possibly imagine. Ask me to set aside the vow and I'll gladly grant your request."

God, she couldn't think, couldn't breathe. Her heart ached with a hunger and need she'd never known, and she tried to marshal the tattered shreds of her will to resist the onslaught of their demand.

Kiervan lifted the lock of her hair and drew it slowly across his lips as he murmured, "Ask me to touch you, to make love to you. Please."

As though from a great distance, she heard herself protest feebly, "This is seduction."

"Aye," he taunted softly. " 'Tis an art you practice well. I wanted you the moment I saw you step from the mists of the Carraig Cor, and with each passing hour, my hunger's grown. You've only to be near to torment me, to make me ache with wanting. Come to me, Alanna. Take from me whatever you will. I'll accept what you're able to give and ask for no more."

She closed her eyes and, choking back tears, gave him the deepest, bitterest of her truths. "I'm afraid, Kiervan. So afraid."

"I know. I'll hold you until you're ready."

In her heart she knew he'd honor that pledge and all the others he'd ever offered her; his word was his bond. That truth twined about one of her own: She loved him and she wanted the joy of loving him completely. She'd lived far too long focusing on *someday*. All she had for certain was today and the happiness she could find in it. To hell with the future and all the what-ifs. Life would sort itself out; it always had.

Kiervan held his breath as she reached out to smooth a wrinkle from the bandage wrapped about his upper arm.

"What about your wound?" she asked. "It's got to be hurting. I don't want to do anything that might make it worse."

He smiled broadly. "I trust you to be gentle with me."

"You're a rogue to the core, Kiervan des Marceaux," she whispered, tracing the line of his stubbled jaw with her forefinger. "Is it wise to take such a dangerous man as a lover?"

"To my way of thinking," Kiervan countered, slipping his good arm about her waist and drawing her against him, "we're well suited to each other."

20

"What about Ashton?" she persisted, drawing her finger down the length of his throat. "And his men? You know they've got to be waiting at the base of this rock."

He pressed his lips against her ear and replied, "I'll not share you, Alanna. Ashton will have to find his own fairy woman."

She placed her hands flat against his chest and drew away just enough to look up into his magnificent eyes. "I mean that they're near, Kiervan. Just down the mountain . . . They could come up for us at any moment."

"We'll hear them long before they pose a true danger."

Her misgivings returned in a sudden, cooling wave. It would only be a matter of moments before Kiervan discovered the thinness of her bravado, how illusory was her confidence. And then he'd be angrier with her than he'd ever been and with more right than he'd ever had. With the last shred of her courage, she forced herself to speak, saying, "But, Kiervan, don't you think—"

"No," he answered, lowering his head to brush his lips over hers. "And for the time being, sweet Alanna, neither should you. Just feel."

Panicked words of refusal melted beneath the warmth and tenderness of his lips, then disappeared in the gentle onslaught of his possession. Alanna ordered herself to keep her thoughts about her. A part of her heard the command and struggled desperately to obey. Another part reveled in the feel of his lips against hers, found the taste of him wondrously, deliciously intoxicating, and demanded more. Yes, the rational part of her admitted as it slipped away, it felt right to be wrapped in the circle of his arm, felt right to trust him, to give herself to him. All was as it should be. In this frozen moment of time, she belonged to Kiervan and he to her.

As her reserve slipped away, she relaxed into the curve of Kiervan's arm and parted her lips in invitation. He moaned low and, laying deliberate, gentle claim to her mouth, drew her hard against the length of him. The warmth and power and completeness of his possession enveloped her and sent her spiraling into a world of potent sensation and untamed hunger. With every beat of their hearts, with every caress of Kiervan's lips, every unhurried stroke of his tongue, the glorious ache within her became more intense, more compelling.

She felt him move against her, felt him shift his stance as his lips left hers to lay a path of kisses across her cheek. Alanna tilted her head, opening for him those places she'd allowed no other man to explore. He caressed the hollow beneath her ear, nipping the tender flesh with his lips and drawing a long sigh from her before continuing his course down to her shoulder. Encountering the edge of her blouse, he murmured a soft curse and paused. She felt the movement of his injured arm in the same instant that he winced and swallowed back a low groan. Even as she straightened in the circle of his good arm, he tried again to reach for her shoulder with his other. Pain etched his brow and drew his lips thin and taut.

"Alanna, perhaps you were right," he offered, his voice rough and uneven, frustration and pain shimmering in his dark eyes. " 'Tis not the time for this. 'Tis not the time for us."

She felt the hardness and warmth of his chest, the steady hammering of his heart, against the palms of her hands. She nuzzled her face into the pillow of ebony curls lying between the open edges of his shirt front. His heart thundered against her cheek as he tucked her head beneath his chin.

"You're wrong, Kiervan," she murmured, breathing deep the scent of his skin: sun and wind and earth and male. "You once told me that you'd allow me to choose the time and place of my surrender. I've chosen now and here."

"Look at me," he commanded, easing away from her. When her gaze came up to meet his, he continued, "I can't use this arm properly. I can't do—"

"Then let me do," she interrupted with quiet resolve.

" 'Tis not the way I want it to be. You deserve to be loved in a feather bed and on soft sheets. You deserve a man who can at least take his boots off without your assistance."

"What about what I might want?" Alanna countered gently. "Doesn't that matter?"

"Can you honestly say that you don't want those things?"

If she had to lead, then so be it. The alternative was simply unacceptable. "Feather beds, sheets, and an uninjured man are only the icing, Kiervan," she said, gathering his shirt into her hands. As she deliberately pulled it free of his breeches, she added with a small, wicked smile, "I'm much more interested in the cake itself."

"Alanna!"

The breathless sound of his protest, his widened eyes, sent a wave of relief and amusement washing over her. Opening the front of his shirt, she declared, "I'm boldly going where I've never been before, Captain. If you'd like to offer some advice from time to time, please feel free. I'll gladly defer to your experience."

"Lord, you never cease to amaze me."

And you, me, Alanna silently replied, sliding her hands beneath the fabric of his shirt and trailing her fingers through the crisp dark curls on his chest, glorying in the warmth of him, in the burnished tint of his skin. Images of him climbing almost naked in a ship's rigging came to her, a vision of a man fiercely his own, unbound by either convention or fear. Her heart hammered and her blood warmed.

The mass of curls tapered to a dark line leading to the waistband of his leggings, and with a slow fingertip, she traced the line down across the sculptured muscles of his abdomen. At her touch he inhaled sharply and the lean ridges of his torso tightened. Beneath the straining fabric of his leggings, his need swelled and rose. She glanced up and found him standing with his eyes closed, his lips set in a grim line.

"Are you in pain, Kiervan?" she asked, studying his face as she rested her hands about the narrowness of his hips.

He opened his eyes and offered her a roguish smile. "God, yes, woman. From the moment I met you," he said, wrapping his good arm around her waist and drawing her against him once more. As his lips captured hers again, his hand slipped lower to cup her, to hold her closer to the pulsing urgency of his need.

The hungry weight within her grew more insistent, more savage. His lips parted at her demand and she felt the tremor which passed through him as she began her determined invasion. He moaned as she slid her hands up and across his chest, up to his shoulders and into the strands of silken hair that tumbled over the collar of his shirt. Threading her fingers through his hair, drawing it over his shoulders, Alanna held him gentle prisoner for her questing lips. The quiver of his longing, his fraying restraint, passed from his muscled flesh into hers, igniting a blaze within her that stole the breath from her lungs and weakened her knees.

Reluctantly she released him and stepped back, her breath ragged. A fire such as she'd never seen burned in the depths of his eyes, a yearning that penetrated her heart and soul. He said nothing, his chest rising and falling in the same fevered cadence as her own, and yet she heard his plea as clearly as though he'd whispered it against her ear.

She stepped from the circle of his arm. Her gaze never left his, never wavered, as she unlaced her midriff band and let it fall to the floor of the cave. She saw him labor to swallow, saw his breath catch in his chest as her skirt pooled about her feet. Alanna stepped out of her boots and kicked them aside. Then, one by one, her remaining petticoats fell away.

A twinge of shyness hit her as she stood before him, her blouse brushing against her bare thighs. "How am I doing so far, Captain? Any suggestions at this point?"

"If your intent is to torture me, you're succeeding well, my enchantress. And as for suggestions . . ."

She sucked in a hard breath and closed her eyes as he traced a line from her chin, down the length of her throat, and into the valley between her breasts. At his touch, a delicious jolt of pleasure shot through her, sending her senses reeling beyond recall. His lips caressed hers for a moment before following the path his finger had blazed only a heartbeat before. She felt the strength of his arm come about her, felt the power of his determination as he gently, slowly drew them to their knees amid the pile of her clothing. Like a feather, she floated down onto her back, riding the currents of Kiervan's masterful touch, trusting his arm to hold her.

Kiervan's lips seared a path between her breasts and then moved upward over the swell of one, teasing, laying a slow ring of fire about the hardened crest. Lost in the fiery tongues of flame dancing through her flesh and branding her soul, she twisted her fingers through his hair and, arching back, offered herself to him. Wordlessly pleading for him to ease the ache, she drew his mouth to her nipple.

His lips, hot and wet, closed about her peak and an intense jolt of pure, excruciating pleasure shot through her. She heard her gasp of surprise, felt Kiervan's lips curve against her skin as he smiled. And then another wave, even stronger than the first, swept through her, tearing a low moan from her throat. Another rode in its wake, its intensity almost too much to bear, its power frightening and consuming. The primitive hunger within her swelled and spiraled upward, bearing her, out of control, toward a dark oblivion. She felt her body arch upward and writhe with the effort to ride the crest, heard moaning words of denial escape her lips.

Vaguely she heard Kiervan's voice, the soft sounds of Gaelic, and then they were lost in another wave, a wave of such sweet, searing savagery that she had no choice but to ride it into a breathless realm of spinning, shattering stars.

She slowly fluttered back to earth, her breath as ragged as though she'd run a thousand miles, an odd sense of an incomplete peace centered low in her abdomen. Kiervan's lips brushed briefly against hers and then drew away. Alanna opened her eyes to find him lying on his side, his head propped in the palm of his hand as he studied her. She'd never seen him happier and yet she sensed that he was only waiting.

"There's a greater pleasure to be had, sweet Alanna," he whispered. "When you're ready."

"I don't think I could survive any more."

He smiled slowly. "Yes, you can. And you'll enjoy it even more than your first journey to heaven." Amusement twinkled in his eyes. "Didn't you like your first sojourn there?"

She drew the strands of his hair over his shoulder, reveling in the feel of them, in the way they lay so softly on his tanned skin. Surely God had never made a more handsome man than Kiervan des Marceaux. "And what makes you so sure it was my first time?" she teased.

He leaned down and placed a lingering kiss on the swell of her breast. Alanna closed her eyes and sighed as pleasure surged through her. "I'm not sure," he admitted, placing another kiss beside the first. "I'm only guessing. Am I right?"

"Yes," she whispered, awed by the way her body responded to the power of his touch, amazed by how quickly the sense of peace evaporated. She slipped her hand beneath his shirt and trailed her fingers down his muscled side. Then with deliberate slowness, she traced the angle of his hip, stopping only when she reached the buttons of his leggings.

"Would you mind too terribly much if I got rid of these things?" she asked, even as she set about the task. He froze and drew a deep breath through his teeth as she worked a button free. Alanna moved down and slipped the remaining button through its hole. As the flap of fabric fell forward across her hand and wrist, Kiervan ground out a low curse in Gaelic.

She glanced up to find his eyes squeezed tightly shut, his jaw clenched, his pulse hammering in his temples. In the face of his obvious agony, bravery threatened to desert her.

"Some instruction at this point would be appreciated," she whispered.

"Can't you hear it?" he asked, his voice tight and raw.

She focused her awareness on the stone enclosure about them. Nothing reached her ears except for the sound of their heartbeats, their ragged breathing. "No," she finally answered.

"Horses," he said, struggling to sit up. "Can you hear them now?"

From the distance came the unmistakable low rumble of hoofbeats. From below their haven came the equally certain sounds of men rousing themselves for battle. She stifled a sigh of frustration as she drew the front of her blouse closed and sat up.

"Would you care to place a bet as to who it might be?" Kiervan asked, climbing to his feet.

"Your uncle?" she supplied, accepting his hand and allowing him to help her to her feet.

"Hah," he scoffed, anger blazing in his eyes as he released her and turned away.

"Maybe it's Ashton."

"Ashton's already at the base of this rock, my sweet. The horses coming in are being ridden hard. 'Tis the sound of a charge we're hearing."

"Paddy O'Connell?"

"It occurs to me that Paddy lacks a bit for a spine. Whatever concerns he might have for our safe arrival are no doubt being shared over ales at Castle O'Connell," he commented while awkwardly fastening the buttons of his leggings. "My money says 'tis Richard St. John. The man's loyal to a fault." He glanced up at her long enough to offer her a mischievous grin and a wink. "In addition to that, I noticed early on that my First Officer seems to have a protective streak where you're concerned. It wouldn't surprise me in the least to discover that he's left the *Wind Racer* and come looking for us."

"He must be a religious sort of man," Alanna observed, bending down to retrieve one of her petticoats. "He can tell when a sin is about to be committed."

Kiervan whirled back and seized her arm. " 'Tis not a sin, Alanna," he growled, drawing her against him. "You must know that. What's between us is no sin. 'Tis as right as God's heaven and all the creatures of His Earth."

"I know," she whispered, offering him a weak smile. "I was trying to be brave about it all and put on a good face."

"You don't have to be brave for me," he whispered, placing a kiss at her temple. "All I'll ever ask of you is honesty."

"Then I'm mad and I'm frustrated and I want . . ." She forced herself to meet his gaze and finish softly, "And I want you."

"And have me you shall, sweet Alanna," he promised, his voice rough. "But not here, not now."

She nodded. She heard him swear as he slipped his arm around her. His kiss was hard and urgent, his possession of her scorching and hungry and deep. Alanna dropped the petticoat and clung to him, savoring the heady taste of his lips, her heart aching for more.

He set her from him with a suddenness that left her shaking. "Unless you set about dressing this instant, Mistress Chapman," he offered with an obviously forced buoyancy, "you'll suffer the acute embarrassment of being rescued naked and in my arms."

"Like that would be so terrible," she muttered, reaching down to gather up the discarded petticoat.

"Then imagine, if you will," he countered, "the horrified expressions on the faces of a shipload of sailors."

She laughed outright. Kiervan winked, then turned and walked toward the opening of their cavern, pulling the knife from his boot top as he went.

Alanna watched him for a long moment and then set about dressing herself, feeling suddenly alone and empty and trying desperately to ignore the inner voice that whispered she should be grateful that fate had just saved her from certain heartbreak.

21

Kiervan drew a deep breath of precious salt air as he guided his horse around the jetty of rocks and onto the open expanse of the beach. In the darker waters of the bay, only a short distance away, the *Wind Racer* lay at anchor. He reined in the animal, his gaze noting every detail of the ship's rakish silhouette framed by the morning sky and his heart filling with happiness.

"Isn't she beautiful?" he whispered. "Don't you think . . . ?"

He frowned as he realized that Alanna wasn't there, and chided himself for not being able to break the habit of talking as though she were constantly at his side. He glanced back over his shoulder at the rough path marking the way he had traveled that morning and wondered how far behind him rode the party Paddy led, wondered how Alanna fared and if she had missed his company as sorely as he had hers since their untimely rescue.

"God, but you are a temptation, woman," he murmured. "And what I wouldn't give to be unconcerned for your reputation."

Shaking his head, he turned his attention back to sea. A smile lifted the corners of his mouth as he watched a longboat pull away from the side of the *Wind Racer* and make for shore.

"But soon, sweet Alanna," he whispered. "Soon I'll bring you aboard my world and then what others might think and say won't matter."

• • •

I'm falling asleep on this stupid horse. I'm falling asleep. Oh, God! I am asleep! Alanna awoke with a start and, centering herself in the saddle, glanced about to see if anyone had noticed her near tumble. Paddy O'Connell edged his mount toward hers, a knowing smile on his face.

Oh, please God, she inwardly groaned. *Don't make me listen to the aren't-you-glad-we-happened-to-be-in-the-neighborhood? story again. I can't take it.*

" 'Tis a rough bit of time you've been through, colleen, to be sure. But 'twill be behind ye soon enough, I promise ye. Castletownbere is but a few hours ahead. 'Twill be a fine meal you'll eat this evenin' an' a soft feather bed you'll sleep in tonight."

Sleep in alone, Alanna silently amended. "I can't wait," she replied aloud, too mentally and emotionally exhausted to think of anything else to say.

" 'Tis a rare bit of fortune we had come that way in search of ye an' Kiervan, to be sure. 'Twas only our thought to ride out to meet ye when we left Castle O'Connell. Not far had we gotten, though, when we heard tales of ye grim meetin' with the bastard Ashton. Imagine, if ye will, our surprise when we discovered that we'd stumbled across the very place where he'd run ye an' Kiervan to ground. And a shame it was the spineless dog ran at the sight of us. There's nothin' more I'd like than to make him stare down the muzzle of me pistol."

Alanna nodded. "I don't know what we would have done if you hadn't come along when you did," she offered, hoping he didn't hear the regret tinting her response. "I guess that's what they mean when they talk about the luck of the Irish."

" 'Twould have been a cold night indeed you'd have spent in that cave," Paddy continued, his gaze sliding first over the assemblage of men riding around them and then into the hills beyond. Almost absently he added, " 'Twould have been doubly hard on Kiervan, what with his arm hurtin' so badly an' all. 'Tis truly an ill-tempered demon he's been since we plucked ye from Death's hand."

"Speaking of Kiervan's arm," Alanna ventured. "Is it healing all right? He's always had some reason to be gone from camp in the evenings, and he rides ahead all day to scout for us. I haven't had a chance to look at it myself."

"Aye, 'tis mendin' well, to be sure. But the captain's flesh appears to be healin' quicker than the wound to his patience. Sore he is still that we refused to sail out of Bantry harbor for Castletownbere."

"It would have been faster." Alanna shifted in her saddle and added, "Not to mention a lot more comfortable."

" 'Twould have meant leavin' valuable horses behind." He turned to smile at her broadly and wink. "An' to be honest, 'tis no more pitiful sight than an Irishman leanin' o'er the gun'les an' makin' an offerin' to the gods of the sea. 'Twas against our better judgment to sail east to County Wicklow to meet ye at the Carraig, colleen, an' 'twas a solemn vow we took when we set foot on land next that we'd not soon make a journey by boat again."

Alanna faced into the southern wind and shook out her hair. Somewhere, perhaps a mile or so away, lay Bantry Bay. She could already hear the gentle lulling sound of the waves, could taste the salty tang in the moist air blowing inland from it. How could the people of an island nation be such pathetic sailors? she wondered. Clearly some other national gene pool had dominated Kiervan.

He was riding down along the shore. No one had said anything when he'd ridden away after the noon meal, but she knew that that's where he'd gone. She'd seen the preoccupied look in his eyes as he left the camp. And just as certain as she was of his destination, she knew for what he searched: the *Wind Racer,* the part of him that would take him back to the well-ordered plans he'd laid for his life, back to the precious cargo of munitions that would buy him all the dreams of a poor bastard child.

"Colleen?"

Alanna blinked and looked down at the massive hand resting lightly on her forearm.

" 'Tis troubled thoughts yer harborin', I can tell," Paddy said gently when she looked up at him. His thick red brows knit in obvious concern, he went on, asking, "Is there a burden ye might be wantin' to lighten with sharin'? Me shoulders are broad, an' if need be, 'tis a silent tongue I can keep in me head."

"No, but thanks, Paddy," Alanna replied with a faint smile. "It's something I have to work through on my own. Sort of like settling the accounts, balancing the ledger, and trying to figure out if there's a net profit from the venture. Two heads would only make it that much harder to do."

He nodded, but the deepening furrow between his brows suggested he hadn't understood much of what she'd said.

It didn't really matter, she told herself, shifting slightly in the saddle to study the mountains rising from the land to the north. She'd lied anyway. The profit-loss statement had been figured the better part of a week ago, on the day after Paddy O'Connell's timely rescue. It hadn't taken second sight to recognize the sudden shift in Kiervan's attitude toward her. Nor had it demanded any great mental effort to understand the reasons for his decidedly cool and distant behavior. His task had been fulfilled. He'd delivered her safely into the hands of his kinsmen. Obviously, what there had been between the two of them was gone as far as Kiervan was concerned.

Accepting the reality of the situation was the hard part. Rationally, she knew that letting their relationship quietly die was for the best. Nothing would keep Kiervan from marrying Eglintine Terwilliger-Hampstead of Charleston, South Carolina. And nothing could justify her being Kiervan's lover until that day, could make it right to give her heart to a man who openly admitted that he wouldn't long cherish the gift.

That her heart couldn't see the plain truth was both frustrating and frightening. Its stubborn refusal to abandon hope made every waking hour pure agony. As if that torment weren't enough to bear, logic and reason had also failed to make any difference to that part of her driven by passion.

Dreams of Kiervan haunted her sleep, leaving her to face each dawn aching, tired, and lonely. And despite the litany of assurances she'd silently repeated for the last five days, accepting the inevitable wasn't getting any easier. Exhaustion had dulled the edges of the pain a bit, she decided. But if she ever got a good night's sleep . . . Alanna drew a deep breath and closed her eyes, admitting for the first time an even more disturbing possibility: the pain might very well be something she would have to endure for the rest of her life.

"Welcome back, Captain!"

Kiervan looked up the rope ladder, returned his smiling First Officer's salute, then climbed from the small craft and up the side of the *Wind Racer*. As he planted his feet on the deck, he cast a quick look about. "Good day, Mr. St. John," he said. "Is all as it should be aboard my vessel?"

"Shipshape and Bristol fashion, sir. Just as you left it."

"Then there's still brandy in my cabin stores," Kiervan replied, heading toward the stairs leading to his berth. Over his shoulder he called, "Come with me, Mr. St. John. We've much to discuss."

As they neared the door to Kiervan's cabin, the First Officer asked, "Would that happen to include the reasons for your somewhat disheveled appearance?"

Pausing with his hand on the latch, Kiervan turned back and cast the man a wholly feigned expression of surprise. "Am I disheveled?"

His friend pointedly surveyed the ragged sleeve of Kiervan's coat and shirt, the bandage sticking out from beneath, and the pale shadows of the bruises on his whiskered face. "Pardon my bluntness, Captain, but you appear to have been trampled . . . repeatedly . . . and by something quite large."

" 'Tis an adventure I'll not soon forget," Kiervan admitted, entering his cabin. He moved straight toward his desk, saying as he went, "Never let it be said that I haven't earned my profit on this voyage, Richard."

He opened the lower right drawer of his desk, removed the brandy decanter, and generously filled two glasses. "Shepherding Mistress Chapman across the south of Ireland has been . . ." Kiervan paused as he considered a variety of words, all of which utterly failed to describe the weeks just past.

"Exciting, sir?" Richard St. John offered with a poorly concealed smile.

Handing him a tumbler of spirits, Kiervan chuckled. "That's one word to describe it, Richard." Lifting his glass, he added, "I wouldn't have missed it for the world."

The man lifted his own glass. "To exciting adventures."

The dark liquid seared Kiervan's throat, and with a deep sigh, he savored the warmth growing in the pit of his stomach. "Lord, 'tis a wonderful feeling to be back where I belong, to feel the deck beneath my feet again."

"Had we reached the harbor at Bantry on schedule, you'd have felt it all the sooner."

Kiervan took a contemplative sip of his drink and met the First Officer's gaze squarely. "Never have I known you not to arrive in a port on time. What went awry?"

"A small matter of frayed rigging that parted when we took full sail. They were quickly repaired, but the effort set us behind enough so that you'd left Bantry before we arrived. I wasn't overly concerned, since I knew I'd find you along the bay itself sooner or later. And I'll save you the trouble of asking. No, the lines weren't frayed from neglect. They'd been partially cut. Either one of the locals slipped aboard to commit the deed—"

"Which is most unlikely."

"Agreed. I lean toward the belief that one of our own crew accepted a hefty purse in exchange for the act. I've been watching. The truth will out eventually."

"When you find him, give him a hefty heave-ho over the side. I don't care how far he has to swim."

"Consider the matter resolved. Now, shall I have water heated for bathing?"

"No," Kiervan replied, swirling the brandy about in the glass before taking another drink. "I'll not be staying aboard and I'd prefer that there be no indications of our meeting."

"I assume an explanation is forthcoming?"

"A few questions first, Richard." Sitting on the corner of his desk and staring into the contents of his glass, Kiervan continued, "You're a man with keen observations. Share with me your impressions of Paddy O'Connell."

"Ah. A puzzling man, our Mr. O'Connell. Protested mightily when we left you to pursue Mistress Chapman on your own, and yet, when we reached Castletownbere, his concern for your safety seemed to matter little to him for the next week. Then, as though suddenly stung by the bee of good judgment, he hastily gathered up a troupe of men and set out in search of you. His concerns appear to be rather erratic at best."

"And how would you characterize the motives for his concern?" Kiervan persisted.

Richard shrugged and took a sip of his own brandy before replying, "That I can't fathom, Captain. His initial reluctance to leave you to pursue the lady was easily understood, but there seems to be no rhyme or reason for his delay in setting out from Castletownbere. I've given the matter of his actions considerable thought and have yet to arrive at a conclusion which satisfies me. What is it about the man that troubles you?"

Kiervan frowned. "I can't rightly say, Richard. He came upon Alanna and myself when the situation had become particularly dangerous with regard to a certain Lord Ashton. In that respect his arrival was most timely. A part of me thinks it was perhaps too timely to have been a coincidence. I also can't help but wonder how he came to be at that particular place at that particular time. Alanna and I could have been anywhere in southern Ireland, and yet he knew to go there.

"Then there is this new matter of the sabotaged rigging to be considered." Kiervan shrugged. " 'Tis only questions and suspicions I have and nothing more."

"Your instincts have proven themselves to be trustworthy in the past, my friend. I think it would be ill advised to ignore them now."

Kiervan tossed the remaining brandy down his throat. "Reason or no, I don't trust Paddy O'Connell. Time will prove me either right or wrong. But until then, I dare not leave Alanna overly long in his care."

"Forgive the audacity, Kiervan," Richard St. John offered, both of his dark brows inching upward, "but it would appear to these eyes and ears that you've developed an attachment to the lady. Most uncharacteristic of you."

"Alanna's an unusual woman," he answered brusquely, suddenly unwilling to share anything more about his time with her than he already had.

Richard St. John cocked his head to the side to study him for a long moment, but when he spoke, he took their conversation in slightly different direction. "And you fear Mr. O'Connell may wish her harm?"

"Not direct harm or I'd have never left her at all. No, Paddy fears and respects her powers as a seer. He also wants very much for her to give a Druidic blessing to his rebellion."

Richard took another sip of his brandy and then nodded. "As do you. George Terwilliger-Hampstead was most precise as to the cost of his lovely daughter and your business partnership."

"Aye," Kiervan admitted slowly, his eyes narrowing as he remembered the rotund lines of his future father-in-law. A bitter taste gilded his stomach.

"But I'm not foolish enough to have put all my eggs in one basket, Richard," he went on, standing. "Do remember, another buyer can always be found in Le Havre should my kinsmen prove either faint of heart or weak of will. A favorable vision from Alanna would only conclude my business sooner."

He opened another drawer of his desk and removed an oilskin pouch. "No, Paddy wouldn't harm her directly," he reiterated, taking a brace of flintlock pistols from the bag and tucking them into the waistband of his leggings at the small of his back. "I'm more afraid that she may become a pawn in whatever game it is that Paddy plays. The harm would be indirect, if not accidental."

"What happened to the pistols you took with you when you went after Alanna?"

Kiervan tucked the small horn of powder and the pouch of shot inside his jacket as he replied, "Taken from me by one of Lord Ashton's churlish minions in the altercation. Certainly regrettable, but they're at least replaceable."

"Hardly," the other man scoffed. "Those pistols cost you a king's ransom to have made. That old Spanish silversmith is most likely dead by now. You'll never have the likes of them again. Unless, of course, you decide to give up the sea and seriously take up smithing yourself."

"Aye," Kiervan agreed, quirking a brow. "I'm not overly worried about them. The possession of them will mark a man for death. If I find them, I'll have them again. Of that you can be sure, Mr. St. John."

Kiervan pulled open the center drawer of his desk and removed the tiny silver earring he had taken from Alanna's lobe the first night he had known her. For a long moment, he studied it, remembering how he had wondered at the contrast between it and the diamond ring and the ruby brooch she wore. Now that he knew her better, the mystery no longer remained. The brooch was no doubt Maude's; the ring a gift from Bill Boyer. The earrings she had chosen for herself, and they suited her best. He put the small piece in the inner pocket of his coat and crossed the room to retrieve his smithing tools from the sea chest.

"There'll be a need for productive diversion once we reach the castle," he explained, catching sight of his First Officer's questioning expression.

"I gather that you're ready to depart."

Kiervan nodded as he moved toward the door. When the other man followed him, he explained, "I ride ahead of the others by some distance, and I'll reach Castletownbere long before they do. I'll have a word with Phelan before their arrival. Perhaps he can put my worries about Paddy to rest. Take the *Wind Racer* into Castletownbere harbor. Lay well offshore and be prepared to sail at a moment's notice."

While two of his crewmen rowed him back to the shore, Kiervan decided that he'd have felt much better about what lay ahead if Richard St. John hadn't looked so grim while watching him leave.

• • •

Worry still nagged at him when Kiervan strode from the great hall and the first of the riders clattered through the gate. Behind them rode Alanna, Paddy at her side. Frowning, Kiervan stepped to the side of the doors, folded his arms across his chest, and considered the drama about to unfold. Alanna seemed so small and frail on horseback, so tiny and feminine when surrounded by the hulking Irishmen. And Lord knew she looked as worse for the wear of their journey as he surely did. That much would be obvious to the chieftain of the O'Connells. What Phalen wouldn't see at first glance was the steely strength and determination beneath her battered surface.

Yes, Kiervan thought, Phelan wasn't the least prepared for the fiery-spirited woman who had just ridden through the gates of his castle, because Phelan O'Connell hadn't deigned to give his bastard nephew even the briefest of audiences. And because The O'Connell didn't countenance challenges of his office or his authority, Alanna would, within the first moments of their meeting, undoubtedly bear the brunt of the chieftain's anger.

There was but one thing he could do to prevent an ugly scene. Kiervan straightened and started down the steps. A few words of warning to Alanna would have to be sufficient.

He reached the cobblestone courtyard and caught Alanna's gaze as the horses neared the wide stone stairs leading up to the massive doors of the hall. She frowned at him in confusion. Then she quickly and resolutely looked away, lifting her chin and squaring her shoulders. Why had she been surprised by his attention? Why had she turned away from him?

He thought she'd understood why he'd kept a good distance from her since Paddy's untimely rescue. Lord, didn't she know that his blood heated every time he so much as looked at her? That thoughts of her made him ache with a need stronger than any he'd ever endured? Alanna was an intelligent woman, the most intelligent woman he'd ever encountered. Surely she could have surmised that staying well away from her the last six days had been the only way to preserve his control and her reputation.

Obviously she hadn't. Kiervan swore at his own presumption. Determined to help her from her horse and set matters right before another moment passed, he stepped forward to take the bridle of Alanna's mount. No sooner had his hand closed about the leather strap than a young redheaded man stood at Alanna's side, his arms raised, his hands open and waiting to slip about her waist.

"The task is mine, lad," Kiervan said quietly. "Stand aside."

Alanna met his gaze for a single second before she turned a smile on the boy, placed her hands on his shoulders, and leaned into his courtly embrace.

Out of the corner of her eye, Alanna saw Kiervan's face darken. Perhaps she'd gone too far in the rebuff. The jealousy game wasn't one at which she was particularly experienced. But her qualms vanished in the same instant. Kiervan had been jerking her chain for the last six days. A little taste of his own tactics would do him a world of good.

"I am Niall, the acolyte," the young man at her side said. "I am at your service and command, milady."

She smiled at him in what she hoped passed for gracious acceptance and let him lead her up the wide stone steps. She felt Kiervan's heated gaze as he fell into step behind her.

22

No sooner had she reached the top step than Paddy took her elbow. Guiding her through the massive doorway, he bent down to speak into her ear. "Phelan O'Connell's a hard man, colleen. Known for his bursts of temper, he is, and for bein' unwillin' to offer an apology, deserved though it may be. Those faults aside, ye needn't worry about breakin' the rules of his court. Few enough he has; I can't think at the moment of any I should be warnin' ye of. Watch the others an' follow their lead an' you'll do fine."

Alanna nodded, finding little reassurance in Paddy's words and already regretting her deliberate dismissal of Kiervan. The castle was huge and gray and cold looking. A shiver passed through her as her burly escort drew her into the dim foyer. Another rippled through her as he led her down the flagstones of the wide hall toward the man seated on the dais at the end of the mammoth room.

The small groups of people gathered in the hall turned as one to stare and then stepped aside to allow her passage. Halfway down the length of the room, her feet suddenly went cold and numb. At the three-quarters mark, panic set in, and it took all of her courage not to pull away from Paddy and run back the way she'd come.

What was it about this place? Certainly it had nothing to do with being indoors after traveling so long. She hadn't felt this kind of dark apprehension when Kiervan and she had gone into the tavern seeking horses and supplies. But then, she reasoned, the tavern had been much like those in the life she had left behind. And living on the road with Kiervan hadn't been so very much different from parts of her other existence. She'd been comfortable with the familiarity of being out-of-doors.

But this place was without parallel in her experience. It was purely medieval; the stark, irrefutable embodiment of a time she didn't know and to which she would never belong.

Paddy drew her to a halt before the man on the dais and inclined his head in the slightest of bows. "Phelan O'Connell, may I present Alanna Chapman, the Seer of the Find whom we have long awaited."

The man who surveyed her from the high-backed chair let not a hint of his thoughts show in his dark eyes. As Alanna met The O'Connell's scrutiny, she couldn't help but wonder what the man had thought when Kiervan had entered his hall for the first time. There would have been no mistaking their common blood. The most casual observer would have known the two to be related. Even as she stood there, she sensed that the people behind her were glancing between Kiervan and the chieftain of the O'Connells in open amazement.

"So you have come to begin the rebellion, have you?"

Alanna straightened and stepped from Paddy's protective grasp. "I didn't choose to come here," she said, facing Phelan O'Connell squarely. "It was Maude's wish that I represent her in this time and place, and so I'll do what I must before I return to my own. As to the rebellion, I have no stake in the matter either way. I don't know exactly how you expect me to help you resolve your dilemma, but I'll do my best."

"And how is it that Maude selected you to travel in her stead?"

"I was her niece." At her words a low murmur rippled out from around the dais. Alanna listened to it, trying to gauge the manner of the reaction even as she added, "Maude passed away several weeks ago, and I'm her only surviving relation."

"Then you are the spawn of Oonagh," the chieftain commented, his tone clearly derisive.

The hair on the back of her neck prickled and a defensive flame ignited in her soul. "Oonagh O'Sullivan was my mother."

He studied her for a long moment, then asked, "And your sire?"

"I don't know and, more importantly, I don't care." Again she heard the murmuring of the crowd at her back.

Phelan O'Connell leaned forward in his chair and considered her as though he were assessing the possible dangers posed by an alien life form. "Paddy tells me you hail from America as does Captain des Marceaux. Is this insolence a characteristic of all those reared in that far clime?"

From somewhere behind her, she sensed the warmth and power of Kiervan's attention. She could feel his amusement and something akin to pride. In that instant, the chill that had come over her as she'd entered the ancient castle evaporated. Alanna arched a brow. "If you're asking how we normally deal with insults, then yes, insolence is a national penchant."

His eyes narrowed. "I will not accept such arrogance from my subjects."

"I'm not your subject." The crowd resumed its muttering. She went on, undaunted. "Mr. O'Connell, if you can agree to treat me with respect, I'll agree to the same and we can pass the time we have to be together without a regrettable incident."

"Are you issuing me an edict, woman?" he growled, his eyes narrowing.

Lord, she silently mused. Even his expressions were the same as Kiervan's. "I'm simply suggesting," she replied, "what I consider a reasonable compromise. One that will benefit us both."

Phelan O'Connell leaned back in his chair with a small smile. He nodded after a moment. "Maude chose her successor well. And when your task among us has been completed, Seer? Where will you go?"

"If a way can be found to do it, I'd like to return to the time and place from whence I came." *Whence?* she silently repeated, her mind reeling back to consider the old-fashioned word. Where had that little linguistic jewel come from?

The sound of The O'Connell softly clearing his throat brought her back with a start to the reality of the great hall. "I can see that you are fatigued by your journey, Seer," he said. "Poor are my manners and lacking is my hospitality for having kept you in audience so long upon your arrival. Rooms have been prepared for you. You have but to make a request of your attendant and it shall be done."

He lifted his hand and motioned for a slim young woman with thick black braids and a freckled nose to come from the edge of the crowd, saying as she did, "This is Hisolda. She will see you to your apartment."

Alanna nodded to the girl and then to Phelan O'Connell. But even as the crowd melted back to allow for the passage of her and her appointed guide, the chieftain spoke again.

"And Seer . . ."

"Yes?" Alanna asked, half turning back.

"Know that I will hold you accountable for the outcomes of your vision. The fate of my clan shall be your fate as well. Should harm befall us . . ."

He left the threat unfinished and a cold, invisible hand squeezed her heart. Alanna swallowed. Attempts to think of a pithy rejoinder or words of reassurance faltered as she fought to control the foreboding washing through her.

"She can't control her visions, Phelan. No more than any of us can control the nature of our dreams," Kiervan said, stepping forward. Alanna turned toward him, finding a wondrous comfort and warmth in the sureness of his stance, in the broadness of his shoulders and the hard expression in his eyes. He didn't look at her, but instead kept his attention focused solely on his uncle. "Alanna merely sees events which will occur. There is naught she can do to alter them. She can't be held accountable for the decisions of Fate."

"She will be, Captain des Marceaux. And lest your own end be bound to hers, you will not again challenge my pronouncements."

Alanna resolutely stepped before Kiervan, effectively placing herself between the two men. She met Kiervan's steely gaze and spoke gently but in a voice that clearly carried through the hushed hall. "I couldn't ask for a more able or dedicated champion, Kiervan. But you've seen me through the journey and your task is done. There's no reason for you to risk yourself or your dreams for me. Our lives aren't bound, Kiervan. We've always known that we have separate paths to follow."

"I won't abandon you, Alanna," he replied quietly, his dark gaze holding hers with an intensity that caught her breath and warmed her blood.

She laid her hand on the lapel of his tattered blue jacket and whispered, "Whatever happens to me, happens to me. There's nothing you can do to change it, and it's pointless for you to try. I have to handle this on my own."

His expression hardened and though his voice came low, it came sternly as well. "I won't argue with you, woman. I'll stand as your protector whether you like it or not. The discussion is over."

Alanna let her hand fall back to her side and stepped away from him. "Then you're a damn fool, Kiervan des Marceaux."

He too stepped back. Then he bowed, sweeping his arm before him in that gesture of open mockery that had so infuriated her the night she'd first met him. Alanna balled her hands into fists and fought back the urge to let him have a good one. When the initial surge of anger passed, a less violent alternative came to her mind.

Turning, she addressed the chieftain. "Mr. O'Connell," she began, "Your nephew has seen me across Ireland, and, I might add, at no small cost to his own comfort and safety. His obligations are done. It would be unconscionable to hold him responsible for my actions from here on out. I ask that you—"

"It was Captain des Marceaux's appearance among us that prompted the necessity of yours, Seer," the older man interrupted, his tone flinty, his dark eyes cold and as hard as his voice. "He will indeed be held to account for the outcome of the affair. And I will counsel you to not again refer to him as my *nephew*. The truth of his claim of relationship has not been established to my satisfaction."

"Then you're a blind man."

A gasp rose from the crowd. Alanna ignored the inner voice that suggested she'd gone too far, pushed too soon. She studied the blazing light in Phelan O'Connell's eyes for half a dozen heartbeats, then, whirling about, met Hisolda's wide-eyed stare and said, "I'd appreciate it if you'd be so kind as to point the way to my room. I've had about all I can stand of testosterone-driven stupidity."

Alanna sat on the edge of the feather mattress and watched the water bearers depart with their buckets. The fire crackled softly in the hearth and an inviting steam rose from the long copper tub as Hisolda closed the door after them.

"All is ready, mistress," the young woman said, gliding back across the room toward her. "We have but to remove your clothing and you shall be in your bath."

"We?" Alanna repeated, arching her brows. Surely this girl didn't intend to help her?

"I will assist you in disrobing."

Yeah, she did intend. Alanna chuckled and shook her head. "I don't think so, Hisolda. I can manage it on my own. But thank you anyway."

"As you wish," the girl replied, opening the doors of the armoire. She removed several tems and draped them over the back of a nearby chair. Then, stepping back, she took up a place near the cheery hearth and clasped her hands in front of her as though preparing to watch and wait.

Alanna considered her, the clothing, the bathtub, and the entire situation for a long moment. "I can take a bath and get dressed again without help," she finally said, sliding off the bed and onto her feet. "How about if you take a break and come back later?"

" 'Take a break'? I'm afraid I don't understand."

"Don't you have something else to do?" Alanna pressed. "You know, eat dinner or something? Talk with some of your friends? Surely you have a boyfriend waiting for you?"

A distressed expression passed briefly over the girl's features. "I am charged with caring for your needs. If The O'Connell discovered that I'd left you on your own, there would be a terrible punishment."

Alanna chewed on the inside of her lip as she considered other options. Defying Kiervan's uncle so soon after having insulted him probably wasn't the best of them, she decided. "Okay," she offered a moment later. "How about if you just went outside into the hallway and waited till I called you? Would that get you into trouble?"

Hisolda's dark eyes widened and darted to the door. Her voice was soft and hesitant when she replied, "It is customary for the lady-in-waiting to assist with her mistress's bath."

Alanna smiled and shook her head. "Not where I come from, Hisolda. I don't mean to be a difficult guest, but no one's bathed me since I was a baby and I'm not about to change that long-standing tradition for you or anybody else. This part isn't a matter open to negotiation. Sorry."

The young woman shifted her weight from foot to foot and glanced nervously between the bathtub and the door before finally saying, "I suppose . . ."

"Good deal," Alanna said on a sigh of relief as she moved toward the door.

As Hisolda crossed the threshold, she paused, turned back, and asked, "Will you be going down to the great hall to sup or shall I have your evening meal brought up from the kitchen?"

The very thought of going back into the presence of Phelan O'Connell sent a shiver down Alanna's spine. "Give me about thirty minutes and then have supper brought here," she replied, gently edging the door closed.

Alanna slipped down in the tub until the hot water came to her chin. What on earth had come over her down in the great hall? The horrible cold that had settled on her had been bad enough to deal with, as had the incredible tension flowing just beneath the surface of things, but calling the clan chieftain a blind man? She must have a death wish.

And why in the name of all the saints had he let her sweep out of the hall and up the stairs like some pompous queen? He hadn't made even the smallest attempt to stop her.

With a long sigh, she closed her eyes. "There's gotta be a payback," she muttered beneath her breath. "And it's gonna be a doozy. A real doozy."

And Kiervan's expression . . . The memory of the troubled look on his face bothered her even more than the certainty of Phelan's retribution. He hadn't wanted her to leave the hall. It had been obvious in the way he'd looked at her, the way his hand had moved slightly from his side as though he'd wanted to reach out and physically hold her there.

Though he'd resisted the urge, she'd nevertheless felt him follow her progress up the stairs, and had felt his regret when she passed around the corner and out of his sight. His regret had been no deeper, no sadder than her own at walking away. Alanna sat up and shook her head to banish the image and the worries it brought with it.

Maude wouldn't have sent her to Phelan if she'd thought the man would do her harm, Alanna reminded herself as she worked soap into her hair. There was nothing to be done but trust it all to turn out as it should.

But had Maude known about Kiervan? she wondered suddenly. Would Maude have cared what happened to him? Alanna slipped beneath the surface of the water and rinsed the lather from her head, deciding as she did that Maude had known all along that Kiervan would be a part of her life in this world. In the dream, Maude had cast her spell about him and entrusted her niece to his keeping. And she'd sent the dream to Kiervan too, so surely she wanted him to know what role he'd been assigned in this little Irish drama. Yes, everything would be all right in the end, Alanna decided. It had to be.

Sitting up again, she felt about for the sheet to rub the water from her eyes. It came into her hand as though someone were—

"Kiervan," she called, smiling as she wiped the linen towel across her eyes. But when she opened them she found an old man sitting in the chair next to the tub. Startled, she jerked the towel over the top of the long copper basin to shield herself.

"I regret that I am not Kiervan," he said with a chagrined smile that deepened the wrinkles of his weathered face. Amusement brightened his clear blue eyes. He added, "I do believe he would be far more welcome at your bath than I am wont to be."

Alanna took a deep breath and silently resolved to handle the situation with all the dignity she could muster. "Who are you? And what are you doing in here?"

"I am Owrd. I am your grandfather."

Alanna sat bolt upright, her eyes wide. A half a second later, she snatched a handful of the sheet and drew it against her pounding chest. "My what?"

His eyes sad, he replied, "Maude and Oonagh were my daughters."

Feeling as though she were teetering on the edge of a yawning precipice, Alanna swallowed back her fear and met his scrutiny. "Then we have to talk."

He rested his elbows on the arms of the chair, then laced his fingers across his frail chest. "Aye, child," he agreed, nodding his white-maned head. "That we shall. There is much I must tell you of your past and even more that I must teach you if you are to ably stand in Maude's stead. And there is little time remaining to accomplish the many tasks awaiting us."

Alanna nodded with enthusiasm, suddenly anxious to begin making the discoveries this man promised. "Okay. Turn your back and let me climb out of this tub. I'm a much better listener when I'm not naked."

Her grandfather chuckled as he slowly pushed himself up from the chair. Straight backed and steady, he walked toward the window as he added, "Your mother was a painfully shy and modest creature. Even as a babe, she disliked being without garments."

Alanna quickly rubbed the linen sheet over her limbs and stepped from the tub. "I'm not shy," she remarked, grabbing the chemise Hisolda had lain out for her and yanking it over her head. "And no one's ever accused me of being a prude."

"You have inherited the best of both my daughters: Maude's boldness tempered by your mother's gentility. You favor your father in appearance though."

With what looked to be a robe in her hand, she whirled about to stare at Owrd's back. "You know who my father is?"

He continued to study the courtyard below. "Was. Like my daughters, he too has departed this realm. But unlike Maude and Oonagh, his soul is surely rotting in the deepest, foulest depths of hell."

"Geez." Alanna shoved her arms into the sleeves of the robe, then tied the silken belt about her waist. "Please tell me that I don't favor him in that regard."

"You do not," he replied. "Of that I am certain. That particular legacy was bequeathed in its entirety to your brother."

For a second she thought the floor might drop from beneath her feet. She blinked and, desperately seeking to anchor herself in the moment, moved to the dressing table. Picking up the brush, she repeated with what she hoped sounded like only polite interest, "Brother?"

"Aye. Neither Maude nor Oonagh mentioned this to you?"

Tugging the bristles through the wet tangles of her hair seemed to help. The floor definitely felt more solid. "I didn't even know they came from across time until I put things together after I arrived here. When I first went to live with Maude, she told me she and my mother had come to America together. I didn't realize that she meant America in the twentieth century."

For a long time, Owrd said nothing, and Alanna turned to study him as she absently brushed her hair. Though he kept his attention fixed on the world beyond her room, he grasped the stone lintel of window with a thin, blue-veined hand. Finally he asked, "Did Maude tell you why the journey was necessary?"

"No. Maude was always kinda cryptic about the family

background. She said I'd know when the time was right and I needed to know. Would that by any chance be now?"

"Are you properly attired, child?" Owrd released his grip on the stone and straightened. "I would prefer to tell you of your father's deeds and confess to my own failings while facing you."

"I guess." Alanna placed the brush back on the table and flipped her hair behind her shoulders. "I'm decent by the standards of my own time."

He turned to face her, and nodded in approval. When he moved to sit again in the chair, Alanna climbed onto the bed and settled herself comfortably. With her legs crossed, her elbows on her knees, and her chin resting on laced fingers, she met her grandfather's calm eyes. "Whenever you're ready, sir."

Without a second's hesitation, he began, his voice strong and evenly controlled. "My daughters were born into a time of great upheaval and sorrow in Ireland. The English preyed upon our people with cruel and heartless joy. Maude was the eldest and possessed both striking beauty and the gifts of a true seer. Oonagh was quiet and, though pretty, content to live in the shadow of her sister."

He lifted his chin. "But it was Oonagh who caught the rapacious eye of an English lord, and when she refused his attentions, he took her as his hostage. Maude came to me, offering to make magic so that her sister might be spared." Tears pooled in his blue eyes, and his voice cracked as he finished, "But I could not accept her offer."

"You knew how it was supposed to happen, didn't you?" Alanna supplied softly, already knowing the truth of it but wanting to somehow ease the old man's burden. "You had a vision and knew that Oonagh was destined to be with the lord."

"Aye, child." His tears dried, and when he spoke again, the light in his eyes came from a distant place. "My heart died a thousand times in consigning Oonagh to the end decreed by the Fates. Eventually Oonagh bore a child, a daughter. The lord tore the infant from her arms and cast it from the window before Oonagh's eyes. The second child she bore him was a son and so was permitted to live. When she conceived a third child, she feared that it might be another daughter. She first thought of throwing herself from the tower in which she had spent four years of her life. In the end she secretly sent word to Maude. Together they planned and finally, with my knowledge and consent, my daughters fled across time to protect the unborn child."

Alanna stared at him numbed by sadness. "To protect me," she whispered.

"Aye," he agreed, his voice matching hers. "And when I watched them depart, I feared that I would not see them on this Earth again, that I would not see them until we are reunited in God's heaven." He closed his eyes and his lips thinned into a line which spoke of pain and loss.

After a long moment, Alanna quietly intruded on his memories. "Did you know I would eventually come to you, Owrd?"

He opened his eyes and she saw that the light within them had grown brighter, saw that the focus of his vision had returned to the present and her. "Yes," he replied with a gentle smile. "That I have known for some time."

Determined to keep him from slipping back into his memories of the past, she deliberately turned their conversation toward the future. "And do you know my fate? Will I be able to get back to my own time and place?"

"The pages of your life have been written, Alanna, my child. While I have not seen the complete course of your destiny, you have no choice but to take the journey. But this is all as it should properly be. There is great disadvantage in knowing the outcome of one's life. Knowing the end cheats you of the glories and lessons to be learned along the way. Your mind's eye must always be on the present if there is to be any joy in the days allotted to you."

It wasn't the answer she'd wanted to hear, but Alanna nodded, knowing in her heart that he spoke the truth. "So . . ." she began, drawing a deep breath. "Who was my father?"

Owrd looked back to the window and the world beyond it. "The lord of Canraterian. Sir Geoffrey Ashton."

She bolted forward on the bed. On her hands and knees, she met her grandfather's steady gaze from across the room. "Then Graeme Ashton is . . ."

The corners of his mouth curved slightly downward. "Aye, your brother" Owrd confirmed. "You have heard of him, no doubt."

Sitting back down and recrossing her legs, Alanna nodded. "Oh, yeah. We've met. And only Kiervan's timely arrival prevented what would have been the worst possible sin."

"Ah, your Captain des Marceaux is an interesting man."

"He's not mine," she instantly corrected. She added in a deliberately dismissive, nonchalant tone, "We shared an adventure or two along the way, but our paths have gone in different directions now."

Owrd shrugged. "As you say, granddaughter." A knock on the door and Hisolda's quiet announcement ended whatever he might have been about to add.

He rose to his feet, bowed slightly in her direction, and started toward the door. "Your evening repast has arrived. I will leave you to enjoy it in peace. Sleep well, my child. In the morning I will return to you and we will begin your lessons in earnest."

Alanna clambered off the bed. "Wait! I have a couple of questions, Grandfather," She waited until he turned back to her. "Will I be able to use the spell Maude gave me to travel back across time to where I belong?"

"It very much depends on the nature of the spell Maude used to bring you here."

Alanna nodded thoughtfully.

"You will need your rest for the work ahead," he added. "Good night, granddaughter."

The cold that had gripped her the moment she'd entered the castle returned after Owrd left her room. Alanna paced past the remnants of her meal for the hundredth time and wished she possessed the peace of mind required to have an appetite. At the thought, her stomach coiled itself into a tighter knot. Rubbing her fingers over her temples and swearing under her breath, Alanna crossed the room to stare out the window at the stars blanketing the night sky. Even as she traced the patterns of familiar constellations, she was filled with a dreadful certainty. Something bad, very bad, was going to happen within the walls around her.

She shook her head and looked about for anything that might distract her. The courtyard lay some twenty feet beneath her window, bathed in the bright light of the midnight moon. Along the edges, small thatched buildings sat in their own deep shadows, silent and empty. No, she instantly amended. Not completely empty. Inside one of them, embers glowed and pulsed with brilliant red flame. Though she couldn't see him, she sensed that Kiervan stood in the darkest of the shadows of that small building and watched her.

As though her thoughts had bidden him, he stepped into the moonlight. Her heart twisted with yearning and whispered his name in a gentle siren's call. She gazed down at him, noting every detail: how he'd bathed and changed his clothes, how he wore a short, dark leather-looking apron, how the moonlight encircled his head with a halo as dark as a raven's wing. He stood with his arms crossed over the broad expanse of his chest and his legs braced, the muscles of his thighs taut and ridged and evident beneath the form-fitting breeches.

"Oh, Kiervan," she whispered, "please don't do this to me. We have no future. Not together."

Looking up, he spied her and raised his hand in greeting, his palm open and toward her as though he could touch her from the distance.

With all the strength of will she possessed, Alanna closed her eyes and stepped back from the window. She blew out the candle and, in the darkness, with fingers still wet with her tears, snuffed out the ember which clung stubbornly to the wick.

23

A lanna followed the white-robed figures of her grandfather and Niall into the clearing just as the sun peeked over the horizon. If Owrd intended to keep this kind of schedule, she groused, she'd be dead of exhaustion long before Beltane rolled around. Two weeks. The time span loomed before her like a dark pit.

"You must practice patience, Alanna. Magic cannot be worked by those whose spirit is demanding," her grandfather said without looking back at her.

She wanted to tell him that she had heard it before, that she hadn't lived with Maude without having been introduced to the rudiments of magic making . . . and failing miserably at them. Instead she drew a slow breath and replied, "I'm trying, Owrd. I really am."

He stopped, turned, and studied her, his expression solemn and his blue-eyed gaze piercing. Niall stood at his side and silently examined the ground between his own feet while fingering the strap of the large white leather bag hanging from his shoulder.

"How much did Maude teach you, child?" Owrd finally asked, his scrutiny no less intense than moments before.

Alanna decided that she had nothing to lose by telling the truth. "Owrd," she began, "Maude should have gotten saint points for the attempt. She never gave up, but . . ." She sighed before continuing. "There's a big difference between what you know up here," she said, tapping her finger against her temple, "and what you feel inside. Know what I mean?"

Owrd nodded slowly, eyes thoughtful. "Then we will start at the very beginning so that you may search for the feeling of truth in the Wittan way. But our beginning will take a few minutes. Niall and I must bring you into the protection and power of our magical place before we may properly begin."

Alanna said nothing, knowing what was to come. She'd done the ritual with Maude a thousand times. She watched in silence as Niall brought the bag off his shoulder and positioned it in his hands so that Owrd could easily reach inside and bring forth the items as he needed.

Breathing deeply and slowly, Owrd offered a small piece of limestone to the north and then bent to reverently place it in the grass. Then he offered a feather to the east before settling it no more than six inches from the rock. He poured water from a skin pouch into a small bowl, offered it to the west, and then placed it just so in relation to the other objects. From the bag he next drew a cow's curved horn and a small leather-wrapped bundle tied with a narrow thong. Alanna watched as he lifted both objects to the south and then turned to hand the cow's horn to Niall.

And the fire, Alanna silently intoned while her grandfather carefully removed the twigs and wood shavings from the bundle and began to lay the foundation for the fourth element. From the horn he slowly rolled a coal into the waiting tinder—a coal, Alanna decided, no doubt taken from one of the many hearths at the Castle O'Connell.

Owrd shot her a reproachful look and she dutifully lifted her chin and banished thoughts of all other places but this spot in the woods.

With his right hand hovering a mere inch or so over the chunk of limestone, Owrd said in clear, resonate tones, "I call upon the powers of the earth to grant firmness and stability to the foundation." He moved his hand to the feather. "I call upon the powers of the air to grant wisdom and the freedom of spirits." With his hand over the small blaze, he said, "I call upon the powers of fire to purify and send forth the power of magic." Alanna expelled a long breath as her grandfather placed his hand over the bowl of water and intoned, "I call upon the powers of water to grant vision and peace to those who walk in the way of Witta."

Owrd rose to his feet and lifted both hands upward. "From the earth, plant, soil, and stone; from the touch of wind and dome of sky; from the crackling warmth of flame's bright cone; from the gentle waters of whispered sighs, I call upon the elemental powers that be to blend and grant their gifts to me. Come now from the direction of your power. Join to protect those who wait in this hour."

Alanna joined Owrd and Niall as they offered the traditional closing to the ritual. "It is done. Thanks be to Lugh."

Owrd turned to her and lifted a bushy white eyebrow as he asked quietly, "And what did you notice in the ritual, granddaughter?"

"They weren't the same words Maude always used."

Owrd nodded and then seated himself cross-legged in the grass. He motioned for Alanna and Niall to do the same even as he said, "It is not the words themselves that are important, but rather the intent of the heart when they are offered to the powers of our Mother. The words merely serve to focus our thoughts in one place and time, to ground us so we may feel the power that flows into and through all of the Mother's creation. The words of magic are always changing and this is as it should be. For magic is nothing unless it is borne on the power that gives all things life, gives all things form and meaning, changes all things from day to day, season to season, year to year."

May the Force be with you. Alanna grimaced. How odd that she'd never made that connection while studying magic with Maude. She glanced between Owrd and Niall. Yeah, if she squinted she could believe that she sat in a clearing with Obi-Wan Kenobi and an unusually quiet version of Luke Skywalker.

"You don't believe in the power of magic, do you, Alanna?"

Her grandfather's words were gently spoken, but they

pulled at her thoughts with a sharp tug. She smiled and shrugged. "Maybe it would help if I put my hair up in honey buns on either side of my head."

Owrd studied her quizzically for several moments, and Alanna sensed that he considered his possible courses. "You bear irreverence as a shield," he finally said. "You do not need the protection, child. There is nothing in magic that will harm you. Accepting the gifts of the earth can only make your spirit stronger."

Maude had told her the same thing too many times to count. Alanna looked out toward the trees that ringed the clearing and replied, "Maybe I just don't have the knack for tapping the . . . Force."

"No. You possess true gifts if only you would allow yourself to trust that which is in you."

Her gaze came back to meet his, and she offered him an apologetic smile before she gave him the unvarnished truth. "I've been down this road with Maude. No matter how hard I try, I can't do it. I'm afraid you're wasting your time trying to teach me."

She knew the instant the words left her mouth that they'd been the wrong ones. Owrd squared his shoulders.

"Then we will go down the road yet again," he said firmly, his manner and tone clearly conveying the shift in his approach to her instruction. "What are the four requirements of magic?"

Alanna mentally geared herself to run through the paces. "A true need, a clear vision, the proper spell, and the ability to charge objects and send your magic to its purpose."

His gaze bored into hers. "Regarding a true need, may it properly be concerning others?"

"Only with their consent and only to achieve a positive end," Alanna replied with the precision of practice. "The Threefold Rule applies to all magic: That which you send out returns to you times three—whether good or bad."

"And the vision? What shapes the images within it?"

"Properly it should be what you hope to achieve with your magic; a detailed image of the results of positive change."

Her grandfather lifted his brow. "Spells?"

"Spells should be done in conjunction with the phases of the moon, the time of day, and the season of the year that support the general purpose of your need and vision. They should be conducted with the appropriate tools, tools that draw and use the powers of the various elements into whose realm you are entrusting the magic." *God,* she silently prayed, *please keep him from asking what phase the moon is in or I'm in big trouble.*

"Very good," Owrd commented with a satisfied nod. "And the ability to charge and send forth your magic?"

Alanna answered, "It comes from two sources: the earth itself and from within you."

"Your left hand, what is its power?"

"It draws things to you," she supplied, lifting her left hand. "It's the receptive hand, the one through which you bring the earth's power into you to enhance what's already there."

"And your right?"

Alanna held up her other hand. "It sends magic outward. It's the hand of projection."

Owrd leaned back slightly, almost as though he wanted to get a better view of her. "And how do you go about twining the powers you draw into you with those always within?"

"You concentrate on the need and the vision until you feel your muscles tighten and begin to tremble." Alanna lifted both brows and fixed her grandfather with another apologetic look before she added, "And then when you don't think you can endure it another second, theoretically, you physically push the energy out through the fingertips of your right hand, sending it toward your goal."

"Theoretically?"

She smiled weakly. "Yeah, well, that's the part I've always had problems with. I can twine and tremble with the best of them, but letting it go—that's another matter."

A patient, almost secretive smile tickled the corners of her grandfather's mouth. "You have sent it outward at least once," he said, "or you would not have crossed through the portals of time."

Alanna laughed quietly and shook her head. Her hands adding emphasis to her words, she countered, "C'mon, Owrd. My coming across time was one of the greatest flukes in the history of magic. I had no need to time travel. I had no vision of zipping back almost two centuries. The first two requirements for magic weren't there. As for the spell, I have no idea what Maude's words were; they were in Gaelic. As for the charging . . ."

The rest of the denial died on her tongue as she remembered standing on the edge of the Carraig and feeling the power of the earth rising through the soles of her shoes and flooding her body; remembered feeling the rightness of the wind as it whipped through her hair.

"Okay," she said somewhat sheepishly, "now that I think about it, I might have felt the power of the earth and the wind." Before Owrd could use the admission to his advantage, she quickly added, "But that alone wouldn't have been enough. I certainly didn't have a need or a vision of the end result."

Owrd tilted his head to the side to study her. The secretive smile remained on his lips when he asked, "For what purpose did you enter the Carraig?"

This one was easy, a nonthreat. "To carry out Maude's wishes," Alanna supplied, "and scatter her ashes to the wind in the manner she wanted it done."

"And did you have a need to do this?" Owrd asked, his brow rising a bare notch. "Did you have a clear vision of carrying out her request?"

"Yes," Alanna answered slowly, remembering the determination she had taken with her into the stone circle. With the memories came an understanding, silent and breathtaking.

"But if your line of reasoning is correct," she whispered, looking at her grandfather in hopeful disbelief, "then it would mean that my being here is no accident, that Maude wanted me to cross. That the spell Maude gave me wasn't for time traveling but for having her will brought into being.

And that means that the spell that brought me here may not be the one that can take me home."

Niall remained as still and mute as a fence post as Owrd leaned over to place his hand on her forearm. "You have great powers within you, Alanna," he said gently, reassuringly. "Maude apparently knew this."

Alanna shook her head skeptically. "But what good are any powers at all if you can't control them? I'm damn lucky I didn't transport myself into the den with Daniel and the lions." Her first meeting with Kiervan came flashing back to her; the warrior standing over her with a sword in his hands and a murderous look in his eyes.

"Had you thought of it, you probably would have done something of the sort," Owrd offered softly, patting her arm. He settled himself squarely and then continued, saying, "The most powerful of all magic comes from entrusting yourself to the forces flowing from the elements. They possess a wisdom humans can never attain. To impose our will on the intent of Nature is to limit Her power and deny ourselves all that She can offer. It is always the better course to ask for a need to be fulfilled and then accept what is given; to trust that the fruits of your magic are those that are best for you."

"Trust . . ." Alanna whispered disdainfully to herself.

"Ah," Owrd retorted, nodding his head. "And at last we come to that which prevents you from developing your power. You do not consciously choose to trust, do you, granddaughter? You trust only when you are denied the chance to think, to consider. Am I correct?"

Alanna's pulse quickened as other images flashed before her, images of the moments she'd shared with Kiervan in the dark room off the pub. She had been forced to trust him then. . . . Her senses reeled before the power of the heady memory.

"And I will give you another truth to ponder, Alanna. You cannot bring yourself to release your power, because you fear what it will return to you."

This had gone far enough. Owrd had pressed too many sensitive buttons already. "No way," Alanna quickly asserted with a wholly feigned smile of confidence. "Why should I fear what comes back according to the Threefold Rule? I've never attempted to send out meanness of any sort."

He spoke as quietly and gently as he had before, but Alanna sensed his growing frustration when he countered, "I have no doubt as to the pureness of your needs and visions, granddaughter. But all things change us, even goodness. To send out your power would be to open yourself to its return and thus to its ability to challenge and change you."

"That's no big deal," she protested with a bright smile belying the pounding of her heart. "Really. I've gone through a lot of changes in my life. I'm not afraid of it. For heavens sakes, look at my present situation. I've traveled through time to find myself in another century and a foreign country. And all things considered, I think I'm doing a damn good job of coping with some pretty radical changes."

"I see it differently, granddaughter," he replied, shaking his head, the patience seeping from his voice. "I see a young woman whose circumstances have indeed changed but who faces them with what I suspect to be the same armor she has used to protect herself in the past. You wield irreverence and bluster with determined resolve in an effort to keep truths at safe distances."

She opened her mouth, preparing to defend herself, but Owrd quickly raised his hand and said, "No, Alanna. Allow me to finish." His gaze held hers. "You wrap your feelings and instincts with rational thought in order to smother them. And those experiences which *have* penetrated your defenses, you pretend that they haven't touched you; you deny your wounds and continue fighting as you always have. You are much like the professional soldier. You know how to battle for your life, but the hours and days between those contests are shadowed with a knowledge you cannot bring yourself to admit—the knowledge that while you are willing to battle bravely for its continuance, you have no life truly worth living."

The words stung. And she'd die before she admitted to anyone but herself that they were basically true. Such nice little inner truths didn't count for much when it came to staying alive. She consciously withdrew behind a mask of cool detachment and then asked, "Are we about done with today's lesson in the gentle art of magic, Grandfather?"

"No," he answered kindly, apparently not the least perturbed by her poor attitude. "I will close our circle here and then you will come with me."

Alanna said nothing as she rose to her feet. She didn't even pay much attention as Owrd thanked the spirits for their attendance and gathered up the tools of his magic. Stealing a glance at the redheaded Niall was as close as she came to admitting that she didn't stand alone in the meadow. His gaze touched hers briefly and in it she could plainly see sympathy and understanding.

As Owrd strode wordlessly across the field and toward the tree line to the east, Niall fell into step beside her. For the better part of a hundred paces, they continued together without speaking. Finally, Alanna couldn't stand the silence another moment and broke it, saying, "You don't talk much, do you?"

"I'm only an apprentice," Niall answered, his voice so quiet that Alanna had to move closer to catch his words. "It is not my place to instruct you."

"So tell me, Niall . . ." She nodded toward the old man striding ahead of them. "Is he about ready to pin my ears back?"

Niall grinned at her, his face brightening until his coppery freckles practically glowed. "No, milady." He sobered slightly to add, "But he knows that there is very little time to train you. And he's frustrated by your stubbornness."

She affected her best Miss Piggy impersonation. *"Moi?* Stubborn?" When Niall rolled his eyes skyward, she chuckled and winked at him. "Well, okay, Niall. Maybe just a little." Geez. She hadn't had any idea of just how badly Owrd had unbalanced her until she'd managed to get her feet back under her.

They entered the shadows of the trees as Niall spoke again. "May I ask you a question?"

"Sure," she answered, ducking beneath a limb and following in Owrd's path. "As long as you understand that I reserve the right not to answer it."

"Everyone says that you possess the power of divination," he offered, falling in behind her. "Is that true?"

"Do you mean like the ability to see the future?" At his nod, she continued, "Well, I suppose so. In a very limited way. I've only seen things twice. Once in Maude's brooch, the Dragon's Heart. And once in the still waters of a stream. But I wouldn't call them long-range forecasts by any means. What I saw both times happened within minutes of the visions. If push came to shove, I'd be hard-pressed to describe them as anything other than a strange flash of intuition. I certainly didn't do anything to conjure them up."

Alanna had almost decided that he didn't intend to respond when he finally said, " 'Tis my understanding that this is often the way of a power as it comes into true being. At first unexpected and short; unbidden and uncontrolled. As the power strengthens, so does the ability to draw on it when necessary."

"Can you do divination, Niall?" she asked as the forest thinned and the crash of waves sounded in the near distance.

"No, I cannot see the future, milady. But it certainly isn't for the lack of effort and desire. I have tried scrying in water and fire, in mirrors and into darkness. Sadly, I've come to the conclusion that I apparently do not have the gift."

"Some gift," Alanna said ruefully. "I'd gladly give it to you if I could."

"I'm not meant to have it, not meant to be a seer," Niall countered with a shake of his head. In the next instant his face brightened with a wide smile. "I think my destiny lies along the path of the healer. With Owrd's help, I am becoming quite skilled in the use of plants and the treatment of various injuries and maladies."

"Now see, Niall. That's the difference between you and me. You can do something useful."

Whatever Niall had been about to say, he swallowed as they rounded a curve in the path and caught sight of Owrd standing on the rocks overlooking the gray-green water of the bay.

"Alanna," he said as she and Niall drew near. "We cannot accomplish our task as long as your spirit remains in turmoil. You must find a peace within yourself, however temporary it may prove to be."

She waited, saying nothing, knowing in her heart that she'd fail whatever exercise he gave her. She didn't have the power that he so desperately wanted her to possess, and his eventual disappoint weighed heavily on her.

"To that end," Owrd continued, "I ask you to cast a spell for yourself. I ask you to walk down to the waters of the bay and then along the shore until you find an object of the sea that speaks to you. Hold it in your right hand as you envision inner calm and an image of what your life will be like when you have claimed it. Let the waves wash over your feet eight times. As the ninth wave touches you, throw the object into the sea with all your might and release the image from your mind."

Alanna nodded and began making her way down the rocks. She'd give Owrd and his magical spell her very best shot. He had such an unshakable faith in her ability to make magic work that contemplating anything less than a wholehearted attempt seemed like the worst kind of cruelty. Alanna frowned as she gained the beach. She knew enough to realize that her grandfather had asked her to cast an attraction spell; that the ritual she was to perform was to draw to her the peace she needed to fulfill her purpose in coming through time. But forming a vision of how she'd be when at peace . . . It all depended on finding the central issue that kept her in knots.

"Like I haven't tried to figure that one out," Alanna muttered, striding down across the hard-packed sand. "If I could have found the answer, I'd have already fixed it."

She stopped at the water's edge, letting the waves ripple over her feet as she deliberately prepared her mind for the task at hand. On each receding wave, she expelled a long breath and surrendered a concern that plagued her heart: her worry of being a disappointment to Owrd, the fear of never getting back to Durango and Bill, her fear of failing the Clan O'Connell at the coming Beltane ritual. It took six waves for her to admit that no matter how hard she tried, no matter how long she stood there, she wasn't going to be able to banish the images of Kiervan des Marceaux from her heart and mind.

She gazed out over the water of Bantry Bay. As though to torture her, a three-masted ship came smartly about the eastern jetty and made for the center of the bay. She watched as its sails were quickly hauled upward; saw the sleek ship turn with a crisp precision that would have made any captain envious.

Alanna shielded her eyes with her hand and squinted at the vessel, trying to make out the name gilded along the ship's prow. She gave up in almost the same moment. The ship was undoubtedly the *Wind Racer*, and just as certainly, it was Kiervan who had the helm. Maneuvering a ship like that would have been just his style. Rakish and confident and beautiful.

"God, but I miss you," she whispered. Memories of the times with Kiervan came to her in brilliant succession, and as they came and went, her regrets and desires twined and coiled into a thrumming knot.

"And it is my peace with you that I must find," she said softly, nodding before the power of the truth.

Alanna looked down and plucked up a bit of shell lying at her feet. Closing her eyes, she conjured a clear image of her hopes . . . saw herself kissing Kiervan and then watching him walk away, felt her own heart's contentment and her soul's acceptance of the sight. Behind and beneath the vision, the tension for resolution built, vibrating through every fiber of her being and shortening her breath. In an almost desperate act to be free of the aching strain, she flung the shell out to sea, out toward the *Wind Racer*. Even as it hit the water and dropped from sight, she realized that she'd forgotten to count the waves as they had washed over her feet.

Alanna closed her eyes. She'd done her best under the circumstances, and she didn't have the energy left to do the ritual again. Every bone and muscle in her body begged for a nap. Slowly she turned and made her way back to Owrd and Niall.

"You have done well, Granddaughter," Owrd said, gathering her into his arms. "The peace will come. You have only to be willing to accept it when it does."

She wrapped her arms about his body and pressed her face into the folds of his linen robe. God, she hoped he was right. She'd never needed or wanted anything more.

24

"*Cachaileith.*"

Alanna turned away from the window as she considered her grandfather. "What?"

"*Cachaileith.* The twelfth word in the time spell. *Cachaileith.*"

Dutifully she crossed to the dressing table, dipped the quill into the inkwell, leaned down, and then phonetically wrote the word after the others he had given her in the course of the last three days. "Two more to go," she said, straightening and laying aside the pen before dusting her writing with sand.

"And as many days."

Again she turned back to study her grandfather. "What happens in two days?"

"Beltane," he answered on a sigh and with a shake of his head. He leaned back in the chair she'd dragged before the hearth for him. "The sacred fire will be lit and you will fulfill the task for which you were sent."

"Oh, yeah," she replied, chagrined that she'd let the central point of her lessons temporarily escape her. "Any idea yet as to exactly how I'm going to go about doing the vision thing?" she added, leaning back against the desk and crossing her ankles in front of her.

He shrugged and a half smile deepened the lines around his mouth. "A way will come when a way is needed. You must have faith."

Feeling frustrated, Alanna shook her head and left the

desk. "As you so bluntly pointed out on our first day of lessons, Grandfather, faith isn't one of my stronger virtues. Neither is patience," she added, crossing the room to stand before the open window. Owrd chuckled and the sound soothed her.

"If we are preparing a listing of your shortcomings, child, then we would be remiss not to add distractible."

Alanna leaned her shoulder against the window's edge. "I'll have you know that I have marvelous powers of concentration. All my teachers have remarked on it."

"Then on what matter is it that you concentrate?" he asked. She didn't have to look at him to know that his eyes twinkled and his brows were raised in mock question. "It certainly is not our lessons. I frequently feel as though I am pouring knowledge through a sieve."

"Okay," she admitted with a repentant smile. "You're right and I'm sorry." She came back to sit on the bed. "I promise to be a better student. Instruct away, dear Grandfather."

"I would be wasting yet more of my effort," he said, shaking his head. "The issues which have you in turmoil must be resolved, Alanna. You cannot perform the rituals if you have not a peaceful mind. You cast the spell into the sea. And I suspect that the solution you seek has already been presented to you."

He rose slowly from his chair and made his way toward the door, saying as he went, "I will leave you now so that you may consider the courses which lie before you and search for the courage to act upon what you know to be the truth. When you have done what you must to calm your spirit and soothe your soul, I will return. We will resume your lessons then."

He paused with his hand on the door latch. "Remember that we have but little time remaining, granddaughter. Do not dwell overlong on the false reasons you have arrayed before you. Do what you know in your heart you should."

Reluctant to have him leave, Alanna asked, "If I were to go to the ball this evening, would I see you there?"

"I shall attend for only a short while. The occasion is for

those younger and more robust than myself. Should you decide to go, you would be, without doubt, the loveliest in attendance, my child, and so the night would be yours to make of as you wish. Decide well and wisely."

Alanna watched the oaken panel close behind him. With a heavy sigh, she dragged herself off the bed and moved toward the window. The mellow rays of the afternoon sun slanted over the stone walls of the castle and into the courtyard.

All day people had streamed in and out through the massive gateway. Beneath her window there was cheerful chaos. Beltane celebrants from across the region, Owrd had explained. Alanna leaned her forearms on the cold stone sill and watched the steady flow of people and carts and animals that jostled through the gates.

The wealthy arrived in carriages or on horseback, their escorts many and well armed. The peasants came in crude carts and wagons or on foot. All who entered the keep were welcomed with food and drink. Owrd had said that the travelers of high station passed into the great hall to partake of Phelan O'Connell's personal hospitality. She could plainly see that those of lesser importance milled about in the dusty courtyard, freely availing themselves of the tables laden with meats and cheeses and cakes, drinking liberally from the kegs stacked and tapped to wet parched throats.

From the throng below rose the sounds and smells of a place of gathering, a place of growing revelry and expectation. *Two days*, Alanna thought. For two days the people had come in a seemingly unending procession. And for two more days the parade would likely continue.

"And then," she muttered ruefully, "on the night of the second day, the eve of the first day of May, I'm supposed to somehow magically determine whether or not the Clan O'Connell should join the revolution against the English."

Whether the O'Connells joined it or not didn't really matter. It would fail, of course. She knew little of Irish history except for the senseless tragedies she'd seen on the nightly news and from what she'd read in the tourist literature she'd picked up with her ticket at the travel agent's office. Inde-

pendence would be the better part of two centuries in coming to the south of Ireland. And the North remained in
British hands even in her own time.

"What if, in the vision, I see the O'Connells joining the
revolution?" she quietly asked herself. "Don't they have a
right to know the course is doomed? Don't I have a moral
obligation to tell them it'll fail?

"And how's Kiervan gonna react if I tell them the truth?"
She pursed her lips and stared into nothing. Finally she
looked down at her hands and sighed. "Easy answer to that
one, Alanna, ol' girl. He's gonna accuse you of trying to
derail his arms deal so that his plans to marry Eggie fall
through. He's gonna accuse you of acting out of jealousy.
Won't that be a fun scene?"

She smiled. "But don't we have the most glorious fights,
Kiervan? And they always end the same breathtaking way."

Remembering stirred her blood, and the hunger she'd
tried so hard to bury deep inside her pounded at her resolve.
Owrd was right. She couldn't run from it anymore. The
time had come to stop being a coward. Her decision made,
Alanna straightened, determined to face the future.

Turning away from the window, she strode toward the
door. She wrenched open the portal and stepped into the
hall. "Hisolda!" she called, looking up and down the shadowed corridor. "Where are you?"

"Here, mistress!" the girl answered, skittering around the
corner with her skirts held high above her ankles and her
eyes wide in alarm. "What is amiss? Are you unwell?"

"I'm fine. Madder than blue blazes but otherwise just
peachy."

"Is it something I have done, mistress?" the girl asked,
sliding to a stop before Alanna. "Or perhaps something I
have not done?"

She noted her maid's flushed cheeks and the rapid rhythm
of her breathing and laid her hand on the girl's arm to reassure her. "It's not you, Hisolda," Alanna assured her. "I'm
mad at myself. Does this castle have a dressmaker?"

Hisolda's braids danced as she nodded. "Yes, mistress.
The best in County Kerry."

"Can she make me a gown for this evening's ball? Is it too late?"

"I know not. I shall go ask."

"Good," Alanna replied, her mind already moving on to other details. "Tell her that I can sew reasonably well and that I'll be glad to assist her if necessary." The girl nodded even as she scampered off in the direction of the great hall. "And Hisolda . . ." Alanna called after the flutter of skirts and petticoats. "On your way back, stop in the kitchen and ask to have water heated and brought up for my bath."

Alanna stepped back into the room in which she'd hidden for the better part of a week and a half. It was well past time she ventured forth. And it was damn sure time for her to take control of her own heart and her own destiny. Kiervan would undoubtedly be among those attending the ball, and she had every intention of going, if for no other reason than to knock the roguish socks right off his feet.

Alanna closed her eyes to keep the room from swaying as Hisolda diligently sewed her into the refurbished gown. "Is it going to work?" she finally asked, almost hoping the young woman would sigh and declare the attempt futile.

"No one will ever know that we've taken in the bodice, mistress. Or that we've drawn up the sleeves."

Alanna studied the cap sleeve that fell from her shoulder. To her way of thinking, it looked a lot like a streamlined balloon curtain. To say that the gown had undergone a major alteration would have been a gross understatement. The pinched-faced, intense little dressmaker hadn't wasted a single motion in her efforts to retrofit what she'd deemed a hopelessly out-of-fashion but serviceable garment. Lord only knew out of whose trunk it had come. Alanna hadn't asked. She'd simply stood silently on a stool in the center of the room while the dressmaker and Hisolda had cut and pinned and sewn and chatted away in Gaelic.

The long train had been removed with a ruthlessness that had taken her breath away, and the full-length sleeves had been slashed off just above the point where they'd turned into a tourniquet. The yards of fabric which had pooled around her feet without the gown's original hoops had been shortened with equal speed and relish, part of the excess easily serving as the pleated capelet which artfully covered the makeshift seams at her shoulders and down the back of the bodice.

"The line turned out very well, don't you think?" Hisolda asked.

Alanna dutifully studied the drape of the silken fabric. She decided that exactly how the dressmaker had managed to so neatly convert the full gathered skirt into one which fell straight from a short bodice would forever qualify as one of the great wonders of the world, right up there with the Sphinx and the Hanging Gardens of Babylon.

Of course, the whole thing was a well-crafted illusion, as the dressmaker had reminded her when she'd departed with her sewing box. The minute she decided to get out of it, the woman had warned, she'd be left with nothing more than a violet-colored silk sack. "Do you suppose," Alanna mused, "that this is the world's first disposable dress?"

Hisolda clipped a thread and stepped back to openly admire her handiwork. She leaned forward to tweak one of the curls in the arrangement she had fashioned atop Alanna's head.

"You look beautiful, mistress," she declared, after another quick inspection. "There'll be no other woman at the ball to rival you. And sure it is that every man will ask you to dance before the night is done."

"Dance?" Alanna felt sick. "Oh . . . my . . . God."

"What is it, mistress?"

Alanna met her maid's worried gaze. "Hisolda, I don't know how to dance."

"Surely you do," the girl scoffed with a relieved smile and a wave of her hand. " 'Tisn't difficult."

"You don't understand." Alanna swallowed. "Where I come from, dancing is usually done without a partner, and you make up the steps as you go along. I've never . . ."

"You needn't worry," Hisolda offered blithely, gathering her scissors and pins into a basket. "You but do what the others do, mistress. Your partner will lead and you follow."

Alanna nodded weakly. Lord, what had she been thinking when she'd launched herself into this little escapade? More correctly, she silently and instantly amended, had she been thinking at all?

The fitting of the corset should have been her first clue that she'd entered waters way over her head. Alanna glanced down at her chest and grimaced. She had enough cleavage for herself and ten needy women. And high . . . The corset practically shoved her breasts over the daringly low edge of her neckline. With a low groan, Alanna closed her eyes and wondered if it was too late to fake a massive headache.

" 'Twill be all right, mistress. You will see."

"Yeah, right." With a quiet sigh, she climbed down off the stool. Her head reeled and she grabbed the edge of the dressing table for support until the room righted itself.

Hisolda handed her a violet wool shawl shot with silver threads and gently admonished, "You must remember to move more slowly and to take shallow breaths."

"I sure as hell can't take a deep one in this corset. You know what's going to happen, don't you? I'm going to pass out halfway down the stairs and roll into the ballroom like a great big purple tumbleweed. Why'd I ever let you two talk me into this contraption?"

Hisolda grinned. "Because at the time, you were determined to make a certain man notice you."

Alanna felt her jaw drop. It took two long heartbeats for her to recover enough presence to offer a protest. "I never said any such thing."

"You didn't have to, mistress. Everyone knows of you and Captain des Marceaux."

"Oh, really?" Alanna asked in what she hoped was a disinterested tone. "And just what is it that everyone knows?"

Hisolda blushed and hesitated before she replied, "They say you're lovers in the midst of a quarrel."

Alanna lifted her chin indignantly. "Well, it's not true."

"What part is untrue?" Hisolda asked, the smile returning to her lips. "That you're lovers? Or that you're having a quarrel?"

Alanna gave the maid the unvarnished truth. "We're not lovers," she stated matter-of-factly.

"But then why are you angry with one another?"

Because we aren't lovers. The power of the simple truth stunned Alanna, and for a moment she stood in the center of her room, numbed by the simplicity of it.

"We're at odds with each other, Hisolda," she admitted, moving toward the door, "because I've been a fool. Because I've wanted everything my way and refused to accept anything less than the perfection of my dreams."

"I think the captain is perfection."

Alanna paused before crossing over the threshold, and turned back. "He's as close to it as I'll ever find. I just hope that I haven't come to my senses too late. Thank you for all your help."

Hisolda dropped into a slight curtsy. "Shall I wait for your return, mistress?"

"Thanks, but no." She draped the shawl across her shoulders and stepped into the corridor. "However this evening turns out, I'd like to have the room unoccupied when I come in."

25

Kiervan waited by the doors leading into the garden, sipping his brandy and nodding occasionally to the vacuous woman who stood before him, fluttering her eyelashes and lamenting the price of silk.

"Do you not find the situation monstrous, Captain des Marceaux?"

He wanted to suggest that his particular situation would improve greatly if she were to seek a different victim. Instead he replied, "Terrible indeed, madam. I cannot imagine how you endure it."

"It is surely the greatest trial of my life, Captain." She laid her hand on his arm, leaned closer, and batted her lashes again. "I would be *ever* so grateful if you happened to bring some with you on your next journey to Ireland."

Kiervan grimaced at the thinly veiled offer and stared at the brandy in his glass as he sought a tactful reply. Heaven spared him the necessity when a sudden hush fell over the room. His companion turned toward the stairway, then rose on her toes in an attempt to peer over the heads of the crowd.

Suddenly a stentorian voice filled the room. "The Lady Alanna Kathleen Chapman." In response a murmur rose from those assembled, and the crowd shifted forward to get a better view of the exotic American creature who had come across time.

Seizing the moment, Kiervan bowed to his thoroughly distracted companion and walked away. Once in the relative safety of the shadows, he leaned his shoulder against a stone column and watched Alanna enter the wide hall. He took in the details of her appearance in a single instant: the high-waisted, low-cut gown of violet silk, the cashmere shawl a shade darker than her dress and woven through with strands of silver, her honeyed hair, curled and loosely piled atop her head, laying bare her long, slender throat and the delicate curves of her ears.

"Magnificent," he murmured, lifting his glass to her in a private salute. As he spoke, the crowd parted and Phelan O'Connell moved forward to take his guest's hands in his.

Even from a distance, Kiervan could see the tension settle into her shoulders, could see her lift her chin in the way she always did when she'd made up her mind to endure something frightening or unpleasant. What had unsettled her? Understanding came to him the moment Phelan signaled for the musicians to play. Alanna couldn't dance; she didn't know how to stand or where to properly place her hands.

His heart cringed for her and he started forward, determined to effect a rescue at any price. Phelan made the effort unnecessary when he leaned down, brushed his lips across the back of Alanna's hand, then straightened, bowed, and graciously set about explaining the rudiments of the dance and arranging Alanna to his satisfaction.

Part of Kiervan sighed in utter relief. Another, more primal side of him seethed as he watched his uncle take Alanna into his arms and move her across the floor. Kiervan stepped back into the shadows, finding some small consolation in Alanna's tight-lipped smile. Despite Phelan's considerable effort, she remained uncomfortable and tense.

Kiervan downed the last of his brandy and studied the empty crystal glass for a long moment. If he had to watch every man in the room gleefully attempt to educate Alanna, this would undoubtedly be the longest night of his life. With that certainty before him, he faced the only two choices he had. He could either drink himself into a blind oblivion, or he could wait a respectable length of time and then spirit her from their midst.

He placed the empty glass on the tray of a passing servant, then stepped from the shadows in search of a suitable dance partner with whom he could pass the necessary time.

If she could make the glass of sherry last for the next few hours, she just might get out of this ordeal with the few shreds of pride she had left. She glanced between each of the three men standing before her and smiled at each in turn, trying not to stare at their short-cropped, fastidiously curled hairdos. *God,* she silently prayed, *I can't take any more of this. Just open the floor and let me fall through.*

As if to add to her torment, one of her persistent admirers chose that moment to bow, permitting her a brief but clear view of the dance floor; a clear view of a smiling Kiervan guiding a petite brunette through an intricate maze of dancers.

Alanna took a long sip of her sherry. The evening wasn't working out anything like she'd planned. Kiervan hadn't come within a mile of her, and for all she knew, he didn't even know she was there. *Just as well,* snipped her inner voice, *acute embarrassment is best suffered among strangers.*

She lifted the glass to her lips and took another small taste of the amber spirit. Damn him for being the ruggedly, roguishly handsome man that he was. And damn her for following his every movement like some lovesick teenager. *And while I'm at it,* she added, *damn those gray breeches and that blasted navy blue cutaway he's wearing.*

"Damn, damn, damn."

"Pardon, mistress?"

With a start, Alanna realized that she'd spoken aloud. Her cheeks warming, she glanced about the semicircle of men. None of them appeared to be particularly upset. "I seem," she began, offering them the first halfway reasonable explanation that came to mind, "to be out of sherry."

"Allow me to replenish your glass," said one, bowing before he took it from her hand.

The second man also bowed. "Would you care for more substantial refreshment, Lady Chapman? I would be honored to prepare you a plate of sweetmeats."

"Thank you. That's most kind of you," she replied as he backed away. *Two down, one to go.*

She looked at the remaining man. "Could you tell me what a lady does with her shawl when she no longer wants to be bothered with it?"

"She allows it to be taken away," he replied, bowing before he stepped behind her and lifted the wrap from her shoulders. "I shall give it into the care of one of the attendants for safekeeping and return forthwith, mistress."

"Thank you ever so much." Alanna smiled sweetly and graciously as he too backed away.

"Very well done, Alanna. I am impressed."

Her heart leaping, Alanna whirled about to find Kiervan leaning against one of the stone pillars, his arms crossed over his chest, one booted ankle crossed casually over the other.

He gave her an amused smile. "Dispatched three hopefuls in a matter of minutes. A skill but few women possess."

Ignoring the deepening warmth of her cheeks, she shrugged and allowed her instincts to take charge. "It's my Scarlett O'Hara impersonation. I only drag it out on really desperate occasions."

She knew that he couldn't have possibly known about Scarlett O'Hara, but his smile broadened and his eyes sparkled with what she knew to be genuine amusement. In almost the same instant, he came away from the column.

"A lady should always come to a ball fully dressed, Alanna," he said, reaching into his coat. "Did your maid not mention that fact to you, or are you determined to set a new social trend?"

She looked down at her gown and then back up at him. "I'm dressed properly, aren't I? What have I forgotten?"

He grinned and cocked a roguish brow. "Your ears are naked, sweet Alanna," he whispered, opening his hand. "Allow me to remedy the faux pas."

"My earrings!"

"One was lost," he explained as she took them from him and began to fasten them into place. "I took the remaining one from your earlobe while you slept in my cabin that night aboard the *Wind Racer*."

"Thank you, Kiervan," she offered, checking to be sure they were both positioned as they should be and fighting back the impulse to kiss him for his kindness. She smiled at him and asked, "Where on Earth did you find another to match it?"

"I've had the time to fashion a mate for it since our arrival," he answered.

"So that's what you were doing down in that little building."

His gaze met hers and he smiled gently. "That and hoping that you'd come in search of me."

"You didn't seem to miss my company," she said softly, mentally kicking herself even as the words left her tongue. She'd been so resolved to say nothing of his distance.

"You have the most beautiful little flecks of green in your eyes sometimes," he said, a mixture of quiet amusement and satisfaction rolling through his words.

A wondrous and dangerous sense of euphoria swept over her, and Alanna seized on the first chance for evasion that came to her mind. "I didn't know you were into silversmithing," she offered, touching the earrings again. "Not exactly what I'd expect a roguish privateer to take up as a hobby."

He shrugged. "I went to visit Riona and Dominica one winter and got caught in Boston harbor when a winter storm set in. Mr. Revere befriended me on my way to the city jail the third night I was in port. I repaid the favor by becoming a student. So why haven't you come looking for me?"

"I couldn't," she managed to get out past the sudden lump in her throat. Another small lie tumbled out. "I seem to have become a prisoner in a stone tower." She could tell by the way the corners of his mouth twitched and his eyes narrowed that he knew full well she'd been a prisoner by her own choice.

"Well," he countered smoothly, "since you appear to have won a temporary reprieve, might I have the pleasure of the next dance, Mistress Chapman?"

Alanna rolled her eyes and grimaced. "In case it's escaped your notice, Captain, I'm worse than miserable at this. I've stepped on the toes of every man who's been either brave or foolish enough to dance with me tonight."

Leaning down, he whispered, "I happen to believe, mistress, that dancing well is simply a matter of finding the right partner."

It took everything she had to keep her hands at her sides, to keep from threading her fingers through the raven strands that tumbled over his shoulders. Leave it to Kiervan not to cut and style his hair as the other men. Did he know how alluring, how tempting, she found him?

Trying desperately to resurrect her Scarlett O'Hara act so that Kiervan wouldn't guess how his presence had affected her, she smiled skeptically and asked, "And you think you might be the right partner for me, Captain des Marceaux?"

"Aye." He offered his arm and his eyes sparkled. "Will you permit me to prove it?"

"All right." She slipped her hand about his forearm and walked beside him toward the floor. "But remember that I tried to spare you," she whispered as they went. "If you limp away, it's your own fault."

He grinned as he stopped and turned to face her squarely. The first notes of a waltz drifted across the room, and when he lifted his hands, Alanna stepped forward into the circle of his courtly possession. Even as she did, he began to move her backward across the floor. Lost in the wondrous power of his smile and the softness of the fire in his eyes, she went with him, only vaguely aware that her feet were moving.

"Has every man here already told you how beautiful you are tonight, Alanna?"

She smiled up at him. "It's been mentioned a time or two."

"Would you care to know what I think?" He gave her no time to reply. "I think that you're no more beautiful tonight than the morning you sat on the riverbank wearing a pair of woolen trousers and a torn shirt."

Alanna felt a wondrous heat flood into her cheeks. After a

long moment, she managed to find her voice. "No one's ever said anything kinder, Kiervan. Thank you."

He drew her closer and she felt the satin of his lapels brush across the swell of her breasts as he bent to her ear. "I should warn you, woman," he said, his voice low. "At the first opportunity, I intend to pull those pins from your hair."

Blood raced through her veins, heated and fierce, and deep within her the long-denied hunger stirred again, demanding succor. In that moment she decided that Owrd hadn't been entirely right. Sometimes there was an advantage to knowing what lay ahead. Knowing allowed one to relax and enjoy the journey itself.

Alanna smiled. "Letting you loosen my hairpins would create a bit of a scandal, wouldn't it, Captain? I have my exalted position as Seer of the Find to think about, you know. I can't let you tarnish my public reputation."

He straightened and chuckled, the sound soft and only for her ears. "Tell me, Alanna, when did you acquire a concern for the opinions of others?"

"I haven't *acquired* one, Captain des Marceaux," she replied, smiling up at him. "I've simply borrowed one for the evening. It seemed like the thing to do under the circumstances and all."

He fought in vain to keep his smile under control. "I'm afraid, mistress, that allowing me to pull the pins from your hair wouldn't be all that much more outrageous than the other acts you've already committed this evening."

"Oh? Like what? My naked earlobes?"

"That and you arrived unescorted." He made a *tsk*ing sound in mock reproach. "A true lady lives by two hard rules. The first is to never attend a social function without a respectable escort. You were marked the moment you entered the hall."

"And the second rule, Captain? I assume that I've broken it too. When?"

"The moment you allowed me to draw you into a waltz. A lady properly concerned about her public reputation would never permit herself to engage in such a scandalously intimate dance."

Alanna glanced about the ballroom. "We're not out here all by ourselves," she observed. "There are others waltzing too. Though not as many as the other dances."

"Aye." He cocked a brow and his voice sobered. "But I'll wager the *Wind Racer* that everyone here's noted that none of the others move together as we do. 'Twould seem to imply a degree of greater intimacy than most, would it not?"

Her step never faltering, Alanna floated before him. Smiling at the second button on his white shirtfront, she admitted, "You're absolutely right, you know."

"About what?"

She looked up at him. "Finding the right partner makes all the difference in the world. Makes me wonder what else you might be right about. Which, in turn, makes me wonder how long you plan to make me wait."

The fire in his eyes burned brighter, and his hand pressed more closely in the small of her back. "Wait for what, sweet Alanna?" he asked, his voice caressing every inch of her.

"For you to pull the pins from my hair."

His smile slowly faded as a different, deeper kind of fire ignited in his ebony eyes and the line of his jaw hardened. He looked away, at a point over her shoulder, and began to move them in that direction. His voice rumbled low in his chest when he replied, "Discretion would suggest a more private place for us to dance."

"Just between you and me, Kiervan," she murmured. "I think it's way too late for discretion."

He muttered something in Gaelic as he whirled her about in a dizzying arc. She laughed and closed her eyes; trusting him, not caring where he took her; reveling in the magical bond which held them in flawless tandem; reveling in the joy that flooded her heart.

And then the air about her suddenly cooled. She opened her eyes to the pale light of the night sky and the realization that they now danced alone. The sounds of the waltz swirled out the doors behind them and carried them into the deeper shadows of the cobbled walkway. Kiervan followed the notes without pause, releasing her hand to wrap both his arms about her waist and draw her closer.

She went willingly, slipping her hands up to rest on his shoulders and surrendering herself to the smoldering promise in his eyes. In the distance she heard the music slow and fade. "The magic . . ." she whispered sadly.

Kiervan solemnly shook his head. "There's no magic in the music, Alanna." With a deliberate hand, he reached up to gently trace the curve of her lower lip. " 'Tis in us."

"Kiervan . . ."

"Will you come to me, Alanna? Will you end my waiting?"

Even in the shadows, she could see the need that flickered across his chiseled features. She leaned into him, twining her fingers through the hair tumbling over his shoulders and drawing his lips down to hers. Never had anything felt as right as standing in the shadows of a castle and offering her heart and soul to a roguish, raven-haired privateer.

26

Alanna sat in the wide stern of the rowboat, hugging Kiervan's coat about her and watching the distance between them and the ship narrow to nothing. Kiervan settled the oars along the sides of the small craft, then stood, his stance square and centered, to grasp the ladder dangling down the side of the *Wind Racer*.

"Just out of curiosity," she began, eyeing the ladder and the distance to the ship above, "how did you get me up there when you brought me aboard last time? I was in no shape to climb up by myself."

A wide grin spread across his face. "I carried you up, slung ignobly over my shoulder like a sack of potatoes."

She smiled at the memory of the threat he had issued in the grove of trees beyond the Carraig Cor. "You are a man of your word, aren't you? Do you plan a repeat performance tonight?"

"Would you prefer it? I can manage."

"Naw. Just let me go up first. That way if I slip, you can break my fall."

"And both our necks." He shook his head. "Richard St. John is a perceptive man. I have no doubt that he'll have anticipated—" A sound from above drew his attention in that direction. "Ah, I see that I was correct. Your throne comes now, my fair princess. This time you shall board the *Wind Racer* in the style befitting you."

She studied the rope net being lowered toward them and

pictured herself being hauled upward like a mess of wiggling fish. "A sling seat?"

"You sound reluctant, Alanna."

The amusement in his voice didn't assuage her fears. "I could climb the ladder, you know. It wouldn't be very lady-like, I'm sure, but . . ."

"You'll be quite safe," he assured her solemnly, catching the netting. As he positioned the conveyance for her, he added, "Mr. St. John has never lost a passenger."

Alanna settled herself into the seat and, gripping the ropes, nodded and said, "Go ahead. Give him the three tugs on the line or whatever the sign is and let's get this show on the road."

She saw him study her for a moment, a puzzled shadow clouding his eyes. Finally he looked to the deck above. At the wave of his hand, she was smoothly lifted from the row-boat and drawn up the side of the ship.

He gained the deck at the same time as another man grasped the makeshift chair in which she sat suspended above the sea and drew it, and her, inward and over the planking.

Kiervan stepped forward to offer his hands, saying as he did, "Mr. St. John, may I present Mistress Alanna Chapman. Alanna, this is Richard St. John, my First Officer and trusted friend."

"A pleasure, sir," she acknowledged with a quick nod while placing her hands in Kiervan's and allowing herself to be extracted from the sling seat.

Richard St. John's gray eyes sparkled as he stepped forward and bowed. "The pleasure is entirely mine, Mistress Chapman. It is a rare woman indeed who can lead the captain on as merry a chase as you have so ably done. I stand in awe of your accomplishment."

She couldn't help smiling at him. There was something comfortable about the man. "I hardly consider myself worthy of such high regard, Mr. St. John If you'll notice, I'm the one who's been caught."

"So it would appear to the casual observer." He bowed again. "Allow me to officially welcome you aboard the

Wind Racer, mistress. Should you have need of anything during your stay, you have but to ask and I shall see it done."

Kiervan drew her to his side as he drawled, "How terribly gallant of you, Richard."

The man lifted one shoulder in a dismissive gesture. "I am simply positioning myself should you prove yourself short-sighted enough to let this lovely creature slip from your grasp."

Alanna placed her hand on the other man's forearm and smiled up at him. "How sweet of you, Mr. St. John." She winked as she added, "I'll definitely keep you in mind."

"I'm no fool, Richard," Kiervan countered, stepping back and drawing Alanna away from his second in command.

Again the man offered a half shrug, but this time it was accompanied by a knowing smile. "That, Kiervan, remains to be seen, doesn't it?"

"Then it's only fair that you know there's undoubtedly many a man in line before you also awaiting my poor judgment. Which brings me to an order I want entered into the log. If a boat comes out bearing anyone from the castle, blow it from the water."

Aghast, Alanna turned in the circle of his arm and stared up at him. "Kiervan! How could you?"

He gazed down at her and cocked a brow while a taunting smile played at the corners of his mouth. "Quite easily. It's simply a matter of powder and shot."

"Kiervan!"

"Very well," he relented with a shake of his head and long-suffering sigh. "Mr. St. John, I rescind the order." He paused, and when he continued, there was no mistaking the seriousness of his command. "Place this in its stead: They are to be permitted to board, but, the moment their feet touch this deck, they're to be clapped in irons. Under no circumstance are they to be allowed anywhere near my cabin. Is that understood?"

The First Officer grinned and nodded. "Aye, Captain. Am I to assume that the latter restriction applies to all hands?"

"Yourself included."

"Aye, Captain." His eyes sparkling, he bowed to Alanna yet again. "Until the morrow, Mistress Chapman."

She let Kiervan lead her away, thinking as she went that Richard St. John looked quite pleased with himself.

Kiervan pushed open the door to his cabin and stepped aside to let Alanna go before him. She walked into the softly lit room. "I like Mr. St. John," she said, looking about the cabin as though searching the room for some diversion . . . or perhaps someplace to hide.

Of course, it would be more difficult now, he reminded himself. He had allowed her time to think. Sensing a gathering storm, Kiervan closed the portal behind them and cursed again the decision not to take her in Phelan's garden.

"Kiervan," she said softly, turning toward him. "I . . . "

He pressed his fingertip to her lips and shook his head. "Not a word, Alanna. We do much better without them."

Alanna smiled and, after a moment, nodded. Kiervan reached out and slowly pushed his coat from her shoulders and let it fall to the floor around her feet. She looked down at it and then back up at him. A tiny smile tickled the corners of her mouth, and in the depths of her violet eyes he saw the shimmering light of desire.

Kiervan took her into his arms and drew her to him. The moment he tasted the sweetness of her lips, he was a man lost to passions too long restrained. She breathed his name as she twined her arms about his neck, and his senses filled with her, the heady scents of roses and woman blending in a mixture uniquely hers, one that he would forever know as Alanna.

Kiervan kissed the corners of her mouth and then upward along the arc of her delicate cheekbone. When he traced the curve of her ear with his lips, with the barest tip of his tongue, Alanna sighed softly and leaned into him. He suckled the tender lobe of her ear, toying with the earring he had made for her before slipping lower to lay gentle siege to the hollow behind her ear. Her hands flat on the planes of his chest, her back gently arched, she offered him her neck as a low murmur came past her lips. The sound resonated through him, feeding a hunger too long held in check.

Bolts of liquid lightning shot through her as his hands wandered down the length of her back and as he boldly stroked her hips. Her knees weak and her flesh trembling, she clung to him and prayed for the strength to endure the pleasure he gave her. His teeth grazed and then nipped at her skin, and through the heady wave that washed over her, she heard him whisper words of Gaelic.

A tiny cry caught low in her throat as she leaned back, opening for him the trail leading to the hollow at the base of her throat. Kiervan planted a lingering kiss there, then blazed a slow, deliberate path across the creamy swell of her breast. She murmured and pressed against him, accepting his possession and offering him what he willed to take. He felt the heated passage of her hands over the width of his chest, felt her hands slide up and around his neck, her fingers twining through the hair at his nape. He drew her closer, holding her against his rising desire as he lifted his head to plunder the sweetest depths of her mouth.

In the recesses of his mind, the near-strangled voice of his conscience reminded him of Alanna's inexperience and the need for a slower pace. Steeling himself, he drew back, releasing his claim to her lips but still holding her tight within the circle of his arms as the frantic pounding of his heartbeat began to ease and his thoughts gained a modicum of coherence.

Her heart vaulted into her throat as he released her and she stood apart from him. Had she been too bold? The rapid rise and fall of his chest spoke more of desire than anger; the tight, determined line of his lips of self-discipline imposed with great difficulty. Still . . . Confused, her breath ragged and her lips throbbing from his kiss, Alanna gazed up into ebony eyes. In them she saw both the glittering promise of his desire and the well-tempered edge of self-control. God, how had she managed to resist the temptation of this man for so long? she wondered. Why had she even tried?

"I'm actually much better at this than it would appear,"

he offered with a chagrined smile, slipping his hands up the length of her back to finger the upper edge of the bodice. "But I've searched everywhere, Alanna, and I have no choice but to ask, where are the buttons to this infernal gown of yours?"

"There aren't any." His brows shot up and she couldn't stifle the soft laughter that bubbled up. "I'm sewn into it. Down the back. You'll have to cut the threads to get me out of it."

"To hell with that." In the same instant, the sound of rending fabric filled the cabin.

Alanna's jaw dropped open. Kiervan grinned at her roguishly as though daring her to protest. He gathered another handful of the cloth and separated the dress all the way to the hem.

"I'd like to see you try that with the corset, mister."

Grinning, he stepped back, drawing the tattered remnants of the dress down her arms. Casting it aside, he asked, "Did you deliberately dress to frustrate me, woman?"

She waited until he had wrapped her in the warmth of his arms again before she replied, "That would imply that I intended to end up here before I even went down to the ball."

"Are you saying that you had no inkling of what would come to pass between us this night?"

"Actually, I was kinda hoping to make you notice."

"A task you most ably accomplished, my sweet. Was it also part of your intention to tumble me into bed before the night was done?"

"I was rather counting on you tumbling me." The color of his eyes darkened and fear pricked at her confidence. She forced herself to swallow. "Which probably makes me one of the most brazen and wanton women you've ever met, doesn't it? Do you think less of me for it?"

He laughed and winked mischievously as he released her and stepped back. While his gaze brazenly caressed her every curve, he unbuttoned and then shrugged the waistcoat from his shoulders. It landed on the floor atop the discarded rag that had been her dress. Alanna stood before him, her own near-naked state fading from her awareness as he leisurely opened his shirt, pulled the tails of it from his breeches, and then undid the remaining buttons. His boots followed his shirt to the floor.

Of its own accord, her gaze traveled over the tanned, muscled planes of his chest and down the thin dark line that disappeared into the waistband of his breeches; then lower to the straining fabric and the proof of his desire. A molten heat surged through her veins, and she silently gasped before the onslaught of its power.

Instincts, ageless and timeless, drew her to him. With a low murmur, she stepped into his arms, closed her eyes, and offered him her lips. He obliged, possessing her with a fierce tenderness that stole her breath and sent her senses reeling. Amidst the maelstrom of dazzling sensation, Alanna felt something settle deep within her soul. A peace came with it and suddenly she understood that Kiervan had been right about the magic; it came not from the music of the waltz, it came from the concert of their hearts. Heaven had ordained this time they had to be together. It was right and all that came of it would be right.

It was between them now as it should have been long ago. There was no need for conscious thought, no need for reserve with Kiervan. She wanted him as she had never wanted any other. The hunger within her had been born of his touch, and only his touch could satisfy it.

Kiervan moaned as he caught her lips with his own and drew her against the length of him. Reassured by the certain, gentle ferocity of his advance, she returned it in equal measure, holding his lips to hers, boldly twining her tongue with his and demanding to explore in her own right.

As she waged her own tender assault, Kiervan moaned again, the sound rippling through her. He held her to him with an urgency that sent delicious shivers of fire through her body. His kiss turned fierce and demanding as his hands slipped lower to cup her and press her belly against his need. In answer, a wild, aching hunger roiled deep inside her, giving her no choice but to heed its demands.

Her hands slipped around his waist and then down to

hold him as he did her. No gale wind had ever driven him harder. Before the onslaught of Alanna's surrender, Kiervan's sense of mastery faltered, leaving him breathless, dazed, and reeling.

Somewhere in the back of his mind the voice of experience warned that the pace of the seduction moved too quickly; that Alanna deserved better of him; that she needed to be well prepared to take him. His hunger begged him to ignore the more sensitive of his instincts, reminded him that allowing Alanna time to think was a dangerous thing. They had the whole of the night, it promised him; the slow savoring of their loving could come later.

Through the pounding beat of her heart, Alanna vaguely heard the quick *ting*s of metal against wood, but, it wasn't until her hair tumbled from atop her head that she fully realized what Kiervan was about. A bubble of joy burst deep inside her, its brilliance shattering the last of the cords which had too long bridled the hungers of her body and soul.

She surrendered all of herself to the mastery of his touch, the sureness of his control, the strength of his arms, and the undeniable force of his unspoken commands.

There was no subtlety in the way he rid her of her chemise. She matched the fevered possession of his kisses and pressed the softness of her curves against his need as he worked to part the strings which bound her into the corset. Only when the back of it finally opened did she turn her lips from his and step away.

He marveled at the woman standing before him dressed only in her lace and gossamer pantaloons; at the regal lady of quality, the woman of depth and substance and will. His gaze caressed the long, graceful column of her neck, and then moved lower, to the dark, rigid peaks cresting her pale breasts.

His heartbeat quickened and he lifted his gaze to note the rosy hue coloring her cheeks, the fire smoldering deep within her eyes. In a single heartbeat, he measured all the women of his past against her and found them lacking; knew then that all the women of his future would fall short.

She smiled up at him and stepped closer, threading her fingers through the curls on his chest. Intoxicating pleasure coursed from her fingertips, weakening his knees and stealing his very breath. Even as he sought to steel his senses, she bent forward and placed a lingering, taunting kiss in the center of his chest.

He drew her to him, seeking her mouth, seeking a respite from the exquisite agony of her slow seduction. She yielded to his desperation, relaxing into the circle of his embrace. Even as she did, her hands slipped down the length of his chest and outward, pausing for only a moment on his hips before they glided back to rest on the curve of his buttocks. Never had any woman taken possession of him with such gentle forcefulness. The muscles across his abdomen were taut with tension as a primal heat pounded through his veins to center low within him and throb all along the length of his need.

Lord, no accomplished courtesan had ever held such an irresistible power over his desires as did the enchantress in his arms. Deep within him, Kiervan felt the tethers of restraint give way. Time suddenly became too short; patience too much to ask. With a single fluid motion, he swept her into his arms and carried her to his bed.

Kiervan gently placed her in the center of the feather mattress. He whispered of her beauty in Gaelic, his hands skimming along the curves of her hips, then down her thighs to where the pantaloons ended with a flutter of lace. He had but touched the top of a stocking when she sighed and gracefully presented him with a wondrously curved leg. Rolling the silk down the length of it, his lips followed languorously in its wake. She inhaled sharply and her foot arched into the palm of his hand. Kiervan glanced up to find her lying amidst the wild tumble of her hair, a smile gently curving her lips as she watched him.

God, but she was beautiful. Would there ever come a time when the merest sight of her did not heat his blood and make him pound with desire? As though she knew his thoughts had wandered from the immediate task at hand, she presented him with her other leg. With pleasure, he stripped the remaining stocking from her as he had the first and then tossed it aside.

Alanna watched him, warmed by the sight of the smooth grace and power of a predator, fascinated with the muscles bunching and rippling across the width of his shoulders as he stripped away her stockings. Suddenly she wanted to touch him, to taste him, to claim all of him for her own for the time they would have together. She needed to know every part of him: the smoothness of his skin, the hardness of his muscled arms, the corded ridges of his abdomen, his hips pressed against hers.

Her hands slipped along the width of his shoulders and then down to caress the planes of his chest. In the next heartbeat, he felt the taunting passage of her fingers across his abdomen and along the edge of his breeches. Every muscle and fiber of his being tightened and quivered with anticipation. He drew a hard breath, his unspoken words of assent mixing with the ragged sound as he closed his eyes and let the waves of extraordinary sensation wash over and weaken him.

And then, with a deliberateness that knocked the wind from his lungs and scattered his senses, Alanna's hands slipped lower. All other sensation fled his awareness as she slowly traced the ridge of his swollen need. Dazed and powerless, he could only gasp in silence when she boldly unfastened the buttons of his breeches. As she pushed aside the fabric and took him into her hands, a rippling shudder passed through him and into his soul. For a second the room spun about him and then righted itself.

"Sweet Alanna . . ." he moaned, gently grasping her wrists and saving himself from the too exquisite sensations of her touch.

Before him, on the bed, Alanna waited, her hair tumbling over the pillows, a knowing smile on her lips. Her eyes were pools of the deepest violet, the innermost color of pansies. He saw the rapid, rhythmic pulse in the hollow at the base of her neck; the ardent rise and fall of her breasts; the dusky rose of her nipples enticing and inviting his hands, his lips; the silent plea shimmering in her eyes. The translucent fabric of her pantalets hid nothing: not the narrowness of her waist, not the gentle beckoning curve of her hips, not the inviting triangle of her femininity.

Lord, he inwardly moaned, had she no idea how enticing was the feast she offered his senses? Like an ancient sailor lost to the sirens' call, he happily surrendered to her. Kiervan reached out and plucked up the ends of the satin ribbon drawstring.

He slowly pulled them in opposite directions, then slipped his hands about her waist to work the gossamer shield down over her slim, silken hips. The fire burning in the depths of her eyes blazed brighter as she deftly accomplished a similar task for him, her hands gliding over the bare skin of his hips and thighs and sending shivers thundering through his flesh.

With a kiss possessive and demanding, he drove her down into the pillowy coverlets. She murmured low, the softness of her curves welcoming the hardness of his angles as he settled into the feather bed at her side. His hand roamed over her freely, almost feverishly, exploring the tautness of her breasts, the satin firmness of her belly. He wanted her, all of her, in ways as glorious as they were undeniable.

His lips seared down across her breast. Alanna gasped, her mind and body remembering in the same instant the wondrous pleasures he had given her in the cave. She felt herself grow taut as he took her in his hand, felt her body yearning for a deeper possession.

A silken curtain of honey-colored hair brushed against Kiervan's cheek as he took the tempting crest of her into his mouth. She moaned as her arms slipped about his neck and her fingers twined through the hair at his nape to hold him a willing captive against her breast. He suckled the hardened peak of her, pulling and caressing with his tongue, his teeth glorying in the little shudders of pleasure that coursed through her body and into his. Suddenly she arched back, his name floating past her lips in the barest of whispers to caress his heart and fan the flames of his desire. He released his prize with excruciating slowness, pulling and flicking his tongue hard and fast across the sensitive tip of the pebbled nub.

With his hands he caressed the curves of her waist and hip, then boldly moved inward to stroke the satin of her inner thigh. With a long, delicious sigh, her legs parted to grant him passage to the dark mound of her moist curls.

"God, but I want you, woman," he whispered, his fingers parting the tumescent feminine folds, his thumb circling, then brushing over the sensitive bud nestled within her curls. She made a whimpering sound and arched upward against his hand in a plea ancient and timeless; arched up to meet his touch, her heels buried in the downy softness of the mattress, her hips angled high and invitingly; reached for him and closed her hand about the heat of his arousal, the rhythm of her possession in harmony with his and igniting within him the fiercest blaze his heart had ever known.

Deep within his loins, Kiervan felt the gathering, the sharp insistence, of his need. Reeling amidst the tattered remnants of reason, he recognized a single, simple reality: the pace of the storm was not his to control, that neither of them had any choice but to ride the raging winds of the tempest.

He caught her hands in his, pinning them to the pillow above her head as he slipped between her thighs. The fit of his hips against her, the press of her honeyed folds against the full, throbbing measure of his desire, sent a keen-edged shudder down the length of his body.

Alanna held her breath as he slowly entered her. Her body tightened, then molded about the heat of him, about the fullness of his gentle, persistent invasion. Alanna looked up at him to see her own wonder and pleasure mirrored in his ebony eyes. He smiled and lowered his head to take her lips with his. And then, with a single swift thrust, he drove into the depths of her, stealing her breath in the same instant that sharp pain pierced the veil of passion cast over her.

She heard herself cry out, but the sound of her surprise and pain were swept into the tender demands of his kiss to mingle with the low, wordless murmur of his apology. And as quickly as it had come, the pain faded away.

He felt her relax beneath him and released his claim to

her lips as her body once more molded about him, welcomed him, caressed him. Then she wiggled down in the feather mattress, drawing him with her, settling herself against him and deepening her possession. He closed his eyes, surrendering to the incredible pleasure of her gentle, provocative demands.

Then, with a growl in Gaelic, he withdrew almost the full length of himself. Alanna's throaty protest was cut short as he returned to the well of her with a tauntingly slow, deliberate fervor. For a moment, brief and exhilarating, he marveled at the perfect sheathing of his body with hers; at the fullness, the completeness, of their union. And then all thought fled before the fervent onslaught of pounding need. Words of desperation, words of promise and love, were lost in the magnificent sensations of moving within her; tattered before the increasing speed and power that followed.

The all-consuming fire rose again between her thighs, and the savage ache too long held captive within her grew as bolts of liquid lightning too wonderful to endure in silence coursed through her. Instincts, primal and compelling, seized control of her body. She gripped Kiervan's hands as she wrapped her legs about his and arched her hips upward, meeting his every thrust, surrendering herself to the pleasure he sent swirling through her body.

From deep within her came a wild yearning that sent scorching heat surging from her womb to every fiber of her being. Her limbs quivered and suddenly she soared upward, caught in a breathtaking, dizzying spiral. Gasping at the swiftness, the intensity, of the wild flight, she cried out, wordlessly begging Kiervan for deliverance. Borne on wave after wave of exquisite sensation, Alanna rode through the swelling darkness of sweetest abandon and into the brilliant universe of a million exploding stars.

Beyond the hammering of her heart and the ragged sound of her breathing, she heard murmured words in Gaelic; realized that Kiervan had stilled within her. Knowing that he awaited her return to him, she struggled to open eyelids strangely heavy.

Poised motionless above her, he watched her, the tumult

of desire glittering in his ebony eyes. Slowly he began again the primeval dance. Alanna arched up, accepting all of him, drawing him into her, reveling in the fierce, primitive sensations only he could stir within her.

His fingers threaded through hers and pressed her hands down into the pillows as he closed his eyes and lifted his face toward heaven. In the same heartbeat, a low growl rumbled in his chest and he plunged into her, hard and fast and deep. With a resonant, shuddering cry, he found his own deliverance and sent her careening, once more, into the magnificent realm of release.

Alanna drifted downward at last, floating on the eddying currents of sated desire, wrapped in the glorious circle of Kiervan's arms. In her heart she knew that no other man would ever fill her body and soul as this dangerous privateer had this night. Tomorrow she would worry about whether making love with Kiervan des Marceaux had been wise. Tonight was for feelings, for delighting in the wonder and joy she saw in his eyes, in the tenderness of his lingering kisses, in the smoky taste of whiskey, the earthy musk of male.

And loving him, she added, nuzzling into the curve of his neck and drifting into contented, blissful sleep.

Kiervan pressed his lips into the silken strands tumbling about her face and inhaled the sweet scent of her. Never had he made love with such savage intensity. And she had returned the fierceness of his demands with a desire equal to his own. He had always known that she was fire, dangerous and consuming. And the hottest fires, he assured himself as he drifted toward the edges of sleep, always burned themselves out with greater speed than the common types were wont to do. Only the worst kind of fool would alter the course of his life's plans in the belief that the fire would last.

27

Alanna drifted gently from the realm of sated sleep. She stretched languidly, reveling in the most complete sense of peace she had ever known. Memories of the night just past came to her and she smiled. Surely no woman on Earth had ever been as thoroughly and repeatedly loved as she had been. And if Kiervan's responses were any indication, surely no woman had ever conducted herself so wantonly either.

There had been nothing gentle about their loving. They had come together each time with a fierceness and a hunger that left them spent and breathless and yet craving more; with an unspoken desperation.

They had shared their hearts as well, she telling him of Oonagh's tale and the depth of Geoffrey Ashton's evil and he laying before her the stories of his travels and the dreams he had woven for Donal and Riona and Dominica. A lifetime of whispers in the dark, a lifetime of loving; all in a single night.

Alanna's smile widened as she rolled onto her back and reached out, searching for the warmth of Kiervan's body. Her hand found only the rumpled bed covers.

Panicked, Alanna bolted upright and searched the cabin for him. He was gone. Even as she fought her fears, she spied Kiervan's sea chest against the far wall. On it, neatly folded, were the clothes she had worn the night she had crossed through the gates of time. Her boots had been placed on the floor beside it.

Well, he didn't have to drop a load of bricks on her. She could take a hint. Alanna climbed from the feather mattress and made her way to the washstand, wincing at the protest of muscles she hadn't known she possessed until that moment.

The water they had bathed each other in the night before had been taken away and fresh provided in its place. Alanna filled the basin, her lips pursed, determined to finish her bathing and dressing as quickly as possible. If, and she suspected it was a big *if*, Kiervan returned, she wanted to be together enough to handle the morning-after scene with some dignity. *Damn hard to do that*, she mused, *while standing in front of him naked.*

Tears inexplicably welled in her eyes, and she brushed them away with the back of her hand. She was being ridiculous, she admonished. Kiervan had far more experience in these matters than she did, after all. Undoubtedly one partner's absence was the easiest way of handling the ever awkward it's-been-nice-it's-been-real-but-it's-over-now moment. No one had to say it this way; it was simply understood. She should be downright grateful that he'd tried to make their parting less stressful.

And parting, she sternly reminded herself, was what she had always known she and Kiervan must do. It was better to do it now, before she became even more comfortable with their physical relationship than she already was. He really ought to come with a warning label, she thought. Something like *Caution. Making love with me could be habit forming.*

She was still reassuring herself when she lifted Maude's cloak from the sea chest. The brooch tumbled from the folds to land at her feet. With a long sigh, Alanna bent and retrieved it. The translucent surface of the stone clouded the instant her gaze touched it, and she stood as though rooted to the spot as she watched the Carraig Cor rise from the mists swirling within the bloodred gem. And then, from the eddying clouds, she saw herself climb up the hill and enter the sacred circle of stones.

The image faded into crimson and Alanna expelled a long

breath. She had been alone in the vision. And she had obviously been returning to the Carraig. Owrd had told her that her destiny had been written, that the time-traveling spell was one she was meant to have. The Dragon's Heart had only proven his prophecy correct.

She had clearly seen a vision within Maude's magical brooch. But more importantly, she had accepted it as a matter of course, accepted it without the slightest twinge of surprise or denial. Somewhere deep within her something had come to center. She smiled, remembering the shell she had cast into the sea, the spell she had cast in her search for a resolution to her inner turmoil. Sometime in the night passed with Kiervan she had found her peace with her abilities. And the Dragon's Heart had just shown her that it would accompany her when she crossed back through the portals of time.

Alanna nodded, the rational part of her accepting the coming end of her sojourn in nineteenth-century Ireland. Still, her heart grieved for all that she would inevitably have to leave behind. She momentarily set aside the brooch. Draping the cloak about her shoulders, she willed her thoughts in less painful directions. She had wondered how she would accomplish the task of foreseeing the O'Connells' role in the gathering revolution. Owrd had promised that the means would come when needed. And it had. Alanna fixed the pin to the cloak and gave it a reverent pat. If she hadn't come out to the *Wind Racer* with Kiervan, she might not have discovered that Maude and Owrd had been right all along, that she could indeed work magic.

"You were to be sleeping when I returned."

She whirled about to find Kiervan standing in the doorway, a huge covered tray in his hands and a wide smile on his face. Her heart turned liquid at the sight of him and the heaviness in her chest evaporated. "I . . ." At a loss for other words, she moved forward to help him.

He shook his head as she reached to take the tray. "I know," he said, kicking the door closed behind him and pointing to the bed with his chin. "Why don't you climb back under the covers and pretend to still be sleeping. That way I can kiss you awake in the manner I have imagined for the past hour."

"But I'm already dressed."

He grinned and cocked a brow. "I rather enjoyed undressing you last night. I'd be most willing to do it again."

She laughed quietly. "You're insatiable, Kiervan des Marceaux."

"Where you're concerned, my sweet Alanna, you are absolutely correct. I'll never have enough of making love to you."

She felt the heat that flooded her cheeks in the same instant that a warning bell went off in her head. He had used the future tense, so obviously he thought they would continue on together for a while longer. She felt a chill pass over her. It would be so easy to stay with Kiervan, to surrender her rational will to the powerful, heady sensations he stirred within her. It would be so easy, but it wouldn't be right. Not for her. Not for him. Not for the woman he intended to marry.

God, why couldn't he have simply stayed away from the cabin? Why couldn't he have sent that nice Mr. St. John to tell her that a boat was ready to take her back to shore? Why in the name of all the Irish saints did he have to make doing the sensible thing so damn difficult?

"Kiervan—" she began, marshaling what little courage she possessed even as she spoke.

He placed the tray in the center of his desk. "You have no need to explain. I understand. Surely you're both sore and tired." He lifted the cover from the tray and put it aside. "But while I can wait, our breakfast can't." He pulled his chair out and motioned with his hand as he added, "Come, Alanna. Sit down and have something to eat with me."

Her mind whirling, she numbly did as he bade. She noted everything he had brought, the fragrant, crusty loaf of bread, the platter of cheeses, the bowl of fresh berries; but it was the green velvet bag tied with the maroon ribbon in the center of the tray that caught and held her attention.

" 'Tis for you," Kiervan supplied, handing her the package.

With a growing sense of misgiving, she opened the bag and poured the contents into her hand. She stared down at the silver Celtic cross that measured nearly the length and breath of her palm, marveling at the intricacy of the Celtic carvings, at the beauty of the polished emerald set in the center of the cross. A finely woven chain trickled from the top of it through her fingers. It was gorgeous, absolutely gorgeous.

" 'Twas my mother's. And her mother's before that."

"I can't." Shaking her head, she handed it back to him. "It's much too valuable."

"I won't accept a refusal, Alanna." He closed her fingers over the pendant and held her hand between his as he gently added, "I give it freely, as you've given yourself to me."

She fought a sense of desperation even as she protested, "But you don't understand, Kiervan. This should go to your daughter. It should be kept in your family." She pulled her hand from his and carefully returned the emerald cross to its velvet bag, saying as she did, "For me to accept this would be wrong."

"Don't be obstinate, Alanna. I want you to have it."

"If I'm being obstinate, it's only because you're being difficult."

"I'm not the óne being difficult," he retorted, angry now. "Or is it simply that you don't recognize the extraordinary nature of what passed between us last night?"

She looked up into the unrelenting light of his eyes. "I'm not stupid," she answered evenly.

"I never said you were. You're the most intelligent woman I've ever met. You also bear the distinction of being the most stubborn."

"Stubborn?" She rose to her feet and faced him squarely.

"No, Alanna," he whispered, slipping his arms around her waist and drawing her to him. "We aren't going to fight. There are other, far more pleasant ways for us to spend our time together."

She pressed against his chest in an effort to keep some distance between them. Alanna could feel the beat of his heart through the palms of her hands. She shook her head and said, "Kiervan, I have to go back to the castle."

He placed a lingering kiss at the corner of her eye. "Why?" he asked softly.

"Owrd's waiting for me," she answered, breathless and weak-kneed at his touch. "I have a lot to learn yet and he's frustrated with how far behind we are in my lessons."

His hands slipped beneath the hem of her tunic, sending a ripple of heady sensation through her. "I'll take you back this afternoon," he whispered, drawing the garment over her head. "I promise."

She offered one last protest even as she allowed herself to be drawn back into his embrace. "I need to go now. I can't . . ." His kiss silenced her words. Her better judgment gave way to the certain knowledge that this would be the very last time she would ever make love with Kiervan des Marceaux.

What he wouldn't give to spend the rest of the mornings of his life lying in bed with Alanna curled against his side, her head resting in the curve of his shoulder. "That's a very serious look in your eye, milady," Kiervan whispered, tracing the beautifully chiseled line of her cheekbone. "What's troubling you?"

"I was just thinking," she answered, her voice distant as she trailed her fingers through the curls on his chest, "about how easy it would be to stay here with you; to not go back to the castle."

He laughed softly. "So don't go. Stay here with me."

She kissed his cheek and then, before he could think to stop her, she rolled out of his arms and off the edge of the bed, saying brightly, "I distinctly recall that you once said I'd make a lousy mistress. Remember?"

"Aye," he admitted, catching her hand. "But you're a wonderful lover. I say we should accept what we have for the moment and not worry about the future. Our courses are set and nothing we do today will change them."

She nodded slowly. A sad light came to her eyes as she drew her hand from his and stepped back beyond his reach.

"My future lies in the twentieth century, Kiervan," she said softly, gathering her clothes from the floor. "Yours is in this time. For us to pretend, even for a while, that the realities don't exist is asking for a broken heart. What's happened between us doesn't change anything."

Lord, why hadn't she simply driven a knife between his ribs? He too climbed from the bed, contemplating the shades of truth before him as he began to dress. In the end he knew in his heart that Alanna deserved the fullest measure.

Both of them had clothed themselves when he finally said gently, "I can't permit either emotions or desire to interfere with a sound business decision, Alanna. I'll marry Eggie when I return to Charleston."

"You don't have to sound so apologetic, Kiervan," she answered, giving him a bittersweet smile. "I understand how you're caught between a rock and a hard place. We're okay as long as you understand that I'm in the same kind of circumstances you are."

Kiervan silently cursed her little bookkeeper's heart, her penchant for imposing order on everything. It would be so easy to put an end to her effort to make sense out of chaos. She stood close enough that he could slip his arm about her waist and draw her back toward their bed, could trace the tempting swell of her breast with his fingers, with his lips. He fought back the urge to reach for her and instead slanted a brow in silent question.

"Kiervan, I can't let what's happened between us interfere with what's right for me either. I have to go back to the time and place where I belong."

His stomach knotted. He stepped to the desk, lifted the cozy from the coffeepot, and then poured them both a cup of the brew before saying, "You're going back to your Bill Boyer."

"If I were going back to Bill, I wouldn't be here with you, Kiervan," she replied, taking the china cup from his hand. "I'm going to call off the wedding and dissolve the business partnership as soon as I get back."

He tightened his grip on his coffee cup and focused his gaze on the distant wall, desperately trying to keep his soaring heart under control. "And what if going back isn't possible, Alanna?"

He watched her lift the cup to her lips, and noted the slight tremor of her hand. "Owrd's given me most of the spell already. I'm only missing the last two words. I'll have them before Beltane, and as soon as I've fulfilled my obligations to Maude, I'll go."

He willed himself to ask, "Is there a particular reason you must return immediately? Can you not go whenever you wish? Can you not stay with me awhile?"

She studied the floor and shook her head. "It'll be easier if I go as soon as possible. The longer I stay with you, the deeper the pain of walking away."

Hurt and angry, Kiervan slammed the cup down amidst his maps and charts. Coffee spilled across the face of his ledger, but he didn't care. She stared up at him, eyes wide.

"You were willing to be my lover last night," he charged. "You agreed while we danced in the great hall. You agreed yet again when we stood together in the shadows of the garden. It was implied in your agreement to come aboard the *Wind Racer*."

"God, you're making this difficult." She closed her eyes. After a long moment, she opened them and resolutely placed her cup beside his on the desk. Steely determination darkened her eyes as she looked up at him. "I did agree to be your lover, Kiervan," she said. "I came here with you willingly, gladly. There's something inside me that wanted to make love with you. No. It's more than that. Something in me *needed* to make love with you. I can't explain it any other way. But I promised you nothing beyond last night. In two days I start back to the Carraig Cor. We don't have a future together, Kiervan. We had last night and this morning. It will have to be enough."

His words came before he could think better of them. "You're asking me to choose between Eglintine and you," he said accusingly.

"No," she answered softly, shaking her head. "The choice you made before you met me is the only one you have, Kiervan."

" 'Tis true that we can't change the past, Alanna. But 'tis equally true that nothing requires us to avoid the joys we unexpectedly find along the paths toward our futures." An image came to him in a blinding flash: an irate Alanna perched on the bank of a stream and protesting the circumstances of his marriage to Eglintine Terwilliger-Hampstead. "Of course," he muttered to himself. "That's it."

He laughed as he found and held Alanna's puzzled gaze. "You have no reason to feel even the slightest twinge of guilt. I'll tell you yet again, sweet Alanna. Please hear me this time. Marriage in this century is unlike marriage in yours. It's perfectly acceptable for a man to take lovers. His wife expects him to, both before and after the marriage ceremony itself.

"And while I've yet to actually meet my intended, I can assure you that in many respects she's typical of women of this time. The only reason Eggie's agreed to wed at all is because, first, she envies her friends' Paris trousseaus, and second, because she's decided that the indignities suffered in the marriage bed are slightly less than those of the public humiliations of spinsterhood. She has no illusions of either love or fidelity."

Even if she'd had a thousand years to consider it, she couldn't have explained why his words hurt as badly as they did. Alanna took a step back and crossed her arms across her chest. "You're the worst kind of cynic, Kiervan."

"I'm a realist," he countered. "I don't want Eggie in the same way I want you. And I'm not ready to allow you to walk out of my life."

Alanna refused to accept his words. "This isn't a matter of what either of us wants. It's a matter of what we can reasonably have. I'd give anything for circumstances to be different." Her eyes suddenly shimmered with tears and she stared at the center of his chest while she resolutely blinked them back.

He stood before her, his eyes dark and soft, and she felt her resolve melting before his wordless plea. Alanna drew a deep breath to fortify her remaining courage. "I think I should be going now. Before one of us does or says something we'll regret."

She didn't wait for him to react, but turned and started toward the door. She was pulling it open when his voice boomed across the distance between them, command resonating through every syllable.

"Don't you dare leave this cabin."

Alanna turned and, with far more poise than she truly felt, replied, "I'm going back to the castle. I have to prepare for the Beltane ceremony."

He stood beside the desk as though nailed to the planking, his hands balled into white-knuckled fists at his sides. "We haven't resolved the matter between us."

"Yes we have, Kiervan," she answered, her voice so soft it barely reached her own ears. "You just didn't get your way."

"Alanna!"

"Thank you for last night. I know they say that a woman always remembers her first lover, her first time. I want you to know that even if you'd been my hundredth lover, I'd always remember how it was to make love with you. It was extraordinary."

Alanna stepped across the threshold and pulled the door closed behind her. From the other side of the portal came the sound of shattering china. Choking back a sob, she raced for the deck above.

Richard St. John had been a true gentleman. He hadn't offered a single comment about her breathless request for immediate transport back to shore. He hadn't asked any questions when he'd provided her a handkerchief with which to dry her tears. He had been utterly silent all the while he'd rowed her to shore. But as she accepted his hand and let him help her from the boat, she knew that he intended to break his silence. She could see the determined glint in his eye.

"If I may speak plainly, mistress."

"Please do," she answered, suspecting even as she did that his words weren't going to make her feel any better about the way she'd left things with Kiervan.

"He's a decent man who truly believes in honoring his promises."

Alanna nodded. "Like the one he made his mother to care for his brother and sisters."

"Would you have done anything less? Asked him to do less?"

"Of course not."

"Has he set forth for you the reasons for his forthcoming marriage to Mistress Terwilliger-Hampstead?"

"Money seemed to be the primary factor."

"Money is certainly a consideration, but it goes beyond that." His gaze went to the *Wind Racer* as he said, "Kiervan knows that he can't sail forever, that the physical demands of it will take increasingly larger tolls. He also knows that if something were to happen to him, were the ship to go down in storm, for instance, then there would be only the investments he's made to support his siblings. While those funds are tidy, they aren't enough to last forever."

"So Kiervan's taking a safer course by marrying his way into a trading company," Alanna supplied. "That way, if something horrible should happen to him, he'll have some of Eggie's daddy's resources going to support his brother and sisters."

"It's not a thing that he's undertaken lightly. Mr. Terwilliger-Hampstead has demanded what in earlier times would have been called a bride price. Never before has the *Wind Racer* carried a cargo of munitions. But Kiervan must be able to pay the sum expected by Terwilliger-Hampstead by this summer, and arms and ammunition are the quickest means to a hefty profit."

Alanna nodded, for the first time clearly understanding the pressure under which Kiervan operated. Damn his sense of honor and responsibility.

Richard St. John went on. "You and I both know that

he's making a terrible mistake in committing to this marriage, to this business arrangement. I've tried to tell him, but he refuses to hear. I had hoped that your presence in his life would make him look at things differently."

"I'm sorry I failed you."

"There's a fine line between determined and stubborn, between bold and foolish. I'm still hopeful that he may yet come to his senses. I ask only that you give him a bit more time to see matters clearly."

She had long known that Kiervan was stubborn. That part of St. John's words had been easily accepted. But no matter what the *Wind Racer*'s First Officer believed, Alanna knew in her heart that all the patience in the world wouldn't make any difference, wouldn't change a damn thing between Kiervan and her. That bitter, undeniable truth hurt deeper than any she had ever known.

Unwilling to crush his friend's optimism, she replied, "All I have is two days, Mr. St. John, and then I have to go back to where I belong."

"Then I'll pray for a miracle." He bowed briefly and said, "Good day, Mistress Chapman."

Alanna smiled weakly, thanked him for his efforts and plain speaking, then watched as he pushed the boat back into the water and set out for the *Wind Racer*. She'd get past the pain, she vowed as she turned and set out on the path leading back to the castle. She wouldn't think about any of it. She'd simply fill her mind with other things. Lord knew she had enough lying ahead of her in the next few days to keep her properly frazzled.

Alanna trudged through the castle's massive doors and moved immediately toward the stairs. She was stopped by a servant waiting at the bottom of the steps like some tin soldier.

"Lady Alanna," the man said, bowing deeply as she neared, "one moment if you please. The O'Connell would have a word with you." He gestured toward the hall.

She grimaced at his words and sighed in defeated acceptance.

Phelan sat in his quasi-throne as he had the day she first met him. Even as she crossed the flagstone floor, she saw the chieftain's furrowed brows and sensed the reason for his obvious displeasure.

"I was told you wanted to see me," she offered, coming to a halt before him.

"We grew concerned when we could not find you last night, Mistress Chapman." He cocked a brow in the same maddening way Kiervan did when he was irritated with something she had done. "Might I ask where you went?"

God, she was too tired, too physically and emotionally drained, to deal with this. Alanna met the chieftain's gaze as she evenly and quietly replied, "With all due respect, Mr. O'Connell, my personal life is just that. Personal."

"Would I be wrong in assuming that you spent the remainder of the evening in the company of Captain des Marceaux?"

"You may assume whatever you like, sir."

He studied her for a long moment before he continued. "I would advise you that the American captain is a dangerous man. He has a reputation for both frequent romantic dalliances and mercenary loyalties. Need I remind you that others' perceptions of one's character and worth are often colored through association?"

Of all the things she had to be worried about . . . If she hadn't been so absolutely wasted, she might have actually laughed at the man's concerns. "And being with Kiervan would tarnish my reputation? Is that what you're saying, Mr. O'Connell?"

"I am saying, Mistress Chapman," he countered, his patience obviously fraying, "that the captain is a persuasive man with specific financial interests in the outcome of your Beltane vision. There are those in this court who are of the opinion that you might allow the captain's charms to influence what you see."

Something inside her brain clicked dully. "Well, Mr. O'Connell, you might reassure them the next time they mention their concerns to you. As charming as Kiervan is, he doesn't control me. No man does. As for the vision, what I see is what you'll get."

"Have I your vow on the matter?"

She managed a pretty good smile and drew a cross over her left breast as she quipped, "And hope to die."

"You offer your pledge lightly."

"Not at all. I'm just refusing to get in a knot about it. I have every intention of being fully honest with you."

"You are an uncommon creature, Mistress Chapman."

She lifted her hands from her side and shrugged. "I'm a seer from another time and place. What else can I say?"

He made a snorting sound and studied her for a long moment. "I sense that there is much you wish to say to me, mistress. Speak freely of what you will."

"You probably wouldn't like it much." The intensity of his stare prodded her on. A spark of life ignited in her as she framed her reply.

"Okay," she said with a sharp nod. "I think you're being foolish in refusing to admit Kiervan's your nephew. He looks and acts just like you. And I know before I say it how weird this is going to sound, but despite his being a rogue and a gun runner, he's a decent, honorable man. I suspect you know what I mean because you were probably just like him when you were younger. If I were you, I'd be damn proud to claim him as family."

"To claim him would make him heir to my properties. I have no other kinsmen."

Alanna paused to consider the unexpected information and then responded, "If it makes any difference, I don't think he's interested in inheriting a thing."

"Then why did he go to the effort of putting forth his assertion of blood ties?"

"He made his mother a lot of promises before she died. Building a bridge to you was only one of them. Truth be known, he'd much rather hold a grudge against you for her exile, but with Kiervan, a promise is a promise. No matter what."

"It occurs to me that you may be the captain's willing pawn; that you are offering me words and assurances he has provided to achieve his own ends. What proof can you offer otherwise?" he challenged.

Alanna shrugged. "None. Except to tell you he's going to be real mad if he ever finds out we've had this conversation. Kiervan doesn't much care for anyone defending or explaining him. He's rather of the opinion that he can do that quite well for himself."

The O'Connell stared over her head into the distance of the great hall, his mind apparently occupied by his private concerns. Alanna shifted from foot to foot and finally offered a small cough in a discreet effort to call him back to her. The moment his gaze lit upon her, she smiled and asked, "May I go now?"

"I recall that you said no man controls you, mistress. You ask for my permission?"

"I'm trying to be polite."

"And if I refuse to grant you my leave?"

Alanna grinned. "We'll stare at each other for a few minutes and then I'll leave anyway."

He too grinned. "I do believe I am coming to understand what Kiervan finds so fascinating about you, woman. Owrd awaits you in your chambers. You had best not delay any longer in taking up your lessons."

Not quite knowing what else to do, Alanna gave him a cheery salute and then headed back toward the stairs. Feeling better than she had all morning, she bounded up the steps, taking them two at a time.

The surge of energy had lasted until noon, and then the deep lassitude that had gripped her after leaving the *Wind Racer* returned. Owrd had shown her no mercy, pouring information into her and making her repeat back to him countless times the rituals and incantations to be performed the following night. When he'd finally been satisfied, he'd ordered her a bath and supper, then kissed her on the forehead and wished her pleasant dreams.

Gowned and perfumed, Alanna paced her room in total darkness. She had thought sleep would come the instant she laid her head on the pillow. In its stead had crept a heavy, almost tangible melancholy. Instinctively she knew that if she could just find some tears someplace, she'd feel infinitely better. But try as she might, even the gentlest of her emotions were trapped behind a leaden cloud that settled over her heart.

28

Alanna brushed the oat flour from her face with an equally dusty sleeve and surveyed the kitchen with one last look. Women seemed to be everywhere, their skirts swirling through the room like roiling clouds as they bustled about, preparing the evening's feast with a precision that would have made a Marine drill team envious. Alanna watched as the last of the Beltane cakes she had prepared and inscribed with the nine-square symbol of the pagan holy day were placed in the ovens to bake. Huge baskets of those already done sat at the end of the large central table. Her work there completed, she wiped her hands on her apron and then removed it, leaving it on a peg set into the wall by the door as she entered the castle courtyard.

Where the kitchen had been the realm of the women, the courtyard was clearly the domain of the men. Every fireplace in the castle had been cleaned out in the course of the day, and bundle after bundle of precious wood had been brought from the land all about to be laid in the grates. Tonight she would light the central fire in the meadow beyond the castle walls, and from it would be taken sprigs of fire to light anew every hearth in the Clan O'Connell.

Alanna had found a strange comfort in the rituals sweeping her through the day, in the welcoming of a new year in ways as old as time itself. She settled herself on a keg in the shade and watched the men who brought buckets of ash from the castle and poured the powdery residue into the bins by the kitchen door, watched other men carry bundled wood on their shoulders through the great gates and drop them into temporary piles in the cobbled center of the open area.

And then Kiervan came through the gates with a bundle on each shoulder, his hair glistening in the late-morning sun, his shirt damp and clinging to the muscles of his arms and torso. Memories of their night together flooded over her, shattering her calm and igniting a familiar fire deep and low within her.

Pride warned her of the danger in remembering so clearly, in wanting more of the heady delight she had found in Kiervan's arms. Common sense whispered of the danger in allowing herself to be drawn again to the warmth of Kiervan's flame. But her heart ached to be set free again, begged to dance just one more time in Kiervan des Marceaux's fierce embrace.

Alanna watched as Kiervan tossed the twin bundles of wood into the heap and turned to study her. She saw the same memories play across his features, saw the same yearning soften the ebony of his eyes. After a long moment, he crossed the yard to stand before her.

Good judgment railed again at her instincts, but she consciously chose to ignore the words of warning. She gripped the sides of the barrel to steady herself as she smiled up at him and softly admitted, "I don't like how we left things the other morning."

With a tender smile, he replied, "Neither do I."

"I wish we could do it over again."

She saw his jaw momentarily tighten, saw him swallow. Then he lifted his hand and brushed the backs of his fingers along her cheek. "You have flour all over your face."

"And you have bark chips in your hair," she answered, surrendering to the urge to reach for him.

With a gentle slowness that took her breath away, he traced her lips with his fingertips. "I have work to do," he murmured, his gaze fastened on hers.

"Me too." She threaded her fingers through the warmth of his silken hair, their path and intent having nothing to do with the bits of wood clinging to the raven strands.

He slipped his hands about her waist and his gaze burned with an intensity that sent a river of warmth coursing down her thighs. "There'll be talk if I'm gone too long, Alanna."

She arched a brow. "Then we probably shouldn't be wasting so much time, should we?"

He grinned and lifted her down from the keg. "Have you a place in mind?"

She smiled mischievously. "I've always heard that stables have a certain ambiance."

"And on a day like today," he added, taking her hand in his, "a bit more privacy than any room in the manor."

Without another word, Kiervan led her into the empty, shadowed tack room at the rear of the stable. The scents of leather, saddle soap, fresh straw, hay, and sweetened oats wafted about them as he pressed her against the smooth planking of the wall, as his lips sought hers in a feverish, demanding kiss, as his hands lifted her skirts and slipped beneath in search of the ties of her pantalets.

She was naked beneath her petticoats. Even as the realization jolted through him, Alanna slid her hands between them and opened the front of his breeches.

"Merciful God, but I want you, woman," he murmured against her lips, struggling against the urge to take her where they stood.

In reply, she gently caught his lower lip between her teeth and took his swollen need in her hands. A primal heat and hunger quivered through his loins. His resistance undone, Kiervan slipped his hands back to cup her, to lift her.

A low string of Gaelic exploded from somewhere in the loft above their heads. Even as they both froze and stared up at the rough-hewn boards, another burst of Gaelic resounded through the barn.

Kiervan glanced down to find Alanna smiling at him, her eyes twinkling with the light of amusement.

"You're blushing," she whispered, kissing his chin.

He slanted a brow and glanced briefly at the loft before replying, " 'Tis a good thing you neither speak nor understand the Irish language. Paddy's . . . requests . . . are . . ."

A woman's voice, rough and demanding, interrupted him and fueled the heat already suffusing his face. "Hers don't appear to be any better," he observed wryly. He sighed heavily and shook his head. " 'Twould appear that this place isn't as private as we had hoped. Under the circumstances . . ."

Alanna nodded and released her hold on his shoulders. "Agreed."

He set her gently on her feet, regretting with all his heart the need to do so. She smoothed her skirts but he sensed that she watched his every move. Fastening the buttons and then tucking his shirt into his breeches, he tried to tamp down the desire still heating his blood.

"Keep looking at me like that, woman," he chided in gentle warning, "and I'm likely to lose my returning, but still fragile, sense of decorum. Paddy and that woman's presence be damned."

"Sorry." Her grin belied the apology. "Will you be all right, Kiervan?"

"I'll be no more uncomfortable than you," he replied, smiling and placing his hands on her shoulders. "Now leave me so I can at least regain the outward appearance of self-control. Otherwise I won't be able to walk across the courtyard without inviting a rash of bawdy comments."

Placing her hand in the center of his chest, she rose on her toes to give him a tender parting kiss. He saw something soft and yielding flicker in her eyes when she stepped away, and for a moment she seemed as though she might speak. Then, with a wink and a resigned smile, she slipped silently past him and out of the stall.

"And I love you, Alanna," he whispered after her.

A low, breathless moan drifted down from the rafters, followed by a laughing answer.

The sun's last bright edge dropped below the rim of the hills to the west, and a cool evening breeze fluttered the hem of Alanna's simple white gown. She scanned the scene before her and tried to convince herself that she had no reason to be nervous. The sacred nine-square grid had been drawn in the meadow, and all but the central patch of sod had been lifted away in the manner prescribed by the Druidic rituals.

It was the expectation so evident in the faces of the people arrayed on the other side of the nine stacks of wood that seemed to bother her, Phelan's especially. If she somehow managed to screw this up . . .

"All is in readiness, granddaughter."

Alanna started and looked up at Owrd. How long had he been standing at her side?

"Have you prepared the tinder, child?"

Alanna tugged the white leather pouch from her rope belt and nodded. "Shavings of rowan, ash, alder, willow, hawthorn, oak, holly, elder, and birch, their proportions equal and combined in the proper order."

"Then it is time to begin," he said, handing her the oaken spindle and oak log socket.

Alanna stepped to the center of the Beltane square, knelt at the edge of the remaining piece of turf, and placed her primitive fire-starting tools in the middle of it. As though she didn't have enough to worry about, Kiervan chose that precise moment to enter the circle of onlookers.

An almost electric shock raced through her body. Would he expect her to jump through the Beltane smoke with him? she wondered. Already most of those present stood as couples; had determined with whom they would share the ancient purification and fertility ritual. Seeing Niall and Hisolda standing together, hand in hand, was a complete surprise.

Smiling ruefully, Alanna fixed her attention on the pouch, opening the bag and positioning it so that she could easily reach the shavings when she had created the required spark. Had she been so wrapped up in the affairs of her own heart that she'd failed to notice those of others? Yes, she resolutely answered. And it was high time to focus on something besides her totally unpredictable relationship with Kiervan des Marceaux.

Concentrating on the immediate task at hand, she blocked the spectators from her mind, placed a pinch of the shavings in the socket of the log, and then fitted the spindle into the hole. She worked the spindle between her palms, and within moments thin wisps of smoke began to rise from the log at her knees. She added a bit more of the shavings and worked the spindle until the scent of burning wood drifted up to tickle her nose.

With the creation of the first inklings of fire, Alanna entered a familiar realm. Adding more shavings and gently blowing on the spark to feed it, she had a respectable flame in no time at all. Rising to her feet, she set about gathering the smallest twigs from each of the nine stacks of wood, being careful to keep them separated. Then, reciting the words Owrd had taught her, she fed the bits of each tree to the fire, one by one. They caught and the flame grew.

A collective sigh rose from those assembled, and she glanced up to see Kiervan's wide congratulatory smile. Lord, but he was without doubt the most handsome man in the meadow that evening. Her mind flooded with memories and her heart thumped wildly against the walls of her chest as the blood coursing through her veins warmed.

Behind her, Owrd made a small sound and she started, remembering the task yet to be completed. She shook her head to clear it and turned back to the piles of wood to gather additional, more substantial, fuel for the Beltane fire.

When she had a blaze strong and vital, she stepped back to Owrd's side and looked up at him. He nodded and then glanced down at her shoulder, at Maude's brooch. A jolt of wary anticipation shot through her, intensifying when Phelan came to stand on her other side. She tried to swallow past it, tried to take a steadying breath. Both efforts proved futile.

As Owrd had instructed, she removed the Dragon's Heart from her shoulder and cradled it in the palms of her hands as she faced the Beltane fire. An unsettling hush fell over those assembled and she closed her eyes for a brief moment to offer up a prayer for a vision, any vision. Slowly she opened them, her gaze focused in the depths of the stone. God, she inwardly wailed, there was nothing there except a reflection of the fire and the silhoutte of Castle O'Connell.

She pursed her lips and looked deeper, willing something else, anything else, to appear.

And then she realized that what she saw was no mere reflection. The castle in the stone was afire. In the shadowed edges of the scene before her, horses charged forward and sabers glinted in the firelight. She stared transfixed and re-pulsed by the horror of panicked people fleeing before the certainty of death and destruction. And then the ruby cleared.

Alanna looked up into Phelan O'Connell's wary eyes. "I saw the castle being destroyed," she provided, drained of emotion.

"By whom? When?" he demanded.

"I can't say. The vision didn't tell me that."

"In your heart, what do you know to be the outcome of the revolution?"

Alanna took a deep breath. On the other side of the fire, Kiervan waited, his arms folded across his chest, his lips a thin line. Her gaze holding his, she replied honestly, "It will fail."

Phelan nodded and then turned to face his kinsmen, his subjects. "The question is resolved," he announced, his voice ringing clearly across the meadow. "The Clan O'Connell shall not join in the rebellion."

A small part of Alanna's consciousness noted the sighs of relief, the suddenly relaxed conversation eddying about her. But the greater part of her awareness remained on Kiervan, on the steely determination and cool calculation that came into his eyes as he stood there, motionless, silently consider-ing her. He felt betrayed; she knew that. He'd hoped to sell his arms to his kinsmen and had invested weeks of precious time in waiting for a favorable vision. And she had let him down. He would have to sail away now; find another revolution, another buyer. And then he would return to America.

And you love him enough to go with him. Alanna started before the power of her own inner voice, desperately want-ing to deny the truth of it. But even as she tried to tell herself that she wouldn't do such a foolish, self-destructive thing, she knew in her heart that what she felt for Kiervan wasn't bounded by good sense and rational thought.

She looked away, remembering that long ago, on her first night in this time, he'd told her that he was a man who took whatever he wanted, neither asking for permission nor offering apologies. He had warned her and she had failed to heed it. Foolishly she'd thought the better side of him would respect her decision to cross back into her own time and place; that in the end, he'd let her run away and hide. But he knew the secrets of her heart, and he wouldn't let her deny them. The next time she stepped into his arms, she'd never leave.

Her mind reeled. From the swirling chaos of her thoughts came a simple fact: she had no choice but to run, to make a break for it while she still had a fighting chance to conduct herself honorably. Even as she struggled to find a sensible course, she saw Phelan pause at Kiervan's side, speak into his ear, and then walk away. Kiervan's expression hardened as he turned to glare at the back of the departing chieftain. Then he glanced at her briefly as though promising he wouldn't be long delayed from his purpose before he strode after Phelan into the darkness.

Alanna grasped the unexpected opportunity. Lifting her robes, she whirled about and looked up at her grandfather. "I have to go back to the Carraig Cor," she said in a rush. "Right now. I can't delay even a single extra second."

"I know. Follow me." He didn't wait for her reply, but simply turned and walked away.

"Come with me," she pleaded, walking at his side toward the already dark edge of the meadow. "Come back with me. I'll take care of you."

He shook his head, his gaze fixed on the darkness ahead. "My place is here. I could not go forward with Maude and Oonagh when they begged me. My destiny lay in this time and place, in preparing for you and the events prophesied so long ago. Neither can I go with you. My end is written and it shall come to pass on this side of the gates of time."

"I don't want to leave you behind. You're all I've got, Grandfather," she pleaded. "Defy destiny. Cross with me."

He said nothing, but continued on a determined course into the night.

Holding her skirts above her ankles, Alanna trotted at his side, her heart twisting and aching. "Owrd," she called. "Did you hear me? Defy des—"

"No," he declared firmly as he stopped in his tracks and turned to face her. "It cannot be done. As my past was here, so is my present and my future. You must go your way without me."

"But—"

"We are wasting precious time." He turned, resuming his course without another word.

Alanna stared after him for a long moment and then looked beyond him. Ahead the dark shadowed shapes of wind-twisted trees rose from a low spot in the meadow. Knowing his destination, she lifted her skirts and ran to catch up with him.

"Then I'll stay," she offered, reaching his side again. "If you won't go—"

"My time is short, Alanna. It was our fate to have but a few days to travel together in this life. And while I have waited long for it, that sojourn is complete. Now your destiny lies away from here. I have prepared for your departure."

"Grandfather . . ."

"Enough, child," he said sharply. "Find either strength or silence."

She followed him into the copse, choking back her fear and trying desperately to find within her even the smallest measure of courage.

"We're here, sir."

"Niall?" Alanna called, skittering to a halt and turning toward the sound of his voice.

He stepped silently from the shadows leading a roan mare. Hisolda emerged behind him, a bundle clutched to her chest.

"She brings your clothing for the journey ahead," Owrd explained before Alanna could ask. "Step into the darkness and permit her to attire you properly."

Numbed, Alanna did as her grandfather instructed; absently obeyed Hisolda's commands as the maid stripped her of the white Druid's robe and dressed her in the outfit she'd worn when she had first climbed the Carraig Cor.

She stepped from the woods, her mind whirling about in search of something, anything, to make the world come right. She heard herself offer words of protest, but she might as well have kept her silence for all the response they garnered. Niall kissed her cheek and asked for the blessings of the Earth Mother to be upon her. Hisolda hugged her fiercely and promised never to forget her. Owrd took her by the shoulders, stared long into her face as though trying to sear it into his memory, then kissed her on the forehead and turned her toward the waiting horse.

Somehow she found herself in the saddle. Niall led her out of the trees on the back side of the small grove and slapped the animal on the rump.

Only when she'd reached the crest of the hill did she rein in the mare and turn to gaze at the valley below. The Beltane fire glowed white and orange in the distance as couples, hand in hand, jumped over the blaze and through the rising smoke. All across the meadow, beads of light bobbed erratically as members of the Clan O'Connell carried portions of the sacred fire to light their own hearths, and to light the hearths of the castle, which sat a dark silhouette against the night sky.

If only Kiervan had been willing to offer her forever. Alanna clenched her teeth, wheeled the horse toward the east, and kicked it gently in the flanks. Kiervan was of the present. Her future, what mending of her heart and soul that could be done, lay on the other side of the Carraig Cor.

29

Kiervan stormed up the castle stairs, taking them three at a time. Damn Phelan O'Connell. Of all the times the man could have asked to speak to him privately, he would choose the one when Kiervan couldn't have cared any less about business. God only knew what the man wanted to discuss and how long it would take. Kiervan needed to get back to the celebrations in the meadow; Alanna was there somewhere amongst the revelers. He needed to find her and convince her that he could make her happy.

Kiervan rapped impatiently on Phelan's door and entered the room at the first sound of the man's answering call. His uncle stood before the fireplace, watching as a maid held a Beltane torch to the wood atop the grate.

Phelan glanced up. "You have the appearance of a storm cloud, lad. Is something amiss?"

"There's a pressing matter to which I need attend as quickly as possible," Kiervan replied, stepping to the side of the open doorway and crossing his arms over his chest.

Phelan smiled and shook his head, then turned his attention back to the maid at the hearth as he observed, "The Lady Alanna is not jumping through the smoke with any other, if that is what concerns you."

The young woman stepped away from the fire and bobbed quickly. "I'll be seeing to the other grates now, milord" she said. As Phelan nodded in acknowledgement, Kiervan suddenly recalled the barn and the sounds coming from the loft. This was Paddy's woman, he was certain. The maid slipped out of the room with her torch and pulled the door closed behind her. Kiervan waited until he heard the latch drop into place before answering, "I doubt neither Alanna's heart nor her fidelity."

Phelan motioned to a chair as he seated himself before the growing fire. "Then sit down and find a bit of patience for an old man."

"I'd prefer to stand," Kiervan replied.

"You inherited your mother's strong will," his uncle said to the flames.

"So, you finally admit that I am Saraid's son and your nephew," Kiervan said bitterly. "What has prompted your change of heart?"

"Something your Alanna said to me, as well as the shame I've borne these many years over my part in Saraid's sad fate. But I am not as full of evil as you believe me to be. I sent for you so that I might tell you the whole of that story. I would make amends to you, lad, and resolve the difficulties between us. I know that is what Saraid would want."

His conscience pricked, Kiervan grasped the back of the chair before him and leaned forward, his eyes narrowed as he considered the man who had sold his mother into slavery. "Speak your peace, Phelan O'Connell, and let's be done with the matter for all time."

Phelan sighed and nodded. His gaze never left the fire as he began, "I came to be The O'Connell too young. I had not the proper kind of wisdom for the tasks confronting me. In the blindness of my youth, I thought that all things were within my power to order as I wished, to mold as suited my purposes.

"Your mother was as headstrong and independent as she was beautiful and intelligent. She would have nothing of my arrangements for her marriage, and we quarreled bitterly over her refusal to be a pawn in my political intrigues. In the throes of a hideous and vengeful anger, I sought to bend her to my will, to frighten her into accepting my design for her life."

"You sold her to the English," Kiervan accused, the words forced through his clenched teeth.

" 'Twas to have been a ruse," Phelan replied, suddenly sounding old and tired and sad. "But my enemies conspired against me and sent my plan awry. When I discovered what had occurred, I sent men throughout England in search of her, and when they brought back word that Saraid had been transported to the American colonies, I sent them there as well."

Kiervan spat out, "Your compassion and concern came far too late."

"What I did was wrong. I know that. I have spent my life trying to atone for the grievous sin I committed against my sister, against your mother. I have long prayed that Saraid found some measure of happiness and love in the life consigned her by my conceited folly."

Kiervan continued to grip the back of the chair, only vaguely aware of the ragged measure of his breathing. "She did."

"The bitterest words you've ever spoken, lad?" Phelan asked, finally turning his attention away from the fire and meeting Kiervan's gaze squarely. Phelan nodded, answering his own question. "I cannot blame you for your anger, for your resentment. A fool deserves the derision of those whom he has injured. A wiser man knows he can do naught to change the past; that he can only make matters right in the present and hope that the future will judge him well for the earnestness of his regret."

Phelan rose to his feet and faced him. "I have legally acknowledged you as my kinsman, as the eldest son of Saraid O'Connell and as my nephew. The record has been written and sealed. I have made provisions for her other children as well; for the boy, Donal, and the girls, Dominica and Riona. But it is you who will inherit this castle and all of my worldly goods. And, should you desire the responsibilities, you are qualified to stand for election as The O'Connell after me."

"I want nothing from you," Kiervan snarled, releasing his hold on the chair and stepping back.

Both of Phelan's gray brows shot up. "And would you have the Lady Alanna sailing the seas with her husband, making a home and raising your children aboard a ship in the rough company of sailors?"

Pain sliced through Kiervan's heart. Through it he answered angrily, "I am to wed another."

Phelan shook his head and ambled toward the hearth, saying as he went, "I see that along with your mother's strong will, you have inherited my penchant for foolishness; a dangerous combination."

With his back to the blazing logs, the old man again met Kiervan's gaze. "Accept a bit of wisdom from a sad old man who acquired it too late to save himself. The heart has a course of its own, and to interfere with it, to place other matters before it, will bring you only unfathomable grief. Marry the Lady Alanna, Kiervan. Fill these walls with the sound of your children's laughter. Let me pass into the next world knowing that I have finally done right by my sister, that I have done what I could to make things as they should have been long ago."

Kiervan stepped from behind the chair, reached for the door latch, and then paused. "Even were it in my heart to grant your request, I can't. As my mother lay dying, I took a solemn pledge to honor her request. I *will* marry well, Phelan O'Connell. I will provide for my brother and sisters so that they'll never know the deprivations and heartbreaks of our mother's life. I've made commitments to that end and they lead me down a path far distant from here."

Pulling open the door, Kiervan turned back and considered the old man standing before the fire, considered the wounds, the tears, his uncle's folly had caused; remembered his mother's last fervent wish.

"Acknowledge me as your kinsman if you will," he replied after a long moment. " 'Twill make my mother's soul rest easier. But pass your worldly goods to another, Phelan O'Connell. Pass them to someone who is content to risk his fortune on the unpredictable winds that buffet the traitorous heart of Ireland."

Ignoring the old man's command to return, Kiervan

stepped across the threshold into the hall and closed the door with a satisfying finality. He stormed down the hallway, his temples pounding, his footsteps resounding along the stone corridor. Cast his fortune with the Irish? The old man had taken absolute leave of his senses. As though Alanna would want to be mistress of Castle O'Connell.

The image struck him with such force that his step faltered and his anger evaporated. He remembered Alanna as she had been in the courtyard that morning: oat flour on her face, her skirt dusty from hours spent in the kitchens, her cheeks made rosy by the heat of the ovens and her desire. Another memory came in the wake of the first: Alanna lighting the Beltane fire in the ancient way, performing the age-old ritual which would bring prosperity and happiness to the people of the Clan O'Connell.

He stopped and turned to stare at Phelan's door. Perhaps the old man wasn't completely mad after all. Perhaps Alanna would be happy as mistress of Castle O'Connell. If she would be content to stay here, to wait, over and over, for his return from the sea, from America and Eglintine . . .

Something within him rebelled at the thought. Swearing beneath his breath, Kiervan whirled around, intent on resuming his original course. He froze in midstep, his attention transfixed by the thick black cloud pulsing from beneath a door midway along the hall, from under the door of Alanna's room.

His heart racing, he dashed forward, seized the latch, and shoved the portal open. As though driven by the very hands of hell, he staggered back, his arms instinctively shielding his face. As the initial blast of heat rushed past him, Kiervan dashed forward again and across the threshold. Covering his mouth and nose with his hand, he sought desperately to see through the pall of dense smoke. The bed was afire, the flames dancing wildly up the bed curtains and leaping across the room to lick at the chairs drawn up before the cold hearth. Whirling about and choking on the smoke, he searched the corners of the room, praying that he'd find nothing. When he'd satisfied himself that she wasn't there, his heart filled with gratitude, and he backed out of the room and pulled the door closed. His Alanna, his sweet Alanna, had not been consumed by the flames. Surely a merciful God kept her in the meadow, safe from harm.

Even as he prepared to raise a cry, others in the castle sounded the alarm. "Up here!" he shouted to those dashing about in the foyer below. "The Lady Alanna's room has been set ablaze."

Phelan was at his elbow even as the summons left his lips. "The barns and storage buildings have been put to the torch as well," the old man said, buckling a saber about his hips. "We are under siege. Find yourself a trusted weapon, lad, and stay close. Protect my back as I will yours and we may yet live to see tomorrow's dawn."

Kiervan reached beneath his coat and drew a pistol from the waistband at the small of his back. It wouldn't be enough, he knew, if they were indeed under attack. He needed a weapon capable of killing more than one man, a weapon that would give him the time and the certainty to find Alanna amidst the chaos.

He and Phelan raced down the stairs together, their strides even and matched, until they reached the bottom. "In the great hall, lad," Phelan shouted above the din as he surveyed the first of the water buckets being passed through the massive doors, "you'll find a choice of swords upon the wall. Get one and meet me in the courtyard."

Kiervan watched his uncle charge through the castle doors and out into the flickering orange that seared the night. For a fraction of a second, he thought to follow him, and in that fragment of time, well-honed instincts for survival seized control. He dashed toward the hall, knowing that securing a weapon had to be his first priority. All the rest wouldn't matter if he couldn't protect himself. He'd do Phelan no good dead. And Alanna . . .

God, he begged, pulling a deadly broadsword from its place on the wall, *let me find her in time. Keep her safe. I love her, God. Please don't let harm come to her.* With prayers still on his lips, he made his way resolutely through the manor and into the courtyard.

All was lost. Kiervan knew the certain, horrible truth the instant he stepped through the castle doors. Phelan stood in the center of the yard, shouting orders into the melee, trying desperately to organize the confusion roaring around him. To their everlasting credit, men and women both raced to obey their chieftain's commands, some joining the bucket brigades in a desperate attempt to quench the ring of fire that threatened to roast them all alive. Others scrambled to the battlements, armed with nothing more than handfuls of stone and implements gathered from the stable and smithy.

Kiervan grabbed the shoulder of a man scurrying to join those who fought the fire. "Take two others with you," he yelled at him, "and bring all the weapons you can carry from the great hall."

The man nodded, yelled to his nearest companions, and ran for the doorway. Kiervan surveyed again the mayhem swirling about him. Women and children were pouring into the keep through the gate, their eyes wide in terror, their voices a shrieking chorus. His mind reeled. They should have been fleeing the fire, not running into the heart of it. Not unless . . .

He swore viciously as he ran for the gates. Halfway there he saw Niall and Hisolda stagger through the archway dragging Owrd's limp form between them. As he pushed his way through the throng to reach them, he reminded himself that Alanna was young, stong, and intelligent, that she could take care of herself no matter how desperate the situation. If only he could believe that would be enough to ensure her survival.

"Where's Alanna?" he bellowed when near enough to Niall and Hisolda to be heard above the din. "Where is she?"

"On her way to the Carraig," Niall gasped, trying to catch Owrd as the old man slipped from his shoulder. "Owrd sent her on well before the English attack."

For a fleeting moment, relief washed over Kiervan. Alanna was safe. And then a steely resolution settled over him. If Alanna truly thought running from him would solve their problems, God help her when he caught up with her.

He shoved his pistol into Niall's free hand, grabbed Owrd about the waist, and heaved the old man over his shoulder.

Glaring at the magician's apprentice, he barked, "Gather the women and children and take them to the shore. Swim if you have to, but get them aboard the *Wind Racer*. Tell Richard St. John to get her the hell out of the harbor."

"But the castle . . ." Niall protested. "We can't leave you here to—"

"Now!" Kiervan roared. "Before you're buried in the goddamned rubble with the rest of them!"

He didn't wait to see if the lad obeyed, but turned away, carrying Alanna's grandfather to the wall beside the gates. With gentle care he lowered the old man to the ground and knelt beside him. Owrd's eyelids fluttered and then opened just enough for Kiervan to see the shadow of death in their depths. Stripping off his coat, Kiervan leaned low and said, "My deepest thanks for seeing Alanna safely away, Owrd."

"She loves you, Captain," the old man whispered as their gazes locked and Kiervan covered his blood-soaked torso. "But she is the wind. Remember both, Captain. It is important."

Kiervan nodded. "Know that I love her too, Owrd. And that I will remember."

A shiver racked the frail old body and for a moment Kiervan thought it might bear Alanna's grandfather through the pain of his end. It passed and in its wake Owrd's jaw tightened. Again his gaze found Kiervan's.

"Your destiny is not set, Captain," he rasped, the effort clearly consuming the last measure of his strength. "But soon you must choose a way. Choose well." The admonition had barely passed his lips when his vision shifted to a place beyond Kiervan's shoulder, beyond the melee surrounding them, and his lips curved upward in a gentle smile. "Maude. Oonagh," he whispered. His smile broadened.

Kiervan saw the light leave the old man's eyes as Owrd's spirit went to join his daughters, and knew that it was done. A small measure of comfort came to him as he drew the old man's eyelids closed. One of Owrd's last deeds had been to see Alanna safe from the English atrocity swirling about him. Kiervan forever owed him a debt of gratitude for that magnificent act of foresight. "Go in peace, Owrd," Kiervan said quietly, rising to his feet. "Know that I will protect Alanna all of my days as you have this night."

A calm settled over him as he turned and started back toward Phelan. There was no point in closing the gates. The English wolves were already within the walls. All that remained possible was to save those he could before the inevitable collapse of Castle O'Connell; before he could consider the field honorably relinquished and then set out after Alanna.

He had taken no more than a few steps when he saw Paddy O'Connell stride from the chaos, a silver-butted pistol in each hand. Even as Kiervan recognized the weapons as his own, as those lost to Ashton in the farmyard, Paddy raised one and fired. In the same moment of time, Phelan tumbled backward, his hands clutching his chest, his eyes wide in disbelief, glazed with the sheen of death.

Kiervan adjusted his grip on the sword and, with grim resolution, bore down on the Irish wolf who had betrayed the Clan O'Connell.

Alanna drew in the reins and dismounted. Her face was raw from the tears she had spilled, from the rough, impatient wiping of her sleeve. She knelt at the stream's edge, and as her horse nibbled grass at her side, she splashed cool water across her fiery cheeks. After a moment she sat back on her heels and sighed. As she gazed at the reflection of the pale moon on the dark, smooth surface of the water, she reassured herself for the thousandth time that what she was doing was right. She didn't belong in the nineteenth century. She didn't belong in Ireland.

And then the mirrored moon darkened to the orange of a thousand suns. Alanna sucked in a breath as before her eyes the color changed yet again, changed to the shimmering crimson of freshly spilt blood.

"No," she whispered, dread filling her as she ripped Maude's brooch from her shoulder. The image was there the instant she sought it; the roof of Castle O'Connell collapsing in a stormy shower of brilliant sparks. Phelan's body lay sprawled in the center of the courtyard, his chest wet and glistening in the firelight, and Paddy lay crumpled beside him, his body slashed, his head twisted at an odd angle. Her hands shook but she couldn't take her eyes from the horror playing before her.

And then she saw Kiervan striding through the melee, bellowing orders to those following him, swinging his sword like a man possessed as he cut a wide swath through the courtyard. He was alive. A wave of such intense relief swept over her that for a moment she swayed, light-headed and weak, barely able to keep her focus on the ruby stone she held in the palm of her hand.

Slowly the image faded. But even as Alanna expelled a long breath, it returned. She watched in abject terror as Ashton rode through the gates of Castle O'Connell, as Kiervan paused before the stable to rally the defenders, as the stone wall behind him bowed and swayed. A high-pitched scream ripped through the quiet of the night when it crumbled and buried Kiervan beneath its weight.

Scrambling to her feet, Alanna shoved the brooch into her pocket. In the same frantic moment, she grabbed the reins of her mount and vaulted into the saddle. She whirled the mare about and, leaning forward over her neck, set the animal to race against the cruelty of fate.

30

Alanna crested the hill, her gaze searching the valley below, trying to see the castle through the driving sheets of silver rain that had started to fall. The fires continued to burn within the walls despite the onslaught of the storm, the glow of danger and destruction a beacon through the pall of smoke and death. She urged the horse on, paying no heed to the still forms lying in the mire of the meadow, nor to those living who jumped at her mount in an attempt to stop her wild ride toward the castle gates. The rain drenched her hair and clothing, numbing her body to the marrow with its cold, and bits of turf and mud spattered her face and hands and clung to her cloak and her leggings.

Good, she thought grimly, leaning forward and rising slightly from the saddle as the horse gathered to leap over a jumble of stone. A harridan on a frenzied ride into the bowels of hell. They'd think twice. She rode full tilt into the yard, recognizing the general shapes of grappling men and the discordant sound of battle as she rode through them. Shouts rang out around her, and men as drenched and dirty as she was snatched at the horse's bridle, at the saddle. Alanna pushed the animal on, her greater awareness on the rubble that had once been the stable wall, on reaching Kiervan.

Even as she reined the animal in, she was already swinging down from the saddle. Giant raindrops pelted her head and shoulders, in the puddles about her feet and on the rocks covering Kiervan. The smell of mud, smoke, and blood filled the air, choking her and making her queasy. Her hands trembling and rivulets of rain running over her cheeks, Alanna bent and lifted a stone from the edge of the pile. Blindly tossing it aside, she reached for another, her heart pounding, her fingers clawing for purchase, her lips forming silent words of prayer. Vaguely she heard her horse whinny, heard the clatter of its hooves as it raced away.

She reached for another stone, and then another, always working her way toward the center, toward the place she had seen Kiervan standing when the wall had come down on him in her vision. In the center of her soul she knew that her love still lived, that beneath the pile of rocks his heart still beat, he still breathed. Had he slipped away, he would have touched her in his passing. She would have felt his farewell.

Lifting yet another block, she gasped and hurriedly cast it away. A portion of Kiervan's boot lay exposed before her, the leather already splattered with raindrops. A grateful sob tore from her as she frantically pushed aside rock after rock, uncovering first his leg, then his chest, his shoulder, and finally his head.

"Kiervan!" she cried, brushing the locks of raven hair from his eyes, tracing the sooty angles of his face. "Can you hear me?" she asked, trying to keep her voice even and calm as her fingers roamed over his head. "It's Alanna. Oh God, Kiervan. Please be all right. Please."

Her fingers caught in a sticky mat on the right side of his skull and he winced and moaned. Despite his obvious distress, Alanna smiled in relief. If he could feel and react to pain, he would be all right. She probed the spot gently, noting the length and depth of the gash, the swelling around it, the tight line about his mouth as she worked. He muttered something in Gaelic.

"It'll be all right, Kiervan," she whispered, leaning across him and shoving aside those few stones still pinning his body to the cobbled courtyard. When she had freed him, she slipped her hands along his limbs and over his chest and shoulders, searching for the telltale signs of broken bones. Finding none, she braced herself and worked her hands down between his arms and his torso. At the end of his right hand, amidst the stones, she found his sword. She drew it from beneath the rocks and laid it beside her, explaining as she did, "I'm going to try to set you up, Kiervan, so I can get you out of this rock pile. Swear all you want. As loud as you want. It's gonna get worse before it gets better."

"Indeed it shall . . . little sister."

Alanna whirled about, her heart beating erratically against her breast, to stare up, open-mouthed, into Graeme Ashton's pale blue eyes. Instinctively she snatched up the sword and vaulted to her feet, planting them on either side of Kiervan, placing herself between him and the personification of evil standing before them.

"The last time we met, you were burying the dead," he said, reaching to touch the thick bandage wrapped about his forearm. His cold eyes darkened and he fixed them on her as he continued, "This time I see that you are raising them. Paddy was most impressed with your capabilities. I can see that my disbelief was unwarranted."

Frantically she sought words with which to do battle. None came. Instead a shudder, cold and hard, raced up her back.

"Your Captain des Marceaux seems to have had an unfortunate accident," Ashton went on, his gaze sliding past her to study Kiervan's still form among the rocks. "It would be less than humane of me to let him suffer any further." He pulled a pistol from his waistband. "Move aside, sister."

"No. You'll have to kill me first."

"How very heroic. Move aside."

She glared at him, willing lightning to stike him down, wishing for the power to pierce his black heart with a look and drop him dead where he stood. "Owrd was right," she said through her clenched teeth. "You inherited all that was evil in our father. What courage and strength it must take to stand there prepared to kill a man who can't rise and defend himself. Just as much courage as it took to tear a baby from her mother's arms and throw it out the window."

"Very well," Ashton replied, ignoring the words she'd thrown at him. "I had thought to dispatch the poor man in order to spare him the torment of hearing your death. But if you would prefer that he bear witness to—"

"You're the vilest, nastiest human being God ever made," Alanna interrupted. "On this side of time or beyond. What a shame our father didn't throw *you* out the tower window. He would have done the world a big favor."

"Oh, you mean all of this might have been prevented?" he said, sweeping his arm in a wide gesture to indicate the destruction all around them. "Nonsense."

He smiled and his eyes glittered with a feral light as he continued, "It isn't much of a sport, you know. The hunting of Irishmen. Getting one to betray his fellow rats for the promise of gold or glory or power is hardly a great challenge, as greedy and traitorous as they are by nature."

"Then why bother?" Alanna asked, her eyes narrowing to consider her brother, her adversary.

"There are some prizes worth the effort of a grand conspiracy." He glanced over at the smoldering shell of the manor and shrugged. "It was rather unspectacular as dwellings go," he said, fixing his attention on her again. "Of course, the Crown will see that I am suitably rewarded for my foresight in anticipating and then putting down the O'Connell insurrection. The new manor will be ever so much grander. And there is also the matter of the lands and the tenants which will come into my hands."

"The O'Connells weren't going to join the rebellion," she retorted evenly.

"Ah, yes. That was a bit of a surprise. I must say that I fully expected you to prophesy otherwise. I truly expected you to give in to your Captain des Marceaux's needs more fully than you did." He shrugged again. "But there will be no one to offer testimony to contradict my own. I dispatched the woman whom Paddy enlisted to start the fires. A lovely little redheaded creature who was most willing to offer her charms in trade for her life. Had they been worth more . . . And of course your dark knight spared me the necessity of having to deal with the matter of Paddy O'Connell myself."

With a bravery she didn't feel, Alanna squared her shoulders and settled the hilt of the sword in her hands. "You can't kill all of us," she declared. "Someone will live to speak the truth against you."

His lips curled in a cruel smile. "I have seen the future. Not only will a new castle sit on this spot, but no charges will ever be brought against me for what has occurred here this night." He stared at her in mock surprise, "Were you not aware that we share our mother's gift of the sight?"

Mom wasn't a seer. "I think there's a great deal of difference between seeing and wishful thinking," Alanna retorted evenly. "You can delude yourself if you want, but I don't think your powers of seeing are all that great, big brother. My guess is, you knew the story of our mother's flight through time, and once you heard Paddy's story about me, you put two and two together. But only after Kiervan and I had gotten away. I also think this whole horrible night is a plan you concocted *after* you saw the possibilities in my being here."

His cocked a sandy brow. "You *are* a perceptive woman. Which has made the game ever so much more interesting than it otherwise would have been." He shook his head and made a clicking sound. "What a pity it is that I must kill you as well as your lover. I truly regret that there is simply no other course. Aside from your rather combative nature and the certain ferocity of your accusations against me, there is also the matter of your possible claims against our father's estates. I am afraid that I have never learned to share very well."

Once again he waved the pistol back and forth and commanded, "Now move aside, dear sister, and let me be on with the necessary tasks."

Her heart leapt into her throat. "No. I won't," she vowed, edging forward and blocking Ashton's obvious attempt to aim a killing shot at Kiervan's upper body.

"Such undeserved loyalty," he sneered.

Alanna shook her head. "It's love, dear brother," she corrected quietly, subtly testing the sword's heft in her hands. "And every measure of it earned."

Suddenly her world exploded in a brilliant flash of red. In

the same moment came a resounding clap of deafening thunder and a thick choking cloud of acrid gunpowder. She felt the scream rip from her throat as terror reverberated through her flesh. Then, time hung suspended, allowing her dazed perceptions to clear.

The smoke thinned and she saw Ashton standing before her with the gun still in his hands, his lips drawn back over his teeth in an vicious snarl. As her heart cried out for Kiervan, she heard her enraged battle cry and, in that same instant, leapt forward and swung the sword with all her might, knocking the discharged gun from Ashton's hand.

He staggered back in a desperate effort to avoid her killing blow.

Her pulse thundering in her ears, Alanna advanced, settling the hilt of the sword in her hands again. Never had she hated with such intensity. Never had she been so determined to see justice done at her own hand. "Find yourself a weapon, you bastard!" she bellowed. "Find yourself something to fight with or I'll back you all the way to Bantry Bay and drown you!"

He scrambled to his left and pulled a thin-bladed saber from the bloody hand of a dead man.

Phelan. Oh God, Alanna moaned. The dead man was Phelan O'Connell.

Alanna took a deep breath and gathered her strength. A clarity as cold as the rain that ran in icy rivulets off the ends of her hair, off her fingers, and along the length of her double-edged sword, took over. Ashton's weapon was obviously lighter and he had both the strength and knowledge to use it as it had been designed. She had the advantage of a longer blade, but its weight and her ignorance of technique worked against her. If their contest went on for very long at all . . .

The heat of hatred and heartbreak returned, sweeping through her in a red rage, turning to cinders all that had ever held her within the bound of reasonable caution. It didn't matter anymore whether she crossed back through the portals of time. Life and death mattered only if Kiervan still lived. And unless she dispatched Ashton, she'd never know whether her brother's shot had found its mark.

Alanna met her brother's gaze. "Had you the gift of the sight, Ashton," she said evenly, "you would have seen the folly of your plan. You would have seen your own death at the end of it."

"At your hand, little sister?" he sneered, advancing with the sword and the same sense of superiority and confidence he had sported at their first meeting. "Do you really think you can best me?"

She watched him and said nothing. Flexing her knees and shifting her weight back and forth between her feet, she gripped the sword hilt tightly and prepared to move in any direction at a moment's notice. She saw the decision in his ice blue eyes a fraction of a second before he lunged at her. She instinctively flicked the blade of her sword up to block his attack, and as his blade slid down along the length of hers to the hilt, she pivoted to the right. The combined weight of her weapon and Ashton's brute force brought the tip of her blade down with alarming speed. Her heart lodged in her throat, Alanna dropped into a crouch and swung the broad sword like a baseball bat at Ashton's legs, hoping to unbalance him enough to let her scramble away and gain some distance.

Even as she felt his sword point tear at the shoulder of her cloak, the edge of hers struck him in the back of his right leg, diagonally just below his knee. His leg instantly buckled and his flesh opened with a smoothness that sent Alanna's stomach reeling. With a scream Ashton fell back, transferring his sword to his left hand as he reached to cover the gaping wound with his right.

"Whoring bitch!" he shouted, suddenly straightening and lunging forward wildly, the sword still in his left hand. "I'll kill you for this!"

She easily sidestepped his attack. "You were going to kill me anyway! Remember?" she shouted back, swinging her blade in a tight circle to catch his and knock it down. The force of her parry drove his sword into the wet cobbles of the courtyard. For a brief second, it made a high-pitched *thwang*ing sound and then snapped in two at a point just beneath the edge of her blade.

With a low snarl, Ashton pitched away what remained of the now useless weapon, spun about, and leaned down to grope among the bodies lying with Phelan's. Alanna settled the hilt in her hands again, cursing the rain that made it slide out of her grip.

"Get yourself another sword, brother," she called above the thunder and the din of the wider battle. "Let's be done with it this time!"

He straightened and whirled in the same motion, staggering only slightly as he tried to stop his momentum with his injured leg. Alanna froze at the sight of the silver-butted pistol he held in his hand. Even as she fought to breathe, a voice in her mind said the powder was rain soaked and wouldn't fire.

"And now the odds are again in my favor," Ashton said, his lips curling back over his teeth. He lifted the pistol to sight along the length of the barrel, aiming the open maw of it at the center of her forehead. "Any last requests, little sister?"

Anger flooded her. "Screw you and the horse you rode in on."

He pulled back the hammer of the flintlock pistol and smiled.

Alanna tightened her grip on the sword hilt and offered up a quick prayer for strength and speed. "While I doubt if it'll make any difference to you, Ashton," she said as her muscles tensed in preparation, "I feel obligated to tell you that the evil you send forth into the world will return to you threefold."

"And I suppose that its return will be at your hand?"

Suddenly in the air to Alanna's right came a high-pitched whine. Instinctively she ducked away from it. Ashton did the same, the muzzle of the pistol swinging out as he sought the source of the bullet. In that split second, she swung her broad sword up and across the distance between her body and his with all her might.

The force of the blow reverberated up the length of her

arms even as Ashton's scream ripped through the rain-sodden air. She closed her eyes, but the effort came too late to prevent the horrible image from burning into her memory. In a distant part of her brain, she heard the pistol fire, but it was nothing more than one small sound in the flood of sensation battering her awareness. She heard the gun hit the paving stones amidst rasping breath and gurgling. She smelled gunpowder, fear, and blood, felt the sword twist in her hands as the point dropped toward the cobblestones at her feet.

Blindly she staggered back, gripping the hilt of her weapon with the last measure of her strength.

Drawing a deep breath, she opened her eyes. Propped against the body of Paddy O'Connell, Ashton sat in a rapidly growing pool of his own blood. Her blow had caught him beneath the ribs nearly cutting him in two. His gaze fastened on her, his eyes glittering with hatred and pain.

"I'll come after you," he said thickly.

Alanna watched the blood trickle from the corner of his mouth. "You're a dead man, Ashton. And it's a damn pity that you can't die a thousand times for the crimes you've committed against innocent people."

A dark bubble grew from his lips, and his eyes widened in denial. Alanna turned away, unable to hold back a sob of revulsion and relief. Her sword clattered to the cobblestones as she raced back toward the jumble of stones and Kiervan.

Kiervan willed his vision to focus again, tried desperately to lift his head just one more time, but his body had given up the last of its meager strength in his attempt to shoot Ashton. He had done all he could. He could only hope that the bullet had found Ashton and that the coward was dying or dead. He felt the pistol slide from his fingers and dimly heard it clatter against the stones. As unconsciousness returned, he heard Alanna cry his name, felt her lips against his, tasted the sweetness of her love. If only he could put his arms around her.

Alanna sensed his fading and for a soul-wrenching moment she thought that he'd died in her arms. But his chest continued to rise and fall, his breaths shallow but even, and where her hand rested against his chest, his heart thrummed gently against her palm. He was weak; he'd lost a lot of blood through the gash in his head. And a concussion was a given under the circumstances. But nowhere could she find a bullet hole. Joy and dread filled her as she quickly considered her options.

Of one thing she was most certain: Kiervan was still alive and it was up to her to keep him that way. She had to get him someplace safe, someplace out of the castle. Beyond that, she'd decide later. Straightening, she quickly pulled the cloak from her shoulders and covered Kiervan, trying to shield him from the pelting rain. Knowing that she'd never manage to drag his weight any distance, and that it probably wasn't the wisest thing to do anyway considering his head injury, she glanced about the embattled courtyard in search of someone who might help her.

As though sent from heaven, Richard St. John and a well-armed landing party chose that precise moment to charge through the castle gates, bringing with them a gleaming circle of sharpened metal and a flashing cloud of gunpowder. Her knees weak with relief, she stumbled from the pile of rocks and staggered toward them, waving her arms, calling above the din, "Over here! Mr. St. John! He's over here!"

The Americans formed a phalanx and, with fixed bayonets and Richard St. John in the lead, forced their way toward her through the battle still being waged. Alanna ran out to the First Officer and breathlessly explained. "The wall fell on Kiervan. His head's . . ."

"The hardest part of him, mistress," he interrupted, grasping her shoulders and giving her a quick, reassuring nod and a thin-lipped smile before handing her into the care of one of Kiervan's crewmen.

The rescuers wasted neither time nor motion. Alanna winced and then protested at the rough way they lifted Kiervan from the rocks and at the way two of them so unfeelingly slung him between their shoulders.

"Survival first," Mr. St. John said as he came past her. "Gentleness and apologies can come later."

As the sailors bearing Kiervan passed them, the sailor

holding her turned and together they fell into step behind them. The others closed ranks around them, and with Richard St. John leading the way again, they cut their own path through the carnage, through the castle gates, and into the rain-cloaked night.

Alanna reached for the gunwale and pulled herself up and onto the *Wind Racer,* into what could have surely passed for a version of Dante's Inferno. She felt Richard St. John's hand slip around her upper arm, but even as he helped her to her feet, she couldn't take her eyes from the screaming, moaning, writhing bedlam spewed across the deck. She caught a glimpse of Niall moving among the battered and slashed survivors, directing Hisolda and others in the sorting and immediate care of the injured, indicating to a group of men those who were beyond his help.

What care Kiervan needed, she would have to provide. Niall had other concerns that rightly demanded priority.

"I've seen worse," the First Officer commented, drawing her toward the doorway beneath the quarterdeck. "Go below and wait. I'll have Kiervan brought to you directly."

He left her abruptly, shouting orders to the crew, motioning some of them to the front of the ship, some of them into the rigging. Alanna stared after him for a long moment, nodding. *Like one of those ridiculous toy dogs in the rear windows of cars,* she sharply admonished herself. There was much to be done, and whether or not she felt capable of the role she was destined to play, she had no choice but to play it and play it well. Squaring her shoulders, she glanced over to where the net bearing Kiervan's silent, limp form was being lowered to the deck. With a deep breath and a fervent plea to the Earth Mother, she headed down the stairs to prepare.

The rolling and pitching of the *Wind Racer* under full sail didn't help matters any. Alanna stumbled across the room to the porthole, the contents of the washbasin sloshing over the rim and her hands, her stomach heaving with the motion and with the overpowering smells of blood and whiskey.

She'd used a good portion of Kiervan's good Irish whiskey to sterilize her crude tools and clean his head wound before stitching it closed. Thoughts of his reaction when he discovered how deeply she'd depleted his supply brought a slight smile to her lips, the first in what felt like an eternity. She climbed up on his sea chest and poured the tainted water through the circular window and into the ocean below.

The worst was surely over, she told herself, climbing down and refilling the basin. She'd cut away what raven strands she'd needed to, bathed the wound, sewn it closed with a sterile needle and whiskey-soaked thread, then bandaged it. He hadn't so much as whimpered once in the whole grueling process. Part of her had been thankful that he'd been unaware of the pain she inflicted on him. Another part of her feared that he'd slipped so far into unconsciousness that he'd never return.

Alanna carried the huge china bowl back across the cabin, and the water sloshed onto the braided rug to mark yet another trip. Maybe he'd stir as she bathed him, she told herself hopefully. Maybe stripping his clothing from him, touching him, would rouse his memories and bring him back to her for just a moment, for just long enough to reassure her that he'd eventually return to full awareness, his mind whole and sound.

The weight of helplessness settled slowly over her when she drew the bed covers over Kiervan's badly bruised limbs. He hadn't stirred at all during her loving ministrations. Standing beside the bed, the tail of one of Kiervan's shirts brushing lightly against her bare thighs, Alanna studied the man before her. Her heart ached to see him so pale and weak. In the silence of the cabin came a truth she had known the instant she had looked into Maude's ruby and watched the wall collapse on him, a truth she hadn't had the time or the calm to face in the hours since. It would be one thing to cross back through time knowing Kiervan lived on this side of it. But if he were to die, that separation would be far too final.

Her heart heavy, Alanna lowered the wick on the oil

lamp, then lifted the blankets and climbed into the feather bed. Wrapping her arms around Kiervan, she pressed her face into the warmth of his skin and silently offered God and all the Irish pagan deities a deal—her happiness in exchange for the life of the man she loved.

31

"You should have seen them, Kiervan," Alanna continued, bathing his face and neck with a cloth. "They came through the castle gates just like the cavalry. All they needed was a bugler. It was impressive. And, I might add, Richard St. John did a damn good impersonation of John Wayne while leading the whole shebang."

He muttered in Gaelic, his parched lips barely moving to form the words, his features drawn by the torment of his fevered dreams. Alanna put the rag back in the basin and picked up the tumbler of drinking water.

"Everything's all right, you know," she assured him, spooning a trickle of the liquid between his lips. "Mr. St. John's taking us to Le Havre. He said we should be in port by the morning after next. He said he was going to run up the distress flags and slip right into a berth without going through the usual protocols, whatever they are.

"Niall says you're going to be just fine," Alanna prattled on, giving him more water. "He thinks I'm nuts talking to you like I do. Says that you can't hear me and that I'm wasting my breath and my energy. I guess he's entitled to think whatever he wants. But I seem to recall reading somewhere one time that talking and touching people who were comatose helped them to get back to consciousness."

"Not that you're really totally comatose, mind you. You're what I think a doctor would call semiconscious. Kinda there but not quite. I sorta figure it this way, if you can hear me, you've got to be getting pretty sick of hearing me rattle on about nothing, and any moment now, you're going to open your eyes and tell me to shut up."

Alanna set the water glass aside and wrung a slight bit of water from the washcloth. "That was your cue, Kiervan," she whispered, wiping the beads of perspiration from his forehead. "Open your eyes and let me have it with both barrels."

Alanna dipped the cloth again, wondering how often she had done so in the last twelve or however many hours it had been since Kiervan's fever had awakened her.

"I know what," she said softly, drawing the cloth down the length of his sinewy arm. "If this doesn't bring you out of it, nothing will. Okay, are you listening? I love you. Did you hear that, Kiervan? I said that I love you. I will always love you."

She dipped the cloth again and began to gently bathe the wide expanse of his muscled chest. "That should give you some ammunition to work with. Now, open your eyes and let's get on with the fight."

His sudden silence disturbed her more than his fevered ramblings. Alanna forced herself to continue.

"But if you think I'm going to tell you that the truth of it is that I won't accept playing second fiddle to Eggie Terwilliger-Hampstead and all her money and social status, you're sadly mistaken, Captain des Marceaux. No siree. And if you think I'm going to beg you to dump her and marry me, you can just think again.

"Okay," she admitted with a shrug. "So it's a massive pride thing. I don't give a damn. You have to come to the possibility of that choice on your own, Kiervan. I can't give you an ultimatum about something this important. If you chose me over Eggie, I'd always feel like I forced you to do something you really didn't want to do. You know, that I took advantage of your weakened condition and all."

He made another soft sound and Alanna paused to study him. "And if it turns out that you're just lying here pretending to be fevered and delusional, mister, I want you to know that I'm making all of this up just to have something to say.

Not a word of it's true. Not a single solitary word. Understood?"

Not that she'd really confessed the truth of her heart to him, she admitted to herself. Whatever she said while he lay unconscious didn't count.

Alanna shook her head, banishing the gray clouds that had settled over her thoughts. "Well," she began with forced cheerfulness, as she dipped the cloth in the basin again and wrung it out, "If you don't mind, I'm going to change the subject. This one's really depressing me and I think I remember the article said that conversation with the comatose should be about positive and upbeat things. It makes sense, doesn't it? Who wants to come back to a reality full of unpleasantness?"

Leaning across him to bathe his other arm, she continued, saying, "How about if we talk about the effects of sleep deprivation and the onset of delayed stress syndrome? I'm well on my way to becoming an expert on those two delightful experiences."

The vision came from the mists, somehow soothing in its familiarity. Kiervan watched in distant fascination as he swept Alanna from certain death, wrapping her in his raven wings and carrying her into the sky. She felt warm against him, her arms circled about his neck, her body moving in rhythm with his own as together they rode the currents above the burnished plains.

And then the land and vision changed without warning.

Kiervan spiraled them down, coming to rest in the lush grass beneath the shade of a gnarled oak tree. And as Alanna released him and stepped back to stand on her own, he suddenly stood before her a man, his hunger and need unbearable, his desire consuming him. Her eyes sparkling with happiness, she took him into her arms, and they tumbled together into the sweet bed of spring grass, their laughter soft and caressing as they loved one another.

He felt his heart swell, felt his soul yearn for the sweetness of surrender. But to give any more of himself up to her would mean a forever of human form; no more could he escape the heartaches and bitterness of the world by flying above it, aloof and alone. He would be tied to Alanna, pledged to suffer with her all the storms of mortal life. And the bubble of panic burst within him. He rose up, spreading his raven wings to the winds and letting them carry him swiftly aloft.

Pain flashed in her eyes as she watched him leave. And then it was gone, carefully hidden beneath a brave mask of stoic independence. But he knew it lay just under the surface of her calm acceptance, and it hurt him to know that he had caused her heartache. The intensity of his own regret startled him and stirred anew the instincts which had driven him to flight. He arched his wings and rode the currents higher, into the winds which could so easily carry him far from the temptation of Alanna's love.

But escape brought no freedom. His heart grew heavier with every beat of his wings, with every mile that came between him and the woman he had so desperately sought to leave behind. Turmoil churned within his soul, darkening his spirit and draining the strength from his flight. He moaned before the onslaught of pain and the truth it bore. Unable to bear the increasing burden of self-deceit, he dipped a wing and dropped, dropped to the gentler, slower currents that would carry him back to the meadows of Ireland, back to where he had flown from Alanna's loving arms.

She would understand his fears. She would accept him for what he was and what he could give of himself. Alanna would love him and demand nothing of him in return.

But the meadow was gone. In its place was the sun-baked plain over which he had first carried Alanna. He circled, searching for her, his heart thundering in his chest, his fear growing. Even as his mind acknowledged the emptiness of the land below, Maude appeared as though from the wind itself. Kiervan swooped low and fast, determined to reach her before she too could leave him to his fate, to the aching hollowness of his soul's desolation.

And then he was a man once more, standing before

Maude. Neither of them spoke and yet words passed between them.

"Where has she gone?" he asked.

"To where you cannot hurt her."

"What must I do to bring her back to me? Tell me and I will see it done."

Maude studied him for a long moment and then shook her head. "The answer is yours to find. Pray that you do not take overlong to reach it."

And then she was gone.

Kiervan awoke with a start that fairly brought him up off the bed. His pulse thundered wildly in his ears. He stared at the planking above his head and tried to sort the memories. The burning of Castle O'Connell, the death of Phelan and Owrd, the betrayal and execution of Paddy O'Connell, he knew to be events as real as they were ugly. But others had an ephemeral quality about them that marked them as unearthly: Alanna digging him from the rubble; the desperate shot that had missed Ashton; Alanna's hands caring for his battered body with the gentleness of angels; Alanna's voice, distant but strong, anchoring him in his tumultuous dreams.

Kiervan closed his eyes and concentrated on the sounds about him, on the movement of the world. He lay in his own bed, in his own cabin aboard the *Wind Racer*. They were at sea. The ease of his vessel's progress spoke of full sails in a night wind. The certainty of her track told him that Richard St. John had the helm. They were out of Bantry Bay and the *Wind Racer* was in capable, trusted hands. How had he gotten to this point?

Alanna. Even as thoughts of her came to him, Kiervan turned his head to search the cabin for her. He clenched his teeth against the explosion of pain in the back of his skull, and his entire body tightened in an effort to endure the white wall of agonizing pain. When it finally eased, he saw her. She wore one of his shirts over her dark green leggings and sat on the floor with her back against the side of his desk, her legs drawn up and her arms wrapped around them, her hair cascading in a wild honeyed curtain about her shoulders as she slept.

"Alanna." He winced at the stabbing pain his voice sent through his head and closed his eyes as he struggled against the rising nausea.

"You're back," he heard Alanna whisper at his side. "I've missed you."

He felt her hand resting on his cheek, felt the warmth of her body as she sat next to him on the bed. Sparks were wheeling across his vision, and although he wanted desperately to give voice to his relief at finding her safe and with him, no sound came.

"Don't even try to talk," she said softly, her fingers brushing over his lips. "The fever broke a few hours ago. Rest now and in the morning you'll be stronger and it'll all be easier."

He felt her begin to rise from the bed, to move away from him, and a wave of urgency jolted through him. "No," he managed to protest on a shallow breath.

"What is it, Kiervan?" she asked, pausing and resting her hand on his chest.

By sheer determination alone, he moved his hand up to grasp Alanna's wrist. "Don't leave me." He felt her pulse tripping through her flesh, felt her hesitation. God help him, he didn't have the strength to fight her if she chose to go. Frustration and fear gripped him.

"I'm not going anywhere," she promised softly.

He heard the caution in her voice, a wariness tinged with sadness, but as she lay down beside him, the need to hold her close overwhelmed his other thoughts. She pressed herself against his side and, resting her head on his shoulder, snuggled into the circle of his weak embrace.

All was as it should be. Finally. Calm settled over him and he surrendered to it, letting it carry him back toward the edges of sleep.

I love you. Kiervan heard the words but in the mists of his mind he couldn't determine whether he had spoken them aloud or merely thought them. In the morning, he promised himself. In the morning he would say them loud and clear enough so that they could be heard all the way to heaven.

Alanna threaded her fingers through the dark hair tumbling over his shoulder and furiously blinked back tears. It was just as well he hadn't heard her declare her love for him. She hadn't meant to say it anyway. The words had simply spilled out when he'd wrapped her in his arms. A tear trickled down her cheek. She brushed it away and marshaled her earlier resolutions.

Kiervan wouldn't need her to care for his injuries after tonight. Tomorrow they would reach the French port of Le Havre. As soon as they docked she'd leave, would find a way back to Ireland and the Carraig Cor. She loved him too much, too deeply, to stay a moment longer, to let herself be drawn into the agony of living with only half of his life to feed the hunger of her heart.

She listened to the sound of his easy breathing, counted the certain, even measure of his heart beating against her cheek. Then she tilted her head to study the hard angles of his face, the dark softness of his beard, the way his lashes lay long and thick on the high curves of his cheekbones. She caressed the strands of his hair between her fingers and let herself remember how his lips felt, how they tasted, how they made her feel.

The sky visible through the porthole had grown light when she allowed herself to ease toward sleep, knowing in her heart as she did that she had wasted the night, that there had been no reason to carefully collect memories of her time with Kiervan des Marceaux. Even on the other side of time, she would be able to close her eyes and see him. She would never forget him, never forget the wonder and the heartbreak of falling in love with her dark privateer.

32

Late-morning light streamed through the porthole as Alanna finished tying her boots and straightened to consider her tunic lying on Kiervan's sea chest. She really ought to change out of his shirt and into her own, she told herself. But the scent of his skin clung to the cotton fabric, and she felt a pang at the thought of leaving that one small physical reminder of him behind. Alanna turned her head and watched Kiervan sleeping for a long moment. No, she decided in the end, he wouldn't begrudge her his shirt.

She was folding her tunic into a neat bundle for travel when the silence of the cabin was broken by a rapping on the door. Afraid that the sound would wake Kiervan, she dashed across the room and pulled open the banded panel. An exhausted-looking Richard St. John stood on the other side.

"Good morning, Mistress Chapman," he said, tucking his hat beneath his arm.

"Good morning, Mr. St. John. Please come in," she whispered, stepping back and motioning him into the cabin.

His own voice dropped to equal the soft hush of her own as he asked, "How is the captain faring?"

"He's much improved, actually. The fever broke shortly after midnight and he's rested well since. His mind should be clear when he wakes up, but I think it's only fair to warn you that he's not going to be in any shape to climb into the rigging for at least a week or so."

"I promise not to push him too hard, mistress." She saw

regret in his eyes as he said, "I was hoping perhaps I might have a word with him privately."

If she had needed a sign from God to reassure her, surely this was it. "Let me get my cloak and then I'll scoot right out of here," she offered. After tucking her bundled tunic into the folds of her cloak, Alanna paused beside the bed and gazed down at Kiervan's peaceful expression, then, leaning down, she lightly touched her lips to his in silent farewell.

"Don't undo all my work," she admonished as she crossed the threshold, her tone and step belying the heaviness of her heart. She paused and glanced over at Kiervan's desk, at the note she'd left for him. Closing the door behind her was the hardest thing she'd ever done in her life.

"Captain, if you don't mind . . ."

Kiervan opened his eyes at the sound of the familiar voice, at the gentle shaking of his shoulder. He winced as he moved his head to look up at Richard St. John, but when he scanned the cabin for Alanna, the pain was but a ghost of what it had been the night before.

"Where is she?" he asked, shifting and gently stretching to ease the incredible stiffness that had settled into his limbs.

"Topside. I asked her to leave so we could speak candidly." The First Officer tossed his hat onto the desk and dragged the chair from behind it. He quickly turned the plain piece of furniture so that the back was to Kiervan, and straddled the seat. "We have a problem," he said simply.

"How so?" Kiervan asked through clenched teeth, fingering the bandage wrapped about his head.

"We came into Le Havre three hours ago, just after dawn, flying distress flags. The harbormaster berthed us without delay. The most seriously injured have already been taken ashore. The authorities will allow the others to disembark shortly."

Lifting his head, Kiervan gently probed along the length of his wound. God, but he would have a headache for days yet. He laid back into the pillows and turned to smile weakly at his friend. "All sounds well. What remains to trouble you?"

Richard hesitated and then frowned as he supplied, "The *Charleston Queen* is also in port."

"Christ Almighty!" Kiervan bellowed, struggling to sit up. The cabin went suddenly awash in the blurring of his vision.

"Save it until you've heard the rest," his First Officer counseled with a rueful smile.

"Lord," Kiervan groaned, dropping back into the bed covers and closing his eyes. "There's more?"

"It seems the flagship of the Terwilliger-Hampstead Line came into port several weeks back, bearing not only its owner, but his lovely daughter as well. Dock talk has it that the delightful Mistress Terwilliger-Hampstead has been to Paris and all points in between shopping for her trousseau."

"Do they know we're—"

"All of France and half of England knows we're here, Kiervan. It's but a matter of time before you're either summoned to the *Charleston Queen* or they come to the *Wind Racer*."

Of all the luck which had cursed him the past weeks . . . Kiervan grabbed the sheets and pushed them aside. "I can't let Alanna and Eggie meet," he gritted through his teeth as he inched his legs toward the side of the bed.

"*Eggie?*" Amusement rang through Richard's voice.

"I'm in no mood for your humor, Richard," Kiervan growled, willing himself up on an elbow and reaching out in an attempt to grasp his friend's shoulder. "Give me a hand up."

"Not a wise notion, Kiervan," Richard observed, shaking his head and leaning back well beyond Kiervan's reach. "If you haven't the strength to climb out unassisted, then you belong right where you are."

"Then I'll do it without you." He hadn't the breath to continue speaking until Richard relented and hauled him up to sit on the edge of the feather mattress. "Does Alanna know about the *Charleston Queen?*" Kiervan asked while waiting for the world to quit spinning about him.

"Only if someone happens to mention it while she's on deck. Why is it so important that she not know?"

"I have no time to explain my relationship with Alanna to you, Richard." He stripped the bandage from his head and dropped it on the bed beside him, ignoring first the searing jolt of pain and then the pounding at the back of his skull. "The matter is far too complicated."

"She seems a refreshingly straightforward woman to me."

"And therein lies the problem," he shot back, pressing his fingers to his head.

"Then what concerns you? If you've been honest with her about your pending marriage, I see no reason to get yourself in knots over their meeting."

"Alanna has consistently refused to even consider staying with me for a while longer," he offered on a hard sigh as he stared at the floor and tried to bring his vision into sharper focus. "But I sense that her resistance to the idea is weakening. With a bit more time, she'll accept the relationship and be content with it."

Slowly he lifted his face until he met his friend's troubled gaze. "But I know this woman like no other, Richard. If she's allowed to meet Eggie, no amount of arguing, no amount of loving, will ever sway her. I don't intend to risk everything on their chance meeting."

Richard quietly observed, "Mistress Chapman deserves better than such cold-blooded manipulation, Kiervan. And you know it as well as I do."

Kiervan pinned him with a murderous look. "Get me something to wear out of the chest and save your sermons for a time when I have the strength and patience to endure them."

The First Officer slowly rose to his feet, but he made no move toward the sea chest on the far side of the room. "Would you care for a piece of advice?"

"No," Kiervan growled.

The man shrugged. "For once in your life be content with what you have, Kiervan. Be satisfied with the bed you've bought. And with the woman and the wealth that comes with it. Don't drag Mistress Chapman into your personal well of misery."

Kiervan glared up at him, his patience gone, his head pounding to the beat of an unholy drummer. "Find Alanna and send her back here," he snarled. "The less opportunity she has to stray, the better. And then go over to the *Charleston Queen* and personally extend my regrets for not calling on them or being able to receive them. Tell them I'll make amends when my strength is properly returned."

"Are those orders?" Richard asked, his tone sharp as he snatched up his hat from the desk.

"They are."

Richard strode across the cabin, slamming his hat on his head as he went. Halfway out the door, he turned back. "There are times, Kiervan, when you test too boldly the measure of our friendship."

"Berate me later," Kiervan said. "For now, do what I need to have done."

The entire wall shook when Richard slammed the cabin door. As the sound passed through him, Kiervan felt his strength go with it. Slowly he crumpled back into the welcoming softness of the feather mattress.

As far as chaos went, it was pretty well organized. Alanna stood at the railing and watched Niall discuss the offloading of passengers with a French harbor authority. Who would have thought Niall spoke French? Shaking her head, she surveyed the Irish men and women bundling what few possessions they had managed to save in the escape from Castle O'Connell, watched the youngest children scampering around the deck, playing games and laughing, apparently unconcerned by the dramatic changes their lives were undergoing.

Alanna sighed. Oh, to be child again, to be able to trust others to be there, to make everything right. But she wasn't a child and even when she had been, her life hadn't been filled with the kind of people who protected her from the unpleasant realities of existence. She squared her shoulders and, reminding herself that rough childhoods made capable adults, turned to consider the wharfside activity.

There were boats of every imaginable shape and size and color in the harbor. Some were in the process of entering and berthing; others in loading and departing. Surely somewhere along the docks she'd find a ship sailing for Ireland. Alanna patted the pocket of her leggings and felt the hard lump of her engagement ring. She needed money to secure passage back to Ireland, and she had to choose between selling the ring and selling the Dragon's Heart to get it. No choice at all, actually. Bill would be furious when he found out. Alanna shrugged and went back to her consideration of the harbor.

Which ships would head across the Channel and into the Irish Sea? How did one tell? Did you wander up and down the docks asking? She considered the rough men working along the wharf below and chewed her lower lip. Perhaps there was a central office someplace where a person could make inquiries and arrangements in relative safety. Even as the possibility came to her, she rejected it. She'd be remembered—a strangely dressed American woman trying to trade a diamond ring for passage to the eastern coast of Ireland. If Kiervan were to decide to come after her, she'd be too easy to find.

But things would be much easier if Niall were to make the arrangements. Yes, she decided. Although she didn't know him all that well, in the time they had been together with Owrd she had grown to like him. Niall had a kind and gentle heart. She could trust him. Alanna turned and strode to midship where Niall and the Frenchman were concluding their negotiations. She hung back until the official walked away and Niall turned to her in question.

"I need your help," she began bluntly. "I have to find a way back to the Carraig Cor, and I need you to make the arrangements for me."

"And what does Kiervan think of your plans?"

"He doesn't know, and if all goes well, I'll be long gone before he figures it out."

"He will come after you, Lady Alanna. You know that, do you not?"

"All I need is a head start, Niall. All I have to do is get to the Carraig with a few minutes to spare. It can be done." Desperation settled over her as she added, "But not if you won't help me."

Niall studied her for a long moment before replying. " 'Tis cowardice to run from difficulties."

Alanna shook her head. "Cowardice is taking the easy road because you can't make yourself do what you know is right," she answered softly, sadly. "If I stayed, it would be as Kiervan's mistress. Is that what you think I should do?"

"Kiervan is a fool, Lady Alanna." His anger showed clearly in his words. "He is a shortsighted fool."

Again Alanna shook her head in disagreement. "He's a man who's had to fight for everything he's ever achieved in his life. Nothing's come easily to him, Niall. And that which he's earned, he can't easily give up. His coming marriage is a prize he swore he'd gain. His pride won't let him throw it away. I can't remake him the way I'd have him be. Then he wouldn't be Kiervan."

"Nor the man you've come to love," Niall supplied with a slow nod. "I understand."

She reached out and laid her hand on his forearm. "Will you help me, Niall? And will you keep my secret for as long as you can?"

" 'Tis indeed a stout heart you have, Lady Alanna," he whispered, his eyes searching hers. Then he nodded. "Yes. I will help you on your journey. When we leave the *Wind Racer,* you must come with us, become one of us for as long as it takes to secure your passage back to County Wicklow. It may take several days. Are you willing?"

She lifted her chin. "Yes, Niall. Whatever it takes."

"Then wait among the women; leave the ship in their midst and I will find you when we reach the dock." He stripped his cloak from his shoulders and handed it to her, saying, "Put this on so that you won't be noticed among them."

"I couldn't ask for a better friend, Niall. Thank you,"

Alanna said, kissing him on the cheek. Then she turned and walked back the way she had come.

It wasn't long before she found herself pacing along the railing, casting nervous glances between the door of the blockhouse and the dock below, her mind playing out worst-case scenarios, all of which ended with Kiervan dragging her back to his cabin, his eyes blazing and streams of rough Gaelic delighting everyone within a mile of the *Wind Racer*. It didn't matter that she rationally knew he wouldn't have the physical strength to do it. Rational wasn't part of their relationship.

Just when she thought she might scream from the tension, a movement on the dock below caught her attention. She watched as a fancy black carriage drew to a halt at the base of the *Wind Racer*'s gangplank. An elegantly dressed man riding on the back of the thing instantly climbed down with a stool in his hand, walked around to the side, set the stool down, and then opened the door while grandly stepping back.

A moment later a portly older man stepped out of the carriage, pulled his waistcoat down over his belly, tugged at the lace dangling from his cuffs, and then turned back to the open door, extending his hand. The woman he assisted from the conveyance was strikingly beautiful even from a distance. Sun had clearly never touched her porcelain skin, and the wind wouldn't have dared to ruffle the perfect mahogany curls that framed her heart-shaped face.

Alanna smiled. When the Good Lord had been handing out cleavages, this woman had obviously been in the front of the line, when the supplies had been plentiful and generously given away. Given the deep cut of her neckline, it was equally apparent that this creature was quite proud of the endowment.

As the older man issued commands to the driver, the woman opened a tiny parasol that perfectly matched her baby blue gown, right down to the contrasting yellow ruffles, and scanned the deck of the ship, her nose wrinkling.

Alanna leaned her forearms on the rail and watched as the two gingerly made their way up the gangplank. No doubt they were father and daughter. And without doubt they were also the richest people she had laid eyes on since her passage through time. She'd seen quite a few in her other life, but none that she recalled had seemed so determined to display their wealth. The money the woman had spent on her dress would clothe everyone aboard the *Wind Racer*, with plenty of change left over. But fashionable or not, Alanna decided that the parasol had to be the most worthless fashion accessory she'd ever seen.

Who were they and why in heaven's name were they coming aboard? The answer came in the low curse of Richard St. John. Alanna turned to find him standing behind her, the corners of his mouth white with tension as he too watched the pair make their way up the wide board connecting the ship to the dock.

He cast Alanna a panicked glance before he took a deep breath and stepped forward, effectively placing himself between her and the new arrivals. As the man gained the deck, the First Officer swept his hat from his head, bowed slightly at the waist, and in an official tone said, "Mr. Terwilliger-Hampstead, what an unexpected surprise. Welcome aboard, sir."

He bowed to the woman then, saying, "Mistress Terwilliger-Hampstead. It is indeed a pleasure. Permit me to introduce myself. I am Richard St. John, First Officer of the *Wind Racer*."

So this was Eggie. Alanna watched as Kiervan's fiancée slowly drew a lace handkerchief from the bodice of her gown. "Pleased to make your acquaintance, sir," she murmured, dabbing at her nose and looking everywhere but at Richard St. John.

"We saw your flags as you entered the harbor," Mr. Terwilliger-Hampstead said, his tone censorious. "And when no word reached us as to the reasons, we came to be certain that no great tragedy had befallen the captain or his ship."

"How kind of you," Richard replied, the customary evenness returning to his voice. "We ran into a bit of trouble in the conduct of our business in Bantry Bay and brought the survivors here. I'm afraid that we have been pressed with matters relating to their care since our arrival. Kiervan had just instructed me to deliver a message to you aboard the *Charleston Queen* when you arrived here."

Mr. Terwilliger-Hampstead lifted a brow. "And where is Captain des Marceaux?"

"In his quarters, sir. I assure you that he would be here in my stead had he not suffered an injury in the course of the Irish fracas. Perhaps another—"

"Has he been disfigured?" Eggie asked, her eyes wide, her handkerchief pressed to her lips.

Alanna bristled, sensing that Eglintine's chief concern didn't lie in the possibility of Kiervan's suffering, but rather in the ghastly chance that she might be forced to marry damaged goods and then have to endure public pity for the rest of her life.

"A blow to his head, mistress," Richard supplied. "When a wall collapsed on him. Aside from a rather nasty flesh wound which will heal without evidence, he is unscathed."

"I'm relieved to hear so," the woman replied.

I bet you are, Alanna silently retorted. She mentally shook herself, angry that Eglintine could so easily stir such raw, uncivilized emotions within her. For all she knew, Eggie could really care about what happened to her husband-to-be. *Not that it's at all likely*. Again Alanna winced, reminding herself that jealousy could make an idiot of even the most sane and rational person.

And jealous she was of Eglintine Terwilliger-Hampstead. The woman was everything that she wasn't: graceful and elegant, a creature of high society and wealth. Kiervan and Eglintine would make a striking couple, would cause flutters of excited conversation wherever they went together. And their children . . .

Pain shot through Alanna. Children rightfully deserved parents who were married, Alanna sternly assured herself as she gripped the railing. She and Kiervan were both bastards born, and to pass that legacy to another generation would be the greatest of selfish cruelties. As much as it hurt her to admit it, Alanna knew in her heart that it needed to be Eglintine who brought Kiervan's children into this world.

A high-pitched sound of distress jerked Alanna from her brooding. She turned in time to see a small child reach for a second handful of Eggie's dress.

Then, before she could anticipate and move to intervene, Alanna saw Eglintine grab her gown and wrench it from the hands of the grinning little boy. He tipped back on his heels and fell flat, his head hitting the deck with a resounding smack. For a half a second he lay there silent and stunned, and then he opened his mouth and let out a piercing wail of pain and surprise.

Alanna dipped past Richard St. John's elbow and scooped the child up into her arms, her rage beyond control as she cuddled him and straightened to meet Eglintine's gaze.

"Your child has soiled my gown," the woman accused, brushing at the fabric.

Alanna felt Richard St. John tense beside her, but she'd passed the point of remaining silent. "Don't worry, Eggie ol' girl," she snapped. "Poverty is no more contagious than compassion."

And with that salvo, she turned and carried the child away without looking back. She handed the squalling boy over to a pair of hands frantically reaching for him. "He's all right," she quickly assured the child's mother.

Her hands were still shaking when, a few minutes later, she was swept along in the crowd of Irish women who made their way to the dock below. And when the tears came, she didn't even bother to pretend they were for anything other than the loss of the children she might have had and loved with Kiervan. With firm resolution she brushed them away and kept her gaze riveted on the way before her.

33

His shirt unbuttoned, his breeches slung low on his hips and only partially fastened, Kiervan paused in the center of the room, holding his boots. He considered first the bed and then the chair Richard St. John had left away from the desk. After a moment he opted for the latter. The bed was simply too soft to hold him upright. The pain in his head thundered and, if he moved too quickly, had a tendency to make the world career oddly and go fuzzy from the edges inward.

Kiervan sat down with a low groan and set his boots on the floor before him. God alone knew why he was making the attempt to dress. When Alanna returned to the cabin, he had every intention of taking her back into the downy cocoon of the feather mattress. The corner of his mouth quirked upward as he pulled on a boot, marveling anew at the formidable power of his desire. No doubt Alanna would balk at the idea of taxing his strength so soon, but he knew that he had only to insist that her loving would aid his healing and she would relent, would surrender to the demands of her own passion.

But first they needed to reach some sort of understanding. He had to be assured that she'd cease her foolish efforts to return to the Carraig Cor. She belonged with him, in this century. He'd get down on his knees and beg her to stay if he had to; would promise her houses wherever she wanted them, servants to wait on her and free her days for whatever pleased her, free her nights for what pleased them both.

Only it won't be every night. His remaining boot halfway on, Kiervan froze at the thought, stunned by the emptiness that came in the wake of the realization. He'd be married to Eglintine. The hours with Alanna . . .

"Will be enough for as long as the fire lasts," he muttered roughly, shoving his foot into the boot. Bits and pieces of the troubling dream came back to him, but he resolutely pushed them away, telling himself that in the scales of decision making, dreams didn't have the same weight as reality. Alanna had an independent nature. To have him constantly underfoot, to spend her every night in his arms, would wear her patience thin. Yes, he told himself, the relationship would last longer if it was punctuated by their occasional separations. And how odd that he'd never before considered ways to prolong an amorous affair.

A knock on the door interrupted his musings. Struggling to his feet, he called, "Enter," as he began to fasten the buttons on his breeches.

His stomach turned to lead in the same instant that recognition came. "George," he forced himself to say evenly, his attention slipping past his soon-to-be business partner to take in the beautiful woman standing on the other side of the threshold. She smiled coquettishly as their gazes met for a brief moment. In the next, hers slid down the length of him in obvious appreciation.

"Mistress Terwilliger-Hampstead," he said, acknowledging her with a slight bow that set the world skidding about him. *God,* he silently prayed, *if I've ever done anything good in my life, reward me now; keep Alanna on deck.*

Behind them he caught a glimpse of his First Officer reaching for the door latch. As Richard drew it closed behind him, he gave Kiervan a quick smile that in Kiervan's mind wasn't quite apologetic enough.

George Terwilliger-Hampstead coughed discreetly, and when Kiervan looked back at the man, the other pointedly stared into the center of Kiervan's chest. Glancing down, Kiervan saw the expanse of skin and dark curls lying exposed between the edges of his shirt front. Even as he began to work a button through a hole, his gaze lifted to Eglintine, curious as to her reaction. She had turned sideways, with her attention riveted on a corner of the ceiling. Kiervan wondered briefly whether her pose was struck more for the effective display of her ample bosom than for any real sense of modesty.

Kiervan stopped buttoning his shirt halfway up. Carefully placing a booted foot on the seat of the chair, he leaned his forearms on his thigh and considered his betrothed and her father. "I regret that you find me in such a state," he offered not at all honestly. "Had I known of your intention to call . . ."

At least George had the good grace to stumble into an apology. "We were concerned after seeing the distress flags bringing you into berth. And when no message arrived, we thought it appropriate to investigate your situation."

Kiervan nodded, ignoring the pain the movement sent shooting up his skull, his awareness fixed entirely on Eggie. Beautiful woman she was; no man would think to declare otherwise. But she utterly failed to stir his senses. Long legged, he decided, and her corseted curves were certainly voluptuous enough, but not at all inviting to his hands. Her thick, dark hair was done in the latest style, but somehow he knew that she'd squeal in protest if he tried to pull the pins from it. He would have bet the *Wind Racer* and her cargo that Eglintine Terwilliger-Hampstead never permitted anyone but herself to choose when her tresses tumbled down her back or cascaded over her shoulders.

"My apologies, George," Kiervan offered, returning his attention to Charleston's preeminent businessman. "My attention slipped to other considerations for a moment. You were saying, sir?"

"I said," George replied, obviously resentful over having to repeat himself, "that we had heard that you had been injured during the conduct of your affairs in Ireland. Is it serious?"

"I'm well on my way to mending, thank you. I gather that Richard St. John informed you of our misadventures?"

"He did, and his account is evidenced by the presence of that ragtag assemblage on your deck."

Eggie had finally deigned to speak? Kiervan looked past her father to where she stood with her handkerchief clutched tightly in her hand at her side, her brown eyes sparking with indignation.

"They barely escaped with their lives," Kiervan explained, trying to settle the sudden impulse to order her from the cabin. "They hadn't time to pack their gowns or tailed coats."

"But, as I am sure you will agree, Captain," she persisted, her tone cool, "such circumstances are no excuse for poor manners and disrespect."

Kiervan arched a brow, noting in passing that the effort seemed to be the only one that didn't create a ripple of pain. "There was an incident as you boarded?" he asked calmly, not really caring if there had been, but knowing that proper manners necessitated at least an inquiry.

"A dirty child pawed my gown." Eglintine indicated the side of her skirt, offering the proof of her accusation for his inspection.

Kiervan could see no more damage than that which would just as likely have been caused by sitting in the carriage on her way to torment him. "You know what they say about Irish children," he quipped, barely able to keep the sarcasm from his tone. "All of them are the spawns of the devil himself and are born but to prey on the sensibilities of gentlewomen."

George Terwilliger-Hampstead drew his shoulders back until his waistcoat rode up over the curve of his considerable belly. "Truly the devil's spawn is most descriptive of the unnatural creature who thought it her place to admonish Eglintine for defending her person and property."

The hairs on the back of Kiervan's neck prickled. "Unnatural?" he asked.

"She had the audacity to address me directly," Eglintine declared, her face a mask of perfect incredulity. "Not only informally, but also shortening my name to a most unflattering length and common association."

His worst fears had come to pass. Not only had Alanna and Eglintine met, they'd apparently clashed. Eggie was obviously the kind of woman unaccustomed to having her sense of self challenged. Alanna was the kind who took no prisoners. There was no doubt in his mind as to who had walked away the victor. A smile twitched at the corners of his mouth. God, what a sight that must have been. And he had missed it.

"I really must insist that you do something about the woman's effrontery, Captain," his future wife persisted. "Why, my very honor has been assailed."

"Your honor isn't the least bit damaged," Kiervan retorted before he could think better of the words. The unexpected honesty felt good. "And if your sense of self-importance has been bruised, it's a drumming no doubt overdue."

Eggie's eyes widened. George looked staggered. Kiervan found the effects of his continued honesty strangely satisfying; it was almost as if a massive weight had been lifted from his shoulders, allowing him to stand straighter. He fought, and failed, to control a grin.

"Now see here, Captain des Marceaux," George sputtered after a moment. He tugged his waistcoat down and fiddled with his lace cuffs before continuing, "No doubt you are suffering unexpected ill effects of your injury."

More likely it is that I'm suffering unexpected ill effects of the company, Kiervan observed. Still, he knew better than to give voice to such incendiary words. That much honesty could well cost him his engagement and the business arrangement as well. Odd, he thought, the possibility of the loss didn't seem to trouble him as much as it had only a short while ago.

"I do seem to have suffered an unusual lapse in hospitality," Kiervan admitted, straightening and removing his foot from the chair. Despite the sudden swaying of the room, he started toward his desk, placing his feet carefully so as not to stumble. "Would you care for a drink, sir? I stock an excellent whiskey," he offered.

"I do believe I will," George Terwilliger-Hampstead answered. "Thank you."

Kiervan opened the drawer, glancing up at Eglintine as he

did. "Mistress? Would you care for a glass?" he asked, knowing full well how the offer would be received. Why did he so enjoy baiting the woman?

She softly chided, "Ladies don't drink, Captain des Marceaux."

Kiervan carefully concealed a smile by turning his attention to his task. "Really? I hadn't noticed." Good Lord, he thought, noting the precipitous drop in the level in the decanter. What had Alanna done with that much whiskey? She'd have had to have bathed in the stuff. *Or bathed me,* he amended, gently crooking his neck to ease the stiffness of his wound.

"I would suggest, Captain," Eggie said silkily, "that you've been in the company of those who might be considered slightly less than ladylike."

It occurred to him that he would have let the velvet-wrapped slur pass had his head not pounded quite so fiercely, might not have taken it as an insult deliberately directed against Alanna had the thought of charity appealed to him at the moment. He poured two glasses of what remained of his whiskey and, handing one to George Terwilliger-Hampstead, met Eggie's gaze square on.

"I'd suggest, mistress," he countered, making no effort to conceal his irritation, "that we have entirely different perceptions of what constitutes a lady."

"Apparently," she countered, tucking her handkerchief into her generous cleavage, "your definition would be broad enough to include the little witch who insulted me earlier."

He gritted his teeth in suppressed anger and replied, "Her name is Alanna Chapman and she is a Seer of the Ancient Find. And I would warn you that I owe my life to her several times over. She not only possesses far greater courage than most men I know, but a depth of compassion and integrity the likes of which most people never attain. Yes, mistress, she indeed meets my standards for being a lady."

"Such a spirited defense," Eglintine retorted. "Is she your doxy on this voyage, Captain des Marceaux?"

The hammering in his head intensified, the beat harder and faster. Sudden calm flowed through him as he answered, "How fortunate that you're of the fairer gender, mistress. Were you a man, I'd have to call you out for that one."

Her father glanced between them. He cleared his throat quietly and then interjected, "I am sure Eglintine meant no slight, did you, my dear?"

"She meant nothing less and we all know it," Kiervan stated, never taking his eyes from hers. She smiled, but in her grin he saw the shadows of a darker kind of happiness, the happiness that came to those who had honed manipulation to an art and found a perverse joy in molding circumstances and people to their own purpose. And then, suddenly, he knew what she was about.

"You misunderstand me, Captain des Marceaux," she said, her voice and manner all sweet gentility. "I've no objections to allowing you to continue your dalliance with the *lady*. As long as you're discreet, of course. I would prefer, in fact, that you feel free to seek out the favors of others with similar charms. It would lessen to a considerable degree the more . . . unpleasant . . . aspects of our marriage."

He smiled slowly, a heady sense of relief washing over him, lightening his heart and brightening his soul. "I do believe, Eggie darlin', that any aspect of our marriage would be unpleasant."

George choked on a mouthful of whiskey and then spluttered, "Are you suggesting—?"

"No. I'm saying it directly," Kiervan replied, his mind clearer than it had been in years. "I no longer find the idea of marriage to your daughter acceptable. I now understand your reasoning in keeping her well distant during the course of our negotiations. An eternity in hell would pass sooner than a single day as her husband."

Fire blazed in her eyes as she slammed the tip of her parasol against the floor at her side. "And I couldn't bear to be shackled to a man who so obviously lacks the essential qualities of good breeding. You, sir, are common."

The grin he gave Eggie was worth all the pain it brought him. "An accident of birth for which I shall be forever grateful." Kiervan lifted his glass in salute. "It's settled, then. By mutual agreement, our nuptial contract is rendered null and void."

"You can't break your word at this juncture," Eggie countered, stepping forward and lifting her chin in defiance. "The bans have been published. My trousseau's been purchased."

Kiervan shrugged and instantly regretted the action. He waited until the pain had dulled slightly and then replied, "I can't be forced to do what my heart finds abhorrent. I regret that the circumstances will cause you some embarrassment, but that's far preferable to a lifetime in which we each daily regret our lack of honesty and courage."

"Consider your decision carefully, Captain," her father cautioned. Setting aside his glass and jerking his lace cuffs over the backs of his hands, he added, "You stand to lose far more than a bride."

Kiervan nodded slowly. "It now occurs to me that when my mother asked for my pledge to marry well, she didn't mean for me sacrifice good judgment and happiness in the pursuit of social position and wealth. Offer your plums and cakes to another man, George. I'll marry for love and nothing less."

"I will see you barred from Charleston harbor!" George Terwilliger-Hampstead thundered.

Eglintine, in her turn, added, "And I'll see your name and the story of your despicable conduct spread throughout the region!"

Addressing first George Terwilliger-Hampstead, Kiervan said, "Do as you will, sir. I care not in the least. There are other ports in which the *Wind Racer* may more profitably trade.

"As for the assassination of my reputation," Kiervan went on, turning to face Eglintine, "You may do as you please as well. Bear in mind, however, that your tale of woe and betrayal will surely result in the raising of glasses through the Carolinas, each man offering his congratulations for my having at long last come to my senses."

"Come, Eglintine," her father said on an indignant huff. "Let us return to our ship at once."

As she swept her skirts about and took her father's proferred arm, Eggie gave him a look clearly meant to put him in his proper place. Kiervan smiled and bowed ever so slightly. She issued her own huff of outrage and allowed herself to be led away.

They were halfway to the door when it opened as if by magic. "Permit me," Richard St. John offered, stepping aside to allow the Terwilliger-Hampsteads ample room for a haughty exit.

Eggie's skirts had no sooner disappeared up the stairway than Richard looked over his shoulder and grinned at Kiervan. "Would you care to wager on how long it will take her to find a French nobleman to take home in your place?"

Suddenly Kiervan felt exceedingly light-headed and the room seemed to be darkening at an alarming rate. "You were listening at the door the entire time, you reprobate," he managed good-naturedly.

"I wasn't at all sure you were strong enough to last out the meeting. And it was a certainty that neither of those two would have dragged you back to your bed if you'd collapsed."

"I think I acquitted myself rather nicely, if I must say so my—" The rest of his words died on the tip of his tongue. Before him, on the desk and propped against his account ledger, sat a piece of folded parchment, his name elegantly penned across the front.

He lifted the paper and opened the fold, instantly noting Alanna's signature at the bottom of the sheet. His stomach knotting in dread, he began to read.

The room tilted up and spun around him. He locked his knees and willed himself to remain upright. He thought he heard Richard say something, but the words were both distant and garbled. "Find Alanna," he whispered. "Find her for me."

The moon had reached its zenith when the last of the search parties trudged up the gangplank. Kiervan closed his eyes and gripped the railing, swallowing back the grief that threatened to choke him. There was no reason to ask. Had they found Alanna, she would be with them. And she wasn't.

Part of him wanted to lie down and simply have done with the effort to live. His heart ached with a terrible emptiness, a hollowness born of his own blind foolishness, a sense of loss that he knew would be with him until the day he died.

"I found this, Kiervan. I thought perhaps you might want to have it."

He opened his eyes to meet the saddened gaze of Richard St. John.

"I chanced upon it in a broker's shop," his friend explained quietly. "I don't know if it's hers, but I recall seeing her wear one quite similar."

Kiervan slowly, numbly looked down. Lying in the palm of his First Officer's hand was Alanna's diamond ring. Kiervan took the ring in his own hand and asked, "Was the shopkeeper able or willing to tell you anything?"

"He paid pennies on its real worth, acquiring it from an Irishman early this afternoon, a redheaded man who apparently spoke impeccable French."

"Niall?"

"I am reasonably certain it was."

"You must have paid quite a bit for it. I'll reimburse you, of course. Thank you, my friend."

Richard nodded. He leaned his forearms on the railing, laced his fingers, and stared down at the dock. After a long moment, he said, "The harbormaster's records indicate that of the ships that sailed this afternoon, three listed ports of call in Ireland."

Tucking the ring safely into his pocket, Kiervan nodded. "Then it's time we sailed ourselves."

"When the wind comes up, Kiervan," his First Officer replied patiently. "You can't bend her to your will. She comes and goes as it pleases her and no one else. When she decides to come again, we'll be ready."

Kiervan blinked and gazed out over the waters of the harbor. "Owrd said Alanna was the wind," he heard himself whisper.

"Who's Owrd?" Richard St. John asked, turning his head with a puzzled expression.

Kiervan tightened his grip about the railing. His heart ached with a pain far worse than that of his head. "God, Richard," he groaned, "I've been such an arrogant fool."

34

Alanna stood in the rutted track with her hands jammed deep into her pockets and studied the Carraig Cor. It looked exactly the same as it had the night she'd first crossed the meadow and entered its circled stones. But the ancient site was all that remained unchanged. She wasn't the Alanna Chapman who had carried Maude's ashes from America. She wasn't the same woman who had found herself lying in the fog, a sword point at her throat, staring up into the blazing eyes of a warrior.

She had come through the portals of time a CPA fulfilling a sacred last request, a fiercely independent woman who had spent her entire life building high, protective walls around her heart. But the walls were gone forever now. Kiervan had torn them down, brick by brick, until she'd no desire but to let him possess her as no man ever had. She was richer for the experience, she knew. Most women would envy her time with Kiervan des Marceaux. But the price had been terribly steep.

With her hands still buried in her pockets, Alanna kicked at a rock. Odd, she mused, for the last three days she'd been obsessed with reaching this place as fast as she could, and now that she stood within sight of her goal, she found herself reluctant to rush up the gentle slope and into the circle of stones. Why? Why was she now hesitant to do what she knew she needed to, what she knew was the right thing? Alanna sighed and shook her head.

Maude had promised her a grand adventure and true

love. Grand adventure? It had been an adventure, certainly. She had crossed southern Ireland by horseback, had sailed on tall ships. She had stayed in a castle and played a part in a ritual older than memory. She'd learned the story of her own beginnings and shared a time with a loving and wise grandfather she hadn't known existed. She had discovered the wonder of her strengths and the depths of her vulnerabilities, knowledge she would have never acquired had she remained safely ensconced in her little office in Durango and safely committed to Bill.

But grand? Owrd was dead. So were Phelan and Paddy. And Ashton . . . her brother. The Castle O'Connell had been burned to the ground. And Kiervan had been surrendered to the needs of his own heart, to the arms of another woman. No, in some respects the adventure had been anything but grand.

And true love?

Alanna scowled at the stars blinking overhead. "Okay, Maude," she answered quietly. "You win on that one. I'll love him forever. No one else'll ever come close to making me feel the things Kiervan can. And I'll go ahead and admit it. You were right about Bill. He isn't the man for me."

She returned to studying the Carraig for a few long moments before looking up again. "I always thought that if you found true love, you got to keep it, Maude." Her voice cracked and she struggled furiously to hold the sense of loss at bay.

Fighting for composure, Alanna glared up at the night sky. "You didn't tell me it would hurt so badly," she accused. "You didn't tell me how empty and alone and lost I'd feel."

But if she'd known beforehand what waited for her, she wouldn't have come.

"You're damned right!" Alanna snapped, staring at the Carraig Cor again. "I'd have passed on the bloody mayhem and death thing. And I sure wouldn't have come through the gates of time knowing that a broken heart was waiting for me on the other side. Thanks a lot, Maude. Thanks a helluva lot for being so damned honest! If you weren't dead already, your life expectancy would be about up!"

And she would never have known loving as she had with Kiervan.

"I'd never have known this much heartache either," she admitted. "I'd never have known how miserable I am because I never would have been as happy as I was with Kiervan."

And she'd been happier with Kiervan than she had ever been in her life. Even when they'd been at each other's throats, when they'd been pitching verbal hand grenades at one another, she'd known in her heart that Kiervan made her feel more alive than any man on Earth. But they'd had times of serenity and contentment too, she reminded herself; times in which she'd drifted along in utter contentment, for the first time in her life not analyzing and planning and living forward of that moment.

Being with Kiervan had brought out the best in her . . . and the worst. And he'd accepted both parts, respecting her for who and what she was. He'd known her heart better than she had herself, had cajoled and pushed and dragged her into wondrous realms she hadn't dreamed existed; his strength and certainty had been hers to draw upon when courage had threatened to desert her. If ever there had been a reason to love a man . . . And love him she did, mind, body, and soul. To be Kiervan's wife, to bear his children, to stand at his side as they steered through the course of a lifetime . . .

"But he's chosen another way," she whispered. "And I can't live with only half of him." She lifted her chin and set out toward the Carraig and the end of her journey.

The pale moonlight did nothing to soften the hardness of the rocks or the difficulty of the task before him. While his horse shifted beneath him, Kiervan's gaze remained fastened on the great pillars of stone rising from the hillock above. He wondered if there was a special direction one was supposed to come from to properly enter the ancient circle. Somehow he'd gotten turned around tonight and come at it from the side opposite the one he'd ascended the last time he'd been here . . . the night he'd met Alanna; the night his life had been changed forever.

In the end, deciding that he could more clearly consider the matter once he reached the top, he nudged the horse in the flanks. The animal snorted, turned against the reins, and danced away from the gentle slope leading upward. When a second and third attempt to get the beast to carry him to the top produced the same results, Kiervan swore beneath his breath, abandoned the effort, and slipped wearily from the saddle.

As he made his way up the hillock, the still-tender wound at the back of his head throbbed unmercifully, and his bruised and battered body punished him for pushing it beyond its limits. A deep exhaustion quivered through his muscles and weighted his limbs when he finally staggered up to the great stones of the Carraig Cor. Pausing on the outer edge and pushing dampened locks of hair back from his face, he filled his lungs with precious air and willed his frantic heartbeat to slow. The *Wind Racer* had made good time, he assured himself. No ship on the sea had the speed of his. The odds had to be in his favor.

And what if he'd arrived too late? What if Alanna had already passed back through the portals of time? Suddenly it didn't matter how the ancient Druids had entered the circle. He stiffened his resolve, took a deep breath, and carried his greatest, deepest fears with him into the center of the sacred place.

He turned about, remembering as he did that Richard St. John had asked him how he'd know if Alanna had slipped away, how he'd know whether to wait for her or return to the ship. He'd assure his friend that he knew Alanna, knew that she would leave him a sign, a final remembrance. Even as he recalled those fateful words, he found what he had most dreaded.

"God, no. Please, no." The desperate cry reverberated around the circle of stone as he stumbled to the altar and plucked the tiny bit of silver from the center. The pain of his body faded as he turned the earring over in his palm and studied the back of it. The post and clasp were thin, too thin to be the earring he'd made for her.

And he knew. She'd left it there on the center stone for him to find. It was her way of saying a last goodbye. She'd left him the earring she'd brought with her through time; taken with her the one he'd made on this side of it.

He swayed on his feet as his heart and his hope shattered. There would be no chance to make things right with her. Never again would he hold her in his arms. He'd never taste again the sweetness of her lips nor dance with her in the wondrous fire of their passions. There would be no children. No growing old together. There would never be another woman for him, no one to love him or for him to love.

Kiervan clutched the earring in his fist and lifted his face to the heavens above him. "Maude!" he cried at the stars, not caring that his grief tattered the sound, "Maude! Tell her to come back!"

Tears welled in his eyes and he furiously blinked them away as he beat back the waves of desolation and futility. No, he wouldn't surrender so easily. Resting his forearms on the ancient Druid altar, he bowed his head.

"Name the price. I'll pay it twice over," he whispered. "Just bring Alanna back to me. Please . . . bring . . . her . . . back. Please."

Alanna paused at the edge of the circle and, with her forehead resting on the cold surface of the wind-smoothed stone, concentrated on all that Owrd had taught her—the movements, the words she didn't understand but trusted to take her back to the time and place where she belonged. The wind rose at her back, its gentle voice whispering assurance and urging her on. She straightened and, just as she had that night so long ago, stepped resolutely into the circle. Just as it had then, the wind again billowed through her hair and tossed the honey-colored strands across her vision. She paused and swept it back with her forearm.

Alanna blinked. He stood in the center of the ring of stones, his forearms resting on the altar, his shoulders slumped forward and his head bent, for all the world looking like a man deep in prayer. How had he gotten here before her?

"Kiervan?" she whispered, her body moving toward him of its own accord.

He straightened as though shot and whirled about to face her. For a long moment, utter relief softened his features. She stared at him, offering up a silent prayer that he'd come to promise her all that she wanted, to promise her all of the dreams she'd thought lost to them.

Then his gaze pinned her and anger flared in his eyes. He flung something away.

His voice was hard and accusing when he said, "You left without saying goodbye."

"It wasn't my first impulse," she said softly. "But probably my best."

"The impulse of a coward," he growled in reply.

"Of good judgment," she retorted, her blood heating as it always did when they argued.

His eyes darkened. "Have I meant so little to you that you could walk away leaving only a note behind?"

"What else was I supposed to do, Kiervan?" she demanded, throwing her hands up in angry exasperation and stepping forward. "Did you expect me to stay around so I could shake your hand and tell you that I'd had a wonderful time? That I hoped you and Eggie had a great life together? That's a helluva lot to ask."

His hands were clenched into white-knuckled fists at his side as he retorted, "So you left me to worry as to what had happened to you. What did *you* expect *me* to do, Alanna? Shrug my shoulders, off-load my cargo, and then blithely set sail for America? Did you think I'd forget you the first moment a fancy bit of skirt crossed my path?"

Far too angry to stand still, she paced back and forth before him, her hands punctuating the air as she gave full rein to her pent-up frustrations. "I know this is way out there, Kiervan, but I thought you *might* decide to try to be faithful to your wife. God knows, if I were your wife, I'd want you to be."

"And I would be."

"Well, congratulations! You've turned a corner, Kiervan. You're at long last capable of seeing that love might not be as fleeting as you once thought. There's hope for you and Eggie after all."

"Not even the slightest bit. I broke the engagement."

"You what?" she asked, whirling to face him, hoping that she didn't look as stunned as she felt.

"I broke my engagement to Eglintine Terwilliger-Hampstead," he replied, adding pointedly, "Had you not run away, you might have been one of the first to hear the news."

"Well, how the hell was I supposed to know what you had planned?" she asked, her sense of aggravation returning. "You never said one word to me."

"That's because I didn't plan it. It simply happened."

With one hand on the altar stone and the other on her cocked hip, Alanna looked up at him in disbelief. "You're telling me that Eggie walked through the door of your cabin and you took one look at her and decided that you'd give up your holy quest for prestige, social status, and incredible wealth? Pardon me if I sound just a tad astounded."

"Yes, Alanna," he answered. "That's precisely what happened. Five minutes after we met, I was searching for a way out of the arrangement. I knew I couldn't endure marriage to her, no matter what the inducements."

"What made you change your mind?" She winced inwardly at the suspicion in her question.

"Do you have to ask, Alanna?" He quickly added, "And before you answer, you should know that Richard described in great detail your encounter with Eggie."

Alanna studied her feet and shook her head, remembering how horribly she'd behaved, how easily she'd slipped to Eglintine's level. "Yeah, I do have to ask," she answered on a soft sigh as she looked up at him again. "I know why I disliked her, but I doubt they're the same reasons you dumped her."

Kiervan cocked a brow. "Dumped her?"

"Got rid of her," she supplied before asking, "So why did you break your engagement to a drop-dead gorgeous woman who came with a rich daddy attached?"

He asked with a smile, "Do you want the *Britannica* or the *Reader's Digest* version?"

Alanna couldn't keep back a smile of her own. "The *Britannica*." She wasn't in any mood to let him off the hook. "Do I need to sit down for this?" she asked. "Is it going to take a while?"

"Yes, it will." He lifted her up and gently set her on the center stone.

"You seem to have recovered your strength," Alanna quipped, trying to marshal her scattered thoughts and slow the beat of her heart. "Apparently even dropping a load of bricks on your head doesn't slow you down for very long."

He was staring into the distant darkness when he said, "Actually, I credit that mishap for bringing me to my senses. Had I had more of my wits about me, I might not have listened to the instincts that saved me from a horrible fate."

"A fate worse than death."

He turned to meet her gaze, his own serious. "You jest, Alanna, but I'm quite serious. I truly thought I could endure a marriage of convenience, that I didn't care about the relationship beyond what could be gained from it financially.

"But then I discovered that it did matter to me, that it mattered very much. I knew that I couldn't stand before God and pledge myself to a woman I didn't want with my heart. I knew that I couldn't bring myself to touch her, to pretend that she roused my desires. I knew I couldn't marry a woman I didn't love."

She resolutely stamped down the hope that his words had stirred. "What about the pledge you made to your mother, Kiervan?" she asked softly, tucking her hands beneath her knees and staring at the ground. "I know you well enough to know that you've neither forgotten nor abandoned it."

He leaned against the rock and rested his forearms on it as he'd been doing when she'd stepped into the circle. Tilting his head, he offered her an almost rueful smile. "I've thought long and hard on the matter the last few days, Alanna. It occurs to me that, were my mother still living, she'd have cut a branch from the willow and taken me to task long ago. She had no patience with what she called the blindness of stubborn male pride."

Alanna grinned and gave him a quick nod. "I think I'd have liked your mom."

"She would have adored you. You're very much like her. Earth and fire." He paused to look up into the night sky, and his voice was barely a whisper when he added, "And wind."

Alanna fought back the urge to reach for him. "I appreciate the compliment," she answered softly, "but you still haven't answered the question. What are you going to do about your pledge?"

He turned his side against the altar stone and, facing her, his expression intent, replied evenly, "She asked me to marry well, Alanna. I will do so. I can do no less."

Alanna nodded and swallowed back the knot rising up in her throat. She couldn't bring herself to look him in the eyes, couldn't bear for him to know just how thin her bravado was as she quipped, "Then I suppose the civilized thing for me to do is wish you success, isn't it?"

"The civilized thing for you to do, Alanna, is to say you'll marry me."

She looked up to find him watching her, his eyes soft and dark. Her heart sang and every measure of her being wanted to grant his request, wanted to be wrapped in the circle of his arms; every measure of her, that is, except her mind—which firmly demanded honesty and caution.

"I'm not rich, Kiervan," she offered in protest. "I'm from another century, from a part of America that doesn't even belong to America yet. I'm—"

"I love you, Alanna."

His simple declaration arrowed into her heart. "And I love you, Kiervan," she whispered, reaching out to lay her hand along the hard curve of his jaw. "With every fiber of my being, I love you. Forever and always."

He closed his eyes and pressed a lingering kiss into the palm of her hand and then looked up at her again. "Yet you hesitate to pledge yourself to me. Why?"

"I'm not the type of woman who can sit at home, tatting lace and watching the children grow up while I wait for you to come home from your voyages across the world, praying every hour of the day and night that you're safe and that I'll get to hold you again. I won't ask you to give up the sea. I can't do that to you. So either I go to sea with you, Kiervan, or I go back through the gates of time," she answered honestly.

"Raising children aboard a ship in the rough company of sailors isn't what I want for my family, Alanna."

"Then we're at an impasse again," she murmured, her heart sinking. "Why do we always end up like this?" She gently withdrew her hand from his grasp.

"Because you're as stubborn as I am."

Alanna lifted her chin and stared straight ahead. "Another strike against the hope of a marriage working for us."

At the edge of her vision, she saw him reach for her shoulder. She looked down and watched him unfasten the Dragon's Heart from her cloak. When he drew back, the soft glint of moonlight on silver and ruby lay in the palm of his hand.

"Look into the stone, Alanna," he commanded gently, offering it to her. "Tell me the future doesn't hold happiness for us."

She took it from him with trembling fingers and covered it. In her heart she knew that the vision was already there. But something within her whispered of faith and trust. Alanna slowly raised her eyes to meet Kiervan's steady gaze, the happiness of her love flooding over and warming her spirit. "I don't need a vision to tell me what the future would hold for us, Kiervan."

Kiervan gently took her face in his hands. She looked up in wonder at the gentle curve of his lips, the light dancing in his eyes. "Would you prefer a lifetime without the passion of argument?" he asked quietly, knowingly. "Without the passion of making peace? I couldn't bear to think of it, Alanna. I cherish the storms with you every bit as much as I do the calm that comes after them.

"I love everything about you, Alanna. I love the way the sun glints off your hair, the way it falls over your shoulders. I love how you lift your chin when you're being brave and how your eyes spark when you're angry, how dark they get when you're worried. I love the sound of your voice and the odd little expressions you use. I love the way you make me smile, how you make me see the world. I want to spend forever in your arms, Alanna. Say you'll marry me."

Her heart swelled in wild delight as her soul soared high into the clouds on wings of heady exhilaration. She tried to nod, but her head wouldn't move; tried to speak, but couldn't force the simple word past her lips.

"Tell me nay, woman," Kiervan whispered as his drew from his pocket his mother's silver and emerald Celtic cross. "Tell me nay or I'll take your silence as assent."

She wanted to laugh, wanted to cry, as he clasped the necklace around her neck. When he put his arms about her and drew her against him, her body at last responded to the yearnings of her heart. "Yes, Kiervan," she answered against his lips, her arms twining about his neck. "Yes."

Through the space between the stones, Alanna watched as a warm glow came to the eastern sky. She snuggled closer to Kiervan's warmth and drew his cloak more tightly about their twined limbs. She touched the Celtic cross lying nestled between her breasts and smiled. The *Wind Racer* would return to the coast later in the day and they would sail for some distant port; where didn't matter to her as long as she stood at Kiervan's side.

He stirred against her and his arms tightened gently around her. "I love you," he murmured into her ear as his teeth grazed the sensitive flesh of her lobe and teased the earring he'd fashioned for her.

Alanna sighed, savoring the delicious quiver he sent coursing the length of her body. She turned in his arms and, with gentle fervor, demanded that he prove it to her yet again.

And when the sun finally broke over the horizon, Alanna caught a ragged breath and grinned up into Kiervan's dark, loving eyes. She had indeed found true love. And the grand adventure . . . The grand adventure was just beginning.

Epilogue

Kiervan looked up from his work as the wagons lumbered through the gates of Castle O'Connell. He set aside the planer and, brushing the wood curls from his sleeves, went across the courtyard to meet Richard and Niall.

"It took you long enough," he said, smiling in welcome as the men climbed down from their seats.

"Then next time *you* go in search of household goods instead," Richard shot back good-naturedly. He withdrew a folded packet of paper from his breast pocket and handed it to Kiervan. "And you can get your own blasted mail while you're at it."

Kiervan glanced down, noted his brother's penmanship, and tucked the correspondence into his waistband.

"Aye," Niall seconded. "Or better yet, we will all go and let the women spend their days and our money in the marketplace while we watch through the windows of a pub."

"It would take considerably less time," Kiervan acknowledged. "Lord knows that no one can acquire as deliberately and frugally as our ladies can."

"And speaking of our ladies . . ." Richard began. Niall looked around the courtyard expectantly.

"Rest assured that they're all quite well," Kiervan said. "They've taken their needlework out into the meadow to work in the shade of the trees at the far end. Alanna said she wanted to exhaust Maude so the child would take a decent nap."

Both men turned at the same time to gaze out the castle

gates. Kiervan laughed and placed a hand on each of their shoulders. "I'll have some men unload the wagons and cart all this very necessary finery inside. You two go and wash the road from yourselves. While you do that, I'll go out and tell your wives that you've grown tired of consorting with shapely women and have decided to come home."

Richard shook his head and grinned. "If your sister didn't have the same spark of deviltry in her as you do, our marriage would come undone from your teasing."

"If she hadn't, Dominica never would have married you in the first place."

Niall cleared his throat. "Hisolda may have the patience of a saint, but I do not. While I'm glad to see you again after so many weeks, Kiervan, I'd much prefer to see my wife. We're wasting time here."

Kiervan grinned. "Richard, I do think the boy needs to cool off. Dunk him and hold him under, otherwise poor Hisolda's going to miss the fun of sorting through all the things you've brought home."

His brother-in-law nodded. "And Lord knows she'd much prefer that to being closeted with our renegade Druid for the next day or so."

Color flooded Niall's cheeks and he stammered about for words to defend himself. Richard threw his arm around his shoulder and turned him toward the castle, saying as he led the younger man away, "You really need to learn the husbandly art of playing hard to get, Niall. If you'll allow me to instruct you on some of the finer points . . ."

Kiervan watched his friends pass through the massive front doors of the central hall and then called several men from their other work and set them to unloading the wagons. Marriage had certainly changed Niall, had made a man out of him, Kiervan mused, leaving the castle and starting across the meadow. Actually, he admitted, marriage had changed all of them. Richard had happily sailed the *Wind Racer* as captain until Dominica had decided to visit Ireland and see for herself the rebuilt castle and her brother's wife and newborn daughter. Richard had come down the gangplank with Dominica on his arm and had never looked back to the sea.

Now they were a thoroughly domesticated lot, he and Richard and Niall. And while they frequently lamented their fates over late-night brandies, they each would freely admit to having it no other way. Life was good, better in fact than any mortal man had the right to expect. They spent their days in honest work on the land, their nights in the strong walls of the castle and the loving arms of their women. Other than children to laugh and play about his feet, what more could a man want or need?

Kiervan studied the trio of women working and chatting beneath the shade of the trees ahead and grinned. Children would soon be no rarity at Castle O'Connell. Alanna's day was close at hand. Dominica would give birth to her and Richard's first child within the next few weeks. And Hisolda would follow her into motherhood less than a month later.

"Good afternoon, ladies," he greeted them, his eyes lingering on his three-year-old daughter, who slept contentedly an arm's length from her mother. She clutched a bouquet of wildflowers in her little hand and, just as her mother was wont to do, smiled sweetly in her sleep. Maude was so like Alanna in so many ways, in her looks and in her temperament. God help the man who ever wanted to take his precious daughter away from him.

He shook his head and turned his attention to the women, letting his gaze slide meaningfully between each of them as he commented, "One would think there was a special magic in the water of Castle O'Connell."

"Hah!" Alanna scoffed with a wide smile. " 'Tis the Beltane fire. You jump through the smoke of fires *I* build and you get results."

He countered, "I would remind you, my sweet Alanna, that Maude's creation had absolutely nothing to do with smoke."

"Kiervan," she warned, her brow arched but her smile mischievous with memories.

He grinned and ceased his teasing as he pulled the packet from his waistband. "This has just arrived for you," he said, handing it to Alanna. "I'm not at all sure that I approve of my wife receiving correspondence from another man."

Her gaze darted to the elegant script labeling the expensive parchment. "Even your little brother?"

"Lawyers have no scruples."

When she rolled her eyes and set about breaking the seal, Kiervan turned his attention to Dominica and Hisolda. "Oh, yes," he moaned, pressing his fingers to his forehead as though a wayward thought had suddenly and painfully returned. "Dominica. Richard is back from Dublin and—"

His sister squealed with delight and hastily began to gather up her needlework. Hisolda did the same as she breathlessly asked, "And Niall too?"

"No. He stayed behind to chase skirts in the marketplace."

"He did not!" all three women chorused.

Kiervan shook his head. "Such excitement to go meet the prodigal husbands. Such hurrying."

Dominica, blushing prettily to the roots of her dark hair, retorted, "It's difficult indeed to hurry when we're carrying this much babe before us."

"Then allow me to assist," Kiervan offered, extending his hands to both of them. He groaned mightily as he helped them to their feet, and then gladly endured their scathing looks. It occurred to him to offer some taunting remark about ducks as they started across the meadow toward the castle.

"Don't you dare," Alanna said softly from behind him. "Dominica is feeling awkward and unattractive enough as it is."

Kiervan held his tongue and turned to study his wife who sat cross-legged, reading the letter. Pregnancy made her even more beautiful. Despite the advanced days of bearing this child, she still moved with a grace that took his breath away, that kept him aching with unfulfillable want.

He went to sit behind her and stretched his legs out on either side of hers. "I thought they would never leave," he whispered, nuzzling her neck and slipping his arms around her to lay his hands on her swollen belly.

She settled back against his chest and lifted the paper so that he could have read the words for himself if he'd been of a mind for such mundane matters. "Donal says that the deposits into the account have been staggering."

"Even after he's taken his share?"

"Stop it, Kiervan," she admonished, swatting at his arm with the letter.

He started to draw away, afraid that his attentions were hurting her.

"No, don't stop that," she protested, catching his hands and putting them back on her belly. As his fingers began again to trail over the swell of her, she rewarded him with a sweet sigh. "Yes. For heavens sakes, keep doing that." She paused and in the silence he felt the muscles beneath his hands tighten and then relax as they had for the last several weeks.

When it had passed, Alanna added, "I meant be nice to your brother; he's earned every penny of his fees. Even as we sit here enjoying the sunshine, he's in some dark, stuffy little office busily working out the last of the financing arrangements for Eli Whitney's firearms company."

His hands sliding over her, he muttered, "Can't you tell that my mind isn't the least interested in business, woman?"

She settled closer against him and lifted the letter again. "And by the way, Donal says to tell you that Riona is cutting a wide path through Boston's eligible bachelors. There's also a personal note in here from Eleuthère. He sends his warmest regards. He also says to tell you that the gunpowder factory is producing revenues beyond his wildest dreams."

"I'm beginning to suspect that Monsieur E. I. Du Pont has designs on more than my investment money. You might warn him that you have a very jealous husband. Now, move that paper aside," he softly commanded, splaying his fingers and massaging her with gentle firmness. "I can't see what I'm doing."

"That feels good," she murmured, putting her letter down in the grass to lean her head back against his shoulder and close her eyes.

"The baby's quiet this afternoon," he observed, trying to keep the sudden concern from his voice. "Is something amiss with her?"

" 'Tis normal, Kiervan. Stop worrying. Saraid will come into this world as easily as Maude did. And like Maude, she'll have ten fingers and ten toes, a strong heart, and her father's lusty lungs. All will be well with her and me."

"Waiting for babies tests my endurance," he growled, desperately wanting far more than he could have of her.

He felt her silent laughter as she retorted, "Believe it or not, you'll survive."

"A man shouldn't properly desire his wife as much as I do at this moment, Alanna. When will this daughter of mine come?"

She sighed and snuggled closer. "Before the night is out, I think."

He felt for all the world like a man struck between the eyes with a broad stick. His heart pounded as he remembered when she'd delivered Maude and how to his mind the pain had been too great, her ordeal taking her far too near the shadows of death. Kiervan gently turned her so that she lay in the circle of his arms. "Why didn't you tell me before now?" he demanded.

"Because you become an idiot during the waiting," she chided, reaching up to circle his neck with her arms. "All your pacing and wincing and teeth clenching is a real pain in the clyde. It'd be different if you actually had anything to worry about."

He took a deep breath and swallowed back his trepidation. "I'll conduct myself better this time."

"No you won't," she said, drawing his lips down to hers. And in her kiss he felt not only the fires of her passion, but the depths of her love and understanding.

Alanna had been right. As she always was, Kiervan mused, holding a pink, chubby little Saraid in his arms and watching the sun rise. They had bound their fate to Ireland, to this beautiful land and the Clan O'Connell. God knew there would be times ahead when he'd have cause to consider the wisdom of that decision, but for now . . . He turned back to the bed and studied the mother of his children.

Her soft smile drew him back to her. Kiervan placed Saraid in her arms and then carefully lay down beside them. With Saraid's fingers wrapped about one of his, he gazed into Alanna's shimmering violet eyes.

"Thank you," he whispered.

"For what?"

"For coming through the gates of time. For loving me. For being stubborn enough to save me from myself. For making me a happy man."

About the Author

Leslie LaFoy grew up loving books and telling stories. From *Bamba, the Jungle Boy* to Early American history, she was hooked. After growing up, leaving home, and earning tons of college degrees, all as a voracious reader, Leslie entered the Real World, and decided to get a job. Looking around at her Real World options, she chose to become a teacher. As a teacher she got to read a lot, which she loved, but she didn't actually have time to write. The decision was difficult, but Leslie left teaching in the fall of 1996 to write full-time. She, her husband, their son, a sheltie, and three cats live on ten acres of windswept Kansas prairie . . . fifteen miles east and three miles north of the Real World.

THE VERY BEST IN CONTEMPORARY
WOMEN'S FICTION

SANDRA BROWN

___28951-9 Texas! Lucky $6.50/$8.99 in Canada   ___56768-3 Adam's Fall $5.99/$7.99

___28990-X Texas! Chase $6.99/$9.99   ___56045-X Temperatures Rising $6.50/$8.99

___29500-4 Texas! Sage $6.50/$8.99   ___56274-6 Fanta C $5.99/$7.99

___29085-1 22 Indigo Place $5.99/$6.99   ___56278-9 Long Time Coming $5.99/$7.99

___29783-X A Whole New Light $6.50/$8.99   ___57157-5 Heaven's Price $6.50/$8.99

___57158-3 Breakfast In Bed $5.50/$7.50   ___29751-1 Hawk O'Toole's Hostage $6.50/$8.99

TAMI HOAG

___29534-9 Lucky's Lady $6.50/$8.99   ___29272-2 Still Waters $6.50/$8.99

___29053-3 Magic $6.50/$8.99   ___56160-X Cry Wolf $6.50/$8.99

___56050-6 Sarah's Sin $5.99/$7.99   ___56161-8 Dark Paradise $6.50/$8.99

___56451-x Night Sins $6.50/$8.99   ___56452-8 Guilty As Sin $6.50/$8.99

___09960-4 A Thin Dark Line $22.95/$29.95

NORA ROBERTS

___29078-9 Genuine Lies $6.50/$8.99   ___27859-2 Sweet Revenge $6.50/$8.99

___10655-4 Public Secrets $16.95/$23.95   ___27283-7 Brazen Virtue $6.50/$8.99

___26461-3 Hot Ice $6.50/$8.99   ___29597-7 Carnal Innocence $6.50/$8.99

___26574-1 Sacred Sins $6.50/$8.99   ___29490-3 Divine Evil $6.50/$8.99

DEBORAH SMITH

___29107-6 Miracle $5.99/$7.99   ___29690-6 Blue Willow $5.99/$7.99

___29092-4 Follow the Sun $4.99/$5.99   ___29689-2 Silk and Stone $5.99/$6.99

___10334-2 A Place To Call Home $23.95/$29.95

Ask for these books at your local bookstore or use this page to order.

Please send me the books I have checked above. I am enclosing $____(add $2.50 to cover postage and handling). Send check or money order, no cash or C.O.D.'s, please.

Name _____

Address _____

City/State/Zip _____

Send order to: Bantam Books, Dept. FN 24, 2451 S. Wolf Rd., Des Plaines, IL 60018

Allow four to six weeks for delivery.

Prices and availability subject to change without notice.   FN 24 11/97